"Why is it your rightful place and not mine. ~~Because of my sex.~~ I spat, sounding far more courageous than I felt in the face of my brother's crackling power. Mine easily rivaled his, but it was quiet, understated, the sort you didn't know was there until it was too late. I could never display mine in such an intimidating manner.

"Yes," said Zeus without preamble. "Because you had the misfortune of being made in our mother's image, and our mother chose to defer to our father. You will be a queen if you wish, Hera, but only second to one of us."

No one challenged him. No one spoke to support me. And as those eternal seconds passed, hatred unlike anything I had ever felt before burned within me. "I will prove you wrong someday," I snarled. "And when that day comes, you will be cast out and fed to the wolves. Do not say I did not warn you."

* * *

Select Praise for
Aimée Carter's
The Goddess Test series

"The narrative is well executed, and Kate is a heroine better equipped than most to confront and cope with the inexplicable."
—Publishers Weekly on *The Goddess Test*

"Carter's writing is a delight to read—succinct, clean, descriptive. *Goddess Interrupted* is definitely a page-turner, one full of suspense, heartbreak, confusion, frustration and yes, romance."
—YA Reads on *Goddess Interrupted*

THE GODDESS LEGACY

AIMÉE CARTER

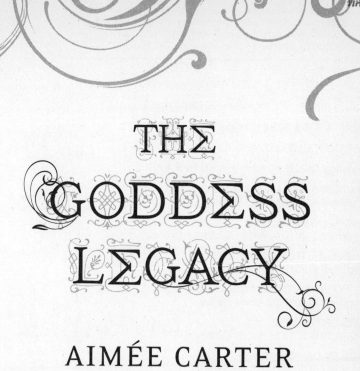

H HARLEQUIN®

entertain, enrich, inspire™

ISBN-13: 978-0-373-21075-6

THE GODDESS LEGACY

Copyright © 2012 by Harlequin Books S.A.

The publisher acknowledges the copyright holder of the individual works as follows:

THE GODDESS QUEEN
Copyright © 2012 by Aimée Carter

THE LOVESTRUCK GODDESS
Copyright © 2012 by Aimée Carter

GODDESS OF THE UNDERWORLD
Copyright © 2012 by Aimée Carter

GOD OF THIEVES
Copyright © 2012 by Aimée Carter

GOD OF DARKNESS
Copyright © 2012 by Aimée Carter

Recycling programs for this product may not exist in your area.

This edition published by arrangement with Harlequin Books S.A.

For questions and comments about the quality of this book please contact us at Customer_eCare@Harlequin.ca.

® and TM are trademarks of Harlequin Enterprises Limited or its corporate affiliates. Trademarks indicated with ® are registered in the United States Patent and Trademark Office, the Canadian Trade Marks Office and in other countries.

www.HarlequinTEEN.com

Printed in U.S.A.

CONTENTS

For Carrie Harris, who is one of a kind,
brilliantly hilarious,
and knows just what to say to vanquish the crazies.
JUICES.

GUIDE OF GODS

ZEUS .... WALTER

HERA .... CALLIOPE

POSEIDON .... PHILLIP

DEMETER .... DIANA

HADES .... HENRY

HESTIA .... SOFIA

ARES .... DYLAN

APHRODITE .... AVA

HERMES .... JAMES

ATHENA .... IRENE

APOLLO .... THEO

ARTEMIS .... ELLA

HEPHAESTUS .... NICHOLAS

DIONYSUS .... XANDER

THE GODDESS QUEEN

PART ONE

In all the years I'd existed, I'd never expected to be free.

I was the daughter of Titans, and as such, I'd always accepted it as fact that they would rule. They were without question the most powerful beings in the universe, after all. They controlled everything and everyone. They were our makers. They were our gods.

But after ten years of rebellion and war in an effort to protect humanity from our father's twisted games, we were the gods now. Still in our infancy compared to our creators, my siblings and I now ruled over the world and all her inhabitants. And as I stared out across the great expanse that was our domain only minutes after our battle had ended, I felt something I thought would end with the war: I felt fear.

It was unnatural. What did we, the captors of Titans, the new generation of gods, have to be afraid of? But the more I tried to picture the future, the clearer it became to me. We hadn't inherited just the Titans' thrones. We'd inherited their responsibilities, as well. And whether or not we were ready for it, the world was waiting for us. Humanity was depending on us to get it right.

Lightning lit up the sky, followed by a symphony of thunder, and I snapped out of my reverie. My youngest brother let out a giant whoop that echoed for miles. "Try to beat that," said Zeus, elbowing my middle brother, Poseidon.

Poseidon scoffed. "That's nothing. Watch this." And with a wave of his hand, the sea below us roared to life, swirling ominously and creating shapes and shadows that danced across the water. Rushing forward, the waves crashed against the cliff we stood on, shaking the very earth.

"Not bad," said Zeus. "But I've seen better."

Before I could blink, Poseidon tackled him to the ground, and the pair of them proceeded to spend the next several minutes trying to pin each other down. If humanity was depending on us to get it right, they were in for several eons of disappointment.

"Don't look so sour, Hera," said Demeter, my sister. She stood beside me, a smile playing on her lips as she watched our brothers wrestle. How she could find amusement in their lack of maturity baffled me.

"Humanity's going to crumble in a matter of weeks at this point," I said. "They need guidance. Protection. Order and help in establishing a life without the Titans' tyranny. Our brothers are not fit to rule."

"We are," said Hestia from the other side of Demeter. Both of my sisters watched them with their heads held high, and they looked every inch the queens the world needed. "As is Hades. Zeus and Poseidon will grow up soon enough, I suspect."

"Never!" cried Zeus, and his booming laughter echoed across the ocean as he managed to gain the upper hand in their wrestling match.

"See?" I gave my sisters a pointed look. "We're doomed."

"I wouldn't go quite that far yet." Our eldest brother, Hades, stepped beside me, his dark hair whipping across his face in the wind. He offered me a small smile, and his eyes glittered with intelligence. Something our other brothers sorely lacked. "You did well, sister. If it hadn't been for you, we would've never succeeded."

My cheeks grew warm. "You're too kind," I said with false humility. I knew as well as he did that by breaking the bonds of the Titans' loyalty to one another, I'd cinched our victory. But the war was over now, and the six of us were a unit that not even I could break. United we had proven to be stronger than even our father, and if we were to have any chance of success, we had to remain that way.

"Hardly. I dare say you should be ruling us all," said Hades.

On the ground, Zeus sat up and shoved Poseidon off him. "Hera, Queen of the Gods?" He chuckled and gave me an enormous wink. "Maybe if she had a king."

He was lucky I was exhausted and weary after battle, else I would've made sure he never had the chance to wink at me or any other girl again. "Are you saying a woman can't rule?" I said.

"I'm saying it would never work." Zeus stood again, offering Poseidon a hand. Once they were both on their feet, they shoved each other playfully and made their way over to the rest of us. "Humanity is used to a king, and Rhea never exercised her rights as queen. They need a leader right now, not a mother."

"I could be a leader," I snapped, and hot anger filled me. Zeus knew never to bring up our mother. The loss of her presence was still too fresh. "I would make a damn good one."

Zeus shrugged and raked his fingers through his golden hair. "Maybe so, but I was the one who led us all to victory. We can all be kings and queens in our own rights, and there's plenty for us to rule over. But as far as a supreme leader goes—"

"Hera won the war for us," said Hades in that quiet, measured voice of his. How he was able to stay so calm in the face of blatant arrogance baffled me. Zeus might have been responsible for the majority of the brute force against the Titans, but he was no more powerful than the rest of us. And he was the youngest and by far the least ready to handle the responsibilities of leadership.

"We all won the war," said Demeter. "We will all rule together, as a council. We will all have equal say, and we will all listen to and respect one another. It is the only way we will not fall victim to revolt, as the Titans did." She squeezed my hand. "Is that acceptable to you, Hera?"

As if I had any real say. But all five of my siblings watched me, waiting for me to yield, and I had little choice. I would not be the one to cut the ties that bound us together.

"As long as it is an equal rule, I can accept that," I said. At least that way the chances of Zeus and Poseidon wreaking havoc were considerably diminished.

Zeus grinned boyishly. "Then it's settled. Let's draw lots for the kingdoms."

"The kingdoms?" I said. "But there are only three."

"Yes," said Zeus with mock patience, as if I were a child who had to be spoken to slowly in order to grasp anything. "Like I said, humanity would never follow a queen."

The edges of my vision turned red, and I clenched my jaw so tightly that I could have shattered diamond between my teeth. But Zeus went on as if he didn't notice, and three gray pebbles appeared in his hand. "Poseidon," he said with a grand bow, as if he were doing him a favor, letting him draw first.

Poseidon narrowed his eyes and touched each of the three stones in turn. "I know which domain you want," he said.

"And you know which domain I want. So why don't you just tell me which one to pick?"

Zeus scoffed. "Where would be the fun in that?" But the middle stone began to glow, and Poseidon snatched it up. As he held it in his palm, a great crash of sea against rock echoed around us, and the stone exploded into a rush of water.

Poseidon grinned. "Perfect."

"Thought you might like that." Zeus turned to Hades next and offered him the remaining stones. "Brother."

Hades eyed him for a long moment, and it wasn't difficult to see what was going on underneath his mask of neutrality. Allowing Zeus to have the sky domain and ultimate rule over the living was dangerous at best. Zeus wasn't ready for it, but if this council was truly to be, then perhaps we could all temper him. Then again, forcing Zeus into the Underworld to mingle with the dead would kill the light inside him, the same light that had rallied us even when we thought all was lost. Zeus wasn't meant to remain among the dead. It simply wasn't his place in the world, and we all knew it. But that didn't mean he was ready to rule.

Without breaking his stare, Hades picked up one of the remaining pebbles and cradled it in his palm. I held my breath, and at last the stone burst into flame, an unexpected light in the dark. The Underworld. Of course Hades would sacrifice himself for our brother's happiness.

Before anyone could react, I snatched the third pebble from Zeus's hand, closing my fist around it. "I will rule the skies," I said. "When you are ready and have proven yourself worthy of kingship, then you may have this stone back."

"Hera—" started Demeter, but Zeus interrupted her.

"Is that what you want? Further anarchy and pain for humanity?" He drew himself up to his full height, thunder rumbling around him. In that moment, a flash of our father appeared on his face, and I took a step back. "You condemn us to another war if you insist on not allowing me my rightful place."

"Why is it your rightful place and not mine? Because of my sex?" I spat, sounding far more courageous than I felt in the face of my brother's crackling power. Though mine easily rivaled his, it was quiet, understated, the sort you didn't know was there until it was too late. I could never display my power in such an intimidating manner.

"Yes," said Zeus without preamble. "Because you had the misfortune of being made in our mother's image, and our mother chose to defer to our father. Because that is the example the Titans set for not only us, but for the world, and we must maintain some order. You will be a queen if you wish, Hera, but only second to one of us."

No one challenged him. No one spoke to support me. And as those eternal seconds passed, hatred unlike anything I had ever felt before burned within me. Not even for Cronus had I felt such disgust. "I *will* prove you wrong someday," I snarled. "And when that day comes, you will be cast out and fed to the wolves. Do not say I did not warn you."

Turning on my heel, I stormed off toward the center of the island. It would be a beautiful place to live if not for the scar of healing earth that led straight into the Underworld, where Cronus and the other Titans now resided. Perhaps it wasn't such a terrible thing that Hades had given up Olympus, after all. At least he could be trusted not to let Cronus escape from the depths of Tartarus.

"Hera!" called Zeus. "Don't be that way."

I ignored him. If he didn't want me there, then I wouldn't be there. But soon enough I heard footsteps behind me, and as they grew closer, I stopped and whirled around. "Can't you take a—"

I stopped. It was Hades, not Zeus, who followed me. In the darkness, he looked far too much like our father for my comfort, but we were all used to it by now. He could change his form, as the rest of us could, but I had no doubt he would keep his natural appearance, determined not to let Cronus dictate who and what he was.

"I am sorry for Zeus," said Hades quietly. "You do not deserve to be spoken to in such a manner."

I swallowed and held my head high. I wouldn't let Zeus get to me. He wasn't worth it. "I won't be anyone's second. I'm better than that. We all are."

He managed a faint smile. "You could never be anyone's second, because that would imply someone was more deserving than you. Never doubt that you are the reason we have won, Hera. You are our true power, and we all know it. It is simply difficult for some of us to acknowledge our own lacking."

A pause, and I deflated. "He'll ruin us."

"Maybe," he allowed. "Maybe not. Time will tell."

"I won't rule at his side."

"I do not blame you." He touched my shoulder. "You deserve better than how he would treat you."

Something tingled down my spine, and his hand felt warm and heavy against my skin. "I could go into the Underworld with you," I said. "You will need someone to help you sort through the souls."

For a split second, his understanding smile changed to one of pity, and I bristled. But before I could react, he said kindly, "Nothing would please me more. As much as I would enjoy your company, however, the Underworld would not suit you. I am fine with the darkness and the quiet, but you, sister, would wither without light. And I cannot do that to you."

"You don't know that for sure," I said. "It would be worth the isolation if I didn't have to be near Zeus."

He chuckled softly. "As I said, I do not blame you. But something better will come along, and in the meantime, you will have an equal voice on this council."

"What if that isn't enough? What if Zeus still finds a way to take over?"

"Then we will deal with that as it happens," said Hades. "I am on your side."

At least someone was. "You're sure I can't come with you?"

He pressed his lips to my forehead. "I would never forgive myself for what that place would do to you. But I will come visit you often, and I promise you will never be alone."

His words warmed me from the inside out, quelling the last of my frustration. "Why do you have to be so good, Hades? Why can't you be more like Poseidon and Zeus? It'd be easier to insist the lot of you weren't fit to rule."

He squeezed my shoulder. "Because if I were, we would be warring amongst ourselves, and we all know what would happen then. Go back to Olympus, Hera. Rest. I will see you soon, and in the meantime, try not to let Zeus get to you. He's overwhelmed with victory and relief, and that does strange things to men."

"He's not a man," I said. "He's a god."

"Then we can expect this to last much longer than it otherwise would." He embraced me for a brief moment before letting me go. "Do not forget your worth."

With that, he turned and walked toward the sealed crack in the earth, his footsteps leaving no trace in the dirt. I watched him disappear until darkness consumed him, and once he was gone, I took a shaky breath and returned to the others. I would never follow Zeus, but as long as Hades was there to introduce reason, perhaps this new life wouldn't be so bad, after all.

★ ★ ★

Sometime in the night, a sharp rap of knuckle against the wall of my Olympus bedroom startled me awake. While normally we did not need to sleep, after exerting our powers as we all had during the final battle, we required rest. Which only made the knock more confusing.

"Come in," I called, sitting up in bed and smoothing my hair. I was exhausted, my body heavy with sleep, but it was hard to shake the sensation of being on edge, as I had been during the past ten years. A knock then could've meant another battle or a turn we hadn't seen coming. We'd devoted every moment to strategizing and watching, and none of us had gotten a proper amount of rest.

The curtains parted, and Zeus stepped through. My stomach turned. Olympus hovered eternally between the blue sky of day above us and the rainbow of dusk below, but even with the golden sunlight that washed across his face, he looked pale. As he should have. If there was any justice in the world, he felt guilty for how he'd treated me and our sisters.

"Hera?" he said softly. "I didn't wake you, did I?"

"Since when have you ever been concerned with courtesy?" I curled back up in bed and closed my eyes. "Be quick about it. I was having a nice dream." One that involved dark hair, silver eyes and a lack of sunlight Olympus would never experience.

Zeus said nothing for nearly a minute. By the time he finally spoke, I'd drifted back to the edge of sleep. "I love you."

My eyes flew open. "Excuse me?"

"I have for a very long time." He stepped closer, reaching out for me as if he expected me to take his hand, but I didn't move. Zeus hesitated. "You are extraordinary, Hera. You are beautiful. You are powerful. And out of all my sisters, I think you would be best suited to stand at my side."

I shook my head. "You have enough women to keep you company, Zeus. I won't be another horse in your stable."

"You wouldn't be. I would devote myself to you and your power. To you and your brilliance. I will forsake the others if you insist I must, but I want to marry you."

For a long moment, I was silent. Any lingering exhaustion I'd felt had vanished, leaving me with bewilderment coursing through my veins. He wanted to marry me? He could barely speak to me as an equal, and he wanted me to devote my life to him? "No."

Zeus recoiled as if I'd slapped him. "What?"

"I said no."

"But—I'm King of the Skies," he said, stunned. Clearly he hadn't expected anything short of a yes. "You could be my queen. You could have absolute power—"

"I don't want to be your queen," I snapped. "And we both know that your definition of 'absolute power' is really absolute power second to yours. I won't be second to anyone, and I will not marry someone who looks down on me for my sex. Now leave."

Silence. Zeus gaped at me, and I stared back. He wouldn't win this one. I would not allow him to put a collar on me and parade me around as an ornament. I was the daughter of Cronus. I should have been a queen, but not *his* queen. A queen in my own right.

At last he left without a word. It wouldn't be the end of it—when Zeus set his mind to something, nothing would dissuade him, as the Titan War had proven—but for now, I needed to rest. We'd only just seen the end of one battle. I wasn't prepared to start another.

On the morning the council gathered for the first time, I spent ages in front of my mirror, searching for any flaws in my reflection. It'd been nearly a month since the end of the war, giving us all time to assess the damage and do what we could to heal it. While our brothers tried to form some semblance of order within their new domains, my sisters and I had roamed the earth, observing humanity and discovering the natural passages between the three realms. Every time we'd found a cave that led into the Underworld, I'd been tempted to go down and visit Hades, but my sisters had insisted he'd be far too busy. I wasn't so sure, but the last thing I wanted to do was burden him further.

Technically Zeus should have come with us, but I suspected part of the reason my sisters had dragged me out of Olympus was to get away from him. He and I had barely spoken a word to each other since his proposal, and for all intents and purposes, he seemed to have dropped it. Unlikely as it was, perhaps he wasn't as thickheaded as I'd thought.

At last, as the weeks had passed, I'd begun to feel at peace with everything. I didn't have to have a title in order to have power. I was who I was; no one, not Cronus, not Zeus, could take that from me.

But now that we were all to gather again, I couldn't shake the giddiness inside me. Maybe it was the idea of our family once again reuniting. We were never as powerful apart as we were together, after all. Whenever I envisioned what the morning would bring, however, all I could picture was one face: Hades's.

At last it was time, and I pushed aside my curtain to leave. Instead of an empty hallway, however, a peacock sat on a satin pillow in front of my rooms, blocking my exit. A gift?

The bird stood, revealing its magnificent plumage of blue, green and gold, and it walked directly into my chambers as if it had been waiting for me. Yes, a gift. But from whom?

I picked up a stray tail feather that remained on the pillow, tickling my nose with its soft ends, and I smiled. Zeus would never get me something so thoughtful. He would try to win me over with jewels and other cold, meaningless things. And that left only one person who would gift me something so extravagant.

Hades.

Was it possible he was as excited about seeing me as I was him? Maybe after a month alone in the Underworld, he'd come to his senses and decided to ask me to be his wife, after all. My excitement increased tenfold, and I all but skipped down the sky-blue and sunset corridor, still holding the feather. At last, a chance to escape. A chance to choose my own destiny. And I had no doubt about it—I would have chosen Hades again and again, until the end of time. Especially over Zeus.

The throne room was set in the center of Olympus, laid out in a circle with over a dozen hallways leading from it, in the shape of the sun and her rays. It had been the seat of our power during the war, untouchable even to Cronus, and it was the one place where we'd all been safe. Now that it was Zeus's domain, somehow the sun seemed darker. But that day, nothing, not even Zeus, could've brought me down.

No, not nothing. The moment I stepped into the throne room, my heart sank. Zeus, Poseidon, Demeter and Hestia were already there, waiting for me, but Hades's throne was empty.

"Good morning," I said, keeping the disappointment out of my voice. He was late, that was all. He had a much longer way to travel than the rest of us.

"Good morning," said Zeus. He'd aged himself a few years, but not even a beard could make him look like a king. "Now that we are all here, I will call this meeting to—"

"What about Hades?" I said. "Shouldn't we wait for him?"

"Hades won't be coming," said Zeus, sounding annoyed.

I lowered the tip of the feather from my nose. "Oh."

Across the circle, Demeter gave me a sympathetic smile. So everyone knew then, even Zeus. Enough to realize that

Hades was at least part of the reason I'd refused his proposal. One of our sisters must have told him, then,

I frowned. Hades felt like a secret, something I opened up when no one was there, and the thought of my sisters discussing Hades and me with Zeus made my skin crawl.

Zeus cleared his throat, and he gestured toward me. "I see you got my gift. Consider it an apology for how I've treated you. I would give you the heavens if I could, but Demeter insisted something simpler would be better."

I nearly dropped the feather. His gift? One Demeter had helped pick out? "Thank you," I mumbled, glaring at my sister. She knew how I felt about Zeus, and encouraging him like that wasn't only cruel to him. It was cruel to me, as well.

The meeting began, a mostly neutral affair with no one raising their voices. Poseidon and Zeus talked about the progress they'd made, protecting their subjects from predators and showing them how best to care for themselves now that they no longer had the threat of the Titans hanging over their heads, while my sisters spoke of what we'd discovered on earth. I remained quiet, however, my gaze focused on Hades's empty throne. His realm was the largest; and after a war, of course he wouldn't have time to spare.

He would come next time, though. He wouldn't break his promise. Not to me.

Hades didn't come the next time, or the next, or the time after that. Finally, nearly a year after the war ended, his throne wasn't there at all.

"Hades has decided to become an honorary member of the council," said Zeus that day. "He will join us when it is important, but otherwise he will defer to our judgment when it comes to matters above his realm."

In other words, he'd separated himself from us, breaking our unity. That pain sliced through me, hot and unyielding, and I had to blink rapidly to keep myself from letting it show. Fine. If he didn't think we were worth it—if he didn't think *I* was worth it, then so be it. We didn't need him. I didn't need him.

But I did, and that empty space inside my chest where hope for a happy life had once been ate away at me. He'd represented everything I'd wanted—respect, compassion, honesty and maturity that Zeus could never hope to obtain. The possibility of life as an equal to my partner. And with one single decision, he'd destroyed all of those dreams.

As soon as the meeting ended, I fled to the earth. It was summertime, and the forest was lush with colors. Green leaves, red and purple flowers, the blue sky and the brown soil—it should've been beautiful, but I was blind to all except Hades's betrayal.

I sat on the shore of a lake and sobbed. My cries echoed amongst the trees, but I was alone. Always alone. My sisters were content with their lots. My brothers each had their own kingdoms to rule. When would it be my turn to have a happy ending? When would I have a chance to live the life I wanted?

The Titan War hadn't been waged just to save humanity. We'd fought to save ourselves, too. I'd fought for my freedom, but what good was freedom when I found no joy in life alone? I wanted to share it with someone, to share the bonds of respect and fidelity, to know that to someone in the world, I was their life. But I would never have that now. Not with someone who could ever hope to be my equal, and I could never be with someone who looked down on me as something less. Hades had been my only hope.

A pitiful cry caught my attention, and I stopped weeping. Only a few feet away, crumpled on the ground, lay a tiny bird no bigger than an acorn. His wing was crooked, and as I peered down at him, he cheeped helplessly.

"You poor thing." Gently lifting the bird into my hand, I stroked his back. Next to the peacock that had become my constant companion in Olympus, this was the tamest creature I'd ever seen.

I touched the broken wing, willing it to heal. The bones eased back into place, and at last the bird righted himself. He seemed to doubt that his wing was fixed; he kept it close as he expanded the other, as if readying himself for takeoff. But instead he remained in my palm, and he cocked his head as he chirped up at me once more.

Despite the heartbreak of the morning, I smiled. "You can fly now, you know. You don't have to stay with me."

He hopped from my palm to the tips of my fingers, and at last he spread both of his wings. As he took off, I felt that same keen wrench in my chest, and it only brought on another fresh wave of tears. Everyone would leave me eventually, given enough time.

But even as I thought it, I felt a featherlight touch on my shoulder, and the bird chirped beside my ear. I wiped my cheeks. "You're back," I said thickly.

Another chirp, and he took a few strands of my hair in his beak. I managed a small smile.

"I wouldn't eat that if I were you. Let's find you some seeds."

The bird and I spent the rest of the day together, exploring the woods around the lake as I tried to find his home. But no matter how hard I searched the trees, I saw no evidence of a nest. He couldn't have been very old, certainly not on his own yet, but I heard no cries of his mother or siblings. So he'd been abandoned, after all.

"We aren't so different, you and I," I said as he perched on my finger. We sat on a rock, sunbathing in the warm afternoon glow. "I'm on my own, as well."

He gave a questioning chirp, as if he understood me. Maybe he did.

"My brother—my friend, he abandoned me, as well." It

was silly, talking to a bird, spilling my secrets, but I had no one else. Not even my sisters were trustworthy anymore. "He promised to come see me, but it's been a year. Not very long in the scheme of things, despite what you may think, but it still hurts."

Nearby, a tree rustled in the breeze, and the bird danced from one end of my finger to the other. He knew he could fly, and that he remained here healed something inside me. At last, someone was choosing to be with me.

"My brother—my other brother, he wants to marry me," I said. The bird tilted his head again, and I smiled. "He's King of the Skies—your king, even if you don't know it. I doubted he could do it at first, you know. We all did, and he proved us wrong, which only makes it hurt even more. Have you ever wanted to be needed so badly that you felt as if your heart would burst?"

He hopped up my arm, climbing until he sat on my shoulder again. I offered him my finger, but he remained.

"Of course you haven't. But my brother Zeus, he only wants me as an ornament. Something to make him look stronger. He doesn't see me—he doesn't love me. He loves my power. And even if I did agree to marry him, he would never be faithful to me. I would never be his equal, and he would insist I bow down to him. That isn't the life I want."

Another chirp, and his warm little body brushed up against the crook of my neck.

"I want to live a life of respect and equality. Of partnership. I want someone to love me for who I am, not what I can do for him. I want someone who keeps his promises. Who doesn't see me as a conquest." I sighed and stared down at the pattern in the rock. "I want to be *happy*."

Without warning, the bird took flight, disappearing into the trees. My heart leaped, and I stood, ready to follow his path.

He couldn't leave, too. I could take him back to Olympus, make him immortal, keep him as my companion—

But he didn't return. The forest was never silent, with the rustling leaves, gentle laps of waves on the lake, and countless other sounds that mixed together in natural harmony, and I strained for any signs of his chirps. Nothing.

A sob escaped me, and I sank back onto the warm rock. So this was how my life would be. Constant loneliness, an ache for something I could never have, and everyone I ever loved would leave me. First my mother, then Hades, and now a creature that I barely even knew. Yet his abandonment still stung as badly as the rest, a reminder of the pain I'd already endured.

I buried my face in my hands, and without any thought to dignity, I cried. For myself, for the life I would never have, for the eons that would never end. For the hope that had been stolen from me time and time again, until it dwindled into nothing.

"Hera?"

I stiffened midsob, silencing myself. The voice had been too muffled for me to make it out properly, but it was male. One of my brothers. Hades?

A twig snapped, and I was on my feet in an instant. No time to wash away my tears in the lake. A figure moved through the trees, at first obscured by shadows. As soon as he stepped into the sunlight, however, I recognized him.

Zeus. Of course. I would never get my way.

"What do you want?" I sank back down onto the rock and drew my knees to my chest. I expected a smart answer, a joke about how I could stop crying now that he was here. Instead he knelt a few feet away, and out of the corner of my eye, I saw the concern on his face. Sincere or not, I wouldn't accept his pity.

"I am sorry." His words sounded heavy, as if he were weighing each one before he spoke. "Not only for how I have treated you, but for how I have thought of you, as well. Father—" He hesitated. "Father was no role model, but I am afraid I took his treatment of Mother to heart. You deserve better, as did she, and for that I apologize."

I shut my eyes. He could apologize all he wanted. It wouldn't change anything.

"You are the best of us all, Hera," he said quietly. "You are the strongest, the smartest, but you are also the most deserving, and—you are the loveliest girl I have ever seen. Not simply on the outside, but on the inside, as well."

That was a lie and we both knew it. Hestia was the kindest, the gentlest, and Demeter was the most even-tempered. I had power, and I had pride. I wasn't content with what lay before me.

But his words washed over me anyway, a small oasis within the desert of my life. Still, I didn't acknowledge them.

"I love you." Zeus set his hand on my shoulder, the way Hades had the evening we'd won the war. "Not as an ornament. Not as a conquest. I see you, and I love you."

I jerked back from his touch. "You were spying on me?"

"Only to make sure you were all right. After the meeting, I was worried—"

"You had no right." I stood furiously and started to march off. "That was a private conversation."

"Hera." There was a command in his voice so reminiscent of our father's that even I couldn't resist stopping and turning to face him. In that instant, my tiny bird took Zeus's place, flying closer to me before he changed back. Zeus was barely a foot in front of me now. "Everything you want, that is what I want to be to you. *For* you."

The magnitude of his deception hit me, and I slapped him. "I don't care what you want to be to me. You will never be anything more than the god who stole my rightful place from me, and the god who tricked me into spilling my secrets."

"They are my secrets, as well." Zeus took my hand with gentleness I'd been certain he wasn't capable of. I pulled away, and his expression shattered. "Please, Hera—I'm lonely. I'm burdened. I want nothing more than someone to share my life with. Not to rule over as the Titans did. But a true equal in every sense of the word."

I shook my head. He was only repeating the things I'd unwittingly told him, and I would not let him worm his way into my heart. "You're lying. You could never be faithful to me, and I will not settle for anything short of absolute fidelity."

"Then you will have it. The other women—they are nothing compared to you, and I only want you. I only need you. I am yours, and I will forever be yours, despite the seasons that pass. I will do anything to prove myself to you, Hera."

"Then give me your kingdom," I blurted before I could think it through. But that was the true test—if Zeus wanted me as badly as he claimed, then why not pit the two things he loved most against each other?

I expected hesitation. I expected bargaining. Instead he nodded, and with the sun as our witness, he knelt before me. "My kingdom is yours. You will be queen, and I will be your king. We will rule together as partners, as equals, whether you consent to marry me or not. From this moment on, it is done, regardless of your choice."

I stared at him. He couldn't be serious. Whatever game he was playing, I was nothing more than a pawn, a way for him to entertain himself while ignoring the responsibilities of his domain.

But he had been a fair ruler so far, and he was no longer the boy who'd led us during the war. In the year since our victory, he had transformed into a young man, one I was nearly proud to call brother. Loath as I was to admit it, even to myself.

"I will never bow at your feet," I said.

"Which is why I am bowing at yours."

"I will not consent to mistresses."

"You are all I need."

"I demand respect and honesty at all times."

"And you will have it, from this moment on."

The warmth and hope in his voice melted the ice around my heart, and at last I allowed myself to relax. Never completely, but enough to feel alive once more.

"I will not give you an answer now," I said at last. "Words are easy to speak, but I want you to show me that you mean this. I will give you one chance. If you break my trust in any way, or if you treat me as anything less than your equal for even a moment, it is over. But if you prove to me that you mean this, that you've changed and are willing to do this—then when the time is right, I will marry you."

Uncertainly flashed across his face, but it was gone before I could comment, and he stood. "Very well. You have my devotion." He brushed his fingertips against my cheek, and my insides fluttered. "I will do whatever it takes to prove myself to you."

"Good." No use allowing Zeus the satisfaction of knowing what his promises meant to me. As Hades had proven that day, a promise was easily broken. "I look forward to your efforts."

"For now, let us walk," said Zeus. "It's a beautiful afternoon, and I'm with the most beautiful woman in the world. It would be a crime to waste it."

Once again, he took my hand. This time I didn't resist.

Zeus stuck to his word. I hadn't thought it possible, but from that afternoon on, he treated me as his equal. Together we ruled his kingdom—our kingdom now, visiting humans, watching over them, intervening when problems became too great for them to handle peacefully. The last thing we needed was a war among mortals, and we both kept busy, putting out fires as they arose. One day they would be able to govern themselves, but not yet.

On top of offering me equality, he showered me with gifts and attention. More than that, he offered me affection as well, never pushing for more than I was willing to give. Soon I began to look forward to spending time with him, and eventually the loss of Hades became little more than a twinge of regret.

Each evening, Zeus asked me to marry him. After each proposal, I said no. But his determination never faltered, and as time passed, I could no longer deny that he'd changed. The days of wrestling in the mud with Poseidon were gone, and I was proud to stand beside him as his queen, as his equal. My affection for him ran deep, and though some nights I wondered what my life would be like with someone I was truly passionate about, I knew I would find no better offer.

So after a day that had been nothing more than average on the surface, yet had been quietly extraordinary because I'd spent it with Zeus—I said yes.

On the morning of my wedding, my sisters helped me prepare. I bathed in the sweetest spring on earth, adorned my hair with the most beautiful flowers in creation and spent hours in my chamber taking every possible step to make sure I was perfect. But only Hestia seemed to share my happiness. Demeter was strangely quiet as she plaited my hair in an intricate style, and nothing Hestia and I said seemed to snap her out of it.

At last, once she'd finished with my hair, I turned to face her. "Say it."

Demeter blinked innocently. "Say what?"

"Whatever it is you're thinking. I can see your disapproval with both of my eyes shut, and I will not have my sister unhappy on my wedding day."

She pursed her lips, and at last she murmured, "I am simply not sure you're making the right decision, that's all."

I knew it was coming, but something inside me snapped. "And why is that?" I said, not bothering to hide the challenge in my voice. She had no right to question my choices. She'd chosen to live her life alone thus far, and I wasn't weaker than her for choosing the opposite.

Hestia quickly stepped toward us. "There's no need to fight. You've made your decision, and Demeter's only concerned for your welfare—"

"My welfare? I daresay it goes much deeper than that, doesn't it, Demeter?"

"Hera—" said Hestia, but I cut her off.

"Let our sister say her piece."

Demeter hesitated again, but finally she said, "Zeus has gone to great lengths to prove he's changed for you. But people don't change like that, Hera—they change because they want to, not because someone demands they do. And I worry that as soon as the wedding's over and the pair of you settle into marriage, he's going to revert back to the person you hate."

"Have you heard something?" I said. "Have you seen him do anything that would make you question his fidelity to me?"

"No, but—"

"He's changed." I stood. "I know him. Not only did he decide to better himself for me, but he's proud of the changes he's made, and he wants to stay that way."

"Hera…" Demeter reached for me, but I pulled away.

"If you had proof, if you had witnesses—but you don't, because he's loyal to me. He respects me, and he would never hurt me in such a way. He would never leave me like that."

"Zeus would say or do anything to get you to marry him," she said. "It's a game to him. I've no doubt he loves you, but that doesn't mean he'll remain loyal as soon as he has what he wants, and you must be prepared for the possibility—"

"It is not a *possibility*," I said. "He's changed, and you will see. You'll both see. Unless you intend on sabotaging his efforts to prove me wrong."

Her eyes widened. "No, of course not—"

"Do you love him? Do you wish you were in my place? Do you have aspirations to be his queen, Demeter?"

My sister's expression hardened. "The only thing I wish is for you to be happy. If that's suddenly a crime or something worthy of your anger, then so be it. I don't regret looking out for you."

"I don't need you to look out for me," I snapped. "I'm Queen. I can look out for myself."

Fire flashed in her irises, and for a long moment, she said nothing as she stared at me. At last, as if it gave her great pain to do so, she curtsied. "As you wish, my queen."

She may as well have slapped me. I didn't want her condescending deference. I wanted her respect. Her acknowledgment that I was more than some silly little girl who saw marriage as the end of aspiration. I wanted her to trust me to make my own decisions, rather than allowing my siblings to dictate it for me. It was my life. What I chose to do with it was my business, and she had no say. Yet with that single gesture, she'd said more about what she thought of my choice than words could possibly express, and I hated her for it.

"Come," said Hestia, touching my hand. "It's nearly time. Zeus will be waiting."

I said nothing as she led me from my chambers and down the sunset hallway. If Demeter wanted to disapprove, that was her burden to bear, not mine. I was walking toward the rest of my eternal existence. If she chose to remain behind me, then so be it.

Hades was waiting for me in the antechamber.

I felt his presence as soon as Hestia left, and until that moment, I hadn't realized how much I'd craved being with him in the time we'd been apart. Warmth washed over me, and I smiled. It was as if I were coming home.

"I missed you." I stepped toward the window, where he stood gazing out across the endless sky. "I was worried you'd decided to separate from us completely."

"Never." He turned, and his eyes swept over me. "You look beautiful."

My cheeks grew warm, and I moved to stand beside him. "I am getting married today, you know."

"So I've heard." His fingertips brushed mine, and I slipped my hand into his without further prompting. "Demeter told me about your argument."

The bubble of happiness inside my chest popped. "She had no right."

"She's only looking out for your well-being," he said. "We've all seen what Zeus is capable of, and we all love you. No one wants to see you hurt."

I shook my head. "He's changed. You haven't been here to see it, but—he's different now. He's proven himself to me again and again, and he loves me." My voice hitched. "That's all I want, you know. To be loved and respected."

"Yes, I know." He squeezed my hand. "You're certain you will be happy no matter what the eons bring?"

I took a deep breath. "He'll stick to his promises, Hades. I know him. And he loves me."

"Love is not always enough, as much as we may want it to be."

His words were a knife, slicing me open and stabbing me in the heart. "It is, if it's with the right person. He doesn't break his promises to me. He doesn't abandon me without a word. He doesn't smile at me and never follow through."

Hades frowned. "I never made you any promises—"

"You did." My voice broke, and I let go of him. "You did, Hades. You promised you'd come visit me. You said you'd be

there for me. You swore I'd never be alone, but I was. I waited
for you, and you never came."

Silence. He reached for my hand again, and I snatched it
away. He swallowed. "I am sorry. I didn't realize—"

"What's done is done." I closed my eyes. I had to regain
control. "You had your chance, and now it's over. Zeus loves
me. He's loyal to me, and he treats me like the queen I am.
He's there for me every single day."

"And is he what you want?" said Hades quietly. "Do you
love him?"

"I wouldn't be marrying him if I didn't." I stepped back,
cementing the distance that had grown between us. I wouldn't
let Hades do this to me, not after all this time. Zeus was the
best I could ever hope to have. Once upon a time, that had
been Hades, but he'd proven he was nothing more than empty
words and promises. I wanted more. I deserved more. "I need
to finish preparing for the wedding now."

He tilted his head in acknowledgment. "I wish you all the
love and happiness in the world, sister. And though I may not
have been there as I should have been, I am here now, and I
will forever be there for you should you need me."

"Thank you," I said softly. It was the most I could give him
in return. "Until then."

"Until then."

PART TWO

The wedding was everything I'd dreamed it would be. Zeus spoke his vows with the authority and compassion of a king, and any doubts Demeter and Hades had managed to plant in my mind vanished. I was happy, and the entire world celebrated our union. That was all that mattered.

Our marriage continued on, much as our initial time together had. We worked side by side, ruling over our subjects and touring the earth, and his loyalty remained with me. Every time he looked at me, I saw the love in his eyes, and it only reaffirmed that I'd made the right decision. I had the life I wanted now, and no one, not Hades, not Demeter, could take it away from me. I would do everything in my power to make sure of it.

Less than a month before I was set to give birth to our first son, Zeus cleared his throat outside the chambers we shared. "Hera?"

I frowned and sat up from my afternoon nap, my rounded belly hindering my movements. He never hesitated to enter. "Yes?"

Zeus stepped through the curtain, his cheeks pink and his

hair windswept. In that moment, he nearly looked like a young boy again, and I set my hand on my belly. Excitement, that was all. He'd nearly burst with happiness when I'd told him about our baby.

"I have a surprise for you," he murmured. "Close your eyes."

Relieved, I did so, trying to guess what it might be. I expected him to set my gift on the bed, but instead I heard the sound of light footsteps. One of my sisters, maybe, though he no longer asked for Demeter's help in choosing my gifts.

"Perfect. Now open them."

As the room came into focus, I blinked. Beside Zeus stood the most beautiful little girl I'd ever seen. Her hair was the same shade of gold as his, her eyes were so blue that they put the sky to shame, and her skin was pink and porcelain. She was perfect in every way.

"Hera, meet Aphrodite," he said, and he ushered her toward me. Aphrodite moved with more grace than the wind, and as she curtsied, her cheeks flushed. "I discovered her among nymphs on an island."

"It's an honor," she murmured. Her voice was like honey, far more intoxicating than mine would ever be. I hated her already.

"A servant?" I said. "How kind of you. I could certainly use someone to help me with the baby."

He cleared his throat. "Er, yes, well—of course, Aphrodite will be here to help you with our son, but not as a servant. As my daughter and a member of the council."

Cold horror washed over me. A member of the council. Zeus wanted her to be our equal. My equal. "But she's a child—"

"She is my child now," said Zeus. "Ours. And she will

grow, as will our son. They will both be members of the council, and perhaps one day she will be his companion."

"But she wasn't born into our family," I said. "She cannot simply join us before we make sure she's suited to rule."

"And how would you suggest we do that?" said Zeus.

I shrugged. "A test, perhaps, to weigh her virtues."

He scoffed. "None of us are perfect, Hera." Something about the way he said it sent a shiver of foreboding down my spine, and I draped a blanket over my lap.

"No, we aren't, but we must all share some key qualities to ensure we're fit to rule. Not us, of course," I said. "But if you intend on adding others to our council, we must make sure it is best for humanity."

Sighing, Zeus patted the little girl on the head. "Very well. We will test her when she grows older, and in the meantime, coming up with the parameters is your responsibility. I expect them to be fair."

"Of course," I murmured. "They'll be fit for a god."

Aphrodite shyly took a step toward me. "Daddy told me all about your baby. Can I touch him?"

I eyed the little girl with distaste. The last thing I wanted was for her to go anywhere near my son, but I felt Zeus's gaze and the hope that emanated from him. He'd done this with the best of intentions. He hadn't meant to insult me with a gift that was far more beautiful than I would ever be. Perhaps he didn't even see her that way, given how young she appeared.

But as she stepped closer, I noticed something ancient in her eyes, something that searched me even as I searched her. She wasn't a child. I didn't know where she'd come from or who she was, but she was not as young as Zeus wanted me to believe.

Without breaking her stare, I took her hand and set it gently over the spot on my belly where my son now kicked. Her eyes widened at the movement, and she giggled. "He likes to move."

"He does," I said. "Perhaps if you are good, when he's born, I will let you hold him."

She nodded solemnly, but that ancient look didn't go away. How could Zeus have missed it? Unless he hadn't. Unless he knew she was older and this was all a ruse.

No, he wouldn't do that to me. He loved me, and he wouldn't hurt me in such a way. We were about to welcome a baby together. But even as I tried to reassure myself, my uncertainty refused to disappear, and my sister's poisonous words returned to me.

"Has Zeus already decided what you're to be the goddess of?" I said. We all chose our assignments—the things we held most dear, the things that came naturally to us. Fidelity for me, of course, and marriage, which I'd chosen after our wedding. Fertility after I'd fallen pregnant. But the council mostly chose for the minor gods that roamed the world.

"Love," said Zeus, and I nearly choked. "She is the goddess of love. There was no choosing involved. She simply is."

"The—goddess of love," I said tightly. "Very well. It certainly suits you."

Aphrodite beamed, and without warning, she threw her little arms around me. "We'll be great friends," she murmured in her childish voice. "I can't wait."

I could. I could wait forever. But the way Zeus beamed, seeing her hug me—I had little choice but to hug back. If it made him happy, I would do it. He certainly did plenty to return the favor.

But that suspicion remained, a small doubt that refused to go away. Before I accepted this little trickster as my own, I would need to make sure that was all Zeus intended for her.

Because although I wanted to trust him, in the face of the unknown, even I had my doubts.

That evening, after Zeus had slipped out of our chambers to tuck Aphrodite into bed, I followed him. My footsteps were silent, and I moved without detection despite the baby I carried. Her room was only one down from ours, where I'd intended the baby's nursery to be, but Zeus had assured me we would be more comfortable across the hall from the baby instead. Perhaps he was more concerned about getting his rest, but the thought of being that much farther apart from my son ate at me.

I bent my head toward the curtain that separated Aphrodite's room from the corridor. If Zeus caught me, I had a dozen explanations on the tip of my tongue, each one a greater lie than the last. But he'd done this to himself, bringing a stranger into our home only weeks before our son would be born.

"I don't think she likes me." Aphrodite's voice, and barely audible at that. I set my hand against my other ear, determined to block out any outside noise.

"Who, Hera?" said Zeus. His voice was like thunder even when he tried to whisper. "She's just a bit surprised, darling. She didn't expect you."

"I want her to love me." The yearning in Aphrodite's voice shifted something inside me. "I want a mother."

"She will be your mother," murmured Zeus. "And I will be your father. You'll never be alone again."

The same promise Hades had made to me. Except this time I knew Zeus wouldn't break it. Not to me, not to this little girl, not to anyone. "I'd really like that," she whispered.

"I know you would." A pause. "Get some sleep. Tomorrow I'll introduce you to all your aunts and uncles."

"More family?" I could practically see her eyes widen in amazement.

Zeus chuckled. "More family."

I stepped away from the curtain and hurried back into the chamber before Zeus could discover me. He wasn't lying, after all. Once again, he'd proven Hades and Demeter wrong.

When Zeus returned to our chamber and lay down beside me, I curled up against him, resting my head on his chest. "I love you," I whispered. "Every part of you."

He kissed my hair. "As I love you. Never forget that."

In that moment, I was certain I never would.

The day Ares was born was the happiest of my life.

As I held that squirming pink bundle, I understood why our mother had refused to fight at Cronus's side against us. No matter how much I loved Zeus, no matter how loyal I was to him, Ares was as much a part of me as my heart. He was mine.

Zeus disappeared hours after Ares was born, presumably to celebrate with Poseidon and Hades. As soon as he'd gone, however, a knock sounded. "Come in," I called.

Demeter pushed aside the curtains. I lay on the bed, curled up with the baby, who slept soundly against my chest. "Hera," she murmured, slipping inside. "He's beautiful. Congratulations."

Regardless of any lingering animosity between us, I grinned. "Isn't he? He looks just like me."

"I'm sure Zeus took that well," she teased. Sitting down on the bed, she touched Ares's cheek. "He almost makes me want to have children of my own."

"Maybe you should," I said. "It's about time you found someone."

She shook her head, and something flickered across her face, something I didn't quite catch. "I wouldn't be very good at it. I think I'd rather plant roots first. Find myself."

"Well, you do have eternity," I said, and she smiled a bit sadly.

"I do." She hesitated and pulled her gaze away from Ares. "I need to talk to you about something, and I need you to not panic or get angry. For your son's sake."

All of the contentment Ares's birth had brought me drained away, leaving me with the same wariness that had plagued me before. "If you're going to tell me you don't think Zeus will be a good father—"

"He already is a good father," said Demeter. "With Ares, with Aphrodite and with Athena."

I made a face. Athena, his child with Metis during the war, before he'd married me. Thankfully, she rarely came around. The thought of being a stepmother didn't hold much appeal to me, and dealing with Aphrodite was difficult enough. "I don't see what she has to do with anything."

"She doesn't," said Demeter. Another moment passed between us in silence. "Zeus has a mistress."

My grip on my son tightened, and burning anger flared up inside me. "How dare you accuse him when you have no proof—"

"Oh, I have proof." Demeter's expression hardened, and she stood. "I've been following him, for your sake. Making sure he remained faithful."

"You had *no right*—"

"I had every right to protect my sister. Whether you choose to believe me or not, all I've ever wanted was for you and Hestia to be happy. You're different from us, Hera—you want things we don't, and sometimes it's hard to see the world the way you do. But that doesn't make me love you any less. And I would never sabotage your happiness for sport."

I swallowed hard. No matter how often we argued, she was telling the truth—she would never hurt me on purpose. And that left me with two options: denial and playing the fool, or acceptance and putting a stop to it.

I'd never been very good at being foolish.

"Why tell me now?" My lower lip trembled, and I clutched Ares. "Why ruin today for me?"

Demeter sank down beside me again, cupping my cheek. "No one can ruin today for you," she murmured. "Your son is healthy and happy, and he already loves you so much."

"So why not wait until after I've had a little time to be happy with him? Why did you have to rob me of that?" I blinked rapidly, struggling to keep myself from crying. I wouldn't give Demeter the satisfaction of seeing me come undone.

"Because," she said, averting her eyes, "his mistress is about to give birth, as well."

All at once, the world gave out from under me, and it was all I could do to remain upright. "He wouldn't. He *wouldn't*."

"I'm so sorry," she whispered, and bitterness and fury unlike anything I'd ever experienced before ate away at me like acid, consuming every good thing left. In my arms, Ares started to cry, but even his fear wasn't enough to make me curb my wrath.

"Who?" I demanded, and Demeter flinched.

"Leto. She's pregnant with twins."

Twins. My eyes flickered shut, and I took several deep breaths, forcing myself to calm down. "That's his plan."

"What's his plan?"

"To take over the council. To override all of us." I opened my eyes again, the fire inside me compressed into a single burning need. "First Aphrodite joins the council. Then Ares.

It's only a matter of time before he asks for Athena to join, as well. And after that, these bastard children of his—"

Demeter shook her head. "We'd never allow it. You know we wouldn't."

"He has Poseidon's vote, and Aphrodite's, and if it comes to it, Hades's, as well. He would never dare upset the balance. Even if the three of us voted against it, we would still be outnumbered. Even if he doesn't manage to do so now, eventually he'll find a way."

Demeter was quiet for a long moment. "Do you really think he would do that?"

"Yes," I said flatly. "He's exactly like our father—greedy, hungry for power, convinced he alone knows what is best. Concerned only with his own wants and desires without any regard for those he claims to love—"

"Hera."

"—and if he thinks I'm going to let him get away with treating me with such little respect, I'll—"

"*Hera.*"

Demeter reached for Ares, and I stopped. He was wailing now, his cries loud enough to wake all of Olympus. Numb, I allowed her to take him. "I need to find her," I said, my arms cold without the weight of my son. "She can't give birth. She can't destroy the council like that."

"It isn't her fault," said Demeter. "I'm certain Zeus lied to her. Even if he didn't, this is a choice he made. She didn't seduce him."

"I don't want to hear it." I stood on shaky legs. "I must go. Watch after him while I'm away."

She opened her mouth, but before she could say a word, she seemed to think better of it. At last she nodded. "Do what you must. I love you."

"I love you, too, sister. Thank you for telling me."

And with that, I exited the room, determined to do whatever I had to in order to stop this atrocity.

Several nights later, Zeus stormed into our chambers. "What did you do?"

The joy he'd emanated since Ares's birth was gone now, replaced by waves of anger that would have frightened any reasonable person. He was, after all, King. But I was Queen, and this war was between equals.

"What do you mean?" I said with mocking innocence. If he was going to dare grow angry with me for protecting the council's interests, for protecting the fairness and equality upon which we'd all agreed, then he was going to have to confess to breaking the most important promise he'd made me. To breaking his vows.

His face went from pink to red to a shade of purple that couldn't possibly be natural, and lightning encompassed his clenched fists. "You know what," he finally said in his thunderous voice. "Leto's been in labor for days."

"And she'll remain in labor for a very long time," I said, cradling Ares as he slept. Odd how my anger affected him, yet he barely batted an eye at his father's fury. "I hardly see why it matters to you. Your son is right here."

"Do not play these games with me," he snarled. "You will undo whatever it is you did immediately."

"What could I have possibly done, and why would I have done it?" I brushed a lock of Ares's hair from his eyes. Such a beautiful baby. He deserved so much more than the father he had.

Lightning cracked outside the balcony, mere feet away from where we lay. If Zeus thought his threats would frighten me into complacency, he was sorely mistaken. At last, however, his shoulders sank, and he reached out for me. "Hera, my love, I'm so sorry. I made a grave mistake—"

I slapped his hand away. "From what I've heard, you've made several *mistakes*. How many mistresses have you had since we married?"

His brow furrowed. "Just one. Just Leto—"

"Liar."

He squeezed his eyes shut, as if he were in pain. "Hera, please—"

"I will not sit here and listen to your lies." I stood, and in my arms, Ares made a small sound. "You may either lie and go or stay and tell the truth. If you want any chance of me helping your precious Leto, I'd suggest the latter."

"I'm loyal to you," he said, his voice breaking. "To you and only you. The others, they're nothing—"

"If they are nothing, then why did you bother with them in the first place?"

"Weakness. Opportunity. I wasn't thinking—"

"That much is obvious."

"Hera, please." Zeus stood and moved toward me, but I backed away. "They're innocent children."

"So is Ares, yet before a week's passed, you've forced him to face his father's infidelities and lies." I walked to the curtain that separated our chambers from the hallway. "I won't help you or Leto. As far as I'm concerned, our marriage is over."

"Then so is your role as my queen."

I stopped, and the darkness spun around me. I clutched Ares to my chest. "My title has nothing to do with our marriage."

"It has everything to do with our marriage, and you know it."

"You can't strip me of our partnership—"

"If you dissolve our marriage, I can and I will," he said in a dangerously soft voice. "I've made mistakes. I won't make them again. All I ask for now is your forgiveness, and that you not take your anger out on the innocent."

"Because of you, none of us are innocent." My eyes watered, and I gazed down at my son. My title or my pride. That was the choice he was forcing upon me. All I'd worked for, all I'd done for the council—or having to stand beside a god who had lied to me about everything.

Our whole family must have known. Certainly Poseidon and Demeter, and Demeter wouldn't keep something like this from Hestia. Though not Hades. Hades would have told me—

I'd chosen wrong. I should've waited. Hades would've never done this to me. I should've listened to him, to my sister, to my conscience—but I'd been blinded by Zeus's promises and my pride. I'd thought I could change him. Clearly I'd been wrong. And now the whole council would suffer for me.

No. I wouldn't allow everything we'd worked for to fall. No matter what Zeus seemed to think, we all had equal say on the council. And as long as those twins never arrived, as long as he never had the chance to place them among us, then he was still only one voice.

"I will remain with you," I said thickly, staring at our son. My son. "I will not forgive you, but I will stay. And in return, you will never see those children or that woman again."

Silence, followed by soft footsteps as he moved toward me. "And you will allow her to give birth?"

"I will relieve her of her burden."

He set his hand on my back, the heat between us hotter than the hottest forge. "Very well. I am and have always been yours."

I turned away from him and stepped into the corridor. "No, you haven't," I whispered, and before he could tell me any other lies, I hurried away, heading for my sister.

★ ★ ★

For the next three days, I waited for news. I avoided my duties both to the realm and to Zeus, wanting to give him a taste of what it would be like to rule without me. Perhaps in the early days he could've handled it on his own, but now the realm was far too big for any one person to rule without things slipping through the cracks. Eventually he would discover just how much he needed me.

I remained with Demeter, sleeping in her chambers and wandering the earth beside her, showing Ares the beauty of the world. He seemed to enjoy it, gurgling and turning his face toward the sun. I avoided the lake where I'd helped the injured bird, knowing that if Zeus wanted to find me, that was the first place he would look. And I would not be fooled by him again.

"It'll get easier, you know," said Demeter as we wandered across a white sand beach, searching for shells for Ares. "Eventually the hurt and anger will fade."

"But things will never be the same again," I said bitterly. "I will never be as happy as I was, believing his promises."

"Happiness is a choice, sister," she said, plucking a piece of coral from the sand. "You have a beautiful baby who loves you nearly as much as you love him. Isn't that enough reason to find joy in the world?"

"Sometimes. Most of the time. But there's a piece of me that will always remain shriveled because of what his father did."

"Then hide it away and never let it be seen, not even by yourself. Focus on the good, and eventually happiness will come as easily as—"

"Hera."

Zeus's voice cut through the ocean breeze, and Demeter fell silent. I stiffened. Finally. "I have no interest in seeing you today," I said without turning around. "Go."

"You did it, didn't you?" He grabbed my shoulder and yanked me around. "You sent that serpent after Leto—"

"I told you I would relieve her of her burden," I snapped, jerking away from him. Ares began to cry. "It isn't my fault you interpreted it the way you did. But it is your fault that you ever put her and those children in that situation to begin with. Consider their deaths to be on your hands."

He set his mouth in a thin line. I expected anger born out of grief and anguish, but I only saw frustration. "That's where you're wrong," he said quietly. "They survived. And you will never find Leto again."

No. Impossible. I stared at him, horrified. Demeter set her hand on my shoulder, but even she couldn't comfort me now. "And the twins?"

"They have joined me in Olympus," said Zeus, and he may as well have squeezed my heart until it was nothing. "When they are older, they too will join the council. Effective immediately, Athena will move to Olympus to help me care for them, and she too will join our ranks."

Athena, Aphrodite, the twins. Four more voices to echo Zeus.

That was it, then, We'd lost. I sank to the ground, rocking Ares as he cried, but my thoughts were anywhere but on that beach. It was only a matter of time before Zeus overthrew my sisters and me entirely.

I didn't know how long I sat there, the sun shining down on me and the waves crashing to shore only a few feet away. Demeter remained by my side, and eventually Ares calmed, but I couldn't find the same peace no matter how hard I tried.

"It's over," I whispered long after Zeus departed. "The four of them and Poseidon will follow Zeus's every word."

"You don't know that for sure," murmured Demeter. "Perhaps they will think for themselves. Athena has a good head on her shoulders, and I can't imagine her being swayed from something she believes in."

"She hates me for replacing her mother. She'll never vote with me on anything, especially against her father."

Demeter hesitated. "Even then, perhaps Aphrodite—"

"She's his favorite." The words stuck in my throat, and I had to force them out. "She'll agree to anything so long as he loves her the most."

She ran her fingers through my hair. "The end of time hasn't come yet. There are still plenty of opportunities to have children and even the numbers."

"He won't touch me now. He'll know I'm up to something. Even he isn't dumb enough to believe I'd forgive him so quickly."

"Then wait," she murmured.

"We don't have time to spare."

Demeter sighed and kissed my hair. "It will work out. I promise you, everything will be all right."

I turned away. After all the broken promises I'd endured from those I loved, her words didn't mean anything to me anymore. "Even if he discards his current mistresses, it'll only be a matter of time before he takes another."

"That's true," she said slowly as the waves lapped our ankles. The tide would force us to move soon. "People don't change."

Or Zeus didn't, at least. "What then? How many more illegitimate children will he have?"

"I don't know," she said softly. "As many as he wants, I suppose."

"And meanwhile, he'll leave me with only Ares. I'll never have daughters, I'll never have another son. Unless—"

I stopped. Of course. Why hadn't I thought of it before? It would be almost too easy, using Zeus's weakness against him, and with patience—

"Unless what?" said Demeter. I didn't answer. "Hera, unless what?"

At last I faced her again, unable to help my grin. "Unless I trick him. Unless I play him like a fool the same way he's played me."

She frowned. "You're miserable enough as it is. Why put yourself in the line of fire all over again?"

"Because when he takes another mistress—and he will, we both know he will—I'm going to make sure it's me."

I roamed the beaches every night for a season. Demeter watched Ares for me, and though we planned an elaborate story if Zeus ever checked in on me, he never did.

I didn't expect it to work. I hoped, and I used my abilities as much as I dared to entice him to come to me, but in all my planning, I never truly thought I would win.

But at last, as the full moon shone down on my changed form, I saw him. He stood framed by the trees in the distance, his hair tickling his shoulders in the breeze, and for a moment I nearly forgot why I hated him. Whether he recognized me or not, I couldn't tell, and I held my breath as he slowly made his way across the sand toward me.

"Hello," he murmured in a voice he'd never used with me. "What's your name?"

Relief swept through me, as palpable as the golden ichor in my veins. He didn't know me. And at last, for the first time in months, I smiled at him.

"Hephaesta," I murmured. "My name is Hephaesta."

Our affair lasted one night, but that was all I needed. I never returned to the beach, and whether or not he came looking for his new mistress, I didn't know. He never showed any signs of distress in Olympus. Then again, I'd been nothing more than a fling to him, and if he truly fell in love with my disguise, then he was a greater fool than even I'd suspected.

My belly grew round as time passed. I made no effort to hide it, and though Demeter reported whisperings and gossip from the other gods, I didn't care. Whether they knew it or not, this was a legitimate child. What they thought didn't matter.

At last, on the morning I gave birth to my second son, Zeus confronted me. I rested with the baby in my bedroom, and he stormed in, startling my peacock into flight.

"What did you do that for?" I said, sighing as the bird took off from my balcony. "We were having a nice chat."

"I'm sure you were." He slammed his fist on the wall so hard that they must've heard it on the other side of Olympus. "Who is he?"

"Who is who?" I said innocently, turning my attention back to the baby sleeping soundly in my arms. "You mean him? This is my son."

"I do not mean the baby," he said through clenched teeth. "Tell me who your consort is."

"My consort?" I tilted my head in what must have been an infuriating show of ignorance. "You're my consort, dear husband. Or have you forgotten? It certainly would explain quite a lot, wouldn't it?"

"Enough," he thundered, and before I could blink, he snatched my son from my arms and stormed to the balcony. The baby started to sob. "I will not be treated this way. I will not be disrespected by my own wife. I will not be played a fool in front of my subjects and my council—"

"*Your* council?" I scrambled to follow, but my empty body was too exhausted and sore to move as quickly as my son's cries demanded. "It is *our* council, or have you forgotten that, too?"

"Do not toy with me," he snarled, and he stood on the

edge of the balcony, balancing my crying son precariously in one arm.

"Give him back." I reached for him, but Zeus sidestepped me. "Zeus, he's a baby, he needs me, give him *back*—"

"Artemis and Apollo were babies, too, when you sent a serpent to kill them." Zeus shifted until the baby was over the edge with nothing but sky below him. "Shall we discover if you whored yourself out to a mortal?"

Icy terror filled me, extinguishing the blaze of my burning anger. "Zeus, no—you can't—"

"You are my wife. You swore fidelity to me. You are the goddess of marriage, and yet you stain the institution with—with this *abomination*."

"He's not an abomination—"

"I will not have him in Olympus as a constant reminder of your infidelity."

My face grew hot. "What about your infidelity? Your lies, your cheating, your whores—why should you be spared the anguish of having to see my son when I must look into the eyes of your bastards for the rest of eternity?"

The breeze that blew in from the balcony shifted into a chilling wind, and lightning crackled. "Is that what you think of our family?"

"*Your* family," I spat. "Not mine. They will never be mine."

"And this—*thing* is?" He glanced at the baby, who was now crying so hard that his face was turning purple.

I rose to my full height. My son was not a thing. He was a person who deserved Zeus's respect and love, though I'd long since discovered he wasn't capable of giving, either. "He's more of a family to me than you will ever be."

I didn't think he would really do it. Zeus may have been a cheater, he may have been a liar, but he'd never physically harmed someone who hadn't wronged him first. But as I watched, helpless to stop it, the baby slipped from his arms and plummeted to the earth.

The edges of my vision turned red, and any lingering affection I had for Zeus vanished. "You will pay," I whispered in a murderous voice. "I cannot kill you, but I will find a way to destroy you. You have my word."

Zeus scoffed, though for the briefest of moments, I thought I saw a flicker of doubt hidden underneath his arrogance and pride. "You brought it on yourself, bearing a bastard in my palace."

"He isn't a bastard." Stepping back, I shed my normal appearance and turned into the girl he'd found on that moonlit beach. "His name is Hephaestus, and he would have been your son."

In the space of a single heartbeat, recognition flickered in Zeus's eyes, and far too late, he reached into the empty sky. "But—"

"Now he will have no father. Not when the one he has tries to murder him. When I return, the entire council will know what you did, I promise you that. And unlike you, Zeus, I keep my word."

Before he could respond, I disappeared. I had to find my son before he did.

Landing on the side of a mountain, so high up that I could see the sea in the distance, I listened. The wail of the wind nearly covered his cries, but nothing in the world, not even Zeus himself, could keep me from my son.

I found him among a bed of sharp rocks, sobbing and squirming against the bitter cold. Though he was immortal, his legs stuck out at an odd angle, and he sobbed as if he were in real pain.

"Oh, baby," I murmured, and I gently gathered him up, healing his legs as best I could. It wasn't my specialty, but

Zeus must have cursed him—that was the only explanation. More reason to hate my dear husband. My hate wouldn't do any good unless I channeled it properly, though.

I would find a way to destroy him, to usurp his power and make sure he couldn't hurt anyone again. Not me, not our children, and certainly not everything the council had worked for. In his thirst for power and control, Zeus had created a rift unlike anything we'd seen since the Titan War. And at this rate, it would only be a matter of time before another one began.

I couldn't let that happen.

I waited. And I watched. And I listened.

Time passed, though I hardly noticed. We grew no older, and Zeus certainly grew no wiser, but I drank in every detail that could be helpful to successfully overthrowing him. He didn't speak to me after the balcony incident, but to my relief, he ignored Hephaestus, as well. Not out of anger or pride— the few times I caught him watching our son toddle around on his lame legs or challenge Ares to an arm-wrestling match, I saw guilt and regret in his eyes.

Good. But no matter how much he longed to be a part of our son's life, I wouldn't let him. And I'd long since poisoned Hephaestus against him, making sure he knew exactly what his father was capable of.

But despite the truth of the matter, in the time I'd been gone to fetch Hephaestus from the earth, Zeus had told the council that I was the one who had dropped him. Out of panic, out of a need to keep his iron grip on the council, out of desire to see me bleed for something I didn't do—whatever his intentions were, Poseidon and his children believed him. And from then on, none of them tried to call me Mother or came to me with their problems. Just as I'd banished Zeus from my life, he'd successfully banished me from his.

It didn't matter. I didn't need him. I was still Queen of the Skies, and that was something he would never take from me.

I spent most of my time with Demeter. Despite our differences, I trusted her, and she knew as well as I did how dire it was that we put an end to his reign of terror as soon as possible. Though at first we plotted together, she grew more and more distant as the seasons passed, until one morning I couldn't take it anymore. It was one thing if she was growing tired of waiting, but she was my only ally. I couldn't lose her support.

"Demeter." I burst into her bedroom. "Sister, I must speak—"

I stopped dead in my tracks. Demeter sat on the edge of her bed, tears flowing freely down her cheeks, and Zeus kneeled in front of her. He clasped her hands in his, and I'd never seen such pain on his face before.

Silence. Demeter looked at me as if she were staring into the eyes of the Fates, but Zeus was the one I focused on. Whatever he was saying to hurt her, I would have his head for it. "Get out," I growled, sounding as feral as any of the wild creatures that roamed the earth.

I didn't need to tell him twice. He stood and hurried past me, and as soon as he was gone, I sank down at my sister's side. "What happened? What did he say? Are you all right?"

That only made her cry harder. She hid her face in her hands, her shoulders shaking with each sob. I rubbed her back, but nothing I said calmed her. Zeus would burn for whatever he'd done to her.

"I'm s-sorry," she managed to choke out several minutes later. "I'm s-so sorry."

"For what?" I said, stunned. What did she have to be sorry for?

But she shook her head again. "I did something terrible. It

was thoughtless and horrible and—I don't know what came over me. Just seeing you with your sons, seeing how happy you were—"

"Demeter." I was anything but happy, and she of all people should've known it. "What are you trying to say?"

She pulled her hands away from her face long enough for me to see her expression crumble. "I wanted a baby," she whispered. "I wanted a family the way you had a family. I wanted to be happy—I want someone to share my life with."

The way Zeus had spoken to her. The way he'd held her hands. My insides twisted with dread. "What did you do, Demeter?" I whispered.

She reached for me, but I pulled away, and she broke down once more. "I'm so sorry, Hera. I wasn't thinking. He offered, and—"

"And you thought that instead of refusing him like you should have, instead of finding someone else, you'd rather betray me by having his child."

Her whole body shook, and she once again buried her face in her palms. For a long time, neither of us said anything. She didn't refute it, and I didn't ask her to. The cold truth settled over my shoulders, icing over what was left of my love for my siblings.

I was alone. I was completely and utterly alone. Even my sister had abandoned me for that fool. Even my sons still called him Father.

I had nothing that was mine and mine alone to love. Zeus tainted everything in my life that had once been good, stealing it away from me like a common thief. Did he hate me so much for challenging him on the island long ago that he was determined to tear me apart, piece by piece? Was this his plan? Marry me, pretend to love me, pretend to respect me, pretend to give me everything I'd ever wanted and then rip it all away?

I couldn't know for sure, but it didn't matter. Whether he'd planned it or not, that was exactly what Zeus had done to me. Though the Titan War had ended long ago, in its place, a new one had been born without my knowing. Maybe without any of us knowing. But it'd been there from the beginning, and now there was no denying it.

Zeus against me. King against Queen. And Zeus thought he'd won, with his control over the council, with his seduction of my sister, the one person I had still trusted.

But he was forgetting one thing: I was more powerful than he was. I'd been the one to win the Titan War. And I was the one who was going to destroy him.

I stood shakily, fighting to keep any signs of my distress from Demeter. "You are never to speak to me again," I said quietly. "You will not look at me. You will not come to me. You will not call me sister. From this moment on, we are through."

"Hera," she sobbed, but I ignored her. She'd had her chance, and though she'd known what the consequences would bring, this was the path she'd chosen. I would not show her mercy for it.

"Goodbye," I said, and without looking back, I walked through the curtains and out of her life forever.

PART THREE

PART THREE

The Underworld was colder than I'd expected. Not unbearably so, but I wasn't used to a world without the sun. Walking down the path to the entrance of Hades's obsidian palace, I clasped my hands together, partially for warmth and partially to keep them from shaking.

Hades was waiting for me in the throne room, hunched over in his black-diamond throne, as if he were carrying an unbearable load. Hundreds of people—dead souls—sat in the pews before him, each watching him expectantly. For what?

"Brother," I said, hating the slight tremble in my voice. I stopped in front of his throne. Though he was the one person I would bow to if he asked, I knew he never would. He was not Zeus.

"Hera." He cracked a faint smile and stood, drawing me into an embrace. It was like coming home. Forget the sun—the coldest pit in the universe would be warm as long as Hades was there with me. I hugged him tightly, only dimly aware of the eyes on us. Let the dead stare.

"I missed you." To my horror, my voice caught in my throat, and he pulled away enough to look at me.

"What's wrong? What happened?"

One look at the concern on his face—genuine, sincere, not born out of manipulation or a need for something else—and the dam inside me burst. As I cried into his shoulder, Hades gestured for his subjects to leave, and they all stood and exited the throne room without a fuss. Where they went or why they'd been here in the first place, I wasn't sure, but I'd never been so grateful to anyone in my life.

At last he eased back onto his throne, taking me with him. I curled up in his lap, not caring that it wasn't proper or that I was married or anyone who came in would assume the worst. Let them. I needed Hades. I needed a friend.

He rubbed my back, not saying a word. Finally, once I'd cried myself out, I rested against him and took several deep breaths. "Demeter's pregnant."

His hand stilled between my shoulder blades, and confusion radiated from him. "Oh?"

"Zeus is the father."

"*Oh.*" His arms tightened around me. "Hera, I'm so sorry."

"Could I stay down here with you?" For the first time in all my eternal years, I sounded like a child. But Hades was the only person I trusted anymore, and unlike the other members of the council, he would never take advantage of my vulnerability. Zeus and Poseidon would have reveled in it; my sisters and the younger generation would have seen weakness. But Hades understood.

"Yes," he whispered. "Of course. As long as you need."

"Thank you." I rested against him, my face buried in the crook of his neck as I inhaled his scent—winter and stone, with hints of a burning fire. It may have taken much longer than I'd anticipated for him to fill his promise, but he finally had. I wasn't alone, after all.

★ ★ ★

I remained in the Underworld for so long that I lost track of the seasons. News came from Zeus's messenger when Demeter's daughter, Persephone, was born, and while Hades went up to visit, I couldn't find it in myself to bother.

Occasionally I met my sons on the surface, sometimes for an afternoon swimming in the ocean, sometimes for an entire week living amongst the trees as we talked. That was the one part about the current arrangement that I hated—missing them. Ares was fully grown now and had taken his place on the council, defending what he thought were my wishes. But I could see Zeus in him, in every step he took, in every word he said, and it was agony.

Hephaestus was quieter, much more reserved, and his limp was a constant reminder of what his father had done to him. I never had to worry about seeing Zeus in him—he couldn't have been more different from that arrogant, insufferable liar. But his limp never went away, and despite my best efforts, Zeus had claimed a stake in his life, as well.

The more time I spent with Hades, the more I grew to appreciate what he did. Day in and day out, often without rest, he listened to the souls who awaited his judgment. Sometimes for minutes, sometimes for hours, and on one memorable occasion, for well over a day. Usually they talked about their mistakes and regrets, but the more I listened, the more I realized that those weren't the parts of their lives the dead lingered on. The happy times—family, love, the moments in the sunshine that didn't seem extraordinary at the time, but remained with them even after death—those were the parts that made them smile. Those were the parts they seemed eager to tell Hades about. Those were the parts of their lives that validated them, that made them feel whole, that gave their life purpose.

I envied them. Even when I was with my sons, Zeus remained with us, tainting everything. My only time away from him completely was with Hades in the Underworld, and I relished it. I remained by his side, leaving only to meet my sons or fulfill my duties to humanity, and there was nowhere else I would've rather been.

Occasionally he asked my opinion on exceptionally difficult cases. With him, I wanted to be gracious. I wanted to show him the compassionate side of me that Zeus had so maliciously ripped to shreds. I wanted to show him I wasn't the ice queen everyone else seemed to think I was. I wanted to be my best.

One day, as I explored the outer edge of the Underworld, I heard footsteps behind me. This was the area where the dead spent all of eternity, and it wasn't unusual to run across them. Each time I stepped through the rock barrier, the world around me was different, and this time I walked along the edge of an island much like the one where we'd defeated Cronus.

"Hera?"

I stilled. I would have recognized that voice anywhere, and it was the last one I wanted to hear again.

Demeter.

"I have nothing to say to you." I could've disappeared and returned to Hades's palace, but I wasn't about to give her the satisfaction of seeing me run from her. This was my home now. She would be the one to leave.

"Hera, I need to talk to you." She touched my wrist, and I jerked away. "Please. It's important."

"Our definitions of *important* are vastly different now, I suspect." I moved away from her, heading toward the ocean.

"Zeus wants to marry off the children," she said. "Including Ares and Hephaestus."

I stopped at the edge of the water, and the waves lapped at my feet. "Excuse me?"

"Zeus—he's decided that Apollo, Hephaestus and Ares will marry Persephone, Aphrodite and Athena."

That bastard. He wanted to do to his own children what he'd done to me. "Tell him I will never allow it."

"He insists he doesn't need your permission—"

"I am the goddess of marriage," I thundered, turning on my heel to look at her for the first time in years. "Any marriage I do not bless will fail."

Demeter stood there trembling, more frightened than I'd ever seen her before. She seemed older now, more like our mother, and for a split second I nearly didn't recognize her. Her skin was paler than before, and she looked as if she hadn't smiled in a decade.

This wasn't my sister. Zeus had ruined her as well, just as he'd ruined me.

In that moment, I felt a spark of sympathy, but I squelched it before it could grow into a flame. She'd watched him do the same thing to me. She should've known.

"Please, Hera," she whispered. "Come back. You can stop this—he'll listen to you. He misses you, even though he doesn't want to admit it."

"Why do you care?" I snapped.

She swallowed. "Because when Persephone comes of age, he wants to marry her to Ares."

The thought of my son marrying her daughter made my stomach turn, as I'm sure it made hers, though for entirely different reasons. Ares wasn't known for his gentleness. "And who would you prefer she marry?"

"Someone she chooses," said Demeter quietly. "Someone she loves."

I took a deep breath, inhaling the scent of the fake ocean. "I will speak with Ares and Hephaestus, and in the meantime, tell Zeus I will never return. I'm happy here, and nothing he offers me will ever change my mind."

Demeter hesitated. "He knows," she said quietly. "And it hurts him."

"Good." The more pain he was in, the better. "I will meet with my sons immediately. Now go."

"Thank you," she whispered. She didn't disappear yet, though. Instead Demeter hesitated, shifting her weight as if she wanted to move closer to me, but thought better of it. "I did it for you, you know. For us."

I scoffed. "You had my husband's bastard for me?"

"To even our numbers. To stop Zeus from taking over—"

"He's already taken over," I said, not bothering to hide my bitterness. "We lost a very long time ago, and I won't listen to your lies. If you'd really wanted to help by having a child, you would've had one with Poseidon."

"Zeus would've never allowed her onto the council then," said Demeter, and though I knew she was telling the truth, it wasn't the excuse she wanted it to be. It was simply another example of how he'd already won.

"I would have fought for her place," I said. "I would've fought for you. Now I have no one left to fight for but myself. I hope you're proud."

An unbearable sadness settled over her expression, and she exhaled, as if breathing out any last hope she had. Good. "Proud is the last thing I am. You of all people should recognize that." She nodded to me once. "Goodbye, Hera. For what it's worth, I will forever be sorry for what I did to you."

I sniffed. "As you should be."

Demeter turned and walked back toward the stone wall. For a moment, something inside me, something I'd buried so long ago that it had nearly suffocated underneath my resentment and quiet rage, wiggled free. And I wanted nothing more than for her to turn around and come back to me.

But she'd made up her mind long ago, as had I. That path was gone now, and no matter how badly I ached to be sisters again, circumstances would never allow it. Not anymore.

As soon as she was gone, I wasted no time. Less than an hour later, I met Ares and Hephaestus on the island scarred by Cronus's imprisonment. "What do you two want?"

Ares scoffed. He was so much taller than me now, and he'd cropped his dark curls short. "I'd rather never marry. I see no point. Unless, of course, it was Aphrodite." He grinned, and Hephaestus scowled. Apparently Ares wasn't the only one who had fallen under her spell. "Wouldn't mind having a go with her."

Yes, Ares was every bit his father's son. "And you, Hephaestus?"

"I wouldn't mind marrying," he said quietly as he watched the waves wash away his uneven footprints. "But I would rather choose my partner."

And Hephaestus was every bit mine. "I'll take care of it," I said, touching his hand. "Zeus is a tyrant, and you both deserve better than this." I wouldn't let what had happened to me happen to them. Even Zeus's daughters didn't deserve it, though my sons had both apparently taken a liking to Aphrodite. But she was not their property, and they had no right to choose for her.

For the first time in years, I arrived in Olympus. After so long in the Underworld, the intense sunlight in the throne room nearly blinded me, but I forced myself to adjust quickly. I would not show weakness.

"Zeus!" I called, my voice echoing down the hallways, reaching every inch of Olympus.

Seconds later, he appeared in front of me. He too looked

older now, as if he and Demeter had chosen to age together. I'd kept my appearance young to match Hades's, and now that I saw Zeus in front of me, the differences between them—both inside and out—became painfully clear. I'd made the wrong decision. And despite the few golden moments my marriage to Zeus had brought me, our sons included, I would have given anything to go back to those minutes in the antechamber before my wedding. I would have given anything to marry Hades instead.

"Hera." His voice had a mixture of caution and relief. "To what do I owe this long-awaited honor?"

"You know why I'm here." Despite his considerable height, I stood toe-to-toe with him, refusing to flinch as he stared down at me. He may have sounded kind and genial, but lightning flashed in his eyes. He hadn't forgiven me, just as I would never forgive him. "You will not have my blessing for any marriage you arrange for your children that they do not consent to," I said. "Nor will any of their marriages produce legitimate offspring."

He tilted his head, as if I were a curious creature he'd never seen before. "You would neglect your duties in such a way?"

"My duty is to bless unions taken on willingly," I said. "Not to condone slavery."

"Is that what you think of our marriage?" He reached out to touch my cheek, and I slapped his hand away. "Do you think of yourself as a slave?"

"Our marriage is nothing now. It clearly never meant anything to you, and it no longer means anything to me. But I will hold you to your vows, and I will not grant you a divorce. You may not marry another woman."

"And you may not marry another man." Though he forced his voice to remain steady, his face slowly turned red, and his fists were clenched so tightly that his knuckles were white. "Is that what you wish? An eternity of loneliness?"

"Is that what you call sharing my sister's bed? Loneliness?"

"No," he said. "And I would imagine you're just as *lonely* as I am."

I bit the inside of my cheek. Zeus had no way of knowing the nature of my relationship with Hades, and I was more than happy to allow his imagination to run wild.

"Is this your endgame?" said Zeus. "Marry Hades and become his queen?"

"I will never be anyone's queen again," I said. "I am a queen in my own right, and neither you nor anyone else on this damn council can take that from me."

"But that is what you want, isn't it?" said Zeus. "To be Hades's wife."

I narrowed my eyes. "I am your wife whether I like it or not. I will not let you out of that contract no matter how you try to entice me."

"So be it, my queen," he said, and he bowed his head mockingly. But as he straightened, his mask slipped, and for a moment I saw his weariness. "If you come back, I will allow the children to marry whomever they want."

"You will allow them to marry whomever they want regardless of what I do or don't do," I said. "Marriage isn't your domain."

"As you have so clearly displayed. Very well. If you wish to start this war—"

"I haven't started anything," I snapped. "You're the one who did this. You're the one who destroyed our marriage, who broke your promises, who did everything you possibly could to make me miserable. This might be a game to you, but I will not allow you to ruin their lives, as well."

I turned on my heel and stormed toward the portal. Before

I could reach it, however, Zeus said in a quiet voice that carried, "You win, Hera. Ares and Hephaestus will not marry anyone they do not love."

Taking a deep breath, I refused to acknowledge him. Just another move in our endless war. A way to twist and turn me until I was unrecognizable even to myself.

"But you do not get to say what my daughters can and cannot do. They are mine, and if our marriage is nothing to you, then your role as their stepmother means nothing, either. You will bless the marriages I choose for them, or I will hold you accountable for treason against the council, and you will be stripped of your title and domain."

"Fine," I snarled. "Do whatever you want with your bastards."

"Oh, I will," he murmured. "That's one promise I assure you I will keep."

Five days later, Hades knocked on the door to my chambers in the Underworld. Despite what Zeus may have thought, I hadn't so much as kissed Hades, nor had I tried. Some relationships took time, and because I would never be able to marry him, I couldn't pressure him into something he may not have been ready for. But I would be there for him, always. That was one thing Zeus couldn't take from me.

"Come in," I called. I sat in front of a mirror, decorating my hair with diamonds. It never ceased to amaze me how many jewels were scattered carelessly around the Underworld, as if Hades couldn't be bothered to pick them up. On the surface, they would have been worth a fortune to any mortal; yet it was just another example of how Hades's values were different. How he didn't care for the material or the conventional. He cared about the forgotten. About people like me.

Hades slipped inside the bedroom. "Hera? Oh. I am not interrupting, am I?"

"No, of course not," I said. "Come help me, would you, please?"

Obediently he moved behind me, and his careful fingers took over for me, placing the jewels amidst the length of my braid. For a long moment, he didn't speak.

"Is everything all right?" I said, watching him in the mirror. He didn't raise his eyes to meet mine. Instead he paused and pursed his lips.

"I have something I must tell you," he said quietly. "And I fear you will not like it."

My insides grew hollow, and the joy that usually filled me when I was with him drained away. "What is it?"

More silence. He took his time finishing my hair, and at last, when he gently set the braid back over my shoulder, he said, "I am betrothed."

My body turned to ice. For a moment I ceased to exist, and he finally looked at me. Not even the piercing stare of his silver eyes could revive me.

Married. He was getting married.

"I have been considering it for a while now. I'm depending far too much on your generosity and guidance, and it isn't fair of me to continue to do so. You have a life on the surface. Your sons, if nothing else, and I cannot endure the guilt of keeping you here."

He thought I didn't like it down here? He thought I stayed out of obligation? "Hades, I wouldn't want to be anywhere else. I'm happy down here. With you."

He shook his head. "That is the trick of this place—it makes you feel as if you are happier than you really are. Down here, you are hiding from your life, and I cannot allow it to continue. You need to return to Olympus. You need to return to our family."

I stood so quickly that my stool flew backward, nearly hitting his knees. "I don't *need* to do anything I don't want to do, and I do not want to leave."

"Hera—"

"No, you listen to me," I snapped. I'd never spoken to him like this in our entire existence, but I couldn't stop myself, not anymore. "I love you. I love you more than I've ever loved anyone. Being with you—being down here with you, ruling at your side, it makes me happy. It gives me purpose. You can't take that away from me."

His expression softened. "Hera, I am not taking anything away from you. We will always be friends, and you are welcome down here at any time. I simply can no longer burden you—"

"You haven't burdened me." My eyes stung with tears. "Please. Let me stay. Don't marry her, whoever she is—"

"Persephone," he said softly, and I froze once more.

Persephone. Demeter's daughter. So this was what Zeus had meant. This was his game. He knew how I felt about Hades, and this was his final move. To take him from me completely. To leave me with no one at all.

Desperation flooded me, and every nerve in my eternal body burned. Without thinking, I leaned forward and pressed my lips to his, pouring every ounce of passion and love and dedication I felt into that kiss. I couldn't lose him.

For one beautiful moment, Hades set his hand on my cheek, though he didn't kiss me back. I couldn't expect him to, not before he was ready. But he would be someday, and when that day came—

"Hera," he whispered, his lips brushing against mine. "You

mean a great deal to me, but Persephone and I have both chosen this. When she comes of age, we will marry."

"But you don't even know her."

"I do," he said softly. "I go up to Olympus often to visit. We may not have the companionship you and I share, but you are my brother's wife, and if I allowed us to happen—"

"What, you'd make him angry?" I wiped my eyes. "You'd cause the council to crack? It's already cracked, Hades. We've already crumbled."

Hades shook his head and reached for me again. I stepped away before he could touch me, and he dropped his hand to his side. "The council has not crumbled, Hera. You have. And I cannot allow us to happen, because it would mean losing you completely. Loyalty, fidelity—those are the things that make you who you are. I will gladly accept the first in friendship and offer it to you unconditionally in return. But I will not allow you to push aside the second, not when it would mean you are no longer you."

I cried openly now. "What does it mean to be me when I have no one? Nobody loves me—"

"I love you," he said quietly.

"Not the way I want you to." My voice was thick, and I had to blink several times to force my vision back into focus. "No one does. I'm alone. And I thought—I thought you understood that. I thought you saw me."

"I do, Hera. I do, and that is why I cannot allow you to break your vows no matter what my bastard of a brother does to you. You're too good for it. You're too good for all of us. We're the ones who don't deserve you."

"Yet I'm the one who's alone." I allowed a single, miserable sob to escape my chest, taking my heart with it. "I can't bless it."

"I know," he said gently. "I would never ask you to."

His kindness only made the ache inside me grow. I'd lost him now, too, no matter how strongly he insisted he would always be there. Once again, he'd broken his promise, just like Zeus.

But now that I knew I couldn't have him, there was one thing I did want. "Please," I whispered, "promise me one thing."

"Anything."

At last I took his hand and squeezed it, trying to memorize the way it felt in mine. "I'm going to make sure Zeus can no longer hurt anyone. Not me, not his children, not humanity, anyone. And I want your support."

Wariness flashed across his face, but he'd already promised me anything, and he nodded. "Of course. Whatever it takes."

I sniffed and wiped my cheeks once more. He pulled me into a hug, and I buried my face in his shoulder for the last time. Whether or not I was invited to the Underworld as his guest, it would never be the same, not with Demeter's daughter watching our every move. Not when he could never return the love I felt for him, not without doing to Persephone what Zeus had done to me. "Thank you," I said softly. "I love you."

"As I love you, forever and always," he murmured. "Never forget that."

I nodded. Nothing in the world could ever take those words away from me, not even my own broken heart.

I needed seven votes. Seven votes to overthrow Zeus's rule, seven votes for me to step up and take his place.

As of the moment I returned to Olympus, I only had three. Hades, Ares and Hephaestus were loyal to me, and there was a chance I would be able to lure my sisters to my side. But Poseidon was firmly in Zeus's camp, which meant I would have to sway one of the children.

I approached my sisters first. I hadn't seen Hestia in a very long time, and though we both sobbed through our reunion, I didn't feel guilty for leaving her behind. She'd never had any trouble finding company, and having vowed chastity, marriage and children would never get in the way of her relationships with our siblings. She was happy—maybe happier than all of us. And the ugly, twisted part of me that Zeus had created hated her for it.

Demeter sat in the corner as Hestia and I greeted each other, and once we'd finished, she cleared her throat. "As thrilled as I am that you have returned to us, Hera, why did you ask for both of us to be here?"

I gave her a withering look, but I couldn't afford anything more. "Zeus has control of the council," I said. I didn't need to attend meetings to know that. "And I suspect your voices are no longer heard."

"Here to campaign?" said Hestia with amusement, but I leveled my gaze at her, and her smile faded.

"I am Zeus's equal. His domain is mine as well, and we both have the capacity to rule. After everything Zeus has done to our family, I want to make it right. I want to give you back your voices. Your power. The respect you deserve."

My sisters watched me closely, their expressions giving nothing away. If I couldn't convince them, I would have no choice.

"Hestia, you want to keep peace within the family, yes?" I said, and she nodded. "The only way to do that is to restore the original council. Perhaps we can keep the others on as… advisors, but we must reclaim our rightful place as rulers."

"But Zeus—"

"Zeus will have no say, not if we have the most votes," I said.

Demeter furrowed her brow. "You're suggesting a coup?"

"I am suggesting we restore order, sensibility and respect. Nothing more. A coup would mean a war, and none of us wants that."

"But in order to avoid it, we must give you power," said Demeter.

"No," I said with more patience than she deserved. "In order to avoid it, we must *redistribute* power among the six of us, equally, as it has always been. If we are successful, Hades has agreed to return to the council as a full-time member."

"Hades supports this?" she said, her surprise in every syllable.

"Hades supports fairness and unity. Hestia? What do you think?"

Hestia crossed her arms over her full figure. She too had aged—had Poseidon, as well? Were Hades and I the only ones who remained youthful? "If what you're saying is true, then I would be supportive of reverting to the way the council was intended to run. Equally among the six of us."

"Thank you," I said, and I squeezed her hand. "Demeter?"

I could see the hesitation in her eyes, the uncertainty on her face, the doubt in the way she hunched her shoulders—she was going to say no. Why? Out of loyalty to Zeus?

Swallowing my pride, I knelt on the floor before her, taking her hands exactly as my dear husband had the day she'd revealed her pregnancy. "Demeter. Sister," I murmured, and her gaze locked on mine. "Let us be whole again. Not just you and I, but all of us. We won't cast Zeus out—simply restore order. Simply fulfill our duties to humanity, the same ones we fought the Titans for."

Still her indecision remained. It was a pity I couldn't use my abilities on my siblings, at least not without them knowing— but I didn't want to force her hand. I wanted her to choose me because she thought it was the right decision.

"I'll bless their marriage," I said quietly. My last bargaining chip, though offering it made a knife twist in my gut. "Be our ally, and Persephone and Hades will be happy."

At last she crumbled. "All right," she said quietly. "You have my vote."

I rose and kissed her cheek. "Thank you." She would never have my forgiveness, and I would never be her sister again no matter how I addressed her, but if she did this for me, I would stick to my word and bless Hades's marriage.

"We still don't have the numbers though, even with Ares and Hephaestus," said Hestia, and I straightened.

"We don't, but we will." I gave them both cordial nods. "Expect a council meeting to be called within the hour." And in the meantime, with a little luck, Demeter wouldn't have a change of heart. But she loved her daughter, that much was obvious, and she wanted the best for her. The only way she could get it was through me.

As I stood outside Aphrodite's room, waiting for the courage to enter, I tried to think of what I was going to say. I had nothing to offer. Nothing to make up for what she would lose if she voted with me. But even during the most heated of debates, Aphrodite had never been particularly vocal. Ruling wasn't in her blood, and perhaps that could work for me.

At last I took a breath and knocked. I would find a way somehow. Everyone had a weakness.

"Just a second!" called Aphrodite, and through the curtain, I heard her giggle. Something rustled, and I thought I heard a male voice murmur something. "All right, come in!"

Wary, I stepped inside. Aphrodite lounged on her bed, practically glowing, and a smile danced on her lips. As I'd predicted, she wasn't alone. Leaning against the wall was Ares. Apparently his interest wasn't simple wishful thinking.

"Hello, Aphrodite," I said. "Ares. Did I interrupt?"

Ares opened his mouth to say something, but Aphrodite quickly cut him off. "Nothing that can't be resumed at a later time. I'm sorry, did you want to speak with him?"

"As it happens, I came to see you." I turned to my son. "You wouldn't mind giving us a minute, would you, dear?"

He sighed dramatically, as if I'd asked him to carry the world. "Fine."

"I love you," I said, giving him a kiss on the cheek. He reluctantly returned it before trudging out of the room. Once he was gone, I moved closer to Aphrodite. "I'm sorry about the intrusion."

"Oh, it's fine," she said, waving her hand. She sat up and ran her fingers through her blond curls. "It's good to see you again. Ares didn't tell me you were coming for a visit."

"That's because I'm not here for a visit." I forced myself to smile as if this were all my idea. "I've returned to Olympus."

She beamed and leaped for me before I had the chance to move away. Catching me in an embrace, she kissed both my cheeks. "Oh, that's fantastic! Ares will be so pleased. He missed you, you know."

"And I missed him." I gingerly removed her arms and sat down on the edge of the bed. "I'm surprised the two of you have grown so...close. Did Zeus decide not to arrange your marriage after all?"

Aphrodite made a face. "Oh, he did, all right. Or—I guess Hephaestus suggested it, actually, though Daddy never gave me the chance to say no—"

"Wait." I frowned. "You mean Hephaestus is marrying you?"

She nodded grimly. "I mean, I'm sure he's a good guy and all, just—not my type, you know? I'd much rather get to choose, but..." She shrugged. "Daddy's the head of the council."

Everything couldn't have been more perfect if the Fates themselves had intervened. Perhaps they had. I didn't blame Hephaestus for this arrangement—no doubt Zeus had orchestrated the whole thing, knowing how much it would bother me to see my son marry a woman who didn't love him. But in doing so, Zeus had unwittingly sprung his own trap upon himself.

I set my hand over hers, the most affection I'd ever shown her. "How would you like to choose who you marry? Or not have to marry at all?"

Her eyes lit up. "You could do that? You could talk to Daddy and convince him otherwise?"

"No," I said slowly. "I could be the one in charge of your marriage. I could be the one with the power to arrange it."

She frowned. "I don't understand. That's Daddy's job."

"Only because he's head of the council." I squeezed her hand. "There will be a vote tonight to decide whether or not to terminate his rule. When the six of us united to form the council, it was always our plan to have equal say. To make things fair."

"Everyone already has equal say," she said, a line forming in the middle of her brow.

"No, we do not," I said gently. "Because Zeus has so many children who readily agree with him, he always gets his way. Like with your wedding, even though you don't want to go through with it. But if we restore the council to its original intent..."

I trailed off, watching her expression flicker as she absorbed my proposition. "I wouldn't be on the council, then,"

"On the contrary, you would all still remain on the council

as advisors. It would just be the six of us who make the final decisions, that's all. As it was when the council first formed."

"Oh." She twirled the ends of her hair around her fingers. "And if I did this, you would let me marry Ares?"

"Or not marry at all, if you so wish," I repeated. "You would have complete control over your life."

Slowly her pink lips twisted into a smile. "And we wouldn't have to sit through all those boring meetings?"

"Not unless you wanted to. All I need is your vote, and it will be settled."

Aphrodite beamed. "You'll have it. This is brilliant—thank you so much, Hera." She captured me in another hug. "I really did miss you, you know."

I patted her hair. It was easy—too easy, and part of me knew I was taking advantage of her ignorance. But I had nothing to feel guilty for. This was the way it was supposed to be. And this was the only way we would restore balance. Zeus couldn't be allowed a monopoly over the council any longer, and whether Aphrodite fully understood the implications or not, it didn't matter. I was doing the right thing.

"I missed you, too," I murmured. And to my surprise, I realized it was the truth.

Everything fell into place. Seven votes, that was all I needed, and now I had them.

Hades. Hestia. Demeter. Ares. Hephaestus. Myself. And now Aphrodite.

I arrived in the throne room long before the council meeting began. I'd missed the feeling of my throne, the power it emanated and the way it seemed to welcome me into its embrace. And as I waited, I stroked my peacock, listening to its soft coos. Everything would be all right. It already was.

I'd won.

The council began to gather shortly after. My sisters first, and then Poseidon and the children. Hades arrived on time, and finally Zeus strode into the room, his golden hair gleaming in the sunlight. There was a new boy now as well, one too young to have a throne, but he sat at Zeus's feet. Another one of his bastards, then. How cute.

"I call this meeting to order," said Zeus, although I was the one who had summoned everyone. He stood, radiating power as he always did, but instead it seemed to form a shield between us. As if he could sense the tension and knew I was his enemy now. "To begin—"

"Pardon me," I murmured with faux politeness, and I too stood. Two could play at this game. "But I believe this is my meeting to direct."

"On the contrary, I am the one who leads them regardless of who called it," said Zeus.

I narrowed my eyes. "And how can you lead us when you do not know what is on the agenda?"

"I think you will find my leadership to be anything but lacking today," he said, and he gestured. "Please, sit."

Every single member of the council stared at me. I caught Hades's eye, and he nodded briefly. It would do me no good to stir up trouble in the minutes before I asked the council to trust me, and though it killed my pride to do so, I sat down.

"Thank you." Zeus stood to his full height. "We are all here today to discuss a dire matter, one that threatens the very foundation of our existence. Treason."

I froze. What was he talking about?

Zeus turned to face me, a golden aura glowing around him. "Hera, have you or have you not spent the day convincing six of our rank to vote to have my children stripped of their thrones and me removed as King?"

It took every ounce of self-control I possessed to keep my

composure. Who had told him? I glanced at Demeter, but she frowned, as confused as I was. Who, then?

Aphrodite. As my gaze landed on her, she looked down at her hands, and her cheeks turned pink. Traitor.

I had no choice now but to go through with it. Zeus could posture all he wanted—if he didn't have the votes, he didn't have the votes. I stood. "I did not realize that discussing a return to the natural order of things was considered treason."

"And what, pray tell, is your definition of the *natural order of things*?" said Zeus.

I drew my shoulders back, every inch a queen. "I wish to introduce a motion to return the council to its rightful state, where only the original six of us shall be allowed to cast a vote. Everyone else may remain on as advisors, but it is only fair and right that we be the ones to make the final decisions. I do not think it is any great assumption to say that lately there has been no variation in the decisions this council has made. The same people—" I focused on Zeus, and then on the cluster of his illegitimate children "—have made each decision, ignoring the voices of others. That is not a council. That is a dictatorship, and I refuse to stand for it."

"It is treason," said Zeus, and thunder filled the throne room. "Wishing to replace your king—"

"You are not my king, nor will you ever be. You are a liar, a thief, and you have no right to rule over us all. You are no better than me, no more powerful than any of us, and you have proven time and time again that you cannot uphold the morals this council demands of its members."

"And you can?" said Zeus.

"Yes," I said with a sniff. "I can."

"As I recall, pride is still considered to be a deadly mark against any candidate," he said. "As is envy."

"As is lust," I snapped. "A crime you have committed more often than I have ever succumbed to pride or envy."

"Then by your own admission, neither of us is fit to rule," he said. "Yet here we are. I will not force my children to give up their rightful places on the council, places they have earned by passing the very test you created, when you yourself could not pass it."

"And I will not back down until equality and fairness are restored."

"Then we find ourselves at a standstill." He folded his hands. "As I am still King, I will allow you a choice. If we take this vote and you win, we will do as you ask. But if I win, then you will be stripped of your title. You will remain in Olympus, where I can keep an eye on you, and you will grant me a divorce."

I gaped at him. "That is completely unfair."

"Is it? Perhaps you ought to consider yourself lucky you are not being tried for treason right now instead." He nodded toward the council. "Tell me, Hera. Would you like to vote on it?"

I looked around the circle. My sisters both watched me, as did Hades. My sons would support me no matter what. And Aphrodite...

Somehow Zeus must have gotten to her. Perhaps in her excitement, she blurted out my promises, not realizing what the consequences would be. Surprise was not an integral part of this, but it would have helped to catch Zeus unaware. And if he had convinced her to change her vote...

I had to take that risk. For the sake of the council, for the sake of equality, for the sake of humanity, I had to try. And at last, I nodded.

"Let us vote."

We went around the circle once. Hephaestus, sitting beside

me, pledged his loyalty to me. As did Hades, as did Demeter, as did Hestia. As I'd predicted, Athena, Apollo, Artemis and Poseidon did not hesitate to vote with Zeus. And Ares voted with me.

At last it was on Aphrodite's shoulders. She sat on the other side of Zeus, wringing her hands uncertainly, and several seconds passed in silence. She couldn't change her vote. She couldn't.

Remember. I pushed my thoughts toward her. *You can have Ares. You can have the love you desire. All you have to do is say yes.*

She looked up at me, her eyes red. *I can't be disloyal to my father. I can't hurt him like that.*

And what about your loyalty to yourself? What about your loyalty to Ares?

She looked at my son, who watched her with the same intensity as I did. Opening her mouth, she started to say something, but on her other side, Zeus set his hand over hers. That bastard. Loyalty was earned, not taken, and if he thought he could control her like that, snatching away her choice—

Power emanated from me before I realized what I was doing. As the invisible tendrils reached Aphrodite, her face went blank, and I slowly untied her connection to Zeus. It was so easy—so simple to remove that hold he had over her. To let her live. To give her freedom.

"Hera." Zeus's voice boomed. Aphrodite blinked, and all of my work unraveled. "What do you think you're doing?"

I gritted my teeth. "Giving her a choice."

In an instant, golden ropes flew from the air around me, binding me to my throne. I gasped, struggling to free myself, but it was no use. "You may not have considered this treason before, but now it is undeniable," said Zeus, his voice echoing with the command of a king. "You are hereby stripped of your title—"

"Daddy!" cried Aphrodite. Hephaestus and Ares leaped to their feet, but Zeus waved his hand, warding them off me.

"—and you will be detained until the council decides what to do with you."

"What?" I said, stunned. "You can't possibly—"

"You abused your abilities to sway a council member's vote against me," said Zeus. "You will be given a trial for your crimes—"

"No!" I shrieked, fighting the bonds once more. They held even tighter, biting into my skin. "I am the queen. You can't do this—"

"Oh, but I can," said Zeus. And before I could say another word, my throne disappeared, taking me with it.

PART FOUR

PART FOUR

For seven days and seven nights, I stayed locked in a small, dark room that even the sun didn't touch.

No one came to visit me. Zeus had undoubtedly forbidden them all. I sat quietly in my throne, biding my time, and I went back through the past hundred years. Would I have done things differently if I'd known this was where I would end up? Would I have tried to be more compassionate, less consumed by pride?

The only mistake I regretted was my marriage to Zeus. I would have changed nothing else.

At last, on the eighth day, I returned to the middle of the throne room without warning. The sunlight blinded me, and though I didn't want to show the council any weakness, I had to close my eyes.

"Hera." Zeus's voice. I didn't bother answering. "We have made our decision. Do you have anything you would like to say before we reveal your fate?"

I didn't speak until my eyes adjusted to the light. Finally I opened them, forcing myself not to squint. I was facing Zeus, and Hades was behind me. But I could feel his presence, an oasis in the storm that was my now.

"I did nothing wrong," I said at last, my voice clear despite seven days without speaking. "My only intent was to protect the council. Nothing more."

"So be it," said Zeus, and he stood. "You have been found guilty of your crimes, and the council has decided effective immediately, you will be stripped of your rank as Queen. You will retain your duties as a goddess, and you will retain a place on the council. But you will no longer help rule my domain. Nor, for one millennium, will you have a vote equal to our own. In the case of a tiebreaker where your vote is necessary, we will allow you to cast it. Otherwise, you will have no say."

I took slow, steady breaths, not allowing my anguish to show. Not only had he stripped me of the power I deserved, the power I'd worked so hard to maintain, but by putting on this show, he ensured none of his children would ever respect me. Perhaps he'd even poisoned my sons against me, too.

"You will remain under the watch of the council at all times. You are never to be alone, and any move of yours to plot against the council or use your powers to sway our decisions will be met with exile."

I burned with humiliation. He'd taken away everything I held dear. He knew what he was doing to me, and he relished it.

"And what if I choose exile now?" I said in as dignified a voice as I could muster.

His expression remained impassive. So he'd expected this. Perhaps even hoped for it. "If that is what you wish, then we will not stop you."

It would be so easy to return to my mother. To remain with her and leave the council behind. It would be a good existence void of this pain, and in that moment, I was tempted. So very tempted.

Hera. Hades's voice whispered to me. *Be strong. Do not give* up. *Remember who you are and what you are capable of. Today is only one day. It is not forever.*

I swallowed, the first sign of emotion I'd allowed. *Did you fight for me?*

I did. As did Demeter.

Will you still be there for me?

A pause, and then, with conviction, *Always.*

I straightened in my throne, holding my head as high as I could. "I will accept your terms," I said. "This council matters more to me than you could ever understand, Zeus, and I will not give up on it. We are united for eternity whether or not we all share the same love for one another, and I will not abandon you. Any of you."

A flicker of disappointment crossed Zeus's face, but he nodded. "So be it." With a wave of his hand, my bonds disappeared, and I stood. I may not have had any power in rank, but I was still the most powerful of them all. I was still the daughter of a Titan, and no matter what Zeus did, I always would be.

In that moment, all of my anger crystallized into bitterness and revenge. It was a cold fury now, tucked deep away inside me, waiting for the day I could finally release it once more. And I would. I had made Zeus a promise, and I would keep it.

But as I turned and looked at Hades, he gave me a secret smile, and a sense of calm washed over me. He was my ally. My partner. My friend. I would be there for him every moment of every day. I would prove my loyalty to him as he had proven his to me. I would not lose him.

And he was right. Today wasn't forever, and neither was a millennium. Time would pass, convictions would fade and soon this moment would be nothing more than a memory. One day, I would set things right. I would be a queen again. And no matter what it took, Hades would be my king.

★ ★ ★ ★ ★

THE
LOVESTRUCK
GODDESS

I like secrets. Daddy's a walking cliché and says that the eyes are the windows to the soul, but I think the secrets people keep are the real way to see who they are.

See, secrets mean someone wants to keep something hidden, and the things people keep hidden are usually the most interesting parts of who they are. Afraid of the ocean? Totally telling. Six toes? All kinds of brilliant. Lusting after your niece? Majorly creepy.

Here's a secret—I failed my test.

I've never told anyone. Daddy knows—he's the one who caught me in a compromising position with a shepherd's son—but he's never said a word about it, either. Technically all the members of the council who aren't the original six siblings have to pass this ridiculous trial that tests our virtues, else we can't be a member of the council, but I think that's crap. Who wants to be ruled over by a bunch of self-important gods who think they're better than everyone just because they could bottle up their natural impulses for a little while?

And why are virtues so important anyway? I mean, I get not being greedy or selfish or too proud, but practically every member of the council's like that anyway, *especially* the six siblings. And I've never seen a more envious group of people in my life. Someone gets something, and suddenly they all hate that person because they got lucky or worked hard or whatever. Why can't everyone just love everyone else? That's what a ruler should do. Rule with love, not fear or intimidation. I love Daddy, but he'd have a lot easier time of it if he bothered to care about other people every once in a while.

He loves me though, so I can't complain too much.

Speaking of love and virtues, why is lust such a bad thing? Everyone acts like doing what our bodies are designed to do is such a horrible thing. Well, no, not everyone. Mostly just Hera. And she's the root of everything, really—she's the reason everyone's so miserable all the time, she's the reason we keep secrets and she's the reason I failed my test. Most important, she's the one who made up these ridiculous virtues we're all tested on in the first place, as if she's followed every single one of them herself (hello, pride), and she's the reason Daddy had to lie to get me a seat on the council.

That takes me to my second secret. My biggest secret. Who is currently trying to force-feed me grapes.

"No!" I bat Ares's hand away and giggle. We're curled up in a nest of silk pillows on my bedroom floor, and the sunlight that pours in from the balcony gives everything a golden glow. I love the way the sunset swirls around my feet, but I love the way Ares traces invisible patterns on my back even more.

"You need to keep your energy up," he says. I brush a lock of dark hair from his eyes. He's beautiful, muscles rippling underneath every square inch of skin, and he looks at me with such intensity that I think his fire will burn me. I'm not so sure I would mind.

"Mmm, but we don't have much longer, and I don't want to waste any more time eating," I murmur. Every place he touches me seems to sizzle, as if just being near each other is enough to spark a blaze. I've never loved someone so much in my life.

No, *love* isn't the right word. I mean, it is, but it's more than that. He consumes me. I'm constantly aware of him when he's nearby, even when I'm trying to focus on something else, and he has no problem exploiting it. That's how we wound up in my bedroom in the middle of the day, minutes before Daddy's supposed to come home.

Sometimes I think Ares does it on purpose.

"Well," he says in that husky voice of his, eternally scratchy from his battle cries. "Then we should get down to business, shouldn't we?"

He kisses me, his lips bruising against mine, and our mouths are a tangle of teeth and tongue. I've kissed a lot of boys before, and none of them affect me the way he does. When I'm with him, I feel *alive,* not just immortal. And believe me, there's a difference. It's easy to be immortal—all you have to do is sit there. But the world passes you by that way, and I don't see the point of existing for eternity if we don't feel it.

Being alive, that's the hard part. That's when my heart beats, my eyes are open and I see and smell and feel and taste and hear *everything.* It's heat, it's fire, it's the crash of the waves and the rumble of thunder. It's an awareness mortals take for granted. I never do though, especially when I'm with Ares.

He's pressing his hips against mine when someone clears their throat. I'm so lost in Ares that the sound makes me jump, and I push him off me. In the half second before I turn to the gauzy curtain that separates my room from the hall, I silently will it to be anyone but Daddy. I'd even take Hera right now. Or Hephaestus.

Shudder. Maybe Daddy would be a better option, after all.

My heart sinks. Standing in the archway, his arms folded

across his chest, is my father. His blue eyes are narrowed, his expression stony, and in that moment I'm sure he's going to smite one or both of us. I can only imagine what I must look like—cheeks flushed, hair mussed, lips swollen from the way Ares claimed them. Terrific.

"Hi, Daddy," I say, hugging a pillow. He says nothing. "Er, you're back early."

Still nothing. I look at Ares for help, but he's leaning back against the pillows with a shit-eating grin that makes me want to smack him. Apparently he's rubbing off on me, and not in the way I want him to.

It's amazing how slowly time can move sometimes, and I sit there, waiting—for what, I don't know. For anything. At last another figure appears on the other side of the gauzy curtain. For a moment, my hopes rise; but the instant Hephaestus limps through the curtain to stand beside Daddy, they burst. Could this possibly get any worse?

No, I take it back. No use tempting the Fates.

"Father," says Hephaestus. He's tall, taller than Daddy, and his arms are thick with muscles from forging. He would be cute if it wasn't for his twisted legs.

Not that I hold it against him, of course. But a girl has to have some standards. Besides, I saw the way he looked at me even before Daddy promised me to him, and I see the way he looks at me now. It isn't as consuming as Ares's gaze, but that love is still there. Gentler, easier, kinder. The sorts of things I don't need when I have his brother.

"Go back to the throne room, Hephaestus." Daddy clenches his fists. Hephaestus has the uncanny ability to make him squirm, something no one else on the council—no one else in the world, probably—can do. Usually Hephaestus takes great pains to stay away from Daddy for that very reason, but apparently today is the exception.

"Ares and Aphrodite weren't doing anything wrong," he says. A truth if I've ever heard one. Maybe he's finally accepted that I don't want to marry him. "He was teaching her how to defend herself. How to wrestle."

I have to bite my cheek to keep my mouth from dropping open. Accepting the fact that I don't want to be with him is one thing, but actually lying for me?

Daddy might have blinders on when it comes to me—most of the time, anyway—but his mouth forms a thin line. He doesn't even bother looking at Hephaestus. "Aphrodite knows how I feel about her having relations with your brother," he says, as if Ares and I aren't here. As if we aren't staring straight at him.

"And why is that, Father?" says Ares. "Why am I not allowed to see her when you spend half your time with mortal women and minor goddesses?"

Daddy grits his teeth. "What I do is none of your concern—"

"Of course it is, when you're upsetting Mother." Ares stands and goes nose to nose with Daddy. He's not as tall as him, but he's physically stronger, and they both know it. "You stop seeing other women, and I'll stop teaching Aphrodite how to wrestle."

The seconds tick by as Ares and Daddy glare at each other. I hug myself, my eyes wide as I wait for someone to blink. Daddy has never treated his sons as well as he treats me, but he's never thrown a punch or a bolt of lightning at them, either. And he can't now—not over me, not over this. It isn't okay.

"Daddy, please," I say, but my plea falls on deaf ears. At last Hephaestus touches their shoulders, as if he thinks his calloused hands are enough to stop them from raging at each other.

"Enough," he says quietly. "This is my battle, Father, not yours, and I choose not to fight."

Ares scoffs. "Coward."

Faster than lightning, Daddy hits him across the mouth. Ares stares at him, stunned, and if time was going slowly before, now it stops completely.

They really are going to fight because of me. Maybe even war. I don't see why Daddy should care so much—Ares has a point, after all. Fidelity hasn't exactly been Daddy's strongest attribute, and it's not as if I'm married to Hephaestus yet. For whatever reason, though, Daddy does care, and this isn't making things better.

But before I can try to stop them, Ares storms out of my room, and that jagged shard of loss burrows itself within me. Not just the loss of his physical presence, but because I know that look on Daddy's face. What little relief I get from this near miss evaporates.

"Aphrodite." His voice wavers, the only sign of how angry he is. "Come with me."

I sigh and stand. Telling him no would only make the situation worse. Daddy walks briskly down the hall, not giving me a chance to catch up with him, but I know where he's going. Before I leave, I pause. "Thanks," I mutter to Hephaestus. "For covering for me, I mean."

He shrugs and brushes his fingertips against my elbow. There's something shy about him, something quiet I don't understand. "It was nothing," he says, and his touch is gone as soon as I register it. All for the better, really. Ares is excitement, passion, fire all rolled into one, while Hephaestus is—

I'm not too sure what he is, but it isn't passion. If Ares wasn't here, maybe I could stomach the thought of marrying Hephaestus, but being forced to settle for subpar when I have perfection right under my nose is cruel.

Without glancing back at Hephaestus, I follow Daddy, taking my time. No point in hurrying toward another talking-to. I've only been in Olympus for a hundred years, but I'm not completely ignorant. When Daddy holds meetings in his office, they're never good.

By the time I catch up with him, the heat in my face is gone. His office is on the other side of Olympus, and in the time it's taken me to get there, I've prepared what I want to say. What I'm *going* to say this time instead of letting Daddy walk all over me. It's my life, not his.

Daddy's sitting behind his desk, gazing into the portal that lets him see what's happening on earth. He's focused on a beach I don't recognize, with tall cliffs in the background. In the seconds before he realizes I'm there, I think I see Hera, but I can't be sure.

"Aphrodite." The portal disappears. "Please, sit."

"I'd rather stand." I'm never rude to him, at least not on purpose, but today I can't find it in myself to hold back. "Why are you doing this to me?"

As soon as I say it, my eyes well up. Perfect. Now he's never going to take me seriously.

Sometimes crying helps though, and at least his expression softens. But this isn't how I want to win. I want him to love me enough to care more about my happiness than he does his war with Hera. "My dear," he murmurs, and he moves out from behind his desk to embrace me. I let him. He smells like smoke and river water, and I don't want to know why.

"Just—" I hiccup. "I love Ares, Daddy. I really, really love him, and he loves me, too."

"Are you sure about that?" he says, and I pull back in horror.

"Of course he does. How can you even say something like that?"

He tries to pull me in close again, but I resist. "I only mean that he didn't seem to be too bothered that I caught the pair of you—er, wrestling. I could easily forbid you to see each other, yet—"

"You wouldn't." I step away from him, and he reaches for me, but his hand grasps empty air. "Daddy, you can't do that to me. I don't care about the issues you and Hera have—marrying me off to Hephaestus just to make her miserable—"

"Is that why you think I chose him?" says Daddy. "Oh, darling."

"Don't 'oh, darling' me," I snap. I've never been so sharp with him in my entire existence. "This is my life, not yours. One son's as good as the other to you anyway, so why don't you just let me choose Ares? Hera will still be angry."

Although, if I was the one making that choice, maybe she wouldn't be. The morning she came to speak with me, the day of the council meeting where we were supposed to vote on whether to remove Daddy as head of the council—Hera tried to give me a choice. Maybe only because she wanted to dethrone Daddy, but I like to think it was more than that. I like to think she really cared—if not about me, then her sons.

I would've voted with her, too. And it's a damn shame she interfered before I had the chance to say so.

"I chose Hephaestus because I thought he was the best candidate," says Daddy. "I see what you and Ares are to each other, and that isn't the sort of love that lasts, my dear. Fire can't burn forever."

I blush. "You paired me up with Hephaestus because he asked you to, not because you thought it through."

"Both of my sons asked," he says. "And I put a great deal of thought into it. You must look beyond the surface, my dear. Hephaestus will love you—"

"Not the way I want to be loved." I wipe my eyes again. I'd give anything to make them stop leaking. "What will it hurt to let me choose?"

"It would hurt you." He reaches for me again, but I sidestep him a second time.

"So you're saying I'm too dumb to choose for myself?"

He frowns. "Of course not—"

"Then let me choose."

"Darling, I have eons of experience—"

"I don't care about your experience." I stomp my foot. I've never actually done that before, and it seems silly even when I'm in the middle of it, but it's strangely relaxing. "I care about my *life*. I love Ares, he loves me, and we want to be together."

Daddy is silent for a long moment. "Do you truly believe that spark will last for eternity?"

I sniff. "Of course."

He watches me. The sun streams in from the balcony, making me see spots, but I don't look away. I can't. There's too much at stake for me to blink.

At last he sighs. "Aphrodite, I am sorry, but I cannot go against my instincts. I love you far too much to let you hurt yourself in such a way. Or allow you to give Ares the chance to hurt you instead."

He may as well have hit me, too. Slowly I straighten, squaring my shoulders and drawing in every bit of my power. "So be it then," I say. "If you won't give me my freedom, then I'll just have to take it, won't I?"

I spin around and march out of his office, holding my head high. To his credit, he doesn't try to stop me, but then again, maybe he thinks I'm too weak to go through with it.

Fine. I'll just have to prove him wrong, then.

I walk purposely through Olympus as I search for Ares. We don't have to stay here. We have a right to rule over our own lives, and if we let Daddy win this battle, he'll keep at it until he wins the war. I love him, but he doesn't get a say in this. Not anymore.

I find Ares in his chambers. Rather, I don't so much find him as I hear him from all the way down the hall. He's yelling at someone, and his voice echoes too much for me to make out the words at first. I hurry to the archway, but I come to a dead stop when I see the scene inside his room.

Everything's a wreck. His bed is overturned, the silk curtains I hung on his walls have been ripped down and the array of weapons he usually keeps so organized are scattered across the floor. A particularly sharp ax is even buried in the wall, inches from the exit into the hallway.

And standing in the middle of the whole mess are Ares and Hephaestus.

"She's *mine*," Ares bellows, and he thumps his chest with his fist. His rage is palpable, and he glows a faint red. "Not yours, little brother—*mine*."

Hephaestus flinches. "You've said that," he says quietly. "But she is not a possession."

Says the boy who asked his father to give me to him. I snort, and both heads turn in my direction.

"Aphrodite?" says Hephaestus. He steps toward me, but Ares blocks his way with a wicked-looking sword.

"Stay out of this," says Ares, giving me a look. That same fire is in his eyes, but this passion isn't for me. It's for the fight.

"Why, so you two can have it out and decide who gets to marry me instead of letting me choose for myself?" I move toward them, sidestepping a massive shield. "Do either of you actually care about what I want?"

Hephaestus opens his mouth, undoubtedly to claim he does care, but Ares cuts him off. "Now isn't the time. I will speak with you once I'm through with Hephaestus."

Ares glares at me, and for once, I don't flinch. I've had enough fighting for one day. If they want to go to war over me, then so be it. I won't be sticking around to see it, or to give the winner his *prize*.

"Fine," I growl, and I turn on my heel and leave. Storming into my chambers, I start to pack. I don't have many things to take—a hand mirror decorated with pearls that a nymph gave me before Daddy found me, several of my favorite pillows and a reflection of Daddy and me playing on the beach. Even though others shower me with beautiful things, the only items I really care about are the ones with love attached to them—with sentimental value. No matter how angry I am with Daddy, I can't leave those things behind.

By the time I'm done, Ares is standing in the archway between the hallway and my room, his arms crossed over his broad chest. He smirks, looking disgustedly pleased with himself. The jerk.

"Oh, so you won the battle then?" I say, bitterness saturating every word.

"Don't be ridiculous. What do you think you're doing?" he says in that hoarse voice I love. I pause. What *am* I doing?

"I'm leaving," I finally say, because it's the truth. "I'd like for you to come with me, but I won't demand it."

He eyes me curiously, as if he's trying to figure out the puzzle in my words. But there's no puzzle. He deserves a choice, just like me. "All right then," he says. "Where are we going?"

With those four words, all of my anxiety vanishes. Grinning, I run to him and wrap my arms around him, showering him with kisses. "I love you so much," I murmur.

He holds me securely against him, his arms strong and his grip firm, as if he's never going to let me go. I hope with everything I am that he doesn't. "Is that a place now?" he teases.

I kiss him again, pouring every last bit of me into it. Words can only say so much, and the way I love him—those words don't exist. "Home," I say. "We're going home."

★ ★ ★

I don't often talk about my life before Olympus. Or at all, really. There's no point. I spent most of it on an island with nymphs, who took care of me as if I was their own. But I wasn't their daughter. I was nobody's daughter, and no matter how much they loved me, the knowledge that my real parents had abandoned me hurt. Daddy likes to theorize that I didn't have parents, that I was born from the blood of a Titan, but that only makes things worse. Who wants to exist because someone was in pain?

But one good thing did come out of my childhood: the island. It didn't have a name when I was growing up, and humans haven't found it yet, which means it still doesn't. It's my safe place, the place I go to think, and the act of taking Ares's hand and dropping onto the island from Olympus makes me feel more vulnerable than I ever have before.

"Wow." At least the first words out of Ares's mouth are appropriate. We stand on a collection of boulders smoothed down by time, and across a clear pool is a waterfall. Vines of pink and purple flowers hang down each side like curtains, and above us the sunset stains the sky.

"This is my favorite place in the world." I squeeze his hand. "Other than wherever you are, of course. And you being here makes it perfect."

Ares wraps his arm around my shoulders, every trace of his earlier wrath gone. Being away from Olympus will do us both some good, but Ares needs it more than I do. He needs to see the beauty in all things, not just in conflict and blood and war.

We stand there for several minutes, soaking in the last of the sunset. As soon as the indigo of night seeps into the sky, I lead him across the edge of the pool toward the waterfall. "Come on," I say. "I'll show you where I grew up."

He follows me, and though he doesn't say anything, I can feel his wariness. None of the gods except Poseidon—and me, of course—are comfortable around water. It isn't part of them, just like the Underworld isn't. But he doesn't complain as we both step through the waterfall, and his bravery is well rewarded. On the other side, in a hidden grotto, is my home.

Over the years, I've brought little things here, and little things add up over time. The nymphs must have known we were coming, because a cozy fire crackles in the middle of the cave, illuminating everything with a warm glow. A nest of pillows inhabits an entire corner, more than enough for both of us. Jewels hang from the ceiling, sparkling in the low light, and my collection of reflections hover on the walls, attached by a thought. If a mortal were to stumble across this cave, they'd be horribly confused. Most of them believe in us, but believing and seeing are two entirely different things.

"Do you like it?" I say. Fresh grapes wait for us on a golden platter, and I lead Ares to the nest of pillows.

"It's incredible," he says, for once not trying to act like he's above it all. "This is where you grew up?"

I nod. "It's my secret place. And you're my secret now, too."

He kisses me with that same bruising passion, his fingers tangling in my hair as he lowers me onto the pillows. The sting of leaving Daddy behind still cuts me, but it isn't forever. Just long enough for him to apologize and let me marry Ares instead.

A choice. Love. Devotion. It isn't too much to ask for, and Daddy will wear down eventually. He has to.

I've never been very good with time. I can tell you how long a day is, of course, and a lunar cycle. But eventually everything sort of blends together no matter how alive I feel.

That's what time with Ares is like—a whirlwind of living. We explore the entire island together as the days trickle by, and for the first time ever, I feel like the center of someone's world. There's nothing like it, being someone's sun, and I lose myself in Ares and our life together.

Years pass—it must be years, because the mild seasons change, and I've nearly forgotten the scent of Olympus—and we have a son. At first I'm not crazy about the idea of being a mother. I'm too young, I still have too much to do before I'm tied down like Hera, and half the time I forget to take care of myself, let alone a baby. But Eros is the sweetest little thing I've ever seen. His blond curls, blue eyes and rosy cheeks are all mine, but his focus and intensity are Ares's. And his chin. Definitely his chin. I've never seen Ares as happy as he is the moment a nymph lays Eros in his arms.

But on the day he's born, my world shifts, and Eros becomes my sun. I think I see it in Ares's eyes, the way he looks at me cradling the baby, though neither of us says it aloud. It's the happiest moment of my life, but it's also the moment our paradise starts to change.

"You still love me, don't you?" I murmur three days after Eros's birth. He's my timepiece now, my moon and my stars, and I won't ever forget a day he existed. I'm curled up in the nest of pillows, cradling Eros as he sleeps. Ares sharpens his sword by the fire.

He pauses, and resounding silence replaces the screech of stone against metal. Somehow the sound doesn't bother the baby. "Why do you ask?"

His reluctance to give me a yes or no answer makes doubt coil inside me, hard and cold and impossible to swallow. "Eros. I just wanted to make sure—nothing's changed, has it?"

He sets his sword down and joins us in the pillows. He

hasn't touched me properly since before Eros's birth, but now he gathers me up, his hand splayed across my back as he buries his nose in my hair. "I love you," he says. "Do you still love me?"

"More than ever," I whisper, and it's the truth. Somehow, even though I thought it wasn't possible, my heart's swelled. I loved Ares with everything I had before, but now there's more—enough for Eros, and even more for Ares.

The fire crackles, and Ares traces my lips with the pad of his thumb. "I have to go tomorrow. There's a war brewing, and I've neglected my duties long enough."

I feel like someone's poured a bucket of cold water over my head, and that doubt returns, thicker than ever. "But—why? You don't need to fight."

He chuckles, but there's no humor in his laughter. For a brief second, he looks at me the way he did in Olympus all that time ago, when he and Hephaestus argued. Like I'm a child. Like I don't understand. "And if I told you that you don't need to love?"

I snort. "That's absurd."

"Then why tell me I don't need to fight?" He kisses my cheek. "I'm taking care of my duties, that's all. The nymphs will be here to take care of you and Eros, and I'll be back soon enough."

"How soon is soon enough?" I say, and he shrugs.

"As long as it takes for someone to win. But I'll think of you every second, I promise."

We both know he won't, not when there's a battle to fight, but I appreciate the sentiment anyhow. And at sunset the next day, he kisses me and Eros goodbye, his lips lingering on mine. A flash of green bursts through the sky, and all that's left of him are two footprints in the sand.

Swallowing tightly, I notice a shell beside the spot where his left heel was moments before. Picking it up, I wash it in the ocean and cradle it in my palm, as if it holds the key to when Ares will return. But it's just a shell, and it gives me no answers. I take it back to the grotto anyway.

I spend the whole night sobbing, even though I'm upsetting Eros. His tears only make me cry harder, and I cling to him as if he's my lifeline. He is, in a way. Ares is gone, however temporarily, and Eros is all I have left until he returns. I need love the way Ares needs war; without him, I'm just immortal again, waiting for that spark to bring me to life once more. But at least he waited until we had a baby to leave. At least he knows I can't be alone.

That in and of itself is a sign of how much he loves me, and I force myself not to forget it.

I go to the beach every day at sunset to wait for him. I make plans for what we'll do together when he returns, and on my bad days, I consider returning to Olympus just to find out where he is. But even though Ares isn't here, Eros is, and watching him grow makes me feel again.

"Eros! Not so fast!" I laugh as I chase my toddler down the beach. The sun beats down on us, warming me from the inside out, and the gentle waves lap at my feet. The only way today could be more perfect is if Ares would come home.

Eros stops at a scattering of driftwood near the entrance to a cave we've explored a dozen times before. Kneeling in the sand, he picks through the crude rope and logs, and I crouch down beside him.

"What are you looking for?" I murmur. He ignores me, but suddenly he beams and pulls something from the wreckage.

"Sell!" he declares, and he sets a white-and-coral spiral

shell in my palm. Out of all the shells we've found on the beach together—one for each day Ares has been gone—this is the most beautiful. I turn it over in my hands, admiring its perfection. I miss him. Badly. And though I'm usually good at hiding it from Eros, seeing this triggers something in me. The love I have for my son isn't the same kind of love I have for Ares, and I want that back. I *need* that back.

While I'm struggling not to tear up in front of him, Eros toddles off again, this time toward the caves. My vision blurs, and I wipe my eyes as I rise. "Eros, no, baby, not without me."

He keeps going, naturally, and I follow him. He's immortal, and nothing can hurt him. That doesn't mean I want him to get lost, though.

As I close in on him, however, I spot something in the sand. Footsteps. Not Eros's small, uneven ones, but large enough for an adult. For a man.

Pocketing the shell, I scoop Eros up and balance him on my hip. He lets out a cry of protest, but I kiss his hair and follow the path toward the cave. The footsteps soon turn to drag marks, as if whoever it was could no longer hold his own weight. Did Ares return without telling me? But why would he leave behind the remains of a raft, and why would he go this way instead of back toward the waterfall?

No, whoever it is must be hurt, and no mortal battle could ever injure Ares. It isn't him.

"Hello?" I call as I swallow my disappointment. No answer. I poke my head inside the cave, smaller than the one we live in, and I have to squint to make anything out in the sudden darkness. "Is anyone here?"

A rough cough. I hold Eros tighter, and with a wave of my hand, a cheerful fire forms in the middle of the cave. Huddled in the nearest corner is a young man dressed in rags. Everything about him is dark: his matted hair, the stubble on his cheeks—even his skin is tanned to a leathery brown.

A horrible smell reaches me, and I wrinkle my nose. Blood. The smell of violence and war. Without letting go of Eros, I approach the huddled figure. Shadows dance on the walls of the cave, confusing his shape, but eventually I make him out.

He's bent in ways a body isn't supposed to be. His legs are mangled, and it's a miracle he was able to leave footprints at all. Part of his chest is concave, as if he had been hit by a large rock, and his breaths are labored. But at least he's breathing. At least he's alive.

"Eros," I say, setting my son down. "I need you to do exactly as I say and follow me home without wandering off. Do you promise?"

Eros nods solemnly, somehow aware of the gravity of the situation despite how little he is. He latches onto my leg, and I wave my hands. It's tricky, and the young man groans, but his broken body rises in the air.

I float him out of the cave, and after three seconds in the sunlight, he passes out. From pain or the shock of being held up in the air without any discernible source, I have no idea. Either way, at least I won't have to dodge any questions.

Even though I know Ares would have a fit if he found out, I bring the injured young man back to the grotto. He moans as I place him on the pillows, and blood browned by time stains his hands. This isn't good. This really, really, *really* isn't good.

I settle Eros in a corner with a basketful of flowers to chain together. I need all the concentration I can get right now.

Apollo?

I push the thought into the sky as hard as I can. Sunset's coming soon, which means so is Olympus as it hovers eternally between day and dusk, and that makes this marginally easier. Unless he's off somewhere wandering the world. Apollo isn't exactly a homebody.

I hold my breath. Not that I need to breathe anyway, but it's the thought that counts. Ten seconds pass, then fifteen, then twenty. I'm about to send it again when—

Aphrodite? There's a tinge of surprise coloring his thought. *What's going on? Are you all right?*

I sigh with relief. *I found a mortal, and he's dying, and I don't know how to heal him.*

Several more seconds pass. *Zeus is watching me. If I go to you, he'll track you down.*

I hesitate and glance around the home Ares and I have made. If Apollo comes, it could mean giving up all of this. Everything we've built, every perfect moment together—maybe even Eros. No telling if Daddy would let him stay in Olympus. I might lose all of this for a single mortal life.

The young man in the corner lets out a soft, agonizing sob, and my heart breaks. Screw it. If Daddy wants to come find me, let him. He will never take my family away from me.

I don't care. He needs your help. I project an image of the island to him, along with an imprint of where it would be from Olympus. The sunset must be close now. *Hurry.*

While I wait for Apollo, I sit beside the young man and touch his cheek—the only part of him that isn't bloody or bruised or both. His breaths come in gasps, but he remains unconscious. From the pain, I think, but I don't understand how he could possibly register the brutality done to his body and still be alive.

As the forest rustles with its nighttime sounds, my brother finally arrives. He kneels beside the stranger, shooing me away, and I sit back on my heels and watch anxiously. It's been too long, I'm sure of it, but Apollo doesn't hesitate. He holds his hands over him, and golden light glows in the space between. I've never seen him heal someone before. I know he can do it, of course, but for a mortal this far gone…was it even possible?

Eros toddles over to me and wraps his pudgy arms around my neck. I pull him into a hug, burying my face in his hair. His curls are the exact same shade as Apollo's. It's a silly thing to think about when a man's life hangs in the balance, but it gives me some small measure of comfort.

At last Apollo pulls away. I don't know how long it's been, but Eros is asleep in my arms, love radiating from him as if he knows how much I need it right now. Maybe he does. My son is gifted in ways I'm just beginning to understand, and I hold him tight. "Is he going to live?"

Apollo nods grimly. He's pale, as if he's poured every last bit of himself into healing this stranger. "I've done what I can. He'll need some time to heal."

"He can stay here." Even as I say it, I can hear the worry in my own voice, but no mortal would dare to harm a goddess. And if he did try, then I'd throw him into the ocean. Something about him, though—the way his face relaxes now that he's free of pain, maybe—tells me he won't.

"Ares won't mind?" says Apollo, and I shrug.

"Ares isn't here." I can have another secret.

Apollo touches my face. Even his eyes are drained of color. "I miss you," he says. "We're all rooting for you and Ares, you know."

I smile faintly. I don't believe him. Artemis, Athena—even our aunts look down on this sort of reckless love. But it isn't reckless if it's real, and I'll take their scorn if it means I get to be happy. They can remain in Olympus with Daddy, alone and miserable and full of cobwebs for the rest of forever. "Stay here tonight," I say.

He doesn't fight me, and soon enough he's snoring in another corner. The fire dims to embers, but I don't move for the rest of the night. I'm too afraid. Any moment, Daddy might find me; any moment, Ares might return. Any moment, the stranger might open his eyes.

Any moment, my world might change forever. Unless it already has.

I force myself to relax. I'm safe for now, and I have Eros. Daddy can't take him away from me. He would never even try, knowing how badly it would hurt me.

Everything will be okay. I have to believe it—for Eros, for this stranger and for myself.

When Apollo leaves at sunset the next day, the stranger is still asleep. While the nymphs watch over him, I gather enough water, herbs and berries to keep him fed for a while—or at least I hope it'll be enough. I don't know how much mortals eat.

For the first time since Ares left me, I don't go down to the beach that day. The perfect shell Eros found joins the hundreds of others we've collected in baskets that line the entrance of the grotto, but I barely think about it as I remain by the stranger's side. One day won't hurt. And this mortal needs me more than Ares needs my misery.

Apollo's handiwork is impressive. The young man's body is straight now, and the worst of his wounds are healed. His skin is still bruised, but at least his heart beats steadily. That's something.

Shortly after the sun sets, the stranger's breathing changes. It grows faster, more labored, and his good hand gropes around for something that isn't there.

"Hold still," I say, touching his knuckles. "You'll hurt your-self."

At last he opens his puffy eyes. Every other part of him is dark, but his irises are a pale gray, the color of stone. "Who…?" He stops and licks his lips. Clearly it's painful to talk, and I know what he's asking anyway. But I can't tell him. He'd never believe me.

"I'm a friend," I say. "Who are you?"

He tries to sit up, and a rattle echoes from deep within his chest. I don't know much about mortal health, but that sound can't be good.

"Lay back down," I say, pushing his shoulders gently. He's in no condition to fight me, and thankfully he doesn't try. "I have food and water if you want it."

He licks his lips again, and I take that as a yes. I pour a trickle of water into his mouth, and though he coughs, he manages to swallow most of it.

"Where…?" His voice isn't as rough now, but it's still hard to make out what he's saying.

"You're on my island. You're safe here, I promise."

"With you." It isn't a question. Even though I'm a stranger to him, he looks at me not as a threat, but like I'm some sort of savior. Maybe to him I am. There's a certain sort of ten-derness in the way he watches me, as if he knows I'm the rea-son he's still alive even though he's barely conscious, and it warms me from the inside out. I squeeze his hand affection-ately. He *is* lucky. If Ares had been the one to find him, he would have had him by the tip of a sword the moment he'd stumbled across his broken body.

"Do you have a name?" I say.

Silence. The young man watches me with those pale eyes of his, and I bite my lip. I'm used to everyone staring at me.

I enjoy it. But something about the way he looks at me—it's like he can see past the beauty, and it makes me squirm.

"Rest," I say. It's the most I can offer him. "I'll be here when you wake up."

His eyes flutter shut once more, and I'm almost relieved. I don't know who he is or where he comes from, but those gray irises speak of things I can't even imagine. There's a reason he survived—a reason the Fates didn't cut the thread of his life. Whatever it is, I vow to make sure he finds out.

For sixteen days, the stranger is silent.

I watch over him while Eros remains in the care of my most trusted nymph, and in my head I call him Cyrus. It doesn't exactly do me much good to name him; chances are it isn't his real name, after all, and I never call him that aloud. But in my mind, Cyrus is more of a person, and it makes me feel better about the risks I took to save him.

Daddy doesn't show up. Not on the first day, not on the second, not half a lunar cycle later. I'm on guard at first, ready to make my case and stomp my foot again if I have to. But either Daddy wasn't watching Apollo closely, or for some reason he's decided not to chase after me. I hope it's the first. The idea that Daddy doesn't care enough to try hurts too much.

Cyrus heals slower than I thought he would, but soon enough he's sitting up. He eats and drinks everything I offer him, but he never asks for more, and I constantly worry that he's not getting enough. Food's important to the healing process for mortals, I know that, but how much is appropriate gnaws at me. I give him an extra bowl of berries, and he eats that, too. But he still heals too slowly.

His silence unnerves me, and I catch him watching me far too often, but it's the love that radiates from him that baffles me. I've always been able to sense love, but this—it isn't the kind of love I'm used to. It isn't made of heat and desire, like Ares's. It's tender. It's gentle, as if he wants to take care of me, even though I'm the one taking care of him. And even though I'm with Ares, even though he could come home any day, I slowly start to give in. I can't help it—it's one of my gifts, the inability to receive love without returning it, but I think even if it wasn't, I would grow to care for him deeply. He's kind, kinder than Ares has ever been, and his presence calms me even when I'm certain Daddy's going to walk through the entrance to my grotto at any moment.

It doesn't matter, though. He's mortal, and even if I let him stay with me until Ares returns, he might die long before then. It's a temporary love at best, and in a way, that helps ease my guilt. And it makes it easier to accept the connection that grows between us, even though he never utters a word.

On the sixteenth day—I know this because every evening Eros brings me a pebble he's found in the pool of clear water—Cyrus sits up and watches me with those eyes of his. They're still uncanny, even though I've had time to get used to them.

"May I have some meat?" These are the first words he's spoken since he asked where he was, and I'm relieved.

"Er, you mean, like…rabbit?" I say. I've never even thought to kill and cook a rabbit. My nymphs would be furious.

"Or fish," he says. His voice is soft, and I have to strain to hear him.

"Fish might be possible." And the nymphs would proba-bly swallow that a little easier. I stand. "I'll go ask my uncle."

"Your uncle?"

I blush. Right. He has no idea who I am. "Er, yeah. I'll be back."

I hurry off. The beach isn't far from the grotto, and Poseidon offers me a few fish for Cyrus. I don't like asking for his help—he's one more person who might tell Daddy where I am—but I don't know the first thing about catching fish. And if meat will help Cyrus heal faster, then so be it. It's not like I haven't risked everything already.

I return with the parcel of fish—which is probably the worst thing I've ever smelled in my entire existence—but Cyrus isn't there. My heart skips a beat, and I drop the fish and hurry outside. "Hello?" I call. Why didn't I ask for his real name when I had the chance? "Where did you go?"

He couldn't have gone far. I look for any trace of footprints, but other than the ones my wet feet leave behind, there are none. Terrific. He's worse than Eros. I turn my back for a few moments and—

Laughter. I stop to listen, straining to hear over the sounds of the waterfall. Yes, definitely a man's laughter. Tiptoeing through the trees, I follow it. What could Cyrus be laughing about? Who is he laughing with? And how did he leave the grotto?

Poking my head around a thick trunk, my mouth drops open. Eros sits in the middle of a small clearing, one he claimed as his ages ago, and he's stringing flowers together. Cyrus sits beside him, leaning against a tree to support himself, and he too is making flower chains.

It isn't just Cyrus who's laughing. Eros giggles, too; the sweet sound of it mostly drowned out by Cyrus's deeper chuckles. I've never seen Eros with anyone other than the nymphs before. The three days Ares was here after our son was born hardly count, after all. But Eros looks happy. Really, really happy. And so does Cyrus.

"What are you two doing?" I say in a playful voice. The last thing I want to do is make them feel as if this isn't okay. I should be wary of Cyrus, especially around my son, but any apprehension I had about him is long gone now.

"Mama!" Eros holds up his flower chain, a mismatch of colorful blossoms. I kneel beside him and kiss the top of his head.

"That's beautiful. Is it for me?" I say, and he shakes his head. Before I can say anything else, he holds it out for Cyrus.

"Yous!" Eros declares. I expect Cyrus to turn it down—Ares would never wear a necklace of flowers no matter who gave them to him—but instead he takes it.

"Thank you," he says, and he ties it around his neck. "How is that?"

Eros giggles, and I kiss his pudgy cheek. "That was very nice of you," I murmur. "Such a perfect little boy."

"He is," says Cyrus. "You're very lucky."

I smile faintly. "I am."

Cyrus ties off the last of his stems. "Thank you," he says. "I owe you my life. I can't begin to make it up to you, the kindness you've shown me, but I suppose this is a start." He offers me his crown of flowers. "It's not much, but it's all I have."

My lips part in surprise. I hesitate, but at last I take it gingerly. He's done good work, wrapping the stems around a thicker vine and securing everything in place. I touch a petal. No man's ever given me something like this before—something they've taken time to make with their own hands. Ares has given me jewels, silks, the finest things in the world. But he's never been able to appreciate the beauty in something so simple.

"Thank you," I say. "It's lovely."

"As are you," he says quietly. "You are the first person I've met who is as beautiful on the inside as she is on the outside."

I have to press my lips together to keep from grinning, and

even then, my cheeks grow warm. "I should get you back to the grotto. I have your fish."

He nods, and slowly he stands on shaky legs. He must be more healed than I'd thought. I watch him for signs of pain, and while he winces some, he manages to make it back to the grotto without too much trouble. I take Eros's hand and follow.

That evening, we feast on fish. I have to eat to keep up appearances, and Eros eagerly tries a few bites before he declares he's full. Cyrus, however, wolfs down three fish on his own, and I take note. Next time I find an injured mortal, fish it is.

By the time Eros falls asleep in my lap, the sun is setting, and I sit beside Cyrus as we watch the fire. It's peaceful, and for the first time since Ares left, I'm not lonely. "What's your name?"

He tilts his head and looks at me out of the corner of his eye. "What is yours?"

I shake my head. I can't tell him. Our names were once a secret, but now that mortals worship us, we're too well known for me to say. He might think I'm a namesake, that my parents wanted to honor a goddess, but he's seen too much. He'll put two and two together, and while I trust him, I don't want to risk him bringing others back to my island.

"I call you Cyrus in my head," I admit. "I don't know why."

"Cyrus?" His lips curl into a small smile. "That's as good a name as any, I suppose. May I choose a name for you?"

I nod. "Just make it a good one."

For a long moment he studies me, his gray eyes reflecting the fire, and at last he murmurs, "Ava."

Ava. The way he says it sends a shiver through me, and I snake my hand through the space between us until I'm touching his. "It's perfect."

"As are you," he whispers. Our eyes lock together, and time

seems to stop. All I see is him. All I feel is him. All I smell and all I touch is him, and all I want to taste is him.

Maybe it's loneliness. Maybe it's the way he looks at me. Maybe it's his laughter or smile or any number of things. But even though I love Ares, I lean into Cyrus and press my lips to his.

It's a soft kiss without the burning passion I have with Ares, but it's still tender. It's still sweet and loving, but a different kind of love—the kind of love that tells me he'll take care of me, and I'll take care of him. The kind of love that wants to hear about my day. That sees me underneath the beauty and still loves me anyway.

I crave it. It's a salve, soothing the wounds Ares has caused. He isn't Ares, he'll never *be* Ares, but in that moment, I'm grateful for it. I don't want the kind of love Ares has given me the past few years. I want this love, the love in front of me, the love I can touch taste smell hear see. Cyrus may not realize it, but the way he feels for me radiates from him, wrapping itself around me. This kiss is an offer, and I want to take it.

"Ahem."

I jump back, jostling Eros. In the doorway, silhouetted by the last vestiges of sunset, is the last person I expect.

Ares.

"I see you've been keeping yourself busy." He spits the words out like venom, and part of me bristles, but another part can't blame him. "Who is this?"

"I—" I swallow and force myself to sit up straight. Ares is the one who left me alone for years. What did he expect? "This is Cyrus. He had a wreck, and he landed on the island. I've been helping him recover."

"And this is your idea of playing healer?" Ares narrows

his eyes, and his fingers twitch toward the monstrous sword strapped to his hip. Brilliant.

Cyrus squeezes my hand. I should pull away, but I need the comfort his touch offers. Clearly I won't be getting it from Ares. "Is this your uncle?" he says, and the idea is so absurd that I snort.

"Her uncle?" Ares steps closer, and the fire casts shadows on his face. "Is that what you've been telling him?"

"What? No," I say quickly, and to Cyrus I add, "this is my— This is Eros's father."

His grip on my hand loosens, and now it's my turn to squeeze. I don't want him to let go. "Oh," he says. "I'm sorry. I had no idea she was—"

"She is," snaps Ares. "She's mine. You have one chance to get the hell away from her before I slit you from nose to navel."

Despite my grip, Cyrus pulls his hand from mine, and he slowly crawls back into the nest of pillows. "I'm sorry," he says again. "I would have never—"

"Not there," growls Ares. "Not in our bed."

"Ares, he's injured," I say. In my arms, Eros makes a soft, keening sound. "He can't go anywhere."

"I don't care," he snarls.

"Well, I do." I stand, taking Eros with me. "You have no right to storm in here and start making demands, not after leaving us. Not after missing Eros's entire life."

"It doesn't seem like you've been left wanting." Ares moves closer until he's only a few inches away from me. He's taller now, stronger than he was before, and his armor is flecked with droplets of blood. They're still wet. "Perhaps Mother was right. Perhaps all you are and all you'll ever be is a whore."

Cyrus's fist comes out of nowhere. One moment Ares is in front of me, and the next he's sprawled out beside the fire.

I gasp and step back. Cyrus is on his feet, his legs trembling with the effort of standing upright, but I've never seen him look so impassioned.

"You *will* speak to her with the respect the mother of your child deserves," he says. "Or you will leave."

Ares scrambles to his feet again, looking both stunned and more enraged than I've ever seen him before. He pulls out his sword, holding it between them as if he's begging Cyrus for an excuse to use it. "How dare you. Do you know who I am?"

Cyrus says nothing. His hands are clenched into fists, and he stares down Ares as if they're equals. But they're not—Ares is a god, and Cyrus is mortal. It's a small miracle Ares hasn't killed him yet, but I'm sure Cyrus will have a one-way ticket to Hades's realm soon enough.

"Stop it, please," I beg. "He'll leave as soon as he's healed, all right? Just don't hurt him."

My protests change nothing. They still stare at one another, as if caught in a silent battle, and I don't know what to do. I clutch Eros closer, and he begins to cry. But there's nothing I can do to comfort him, either. I'm helpless.

At last, Ares's mask of rage slips, and he begins to laugh. It's a mocking sound though, the kind of empty, haunting laugh that isn't a laugh at all. "You," he says. "You sick, twisted bastard. Aphrodite has no idea, does she?"

I frown. "No idea about what?"

Ares shakes his head, his focus still locked on Cyrus. "Would you like to tell her, or shall I?"

I expect Cyrus to deny knowing what he's talking about—after all, I've been with him for sixteen days. Ares only arrived moments ago. But instead Cyrus's expression crumbles, and he turns to me. "I'm so very sorry for my deception."

"What deception?" I look from one to the other, my heart pounding. "What are you two talking about?"

Ares sheaths his sword. "He isn't mortal," he says. "He's been lying to you all this time, haven't you, brother?"

My mouth drops open. Cold horror washes through me, so icy and real that I shiver, and I stare at Cyrus. *"Brother?"*

Ares smirks. "I'll be outside while the two of you sort things out. But when I return, I expect him to be gone."

He slips out of the grotto, leaving Cyrus and me alone. No, not Cyrus. Never Cyrus.

"Hephaestus," I whisper, and he stares at the floor. "You lied to me."

Anyone else would deny it. He didn't really lie, after all—he never told me his name. He never claimed to be someone he wasn't. But he never told me the truth, either. He pretended not to know me, and his mortal form alone was an intentional deception.

Hephaestus nods. "I'm sorry."

"But—you're mortal," I say, dazed.

"I've been searching for you ever since you left, and I scoured the world looking for this place. The only way I could blend in was to take a mortal form. I knew my boat might crash. I knew I might feel pain. It was a risk, but for you…" He clears his throat. "Please forgive me."

"I don't…" I trail off and stare at him as if this is the first time I've ever seen him. It is, in a way. "Why are you here?"

He grimaces. "Because I want you to have the life you deserve. I'm not very good with words, but I love you, Aphrodite. I've loved you my entire life. Not because of what you look like, not because of the horrible arrangement my father made, but because of who you are underneath. You radiate. You're sunshine. You make the world a brighter place just by existing. You see the beauty underneath the surface, and the way you love—I've never seen anything more inspiring. And what you've done for me on this island…" He shakes his head. "You risked your safety to heal me. You took extraordinary measures when anyone else would have left me to die. You gave hope to the hopeless, and that is the person I love. I only wish you would let me show you."

I open and shut my mouth, speechless. What am I supposed to say? What does he expect me to do? Up and leave this place just because he found me and tricked me into caring about him? "Nothing's changed, you know," I say in a shaky voice that betrays me. "I still love Ares."

"Even though Ares loves himself more than he could ever love you?"

I recoil. "You have no idea how much Ares loves me."

"I know he left you alone with your baby son," says Hephaestus. "I know he's been gone long enough for you to feel lonely and betrayed."

"You don't know that," I mutter.

"I saw how you looked at him when he came back. If you truly loved him the way you claim, it would have been an entirely different look," he says. "You can love more than one person, you know."

"I love Ares. *Just* Ares." I say this more forcefully, as if I'm trying to convince both of us. He frowns, and I know he hears it, too.

"Love isn't just passion and noise and lust," he says. "Love is the way you feel for Eros. Love is the way I feel for you, the way you fill something inside me whenever you so much as walk into the same room. Sometimes love is quiet, lingering in the background until you least expect it. But love is always there for you. Ares hasn't been."

It's my turn to look away now. The way he talks about my relationship with Ares as if it's only temporary, as if it isn't the best I could have—I don't know how to swallow that.

"Aphrodite," says Hephaestus, and he reaches for my hand. His fingertips graze my knuckles before I pull away. "Love is an action, not a word."

"I don't need a lecture on what love is." I hiccup. I'm crying now. "I'm the goddess of love. I know what it is better than anyone else."

"Then prove it," he says. "Come with me. Or tell Ares he isn't welcome anymore. We can stay on Olympus, we can stay here, or—or if it's what you want, I will leave you in peace. Just don't let him do this to you. He's hurt you enough already, and you deserve better. You *are* better."

My vision blurs, and I can barely make out his face anymore. Just those piercing gray eyes that aren't really his. "I'm not," I whisper. "This is my home. Ares is my home."

"Your home is love," he says. "I could be that love if you'd let me. I want to be there for you and Eros. Not when I feel like it, but every moment of every day for as long as you'll both have me. Let me love you. Please."

I hiccup. I must look like a disaster, but Hephaestus's focus hasn't shifted. If I do look awful, he doesn't care. "I can't choose," I whisper. "Please don't make me."

He takes my hand again. This time I let him. "If he matters that much to you, then with me, you would never have to choose. As long as it's what you truly want and as long as he never hurts you again, you're free to love him as much as you'd like."

I don't understand what he means. No, I do understand—I understand what he *thinks* he means. But Hephaestus is Hera's son through and through. Going into the kind of relationship he's talking about—the kind where I could still love Ares and Hephaestus wouldn't mind—will be too much for him after a while. Maybe immediately. Maybe a few years. Maybe a few centuries or eons. But one day, Hephaestus will wake up and realize he doesn't want to share me. Or he'll give me the option of seeing others in the hope he'll be enough.

"For me—" I hesitate. "For me, love isn't something you only give once, and then it's gone. Love is everywhere. Love is everything."

He raises my hand to his mouth and kisses my knuckles. "I know. I have no interest in stifling you or loving a version of you that isn't real, and to ask you to commit to me and only me…" He shakes his head. "It would go against your very nature, and I'm all right with that. More than all right. It's part of what I love about you. As long as you're happy, I'll still be there for you regardless of who else you choose to love."

I swallow. It seems impossible, but maybe he does understand. Maybe that's the difference between him and Ares. After all, it was Ares who left me for what he thought were adventures more exciting than our life together, while Hephaestus scoured the earth trying to find me. If I left this island, would Ares do that? Would he search until he found me, no matter how long it took? Would he exchange his immortal form for pain and hunger and thirst just to have a chance of being with me?

I don't know. I can't think. Everything spins around me until I have to squeeze my eyes shut, and even in the darkness, I can see Hephaestus's face. I can't do this. I can't choose. No matter what Hephaestus says, one day he'll grow jealous. It's natural. Even if he wouldn't on his own, Hera will poison him against me, and our days would be numbered. And

Ares—with him, I don't even have the illusion of choice. But at least he loves me. At least he came back to me.

After years away without a second thought, while Hephaestus searched endlessly just for a chance to tell me he loves me.

Dammit. I bite my lip, and in my arms, Eros lets out another soft cry. That's enough to draw me back down to earth. He's my sun, my rock, my world, not Ares. Not Hephaestus. He's the thing I love most in this world. And no matter what choice I make, I will always have him.

That doesn't make it any easier, though.

"Please go," I whisper after an eternity passes. "I need to be alone."

My eyes are shut, but I feel the heat of Hephaestus's palm hovering over my cheek. He doesn't touch me, and I'm grateful for it, but I still feel a keen wrench of loss when he pulls away. "I'll always be here for you and Eros, no matter who you choose," he says. "Never forget that."

I'm quiet as his uneven footsteps echo through the cavern, and at last it's silent, save for the crackle of the fire. I sink into the nest of pillows and hold Eros tight. He seems to understand my turmoil, and he wraps his pudgy arms around me. I sigh into his hair. What am I supposed to do?

"I see he's gone."

My eyes open. Ares stands beside the fireplace, warming his hands. He stills wears his armor. What good he thinks it'll do him here, I have no idea.

"I'm not surprised you didn't recognize Hephaestus," he says. "I didn't until he punched me. He has a slight twist to his roundhouse—a sort of signature. Took me a moment, but I caught on soon enough. Ridiculous, isn't it? Bastard must be desperate, barging in while I'm gone, trying to wreck our life together."

I snort. "What life together?"

The words are out before I can stop them, and Ares looks as if I've slapped him.

"What do you mean?" he says in a cautious voice, the one that means he's seconds from flying into a rage.

"I mean—" My voice breaks, and I clear my throat. "I mean you haven't been here. In the past two years, you haven't even bothered to check in on us, to visit Eros to make sure he knows who you are—none of that. You left me. You left *us*."

He gapes at me, and the silence between us is so heavy that I think it's going to suffocate me. At last he clenches his hands, his face growing redder by the moment. "I have duties. I don't abandon them."

"Are you saying I've abandoned mine?"

"Of course not." His jaw is clenched now, too. "I came back to you."

"For how long? Another three days? A year? Two? How long before you leave us again? And how long will you be gone next time? Two years? Ten? A century?"

He slams his fist into the rock wall so hard that the earth around us trembles. Eros starts to sob, and I cradle him.

"If that's the way you want to see it, Aphrodite, then be my guest. But don't you dare act like I'm the villain. I wasn't the one who kissed my husband's brother."

"You—" My voice shakes. "You're not my husband."

"I would have been. I wanted to be. I came back to propose, you know. To tell you we were going to face Father and make him see that together, we're undefeatable. Apparently I was wrong."

He storms out of the grotto, once again leaving Eros and me. I don't call after him. I'm too stunned for that. Was he really coming back to marry me? To have a life together, one I'd always dreamed about?

Or did he say that in the heat of the moment to make me feel even worse than I already do?

I hate myself for second-guessing him. I hate myself for thinking he's capable of that kind of emotional brutality. But I've seen the blood on his armor, and the sword isn't his only weapon. Ares always wins his battles, no matter the cost.

I spend the rest of the night crying silently. Ares doesn't come back, nor does Hephaestus. I don't expect them to, not really, but part of me hopes they will. A very large part of me. I can't decide who I want to see more though, and that's the part that hurts the most.

The next day, Eros and I play on the beach, and this time, when sunset comes, we don't go back to the grotto. I gather him up in my arms, and staring into the rosy sky, I push myself upward toward Olympus. Toward home.

I don't know who I'll see or what I'll find, but I do know one thing for sure: this has to end. And before it can, I have to make the hardest decision of my life.

I land in the middle of chaos.

On the floor, Ares and Hephaestus are locked together in battle while the council all shout over one another, forming a symphony of noise. Hera is the most vocal, despite her recent shaming and demotion, and she stands beside her throne, yelling so hard that her entire body glows with power.

Though she looks back at Zeus every few sentences, the majority of her anger's directed toward Ares and Hephaestus. The sunset floor is cracked, and Ares throws punches faster than I can follow. Hephaestus, on the other hand, is only acting defensively, covering his face and eventually wrapping his thick arms around his brother. At first I don't understand why he'd want to embrace Ares in the middle of an epic fight, but when Ares flails, unable to hit him, I get it.

"Stop it!" I cry, and at the sound of my voice, both of them look at me. Hephaestus turns red, clearly embarrassed to be caught, but Ares only narrows his eyes.

"Let me go," growls Ares.

Hephaestus hesitates. "I will let you go if you promise to do as Aphrodite says."

Clearly Hephaestus doesn't believe it'll actually happen, but Ares nods, and reluctantly Hephaestus releases him. For a moment, we all hold our breath, waiting for Ares to strike again, but instead he stumbles to his feet and trudges to his throne. Hephaestus takes a moment to recover on the ground, and he slowly follows. His eyes never leave me.

As they're getting settled, Hera whirls around to face me. Her entire being burns with fury, and my heart races. I've never been so afraid of anyone in my entire life. "How dare you set foot in Olympus after what you've done," she snarls. I take a step back toward my throne, on the other side of Daddy. My stomach turns. Maybe I made a mistake, after all. It isn't too late to return to my island, but the way Hephaestus watches me—I can't go, not now.

"What did I do?" I say, cradling Eros as I perch on my sea-shell throne.

"Were you not paying attention just now?" she hisses, and before she can lay into me even more, Daddy interrupts.

"My sons have destroyed a significant portion of the palace in order to settle a tiff that you apparently caused." His voice is as empty as his expression, and that twists the knife in my stomach. Couldn't he at least pretend to care?

"Not to mention put them both in danger," says Hera. I see

it now, the fear in her eyes—I hear it in her voice, as well. It isn't all anger. I hug Eros tighter.

"They're immortal," I say. "Any damage wouldn't be permanent."

Hera glances at Hephaestus, and I know what she's thinking. Once upon a time, immortality didn't protect him. Who's to say it wouldn't happen again? I don't know the whole story—no one but Hera does, and she's never bothered to talk to me about it. But I know it had to do with a fall to the earth. And if they've really destroyed part of Olympus…of course she's upset. Any mother would be.

"I'm sorry," I say. "I was just trying to help him—"

"It's my fault," says Hephaestus. "I tricked her into thinking I was someone else."

"Did you trick her into falling in love with you, as well?" growls Ares, and the two glare at each other.

"You should've never returned," says Hera. "You've never been anything but trouble, and the pain you've put my sons through—"

"Hera," says Daddy in that commanding voice of his, the one none of us can ignore. "Leave us. The rest of you, as well."

The other members of the council grumble, but one by one, they leave. As Artemis passes me, she touches my elbow. At first I think it's a sign of affection—maybe someone's missed me, after all. Instead she leans toward me until her mouth is next to my ear. "Honestly, Aphrodite. How can you call yourself the goddess of love if you can't even make up your mind?"

I bristle. As if she knows the first thing about love. "You can love more than one person, you know," I snap, echoing the same words Hephaestus said to me the night before.

She sniffs haughtily, and I'm about to tell her where she can shove her attitude when Daddy says, "Artemis. Go."

Giving me one last look, she follows Apollo and little Hermes, who isn't so little anymore. They join Demeter and her daughter, Persephone, and the five of them enter a corridor we rarely use. No one heads down the hallway that leads to our chambers. That must be the part of Olympus that Ares and Hephaestus destroyed.

"Who?" says Eros, pointing toward their group.

"That's Persephone and Hermes," I say. "Maybe you can all be friends." If the council lets me stay. His little face scrunches up like he's considering it, and he leans back in my arms. Having friends will be good for him, as long as I can find a way to shield him from the worst of the hatred in this place. Keeping him away from Hera is a start.

As soon as the three of us are alone, Daddy reaches for my hand. "I missed you," he says. "Never leave me again, my darling."

I press my lips together. I don't know what to say to that. "I'm sorry. For leaving the way I did, I mean. I didn't think I had any other choice."

"I understand. When I was your age, I would've done the same thing." He smiles. "Speaking of youth, I'm afraid I haven't had the pleasure of being introduced to this handsome young man."

"This is Eros," I say, snaking a protective arm around him. "Eros, this is Zeus, my daddy."

Eros's eyes go wide, and he sticks his thumb in his mouth. I ruffle his hair. Nothing to be afraid of, or at least I hope there isn't.

For a moment we sit in companionable silence, both of us watching Eros. He pretends to be shy, but I can feel him glowing as he laps up the attention. Such a ham. The moment can't last forever though, and eventually Daddy sighs.

"What are you going to do, my daughter?"

I stare at Eros's golden curls. I thought coming back to Olympus would give me some answers, but I'm as confused as ever. "I don't know. I love them both."

"But you've only been with Hephaestus for a short while."

I shrug. "Doesn't matter. I can feel the way he loves me. It's—warm. Gentle. Steady. And I want that, Daddy. I really do."

"Then what is the problem?"

The words catch in my throat. "I love Ares, too."

"And what is the difference between them?"

Everything. "Ares—I know who he is. I know *what* he is. I know he blows hot and cold, and I know he's sometimes unreliable, but when we're together, it's like—it's like the entire world's on fire."

"And Hephaestus?"

My cheeks turn pink. My father is the last person I want to talk to about this, but he's the only one who can possibly understand. "With him, it's just the two of us. Everything else goes dark, and no matter what we're talking about, even if it's something silly, it's warm. Always warm." Never cold like it is sometimes with Ares.

"Then it seems you have a choice to make," he says. My eyes water all over again.

"How?" I whisper. "Everyone thinks I'm—I'm a whore for loving both of them, but I can't help it, Daddy."

"Oh, Aphrodite." He moves into the space between our thrones and captures me in a hug. "You have nothing to be ashamed of no matter what your mother or sisters try to claim. You're so full of love in a way they'll never be, and it's natural you love both of my sons. Some people are built for monogamy. They see love in one person, and they devote themselves entirely to that love. But people like you and me, we see love everywhere, and we know what a waste it would be to pass it by. That doesn't mean we love our partner any less. It just means we share our love with others, as well."

I sniff, and Daddy produces a piece of cloth. I take it and dab my eyes. "But what happens when it hurts our partners so badly that they don't want to love us anymore?"

For a moment, Daddy's silent. I shouldn't have asked. I know exactly what happens then—I've seen it in Daddy's marriage to Hera. We all have. "Then maybe they simply aren't the ones we're supposed to be with."

"How am I supposed to choose?" I mumble. "Hephaestus says he's all right with it, but I think he's secretly hoping he'll be enough. And Ares—he doesn't want me to be with anyone else at all."

"I don't know, my darling," says Daddy, running his fingers through my hair. I've missed that. I've missed him. "What I do know is that it is a choice you'll have to make. I made the mistake of trying to force you into something you didn't want once, and I won't do it again. You have my permission to decide. But be careful, and think it through—whatever choice you make will define this part of your existence. Maybe all of it. Make sure it's someone you want to be tied to forever. My sons love you in very different ways, and love can either be a gift or a curse. Try to choose the first, if you can."

"Which one's that, Ares or Hephaestus?"

"That's for you to decide." He kisses my forehead. "I'm glad you're home."

When our conversation is over, I carry Eros into the corridor where Persephone and Hermes disappeared. He's never had the chance to make friends before, and I want that for him. I don't want him to be alone.

"Heh!" cries Eros, suddenly struggling in my arms. I blink, making my teary eyes focus, and I spot a bulky figure looming far down the hallway. Hephaestus.

I hug Eros tighter. I'm wrong. He does have a friend. And if Hephaestus meant it when he said he'd be there for us always, no matter what—

"Aphrodite?"

I turn. Ares stands in the middle of a guest room, looking weary and more miserable than I've ever seen him. The spark's still there when his eyes meet mine, but it's lessened somehow. And that hurts me. Badly.

Hephaestus forgotten, I slip into the chamber and set a squirming Eros down. He takes off on his little legs, and I start to follow. When he turns left, however, I know where he's going, and I force myself to stop. Hephaestus will watch over him. I need this moment with Ares.

"He's big," says Ares roughly, and he sits on the bed. I hesitate. I don't want this to be purely about sex. I want him to love me the way Hephaestus does, too. And maybe he does—maybe the heat's overshadowed the rest of it for so long that I can't recognize the warmth anymore. But the way the spark between us has lessened…

"Yeah, well. That's what happens. Babies grow up." I lean against the wall instead. "I wish you hadn't gone away."

He furrows his brow. "I wish I hadn't had to."

"You'll always have to leave at some point, won't you?"

"But I'll always come back to you."

I believe him. He squints at me as if it hurts him, as if I'm still his sun and I'm shining too bright for him to face me head-on, and the ice around my heart melts. I've been so busy thinking about what I want that I haven't stopped to think about how this must be hurting him.

"I'm never going to be like your mother," I say softly. "I'm never going to be able to devote myself to one person no matter how much I love them. You have to leave to do your duties, and this—this is my way of doing mine."

He swallows. "I know. I don't like it, but I know."

"It doesn't mean I love you any less," I say. "I don't. I love you so much it hurts. But—I can love other people without my love for you fading. If anything, it only makes me love you more."

His mouth forms a thin line, and he stares at his hands. I've never seen him so undone before. I'm used to his rage, his fire, but this quietness is unnatural. And I'm the one who did it to him.

"Do you...do you still love me?" I say in a small voice, and his head snaps up. He rises without a word. Crossing the space between us, he embraces me.

"Always," he murmurs. "I still want to marry you, Aphrodite. You're perfect. You're beautiful. My favorite moments are when I'm with you. I don't want that to end."

"It never has to," I promise. Something twists inside me, though. Beautiful, perfect—the things I am to everyone else, as well. It shouldn't bother me, but it does, and I hate myself for it.

He hesitates. "But I can't marry you when you're still seeing him. I need you to understand that. Anyone else—I don't care who, you're free to do whatever you want as long as you love me most of all. But Hephaestus..."

I grow still. I expected this, of course. Ares sees the world in black-and-white, and no matter how happy Hephaestus makes me, Ares doesn't want to compete with his brother. After all, he might lose. I understand that. It hurts, but I understand. And at least he isn't lying to himself.

"I love you," he says. "I love every part of you, except the part of you that—cares for him. I want to marry you. I *will* marry you, and we'll spend our lives together. But in order for us to be happy, you can't see him anymore. That's all I ask."

My heart flutters. It may be the only thing he wants, but it's not exactly a small request, and the thought of never seeing Hephaestus again—of never feeling that warmth, of never getting to be with him—makes me ache in a way I've never ached before.

Ares or Hephaestus. The love I want or the love I need.

It isn't fair. But Daddy's right—whatever I choose is going to define the rest of my life. There will always be battles, and there will always be war. No matter how often Ares promises he'll be there for me, he *will* leave. Probably more than I realize. So that's my choice—a life of intermittent fire, of waiting for Ares to return home from whatever battle he's disappeared to, or a life of steady warmth. Of companionship.

And maybe Hephaestus isn't lying to himself. Maybe he is willing to share me in a way Ares isn't.

I hesitate. "I love you and Eros. I love our family. If I could only know one truth in my life, that would be it. But—if I didn't marry you…if I did what Daddy wants…"

Ares stiffens, and his warmth turns to ice. I expect nothing less, but it still hurts.

"I could still be with you," I say. "We wouldn't lose anything."

He hisses and pulls away. "Do you really think that? If you belonged to him—"

"Belong? I don't *belong* to anyone, Ares."

"Of course you do," he scoffs. "You belong to me."

I slap him. Hard. The sound of skin against skin echoes through the chamber and undoubtedly down the hallway, but I don't care who hears it. "The only person I belong to is myself."

He touches his cheek. I didn't hurt him, of course, but that spark in his eyes is back, and he steps toward me. "You know that isn't true. Mother belongs to Father, Persephone will belong to Hades once they're married, and you'll belong to me. If you choose Hephaestus—" he spits out his name like it's poison "—then you'll belong to him, as well. That's how marriage works."

I draw myself to my full height. "Then I won't marry anyone."

He grabs my shoulders, his fingers digging into my skin. Before I can protest, he kisses me, nipping my lower lip and pressing his body to mine. "Fine," he growls. "Then you'll still be mine."

Using every ounce of strength I have, I shove him off me. "*No.* And if this is how you're going to treat me, then it's over."

He laughs his humorless laugh. "Yeah, right. You'll be begging to come back to me soon enough. It's who you are, Aphrodite, and Hephaestus will never understand."

I spin on my heel and head toward the archway. "That's what you think."

But even as I storm out of the chamber, I can feel that fire between us. It'll always be there, whether we're married or not, and nothing I do will ever quench it. The faster we both accept it, the better.

Hephaestus and Eros sit in the middle of the hallway several rooms down, close enough that they must have heard everything. Eros is oblivious as he plays with a stack of wooden blocks, but Hephaestus meets my eye, and I see understanding. Something Ares has never shown me.

"Ask me," I say, kneeling beside them. Hephaestus says nothing. "Ask me, or I'll ask you."

He shakes his head. "I won't ask you to marry me when you're out for revenge against my brother."

My mouth drops open. "But that's not—"

"It is," he says quietly. "I know how you feel for him. Ares is a brute at times, but you still love him, and I respect that. I won't make things worse for both of you by marrying you just to make him angry."

I brush my fingers through Eros's curls. "I just— I want someone to love me. Not as a trophy, but as myself."

"Someone does," he says, and silence lingers between us. "One day, once you've had time to sort out your feelings, I will ask you. But in the meantime, I don't need that commitment in order to love you, and I don't think you need it to love me, either."

My chin trembles, and he brushes his fingers against my cheek. He's returned to his immortal form now, twisted legs and all, but I don't see those anymore. Well, I do, but not as much as before. I see him now, the way he sees me. I see what's underneath his ugliness, just as he sees what's underneath my beauty.

"I choose you," I whisper, wiping my eyes. "Not because I'm fighting with Ares, not because he left or—or any of that. I choose you because of the way you look at me. The way you touch me, the way you talk to me, the way you respect me and see *me*. I love how you are with Eros. I love that you care about him even though he isn't yours. I love that you say no when anyone else would say yes, just because you know that somewhere down the line, I might get hurt."

"That's all I care about," he says. "Your happiness. Your freedom. No matter how you feel for me or my brother."

"I'll always love Ares. I'll always have something with him—"

"I know," he says, and he lowers his eyes. "I'll never begrudge you that. I've seen what jealousy does to love, and I will never hurt you that way. It's part of who you are, and I love every piece of you. Even the part that loves my brother. And if you decide you want to go back to him, then as long as you're happy, I'll accept it."

I have to blink rapidly to keep myself from crying. "Let me finish," I say, touching his cheek. "I'll always love Ares, but his love is the kind of love that consumes. I may not know everything about you yet, but I do know the way you love, and that's the most important part. We'll have eternity to learn the rest."

He sets his hand over mine. "And how do I love?"

I hesitate. "Your love—it's the kind of love that feeds and grows, the kind that's steady no matter what. It's warm, it's inviting, it's accepting, and that's the love I want. That's the love I need."

He smiles faintly, tracing the edge of my jaw. "And you will have it as long as you wish. It will always be there for you, just like I'll always be there, as well. When I ask you— and I *will* ask you—I want you to be sure. I'm willing to wait as long as it takes."

I shake my head. "I *am* sure."

"Then show me," he murmurs. His face is only inches from mine now. "Show yourself."

I close the distance between us. Just as it was back in the grotto, kissing him is easy, simple, as natural as existing. But I'm more aware of this moment than I've been of anything in my life. The way his lips feel against mine, his taste, his smell—all of it. Most of all, I'm aware of the warmth that wraps around us, binding the three of us together. Eros is my sun, Ares is my fire, but Hephaestus is my rock, my foundation, and no matter where I go or what I do, I will always come back to him. I know that now.

I may spend eternity torn between two brothers, but that isn't such a bad fate, really. One day Ares will get over himself, and he'll come crawling back to me. When that day comes, I'll forgive him, and we'll be as passionate about each other as we've always been. But I won't give up this love for anything, and until Ares accepts that, he'll be the one missing out. Not me.

"There," I whisper as I break the kiss. "You'll have that as long as you want it, as well. I may love others, but if you let me, you will always be my home."

He smiles and kisses me again. "I'd like nothing more."

I try to move closer, as close to him as possible, but I accidentally knock down the block tower Eros has created instead. "Mama!" he cries, indignant, and I laugh.

"I'm sorry," I say, settling back down and pulling him into my lap. "Let's build another one together, okay?"

He huffs, but as Hephaestus begins to form the foundation, Eros's anger is forgotten, and he gleefully reaches out to help. Together the three of us start to build, and as I watch Hephaestus's steady hands set each block into place, I know I've made the right choice.

★ ★ ★ ★ ★

GODDESS

OF THE

UNDERWORLD

PART ONE

PART ONE

For the first sixteen years of my life, Mother told me my wedding day would be one of the happiest in my eternal existence. That the birds would sing, the air would smell like flowers and the sun would shine. Every last detail would be perfect.

Like an idiot, I'd believed her.

The sun didn't shine in hell, and unless bats counted, there weren't any birds in the endless Underworld palace, either. To make things worse, the infinite rock surrounding the cavern weighed down on me, growing heavier with every passing second. I was trapped, literally and figuratively. And I had no idea how to dig myself out of this one.

Mother did manage to keep her word about the flowers, though. As I paced from one end of the chamber to the other, eleven steps in each direction, I had to zigzag my way around the endless bunches of wildflowers that covered every available surface. The perfume was strong enough to knock out Cerberus, but at least it didn't smell like death.

"Persephone?" Mother poked her head into the room. Given the way she glowed, I would've guessed this was her wedding, not mine. "It's time. How are you feeling?"

She knew exactly how I felt about all of this. She didn't want the truth—she wanted false affirmation that I was as happy as she was. "I don't want to do this," I said. No use holding back now.

"Sweetheart," said Mother in a tone she must have thought was understanding, but was really the same one she'd used to convince me to do this in the first place. She stepped inside the chamber and closed the door behind her. "What's wrong?"

"What's wrong is that I don't want to marry Hades." Searching for a place to sit, I spotted a chair in the flowered jungle, but a bouquet of purple blossoms already claimed it. I huffed and sank to the floor instead. "You told me the Underworld wasn't so bad."

"It isn't." She knelt beside me. "You've only seen the palace. There's an entire world out there—"

"It feels like a cage. It's heavy and unnatural and—I want to stay in Olympus with *you*." My voice hitched, and I blinked rapidly. Breaking into tears would've been a surefire way to make Mother believe I was simply too emotional to think clearly. I'd never thought more clearly in my life, though.

Mother wrapped her arms around me, and for a moment I allowed myself to lean against her. "You've known this was coming for a long time, my darling. I would never allow this if I wasn't absolutely certain you would love him."

"But I don't." Didn't she understand that?

"You will, in time."

"What if I never do?"

"Persephone, look at me." She tilted my head upward, and my eyes met hers. "You will. Trust me." Her confidence should've sparked the same in me, but I was empty. "I'll come visit you all the time. This is the beginning of the rest of your life, not the end."

She was wrong—it was the end of everything that mattered.

The end of days picking flowers and soaking in the sunlight, the end of nights sitting in her lap as she told me stories. A deep ache filled me, and I swallowed hard. No crying. Not today.

"I am so proud to call you my daughter," she murmured. "Eventually you will understand why I asked this of you. In time, you will be happier here with Hades than you could ever be with me in Olympus."

Mother had never been so wrong so many times in a row before. I couldn't be happy, not in this underground cavern. Not without the sun. Not without her.

"Hades loves you already, my darling. He is quiet, and he doesn't love out loud like you may be used to, but that doesn't make his love any less strong. You've seen the way he looks at you."

Reluctantly I nodded. I'd seen it, that piercing stare when he thought I wouldn't notice. The way his eyes seemed to follow me as I moved across the room. Not in a predatory way, but as if he was concerned. As if he cared. Maybe he secretly wasn't crazy about this whole thing, either.

"Do you trust me not to hurt you?" she murmured. "Do you trust me to want only the best for you?"

I loved her. I trusted her. And her pride filled me in a way I was certain Hades's so-called love never could. But maybe she was right—maybe in time I would love him. Maybe if this wasn't an arranged marriage, I would've loved him anyway. But she and my father had stolen that chance from me.

"You'll find happiness here," she said. "You'll find your purpose, and I will never be far. We all have roles in our lives, Persephone—roles we may not initially enjoy, but roles we soon realize are necessary. You were born to do this, my darling, and Hades loves you. Trust me when I say that. I love you too much to ever allow anyone to hurt you, including myself."

I swallowed. She did love me. Out of everything in the

world, that was the one thing I knew to be completely, un-equivocally true. And because of that, I let her help me up, my legs unsteady beneath me.

"My beautiful girl. The love of my life." She plucked a purple blossom from the bouquet in the chair and secured it in my curls. Strawberry-blond now, as autumn set in. "You are perfect."

I ached to believe her, but as she led me into an antechamber, a melody from the strings of Apollo's lute filtered through the air. And instead of reminding me of harmony and love, the notes were mournful to my ear, fitting perfectly with the bleakness of this realm.

This wasn't my wedding. It was my funeral.

She looped her arm in mine, and a pair of double doors opened, revealing the throne room of the Underworld. With its obsidian pillars and curtains of black-and-gold that hung from high windows, it was nothing like the throne room of Olympus. Nothing like my home.

Mother stayed with me until we reached the front of the throne room, where Hades stood between a pair of diamond thrones. His, a black one I'd seen countless times during council meetings, and mine. White diamond—a present from Hades, welcoming me to the Underworld. And from the council, welcoming me as their equal.

But I would never be their equal, and they knew it as well as I did. An equal would've been allowed to make her own decisions, not pawned off in an arranged marriage at sixteen. If they thought I would lie down and take it, they were dead wrong.

"I love you," whispered Mother. I stayed silent. Taking my hand, she placed it in Hades's, his skin warmer than I expected. His silver eyes met mine, and a shiver ran down my spine.

I was his for eternity now.

★ ★ ★

I couldn't hide behind the wedding forever. The other members of the council seemed to enjoy themselves, dancing and drinking well into the night. Hera remained close, eyeing me every so often, but she didn't speak to me. Could she sense the mountain of anxiety forming in my chest? Could she see my fear growing with every moment I remained inside my stone cage? More than the rest of us, she cared about marriages being successful. Could she tell how much I hated mine already? Did she regret giving her blessing?

I wished she hadn't. Maybe then my parents would've never forced me into this. I was hours into my marriage, and already I felt weighed down by rock and invisible chains. Not exactly an auspicious start.

At last only Hades, me and Mother remained, and after Hades excused himself for his chambers—our chambers now—she pulled me into a tight hug. "He loves you," she murmured. "I know it may not feel like it, but he would have never married you if he didn't."

I buried my face in her shoulder. It wasn't his love I was concerned about. It was mine. For as long as I'd been aware of what marriage was, I'd known I was promised to Hades, and I'd been absolutely certain I would love him by now. Enough to be content, at least, if not thrilled. And while I tried to grab on to the single wisp of love I may or may not have felt for him, it was beyond my reach.

But it would come closer the more time I spent with him, the more smiles and words and touches we shared. It had to. Aphrodite hadn't chosen her husband either, after all, and now she'd spent the entire day cuddling up to him. And Hera, who *had* chosen hers, was completely miserable.

So maybe Mother was right. Maybe love was in that room, waiting for me, and all I had to do was go in there and get it.

"You'll come visit me?" I said. "Or I could come visit you."

"Both," she said, kissing my cheek. "All the time, as much as you want. Just make sure you don't neglect your duties down here, darling. And remember—happiness is a choice, but so is misery. Choose wisely."

She let me go, and I reluctantly dropped my arms. Giving me a reassuring smile, she turned to go, but before she reached the door, I blurted, "It'll be okay, right?"

Mother looked over her shoulder. "It already is. Go to your husband, Persephone. Give him a chance to make you happy."

She left, the door closing behind her, and I exhaled. Hades was really my husband. My king. I was married now, and things would never go back to the way they'd been. This was my life now.

Time to face it.

The door into Hades's chambers opened easily. I stepped inside, expecting it to be dark and dank, like the rest of the Underworld, but instead the large room was lit with dozens of floating candles. They cast a soft glow on the plush bed, where Hades sat waiting for me, and a fist wrapped around my guts. This was it.

"Persephone." He rose and offered me his hand, his silver eyes searching mine. I didn't know what else to do, so I threaded my fingers through his. We were friends, sort of. Growing up knowing who I was going to marry took the choice out of it, sure, but it'd also given me a lifetime of getting to study him. Mother was right—he was a good man. He did love me. And being here with him wasn't the worst thing I'd ever experienced.

I stared at him for the space of several heartbeats, and at last I whispered, "I'm sorry, I'm not—I'm not really sure what to say."

He smiled, crinkles appearing around his eyes. "Then allow

me to break the silence by saying how lovely you look tonight. You always do, of course." He touched one of my curls. They would change with the seasons, auburn in the coming months before turning black for the winter solstice, and then as spring came, they would lighten to brown. Finally, in the summer, I would be blond. It'd never served a purpose before, but now I would never lose track of the seasons in the Underworld.

I sank onto the edge of the bed. It was strange being alone with him—despite Mother's insistence that he and I get to know each other, she'd always been present. He felt older somehow, and power radiated effortlessly from him. As he sat down beside me, however, he gently cupped my hand in both of his.

"You're nervous," he said. It wasn't a question, and he didn't wait for me to answer. "I am, too."

I scoffed. "You're King of the Underworld. What do you possibly have to be nervous about?"

He hesitated, brushing his thumb against my knuckles. The gesture was almost intimate in its simplicity, and a shiver ran through me. "I am nervous that I cannot give you everything you deserve."

"What do you mean?"

He squeezed my hands. "You could do so many things with your existence, yet you are down here with me. I cannot tell you what that means to me. No one..." He paused, and the cords in his neck stood out. "No one has chosen me before, not because of who I am. Not for pure reasons. That you are willing to try is everything I have never had before."

Warmth filled me, and I inched closer to him. It wasn't so hard to see his life through his eyes, all those eons of loneliness. "I'm going to try," I promised. "I want—I want to be with you."

I wasn't sure I did, really, but I also wasn't sure I didn't. I would've liked the choice, but that had always been out of my control. This—the here and now, how good we were together, that was at least half in my control. And knowing Hades was willing to try to make this work made all the difference.

"I know that this marriage will take time to settle for both of us, but we will grow together. We will learn together," he said, raising my hand to his lips.

Yes, we would. Underneath his piercing gaze, I relaxed. It would be all right. Mother knew what she was doing, and she would've never married me off to Hades if she wasn't absolutely sure we would work. But even as I thought it, I grew painfully aware of the stone surrounding me. No matter how I felt about it, I was still trapped down here. Fooling myself into being happy wouldn't change that. It wouldn't give me my choice and freedom back.

I straightened and took a deep breath. Yes, it would. Happiness was a choice, exactly as Mother had said. And this was a choice I could make.

I didn't ask. I didn't hesitate. Instead I leaned in and kissed him full on the mouth, the kind of kiss I'd never given anyone before. The kind of kiss Aphrodite gave to Hephaestus. The kind of kiss I wanted Hades to give to me.

It was warm and wet and not what I expected, not at all. It didn't sizzle or sparkle or make me love him. It didn't open up a whole new world of possibilities. It was just that—lips against lips, a soft mouth against my own. And to make matters worse, Hades didn't kiss me back.

I opened my eyes. His were open as well, cloudy with questions, but I didn't give him the chance to speak. I knew what he would say if I did—was I sure I wanted to do this now? Did I want to wait until we knew each other better?

But I wanted that love. I *needed* that love to make the rock melt away, to make everything not so bad. And if I could make myself love him as much as he loved me…maybe it would all be okay. Maybe this wouldn't be a prison.

So I kept kissing him. My hands fumbled down his front, pushing away his clothes and brushing against his warm skin. I could do this. I *would* do this, and once we were together in the most intimate way possible, it would all click. We would be happy, and it wouldn't be an illusion. It would be my choice.

As I drew him down onto the bed, however, he broke away. "Persephone—"

"Don't," I said. "Please."

His Adam's apple bobbed, but he fell silent. I kissed him again, pulling him as close to me as possible. I'd never had someone pressed against me like this before, and his body was solid, weightier than I'd expected. Not that I'd expected much, but it still felt foreign.

I didn't let myself stop. Soon enough we were both completely undressed, and as he settled over me, I pushed away every last shred of fear that haunted me. We were doing this together, and no matter how exposed and terrified I was, lying there in his bed, I would not back down.

One night of swallowing my fears, one night of being with him like this, and that wisp of love would turn into a howling storm. I just needed to get through tonight.

"Do it," I whispered, and when he opened his mouth again, undoubtedly to protest, I silenced him with a burning kiss.

Everything would be fine. Better than fine.

It had to be.

It wasn't fine. It wasn't even close to fine.

Our bodies didn't fit. Maybe it was my virginity, or maybe he was unnaturally blessed, but whatever it was, it was hot, sticky, uncomfortable, awkward, everything it wasn't supposed to be. And had I not been immortal, I was sure it would've been one of the most painful experiences of my life.

To make matters worse, he didn't seem like he knew what he was doing, either, and we both fumbled through it. It might've been intimate, but it wasn't sexy or loving. It was all physical, nothing emotional, and by the time it was over, I was struggling to hold back tears.

Hades rolled off me, his chest heaving. As his eyes searched mine, his brow furrowed, and he brushed his fingers against my cheek. "I'm sorry."

I shook my head, too close to breaking down to speak. It wasn't his fault. I'd been the one to pressure him into this, to force us both before we were ready. But the part of me drowning in anger and disappointment blamed him. He could've done what I hadn't had the courage to do and walked away. He could've said no to my father when he'd suggested this marriage to begin with.

"It will get better," he whispered. "I love you."

Silence surrounded us, and I knew without asking that he was waiting for me to say it back. To offer him one small affirmation that this wasn't a complete disaster. But it was, and a tear slid down my face, too fast for me to catch it.

In the glow of the candlelight, Hades's expression crumbled. He knew what my silence meant, and for a moment, he seemed to fold into himself. His shoulders hunched and his head bowed, and his fingers dug into the sheets. I didn't offer him any comfort. I couldn't. I'd only be lying to us both.

At last Hades came to life and pulled a silk blanket up to cover me. He didn't try to touch me, though he did watch me for a long moment. I turned away. I didn't want his guilt as well as mine.

Eventually the candles burned out, or maybe Hades extinguished them. Either way, in the darkness, the rock weighed down even heavier around me, and I could barely breathe.

I couldn't do this. I couldn't be here with a man I didn't love. Married or not, his queen or not, I was a person, not an object, and my parents had had no right to do this to me in the first place. But here we were, both of us victims, both of us painfully aware of the wall between us now. It hadn't been there before the wedding, but now, because of me, because of my parents…

I didn't sleep, and judging from Hades's breathing, neither did he. At last, when it was time to get up—how Hades could tell without the sun, I had no idea—I waited until he dressed and disappeared before I got out of bed and bathed. I had two options: I could stick around and accept my fate, or I could fight for my freedom.

No contest.

As soon as I finished washing off any last trace of the night before, I hurried out of the bedroom, nearly crashing headfirst into Hades in the hall. Though he carried a tray, he managed to sidestep me without dropping anything. For a long moment, we stared at each other.

"Where…" He paused and clutched the tray, loaded with my favorite fruits, breads and cheeses. He was bringing me breakfast in bed. "Where are you going?"

Another wave of guilt washed over me. Even after last night, he was still trying to make me happy. "I—I need to see Mother," I said, my voice hitching. "Can I…?"

"Of course." He set the tray down on an end table and reached for me, though he pulled away at the last second. "I'll take you up to Olympus."

I followed him through the hallway to the private entrance, and together we walked down the cavern path that led to the portal between realms. Seeing the rock around me only made the weight on my chest worse, and by the time we reached the crystal circle in the ground, I could barely see straight.

"Are you all right?" said Hades, touching my elbow. Though it wasn't much, it was enough to remind me of the night before, and I shuddered. He immediately dropped his hand.

"I'm sorry, I just—I need to—I need to go to Olympus. Can you show me how?" Technically, before my wedding and coronation, I'd been unable to, but now, as Queen of the Underworld, I had that power.

"Yes," he said slowly. "Of course. I have to touch you to get you there. Is that all right?"

I nodded, and he set his hand on my back. It was a familiar touch, the kind only two people who knew each other well could share, and his skin burned against mine.

Why was it this bad? Sure, the night before hadn't been at all what I'd been raised to expect from watching Aphrodite and her lovers, but plenty of people had gone through worse. So why did the very thought of him make me sick to my stomach?

"Like this," he said quietly, and I felt a rush of power emanate from him, dark and rich and completely repugnant. But there was no escaping him as we raced upward through the rock, and by the time we burst into the open sky, I was nauseous. From the journey, from the Underworld, from Hades's touch or ancient power, I didn't know, but all I wanted was to go home.

At last we landed in the middle of Olympus, and I broke away from him and ran as fast as I could. Through the throne room, into the hallway, toward Mother's room, everything around me a blur. The golden sunshine that reflected off every inch of Olympus seemed to fill me from the inside out, and by the time I burst into her chambers, I was glowing. "Mother!"

"Persephone?" She stood and opened her arms, and I melted

into them. "I didn't expect to see you so soon. Is Hades with you?"

I nodded, and something about hearing her voice and feeling her familiar presence made that dam inside me snap. I broke into rough sobs, clutching her as hard as I could. I wouldn't let her go again, not for anything.

Somehow Mother managed to guide me to her bed, and together we sank down. "Sweetheart, what's wrong?" She tried to pull away, but I held on. "Surely it wasn't that bad."

But it was. I couldn't explain it to her—I couldn't even explain it to myself—but in that moment, I would've rather faded for eternity than go back to the Underworld with Hades. I didn't belong there. We didn't belong together, and it was all a mistake—a stupid mistake that Mother could fix.

"Please," I gasped between sobs. "Don't make me go back there."

Her arms tightened around me. "What happened? Darling, if you don't tell me, I can't help you."

I opened my mouth to try to find the words, but before I could say a single one—

"Persephone?"

I looked up, my lower lip trembling. "Father?"

Zeus stepped into the room, his brow knit and mouth turned downward. Father or not, I'd never spent much time with him beyond what little bonding assuaged his guilt. But I would've taken his awkward hugs and nasty temper a thousand times over before I went back to Hades.

"Persephone, your husband is waiting for you in the throne room," he admonished. "He's quite worried."

I sniffed, refusing to lessen my grip on Mother. "I can't go back there. I can't *breathe*."

"Don't be ridiculous. You're a goddess. You don't need to

breathe," said Zeus. "Now, explain to me what this tantrum of yours is all about."

"Zeus," said Mother in a warning tone, but he didn't budge. He stared at me, his blue eyes stormy and his arms crossed over his broad chest. I'd never been afraid of him before, but tension crackled in the air sure as lightning. One wrong word, and daughter or not, he'd treat me like a traitor.

"I can't—" I hiccupped. "The rock's too heavy, and—Hades, we—" My face grew hot. "Please don't make me go back."

"You have no choice in the matter," said Zeus. "You are Queen of the Underworld now, and that is not a crown you can give up."

"I don't care, just—please. I'll do anything," I begged. "I can't go back."

Mother sighed. "You've been there all of one night. Things will get easier. I know it's a change from Olympus—"

"Have you ever spent the night down there?" I said, and she hesitated.

"No, but—"

"I *can't*, Mother. *Please*."

She frowned and shared a look with Zeus. "Your father's right. You're Queen, and like it or not, that is not a role you can relinquish. Regardless of your marriage, Hades needs your help ruling, and you've already made a commitment. You cannot back out of it no matter how different it is from your expectations."

My entire body felt as if it had turned to stone. I'd expected opposition from Zeus, of course. He was never agreeable about anything. But my own mother…

"You don't understand." I pulled away and stood on trembling legs. "It's not natural down there. It's—cold and dark and twisted, and I can't *breathe*—"

"Again with the breathing," said Zeus, and Mother shushed him.

"—and I don't love him, Mother. I can't spend my life down there."

"Love?" Her confused expression morphed into a sympathetic one, and humiliation coursed through me. I didn't want her pity. I wanted her understanding. "Persephone, love has very little to do with it. Hades loves you, of course, but your love for him won't come immediately. You must give it time."

"But how can I love something completely unlovable?" My voice broke, and I wiped my cheeks angrily.

"You can, and eventually you will. In many ways, Hades is the most loving of us all," said Mother. "Do not be fooled by his dark kingdom. There is beauty in it, and despite a difficult night, things will get easier. Happiness is a choice—"

"And I choose not to be." The words came out as a broken sob. "You're going to do this to me? You're going to damn your only daughter to a life down there with him?"

Mother faltered. "Sweetheart, please. Tell me what brought this on."

But I couldn't. I didn't know what specific thing was behind the wall of hatred and anger inside me. I didn't know what made me want to run, but that didn't make it any less real. "He just—" I shook my head. "It isn't right."

"Take it one step at a time," said Mother in what she must've meant to be a soothing voice, but it made me shudder. "If you didn't enjoy consummating your marriage, that's natural. The first time is almost never—"

"It isn't *about* that."

"Then what is it about?" She reached for me, but I stepped back. My entire body trembled so badly that I had to struggle to stay upright. It was as if I was fighting an invisible force just by being in the room, and I didn't know how to stop it.

"I just—I don't belong there. I don't know how else to explain it."

Mother and Zeus exchanged another look, and Zeus cleared his throat. "You will return to the Underworld with Hades, and you will obey him as you would obey me. He is your husband now, and you will not dishonor me by evading your duties. Do you understand?"

My eyes watered until I couldn't make out his features. But I knew that voice—it was the voice of a king, the one he used when we had absolutely no choice. The voice he'd used to tell me I'd be marrying Hades on my sixteenth birthday no matter how I felt about it.

I couldn't respond. Every time I opened my mouth, that wall of hatred and resentment was there, and finally I dashed past him and fled the room. I couldn't do this no matter how often he threatened me, and the fact that he and Mother refused to so much as consider my feelings—it wasn't fair. I needed to get away from that unyielding revulsion. I needed to get away from my life.

As I ran down the hallway, I nearly barreled headfirst into Hera. Had she been there the entire time? Our eyes locked, and she opened her mouth to say something, but I regained my footing and rushed past her. I didn't care if she'd overheard. I didn't care if she empathized with being trapped in a loveless marriage. There was nothing she could possibly say or do to change my parents' minds, and I didn't need pity. I needed an escape.

At last I made it to the throne room. A few feet from the portal, Hades waited with Hermes, who wore a bewildered expression. As I stumbled onto the crystal circle, Hades moved to join me, but Hermes darted in front of him, blocking his way. Whatever his reason was, I didn't have time to find out.

I dropped from Olympus, the wind rushing through my hair and whipping it across my face.

Freedom. And free-falling, apparently. I'd never used a portal by myself, and I opened my mouth in a silent scream. So maybe not waiting for Hades hadn't been the best idea, but I would've rather plummeted to earth than let him join me.

I expected a crash landing, the sort that would leave an indentation in the ground for curious mortals to ponder, but as my feet touched the earth, I stopped. No hard landing. No real impact. I didn't even leave footprints on the grass.

Breathing a sigh of relief, I ran my fingers through my tangled hair and looked around. I stood in a meadow full of purple flowers that danced in the breeze, and it was warm despite the late hour of wherever it was I'd landed. A beautiful summer evening.

Why couldn't Hades live on the surface? Why did he have to be near his subjects at all times? Zeus certainly wasn't. I sat down heavily in the middle of the field, passing my hand through the tall grass. This was my home, surrounded by warmth and nature and life. Not encased in stone.

The wind picked up for a moment, and something rustled behind me. Hades, no doubt, coming to reclaim me and drag me back to that dark place. I refused to turn around. He couldn't have me, not anymore.

"Persephone?"

I exhaled. Not Hades. "Hermes? What are you doing here?"

"You're upset," he said as he moved to sit in front of me. We'd grown up together, babies compared to the rest of the council, and seeing him now made me more homesick than ever. "Did Hades hurt you?"

He was the first person to acknowledge that maybe this wasn't my fault, and my heart swelled in gratitude. "N-no." I hiccupped. "I just—I can't go back."

He took my hands, his fingers smooth and cool. That small gesture of affection was enough to make me break down all over again, and I rested my head on his shoulder as I cried. I hated feeling like this—I hated not having the courage to give Hades a chance. But it wasn't him. It was the feeling of being suffocated, smothered, burned out before I'd had the chance to live. Why hadn't I questioned my parents earlier? Why hadn't I demanded a chance to get to know Hades and the Underworld better? Why hadn't they given me a choice?

Because they'd known what I would say if they had. They must have. Mother knew me better than I knew myself, and my trust in her—the same trust that had made me take the plunge into this marriage—was too absolute for me to question it before. Even now I second-guessed myself. Was I being hasty? Should I give Hades a chance? Did I even have a choice?

No, and that only made me cry harder. I didn't have a choice. Whether I liked it or not, I would have to return to the Underworld. Unless—

My eyes flew open, and I sat up. Hermes straightened as well, but I spoke before he could utter a word. "Run away with me."

His lips formed a perfect circle. "What?"

"You heard me. Run away with me. We can go someplace they'll never find us, like Aphrodite and Ares did, and—and we can be *happy*."

"Wait." He pulled away from me. "You mean you want—you and me—"

I shivered. After last night, I never wanted to have that sort of relationship with anyone ever again. "No, I mean—as friends. Brother and sister, whatever we are." We weren't, technically, since Zeus had taken different forms to father us and we had different mothers. But I needed someone else to love me. I didn't care what kind of love it was, as long as it meant I could get away from Hades. "Please."

Hermes hesitated, and I could see the wheels turning in his head. Hope blossomed inside my chest, pushing aside the coldness and despair. He was considering it. He was really considering it.

"Persephone…" He took my hands in his again. "You know I want nothing more than to see you happy, but Zeus already forbade anyone from interfering with your marriage. If we left, Zeus and Hades would both hunt us down, and I'd get a lightning bolt to the skull for sure."

My heart sank, and that delicate bubble of hope deflated. "He really ordered everyone not to help me?"

Hermes nodded. "I'm sorry. But maybe you and Hades could talk it out. You could just be his queen and not his wife, right? He needs you to help him rule, not warm his bed."

I squeezed my eyes shut, fighting another wave of tears. I was never getting out of this. Not now, not in a thousand years, not ever. Not as long as Zeus treated me like property and Hades went along with him. "He would never agree," I whispered.

"So don't give him a choice." Hermes tucked a lock of hair behind my ear, his touch so gentle that I shifted closer. "Just tell him. You're stronger than you think you are, Persephone. Never question that. You can do whatever you set your mind to, circumstances be damned."

"I wish—" My voice broke, and I swallowed thickly. "I wish I were like Aphrodite. I wish I had the strength to do what she did."

"Maybe someday you will," he said. "You just need to find the right person is all. If Hades isn't it, then there's nothing wrong with that. This doesn't have to be forever if you don't want it to be."

I snorted despite myself. "Everything in our family is forever."

"Only the good things," he said. "We usually find a way to fix the bad ones."

"Don't see how anyone would agree to let me off the hook if I don't even try."

"Then try. Do whatever you have to do to prove to yourself and the rest of the council that it isn't a good fit."

"Hades will never let me go," I mumbled. "Not now, not in a hundred years, not ever. He loves me."

"If he really loves you, then once he understands how miserable you are, he will let you go," said Hermes. "Just because he's a good guy doesn't mean he's a good guy for you."

I shook my head. "You can say all the pretty things you want, but that won't change anything."

"You're right," he said. "The only one who can change any of this is you. You just have to try."

"But I already did."

"I know. They should've listened." He pulled me into a hug. The weight of his arms around my shoulders was a comfort, and I managed to relax against him. At least I had someone on my side.

A moment later, the breeze picked up again, and I sensed a second presence in the meadow. The sun dipped beneath the horizon, and Hermes stiffened. I didn't need to turn around to know who it was.

"Please," I whispered one last desperate time. "I'll do anything."

"I can't. I'm sorry." Hermes's voice was low and his words rushed. "Listen—I'll visit you all the time, I promise. You won't be alone. Just do me a favor and give yourself a chance, all right? Do whatever you have to do to be happy, even if that means upsetting the council. They've already had their say. Now it's your turn."

I pressed my lips together. Being that kind of selfish went against everything Mother had taught me. Be there for others; place their happiness above my own; be content with my life; don't be greedy or envious or unkind; appreciate the warmth and love around me, and don't covet what I don't have.

But how could I appreciate what wasn't there? Hades may have loved me, but what did that mean if I couldn't feel it? He could love me more than anyone loved anyone else in the entire world, and it still wouldn't help if I didn't love him back. Maybe in time I would adjust and grow to love him, but right now, all I could think about was the rock weighing down on me and the feeling of Hades's body over mine. And I didn't have the patience to wait.

"Promise me, Persephone," whispered Hermes, and at last I nodded.

"I promise."

Behind me, something—rather, someone—cast a shadow over me with what little daylight remained, and I shivered. "Hades."

"I am sorry to interrupt," he said quietly, and there was something about the way he said it that made me think he really was. "If I could speak with you alone, Persephone?"

Hermes nodded, and before I could protest, he untangled himself from me and stood. "I'll see you around," he said to me, and at least I knew he wasn't just saying that. At sixteen, he was training for his role on the council, as I was, and part of that included guiding the dead down to the Underworld. Chances were good I'd see him often, and that one reminder was enough for me to breathe easier. It wouldn't be just me and Hades down there. I had to remember that.

Once Hermes walked off into the woods, Hades knelt

beside me. His long, dark hair, usually so impeccable, was mussed, and his fingers dug into his thighs. "I owe you an apology."

Not this again. "You don't owe me anything," I mumbled, staring down at a lopsided blossom. "I'm sorry I ran up here."

"Do not be," he said. Neither of us could look at the other. "What happened last night...I promise you it will not happen again, not unless we are both willing and prepared."

His words twisted something in my gut. I'd been willing last night. Nervous, but willing, and determined to get it over with. Had he not been? Had I taken that from him? Was that part of the reason why things were so terrible between us?

"I don't..." The words stuck in my throat, and I struggled to swallow them.

Just tell him.

Hermes's voice echoed through my mind, gentle but unyielding, and finally I opened my mouth and blurted, "I want a separate bedroom."

Hades blinked, clearly startled. "Is there something wrong with—"

"Yes," I said before I lost my nerve. "I'm scared of you. I'm scared of this. And if I can't stay up here, then I don't want to stay with you down there."

He stared at me, speechless. For the better part of a minute, his eyes searched mine, and I refused to look away. I couldn't back down no matter how much it hurt him. Maybe this was a step in the wrong direction, maybe this was exactly what we didn't need, but I needed a space of my own. If I stayed with him, I would crumble. And I rather thought he would, too.

"All right," he said, his voice cracking. "If that is what you want..."

"It is," I said. "I'm your queen, and I'll rule at your side as much as you need me to. But if you want me at my best, then I can't be your wife. Not yet. Not until things are better."

For the briefest of moments, his expression shifted into pain and self-loathing, and guilt rushed through me as I nearly took it back. I could try. I had it in me. But even as I opened my mouth, that wall reared up inside me again, forming a barrier between us so strong that no amount of guilt could break it. I couldn't be his wife. Not now. Not if I wanted to have any chance of surviving this.

"Someday they will be," I said. "We can work toward it. Just—give me a chance to adjust, okay? And in the meantime, we'll be friends."

His expression relaxed enough to let me know I'd said something right. "Very well. We are friends."

Hades stood, offering me his hand, and I reluctantly accepted. Not because I needed his help, but because he needed some small amount of hope. I couldn't crush him completely.

"I want you to be happy," he said as the warm breeze danced around us. "From the moment your mother introduced us, my joy was tied with yours, and I promise you that despite my mistakes, everything I do is to please you."

I nodded, wishing I could say the same. But my happiness was my own, and I couldn't be responsible for his, as well. "Thank you," I said quietly. "Before going back, could we go somewhere warmer and walk around a little?" It was dusk here by now, but it was still morning back home, and I was desperate to feel the sun on my skin again.

"Of course." He slipped his hand into my elbow, and while that small amount of contact was enough to make my skin prickle, I didn't pull away. I hated the resentment and anger that prevented me from loving him the way he loved me, but no matter what Hermes said, I lacked the strength to conquer it. All I could do was open myself up to my new life and hope that in the end, it would be enough.

I tried.

I tried harder than I'd ever tried anything before. Every morning I let Hades bring me breakfast in my new bedroom two doors down from his. Every day I forced chitchat as he taught me more and more about what it meant to rule the Underworld. Every evening I sat with him as we read or talked about our shared day, and I tried so damn hard to love him that as time passed, I grew more and more certain that one day my heart would burst.

But the wall of resentment inside me didn't budge. Nothing Hades did or said wore it down, and no matter how hard I tried to work around it, it was always there. It was as if someone had cursed me into never falling in love, or at least never falling in love with Hades. We'd been friends before this, as much as we could've been, but even that was gone. Every tie that connected us had been severed, and that wall in my chest blocked every attempt I made to create new ones.

I was stuck. *We* were stuck. Whenever I looked at Hades, I could see the pain he carried with him, building up slowly from our restrained time together. But how could I explain my unnatural hatred toward him? Wouldn't it hurt him more if I told him that I didn't want anything to do with him? That I hated him so much it physically hurt me?

I had to pretend to care. And part of me did—I cared about how badly I was hurting him. I cared that I was lying to him. I cared that he was just as miserable as I was, if not more so. But every time we could have moved into the realm of something more, that wall was there, ever looming, ready to stop me.

Hades tried everything. Breakfast in bed, lavish gifts, even giving me free rein over the palace's interior decorating. I had a large patch of rock to work with outside as well, and over the years, I created a jeweled garden. It wasn't anything like the real thing, but it gave me time alone, time I needed to think, and Hades showered me with praise for it.

But nothing worked. We were frozen, not because of him, but because of me. And I didn't know how to fix it.

The days were endless, and though the seasons passed on the surface, nothing but my hair color changed in the Underworld. The rock pressed down on me constantly, trapping me without mercy, and the few times Hades brought me to the surface didn't make up for my prison. Mother only visited once, shortly after my tantrum in Olympus, and even then it was simply to make sure I was behaving.

Hermes, however, stuck to his word. Whenever he came down to train with Hades, he spent a little time with me. Playing games, talking, exploring what few parts of the Underworld I was willing to see—he was my lifeline, and things seemed a little brighter when he was there. He was the reminder I needed that life hadn't stopped completely. That there was still a world up there teeming with it.

One afternoon, I sat in the middle of the observatory, a long room at the very top of the palace that looked out across the vast cavern. It'd been empty when I'd discovered it, but I'd created an armchair for comfort, and the fireplace crackled with flames every time I entered. The entire length of the outer wall was made of glass, and I spent as much time up there as possible. One of my gifts was the ability to see the present, and sometimes, especially after a hard ruling, I liked to sit up there and go from afterlife to afterlife, reminding myself that what we did wasn't all bad. People lived whatever lives they wanted on the surface, and as Hades reminded me again and again, it wasn't our job to judge that. It was our job to judge what they thought was right. What they thought their afterlife should be. Most of the time, a soul went directly to their afterlife without any contact with Hades and me. But sometimes they were confused or didn't know or couldn't rectify their beliefs with their actions, and that was where we came in.

It was exhausting, judging eternities. But I did the best I could.

A soft knock cut through the room, and I pulled myself back into the present. I'd been watching a girl walking hand-in-hand through the woods with a young man. She'd clearly loved him in her life, and the fact that they'd found each other even after death…I envied her. I envied her so badly that I hated her. "Come in."

Someone slipped inside—no, not just someone. Two sets of footsteps too light to be Hades's echoed through the room. Frowning, I twisted around in my chair. Hermes walked toward me, and behind him, Aphrodite followed.

"Afternoon," said Hermes, giving me a boyish grin. "You look like hell."

"I feel like hell," I muttered, trying to push the thought of the girl away. She was mortal and dead, and she'd probably never held a jewel the size of a fist in her life. She was happier than I would ever be though, no matter how many gifts Hades gave me. "What are you two doing here?"

"What, I'm not allowed to come by anymore?" he said, perching on the arm of the chair. Aphrodite wandered toward the window, setting her hand on the glass and smudging it. I winced, but the unseen servants who staffed Hades's palace would clean it later.

"You know what I mean," I said. "Why did you bring Aphrodite?" She practically glowed with eternal satisfaction, and seeing her only made the fire of jealousy inside me burn even hotter.

"Because I think I can help," said Aphrodite, turning to face us. "If you let me, I mean."

"Help how?" I said warily, finding Hermes's hand. I didn't trust Aphrodite, for all her good luck and happiness, but I did trust him.

"Hermes mentioned you've been having trouble adjusting," she said with a hint of mischievousness that probably drove every man on earth wild. "How often do you and Hades sleep together?"

Just the thought of sleeping with Hades again made my skin crawl, and I narrowed my eyes. "Once. To consummate the marriage. If you tell my mother, I'll rip your hair out."

Aphrodite blinked, clearly stunned. "Why haven't you two slept together since?"

I shrugged. I'd spoken to Hermes about this a few times, but it never got easier. And I didn't know Aphrodite half as well as I knew him. "I don't know. It's just—I don't love him. And every time I think about doing that kind of thing with him, it's like a wall forms. I can't move past it no matter how hard I try."

"A wall?" she said, frowning. "But weren't you two friends before you got married?"

I nodded. At least someone understood how little sense all of this made. "I don't like the Underworld. It makes me feel trapped. And sleeping with him—it was horrible."

"Everyone's first time is horrible. Except mine, but, you know. Goddess of sex. Can't really help it."

"How did you do it?" I blurted. "How did you make yourself fall in love with Hephaestus?"

"I didn't make myself," she said. "I didn't want to at first, you know. I mean, that's why Ares and I ran away. But in the end…" She shrugged. "Heph and I just fit together. We work, you know? There's really no substitute for that. I have lovers on the side, of course, but in a way it helps us."

Hermes snorted, and Aphrodite gave him a look. "I'm serious," she said. "I love him. I love what we have together, and he'll always be my home. At the end of the day, it's because of my affairs that I stay with him. It's because of them that I don't feel trapped."

If only it were that easy for me. I stared at my hand intertwined with Hermes's. "Hard to have an affair when I'm stuck down here the entire time," I mumbled.

"They're not for everyone," she agreed, twirling a lock of blond hair around her finger. "But there are other ways I could help you, if you'll let me."

"Help how?" I said. "Make me fall in love with him?"

She scoffed. "No one can make anyone fall in love with someone else. In lust, sure—Eros is really good at that. But I mean trying to help you break down that wall. Giving you a little nudge in the right direction."

I had no idea what she meant, and the more she talked about it, the tenser I became, until Hermes had to practically yank his hand from mine. While he was busy flexing his fingers, I said, "I don't know."

"Of course you do," she said. "You want to love Hades, right?"

I hesitated. I wanted to have the chance to choose for myself, and if that included falling in love with Hades, yes. But what if it didn't? What if, given the choice, I would've fallen in love with someone else? "I don't know what I want."

"You want to be happy. That's what everyone wants. And if you can't get out of this mess—"

"You don't know that I can't. Maybe Hades will change his mind and—"

"It isn't his mind to change," she said, and the moment she

said it, her eyes widened, and she pressed her lips together. What the hell was she talking about?

"Aphrodite," said Hermes in a warning voice. "Spill. Now."

She sank onto the other arm of my chair, her expression falling. How was it possible that she could look so damn pretty all the time no matter what mood she was in? "Daddy decided you had to marry Hades because he was jealous that Hera was spending so much time with him, and he didn't want her to get any ideas."

My eyebrows shot up. "Wait, *what?*"

"It's exactly what it sounds like," said Aphrodite. "Hera spent some time down here, remember? And Daddy was afraid she was having an affair. She wasn't, of course, but it's obvious she loves Hades—"

"As a brother," I said. Everyone knew that. "Not as a husband. She's *married*."

"Yeah, well, so am I." She gave me a little grin. "And whether Hera likes it or not, she's as fallible as the rest of us. She just doesn't act on it, that's all."

I shook my head. The idea of Hera being in love with Hades was ridiculous. "I don't believe you. She might love him, but that doesn't mean she's *in* love with him. He's a nice guy, and Zeus isn't. No wonder she ran down here to get away from him."

Aphrodite inspected her nails. "If that's what you want to believe, so be it. I could be wrong."

"You are," I said. "And even if you aren't, Hades loves me."

She arched an eyebrow. "So although you don't love him, you relish the fact that he loves you."

"Not relish." The word sounded bitter on my tongue. "Just—it's a fact. He does."

"Yes, he does," she conceded. "More than he's loved anyone. And this is hurting him as much as it's hurting you—"

"You think I don't know that?" I snapped, my temper frayed. Whether it was from her spreading lies about Hera or the way she treated all of this like a game, I didn't know. Maybe it was jealousy. But either way, the thought of accepting her offer made me sick to my stomach. "I don't need your help, Aphrodite. If this is going to happen, it won't be because you decide it should."

She frowned. "That's not how—"

"I don't care, all right? All I want is my life back. And if you can't give that to me—if the only other alternative is tricking me into feeling like I love him even though I don't—then no thank you. I don't want to be a slave to illusion."

Two pink spots appeared on her cheeks. "Fine. If you're not even open to the idea, then there's no point."

"You're right, there isn't."

Huffing, she stood and ran her fingers through her hair. "I'm going back to Olympus. Hermes, are you coming?"

"Go on. I'll catch up," he said, and though he'd been quiet for most of the argument, he took my hand again.

Aphrodite stormed out of the room, and as soon as the door clicked behind her, a dam broke inside me. All of the frustration and anger and despair I'd swallowed since the day I'd married Hades flooded out, and I burst into tears.

After a moment's hesitation, Hermes pulled me into an awkward hug, and I buried my face in his chest. It wasn't fair. Aphrodite thought she had it all figured out, but she wasn't stuck down here. She could leave whenever she wanted, and she had a husband she loved as much as he loved her. Her arranged marriage had worked.

But mine was failing. I'd tried everything—forcing myself to love Hades, letting myself grow into it, and everything in between. Nothing was working, and I was never going to have the chance to live the life I wanted.

And of course it was Zeus's fault. Everything was. I'd never been ashamed to be his daughter before, but now, knowing what he'd been willing to do in order to protect his own interests, to keep Hera as caged as I was—

"Hey," said Hermes. "You're all right. Everything will be okay."

But no matter how many times he repeated it, he was wrong, and neither of us could change a thing. "This can't be my eternity, Hermes."

"It won't be. I'll do whatever I have to do to make sure it isn't."

I held him tighter, my shoulders shaking with sobs. I wasn't supposed to break down like this. Mother had raised me better—she'd raised me to adapt, to accept that not everything would go my way, but I couldn't be that girl right now. Somewhere in the middle of that bitterness and pain, I'd given up on her, and now the only person I could be was me.

At last I managed to stop crying, and he kissed the top of my head. "You're my best friend," he said. "You matter to me. You matter to all of us, even if it doesn't feel that way. Don't forget that, all right?"

I nodded. Even when everything else was falling to pieces, Hermes would be there. I was sure of it.

Once he left, I took a shaky breath and righted myself, gazing out across the cavern. The River Styx flowed through the stone, carving a path older than all of us. What would it be like to be on the other side? To live knowing there would be an end someday? Mortals didn't all know about the Underworld, and those who did only suspected, really. They believed, but they'd never been down here, and once they died, they never left to tell their family and friends about it. What would it be like to face that inevitable unknown?

In a way, I envied them. No matter how terrible their

lives were, they would have a chance to escape it in the end. I wouldn't.

Closing my eyes, I let my mind drift. I couldn't stomach going back to the happy couple in the woods, so instead I focused on someone I wanted to see—Hermes. I slipped into a vision, viewing the present as it was happening, and my heart skipped a beat. Hermes stood in the throne room, empty except for Hades, and he stared my so-called husband straight in the eye.

"If you don't let her go, she's going to wither. You know that. You see it every day. So why delay the inevitable?"

Hades frowned. "You speak as if you know exactly what is happening."

"I know you love her so much that you're in agony," said Hermes. "I know she doesn't love you, but she's trying to force herself to anyway because she knows how much it's hurting you. I know you're doing everything you possibly can to make her happy, and I know despite that, she feels trapped down here. And I suspect that you feel caged, too."

I held my breath, wavering between anger and relief. At least someone was finally saying everything Hades needed to hear, but it should've come from me. Not Hermes. I owed Hades that much.

But I couldn't interact with the present; all I could do was watch, and though it occurred to me that I could end this vision and join them, I was too much of a coward to do so. This way, Hades could make a decision without my interference. Or at least, that's what I wanted to believe.

"And what would you have me do?" said Hades quietly. "Abandon her? It may be difficult for both of us, but given time—"

"You've both had plenty of time," said Hermes.

"One cannot expect change to happen quickly. It may take centuries, eons—"

"You'd do that to her?" said Hermes. "You'd trap her down here for that long, knowing how miserable she is?"

Hades hesitated. "It is none of your concern."

"When my best friend feels like she's being held hostage, it is damn well my concern," he snapped. I winced, and so did Hades. Wrong choice of words for sure, but in a way, it was the truth. Except now I knew that it wasn't Hades holding the key.

"Leave," he said in a low voice that by itself wasn't much, but combined with the thrum of power that filled the throne room, it was deadly. Hermes opened his mouth as if he was going to protest, but at the last minute, he closed it again and turned on his heel.

When the door slammed shut, Hades closed his eyes and took several deep breaths. Whether to calm himself or work up enough courage to talk himself into something, I couldn't tell, but after three heartbeats, he disappeared.

Oh, hell. No doubt where he'd gone. I pulled myself back into the observatory just in time to see Hades arrive beside the armchair. So much for privacy.

"I am sorry, I didn't mean to interrupt," he said, a hint of a break in his voice. Whatever he was thinking, he was struggling with it.

"You didn't," I said, straightening. "I was just—you know. Watching."

"Anyone in particular?" he said, and I shook my head. No need to let him know I'd heard everything.

He stood there awkwardly for a long moment, his hands folded in front of him, and together we stared out the window. At last, when I was certain he wouldn't say anything at all, he cleared his throat.

"Are you happy?"

I blinked. He really didn't know? "No. Not because of you," I added hastily. "But—it's this place. It's suffocating." Whether my hatred for the Underworld had become nothing more than an excuse or if it really was the root of my unyielding bitterness, I didn't know. And I didn't particularly care either way. I'd already done everything I could think of to fix it.

"I see," said Hades, and another moment passed before he said, "What would it take to make you so?"

I hesitated. A thousand thoughts came to mind, each more ridiculous than the last, but there was only one thing I really wanted. "I want a choice," I said. "I want the chance to choose this life for myself."

"And how would I be able to give that to you?"

"I—" I paused. If I lied now, I might never have another chance like this. We might never have another chance like this, and lying would only bring more pain in the long run. "Freedom. Let me go. Give me a divorce."

Agony I hadn't expected flashed across his face. Whatever I was to him, it was more than I'd realized. Much, much more. That wasn't the pain of a man losing his pride. That was the pain of a man losing everything he loved.

"I cannot do that," he said, his words little more than a whisper. "If it were in my power, I would give you everything you desired, including a divorce. But the bonds that tie you to the Underworld as its queen are stronger than even I am."

Any and all hope drained from me, leaving me hollow and numb. Whether it was true or not, of course he would hide behind my vow to the Underworld. If I'd been capable of shedding more tears, I would have, but as it was, I was completely empty.

So this was it. This was my life from here on out—a slave not only to a husband I didn't love, but to a realm I hated with every breath in my body. Everyone would have a happy ending except me.

And Hades, I realized, glancing at him out of the corner of my eye. His fate was tied with mine, and he looked almost gray in the low candlelight. This wasn't just my life we were talking about. It was his, as well.

He'd known what he was getting into when he'd agreed to marry me, though. He knew this was a possibility, that I would never love him. Or maybe it'd never occurred to him. Either way, he'd made his choice; he'd had one to make in the first place. I hadn't.

I started to stand. I wanted to be anywhere but there—even his bedroom would've been better than this, as long as he wasn't there, too. But as soon as I straightened, he turned to me, his eyes glistening in the firelight.

"What if..." He swallowed. I'd never seen him at a loss like this before, and it broke every good thing inside me. "What if I were to give you a choice?"

I folded my arms over my chest, hugging myself. "You just said you couldn't."

"I cannot allow you to leave permanently," he agreed slowly, his focus fixed on something over my shoulder. "But if you were to return and help me rule on a regular basis..."

My heart began to pound. "What do you mean?"

At last he looked at me, and his silver eyes, so crowded with everything he couldn't say, sent a shiver down my spine. "If I were to give you half of every year to do with as you will... would that make you happy?"

Half a year. Half of the rest of my life. Was he serious? I watched him closely for any signs it was an empty offer, but everything about him was sincere. "Yes," I said, a thread of hope weaving its way through me. Freedom. Real freedom, even if it was only temporary. "That would make me happy."

He nodded once, twice, three times, as if trying to convince himself. "Then—that is what I will do. From sunrise on the spring equinox to sunrise on the autumnal equinox, you may spend your time wherever you would like. In Olympus, on the surface, even—" He cleared his throat. "Even down here, if you wish."

We both knew that wouldn't happen, but I took his hand anyway. "Thank you," I whispered. "I can't tell you how grateful I am."

I couldn't let myself believe it, not yet, not until I felt the sunshine on my skin and the wind in my hair, but the crushing look of loss on his face all but confirmed his offer was real. "You do not have to," he said. "Your happiness is all the thanks I need, and it is all I ask in return. Just come back to me."

Against my better judgment, knowing it might only hurt him more, I stood on my tiptoes and kissed his cheek. It was the most intimate contact we'd had since our wedding night. "I will. Thank you."

Rather than blush or give me a boyish smile, as Hermes might've done, Hades let go of my hand and stepped back. Without saying a word, he gave me one more tight nod, and the next moment, he was gone.

I sank back into my chair, elation and dread tumbling around inside me. Finally I would have what I wanted—a chance to live my own life, even if it was really only a half life. But at the same time, the pain on Hades's face, the thought of what Mother would say—

No. I was done worrying about what everyone else wanted for me. This was my life, my world, my future, not theirs. And now that I had a second chance, I wasn't about to give it up again. Not for anyone.

PART TWO

True to his word, Hades brought me to the surface on the spring equinox. He'd said little all morning, and as we arrived in a cool meadow, he was silent. As soon as we were on steady ground, he dropped my hand, and I hesitated.

"Thanks," I said at last, and I gave him what I hoped was a reassuring smile. "I'll see you soon."

He nodded once, and before I could say another word, he disappeared. I took a deep breath, inhaling the scent of nature even as a fist tightened around my heart. But I would come back to him eventually, much happier than I had been, and in the meantime, I could do what I wanted. We both lost, yes, but we both won, as well.

"Persephone?" Mother's voice cut through the dewy morning air, and I wasted no time. One moment I stood alone in the middle of the meadow, and the next I barreled straight into her open arms. It didn't matter that this was only temporary. Being here with her made me soar.

"I missed you," I mumbled into her chest, and she wrapped her arms around me in a secure embrace.

"As I missed you," she said, but there was a hint of something I hadn't expected in her voice—disappointment.

I clenched my jaw. If what Aphrodite had said was true and Mother and Zeus had married me off to Hades as some sort of twisted revenge on Hera, then she had no right to be disappointed. None at all.

But even that momentary spark of anger couldn't ruin the morning, and I slipped out of her hug and took her hand. We had two entire seasons to talk. Right now, I was going to relish my freedom and forget every awful feeling that had built up inside me in the Underworld. I wasn't going to waste this, not for anything.

"Come, my darling," she said, leading me into the forest. "Let's go home."

Home turned out to be a small cottage on the edge of a clearing deep in the woods. By the time we reached it, I had no idea where we'd gone or how we'd gotten there, but I didn't care. As long as it wasn't the Underworld, I would follow her anywhere.

It was small, one room divided into a cooking area, a sleeping area and a place to sit. Flowers and herbs hung from the rafters, creating a dizzying scent, and everything was handcrafted, as if she'd hired mortals to build it for her.

Zeus would've hated it. I loved it instantly.

We settled in, but the roof over my head reminded me of my constant claustrophobia in the Underworld, so soon enough we moved outside. Together we tended the tidy garden, and sometime in midafternoon, I worked up the courage to ask the question that had haunted me ever since Aphrodite had mentioned it.

"Did you marry me off to Hades because of Hera?"

Mother looked at me, her eyes wide, and her mouth formed

a small circle. Dirt streaked across her face, and in her hands she cupped the beginnings of an orchid encased in earth. "What?"

My cheeks burned, but it was too late to back down now. "Someone told me that you made me marry Hades because Zeus wanted to make sure he wouldn't have an affair with Hera."

She said nothing as she gently set the flower in its new home. Once it was properly in place, she sat back on her heels and wiped her hands. "Who told you that?"

I shook my head. I may have envied Aphrodite to the point that it actually hurt, but I wasn't about to betray her trust. "A reliable source."

"Ah, yes. The world seems to be full of those." She sighed. "It's no small wonder that Hera isn't happy about your marriage. You know how she feels about Zeus's illegitimate children. I don't blame her in the slightest, and a very large part of me feels a great deal of shame for betraying her in such a way. But I can't regret it, not when the result was you."

She set her hand over mine, and while I didn't pull away, I didn't take hers, either. "You're avoiding the question."

Mother pursed her lips. "I don't know what to tell you, my darling. Only that I arranged your marriage because Hades is a wonderful man, and I could think of no one who could possibly love you more."

"So Zeus had nothing to do with it?" I said. She hesitated.

"Zeus was the one to suggest him, certainly, but—"

"Is Hera in love with Hades?"

She blinked. "What makes you say that?"

"Is she?"

Mother rubbed her cheek, causing the streak of dirt to spread. "We all love Hades very much. Perhaps it is because he is the best of us all, or perhaps distance has something to do with it. We know each other so intimately in Olympus, but Hades is removed from us, and it is easy to forget his flaws. As far as I know, however, while Hera loves Hades as a brother, she has no interest in him as a lover. She is faithful to Zeus, as much as that pains her."

That was sort of an answer, at least. A half answer, but an answer nonetheless. "So Zeus didn't suggest I marry Hades simply because he wanted to make sure Hera was kept on a tight leash?"

Mother laughed, but there was something oddly humorless about it. "Oh, sweetheart. Hera does only what she wants. If she wanted Hades as a lover, she would have him, but she is far too devoted to her duties to ever betray the council that way. Zeus and I discussed all of our options, and in the end, we thought Hades would be the best match for you."

"And Hades? What did he think?"

"He was intrigued," she said. "He needed help with his duties, with the way the world is expanding, and he agreed so long as you were willing."

Willing. Funny how my definition seemed so different from my parents'. At least now I knew that if Hades had been aware of my hesitations, he would've never gone through with our marriage. That was a small comfort. "Did it never occur to you that I might want to decide on my own?"

"Darling." She squeezed my hand. I didn't squeeze back. "Yes, it occurred to me. Many, many times. But I was so certain you would love Hades as much as we all do, and he was in desperate need of help. I can't tell you how deeply sorry I am that your marriage has caused both of you so much pain, but I haven't given up hope yet. None of us have. And perhaps this time away will do you both some good."

I was silent. If that was the reason she'd agreed to this summer—because she saw it as a way to convince me a marriage with Hades wasn't so bad after all—then I had nothing more to say. I would be his queen for eternity; if Hades couldn't sever that tie, then there was nothing anyone could do. But this half year was mine to live as I wanted, not to pine over a husband I didn't love or a realm I hated.

I loved Mother. I loved our family. But the more I opened my eyes to the world around me, the more I began to realize that she and I wanted very different things for my life. And I was no longer afraid to tell her no.

Hermes came to visit that night, long after the sun had set. Mother answered the knock on the door, but when she invited him in, the suspicion behind her smile made me nervous. It wasn't the kind of smile she gave guests—it was the kind she gave Hera when they were forced to play nice. I intercepted them, looping my arm in Hermes's. "Why don't we go for a walk?" I said, and he nodded.

"That's what I was going to suggest, actually."

I forced a grin. "Perfect. We'll be back soon, Mother."

Without giving her a chance to protest, I led Hermes out of the cottage and through the garden. As soon as we ducked into the forest and out of Mother's line of sight, I exhaled.

"I'm sorry," I said. "She's been on edge."

"Don't apologize." Hermes stepped over a fallen tree and offered me a hand. I didn't need his help, but I took it anyway. "She's rooting for you and Hades to work out. Everyone is."

"I'm not so sure it will," I admitted.

"Maybe it will, maybe it won't," he said. "But right now you're not going to think about him at all, because I have a surprise for you."

I brightened. Hades brought me surprises practically every other day, but the thrill of anticipation ran through me anyway. It meant more somehow, coming from Hermes. "What kind of surprise?"

"That's a secret," he said with a grin. "It does come with a price, though—you have to trust me and close your eyes when I say so."

I raised an eyebrow. "You expect me to let you lead me through an unfamiliar forest in the middle of the night?"

"And I expect you not to peek, either."

I sighed dramatically. It wasn't that I didn't trust him—I did, and a few falls wouldn't exactly hurt either of us—but what little control I had lately was precious to me. And he must've known that. "Oh, fine," I said. "Just don't get us lost."

"Me, get us lost?" He snorted. "I'm more likely to get us killed."

"And that's supposed to boost my confidence in you how?" I said with a grin. I hadn't felt this good in ages.

At last, as we approached a clearing, Hermes stopped. "Close your eyes," he said, and I obeyed, my heart flutter-ing. He may not have had access to the riches Hades did, but that made this all the better.

Step by step, he led me through the remaining trees, art-fully avoiding every stone and root. The air changed once we reached the meadow, cooler now that the forest canopy wasn't above us. "Can I open them now?"

"Almost," he said. "Just two more steps and…now."

I opened my eyes and gasped. At our feet was a midnight picnic, with fruits and meats and nectar, but that wasn't the part that took my breath away. Above us, the night sky twin-kled with countless stars, somehow brighter and more stun-ning than I remembered. Away from the light of dusk, they glittered, and I sank to the ground beside the picnic. I'd never seen anything more beautiful in my life.

"It's incredible," I whispered. "You've no idea how much I've missed this."

"I figured you might like it," said Hermes, and he sat down beside me. "Zeus likes to create fables to go along with them, you know. Most of them are based on us. Like that cluster right there—the Pleiades. One of the stars is called Maia, after my mother."

"Do I have one yet?" I said, and he chuckled.

"Not that I know of, but I'll make sure to get right on that."

I grinned, but that soon faded into a wistful smile. "No one's ever done anything like this for me before."

"What, show you the stars?" he said, and he offered me a pomegranate. My favorite fruit, and the kind Hades brought me for breakfast every day. I shook my head. Not tonight. Not while I was on the surface. I didn't want that reminder.

"Do something nice for me that didn't have strings attached," I said.

He shrugged, but even in the darkness, I could see his ears turn pink. "It's just a picnic."

It wasn't, though. All of Hades's gestures, all of his gifts, they weren't things I wanted. They were things he'd hoped I would like, but I hadn't *needed* any of them. This, however— the stars, the open sky, the taste of freedom no matter how fleeting it was—this was what I'd been searching for.

I lay in the grass, picnic forgotten for now as I stared up at the sky. Hermes lay beside me, and I groped around until I found his hand. "I heard what you said to Hades."

Silence. "You did?"

"Yes." Tearing my gaze from the stars, I looked at him. "Thank you. For sticking up for me, for saying what he needed to hear—"

"Zeus wasn't happy with me," he admitted.

"Zeus is never happy with anyone. He didn't punish you, did he?"

"Just a verbal thrashing in front of the council. It happens."

I brushed my thumb against the palm of his hand. "I know it isn't much, but I would've never been this happy again if it wasn't for you."

He met my gaze, a small smile playing on his lips. "That's all the thanks I need."

I wasn't sure who moved in first, or if we both got the same idea at the same time. I wasn't sure it even mattered. One moment we lay there side by side, and the next he was kissing me, and I was kissing him, and the whole world seemed to go quiet.

This wasn't just lips against lips; this was warmth and comfort and safety and knowing he cared enough about me to risk his own neck. Not because he needed help ruling, not because I was promised to him, but because he saw me, flaws and all, and he cared anyway.

I wrapped myself around him, wanting to be closer to someone for the first time in my life. This wasn't like my wedding night; there was no pressure, no expectations, and I wanted this. I wanted him.

He didn't stop me, and I didn't stop him. At last I understood what Aphrodite was always going on about and why Zeus tested Hera time and time again. This warmth, this comfort, this all-encompassing love—this was what I was meant to feel. Not hurt or guilt or chains. I kissed him deeper, needing to be as close to him as possible; and underneath those glittering stars, he set me free.

As long as I had this, I always would be.

I returned to the cottage at dawn, my hair tangled and my step lighter than it'd been since I'd first entered the Underworld. Mother took one look at me, and her face fell.

"Persephone. You didn't."

I breezed past her. I'd cleaned up in a stream, of course, but I needed my comb. "Don't worry about it, Mother."

"Of course I will. This is your marriage." She followed me through the small cottage. "Sweetheart—"

"Don't." I whirled around to face her, brandishing my comb like a sword. "I'm not with Hades right now. I haven't been *with* him since we got married, and right now, I can do whatever I want. I'm *supposed* to do whatever makes me happy."

"Even if it destroys him?" she said, and I shook my head.

"You don't get it, Mother. He made this choice, and it isn't my fault he loves me, all right? It isn't my fault we can't be happy together. I've tried, we've both tried, but it isn't working."

She sat down on the edge of the bed, and I pulled the comb angrily through my hair. Leave it to her to ruin an otherwise perfect night. "Do you even intend to go back?" she said quietly.

"Of course," I snapped. "I won't abandon him, but I'm not going to waste this chance, either. I finally get to be *happy,* Mother. Why aren't you okay with that? Because it isn't the happy ending you wanted for me?"

"Because it isn't a happy ending at all," she said, as gentle as ever. "And as long as you continue down this path, you'll never find it."

"And you think I will with Hades?"

"Yes. Otherwise I would have never asked you to marry him."

"You didn't ask me to marry him. You *told* me. And you were wrong, Mother—I'm sorry, I know it must break your heart, but you and Zeus were wrong. We aren't happy. I'm not happy, and the more you try to pretend, the more it's going to hurt all of us. So just let it go, all right?"

I stormed into the cooking area, starting the fire with a wave of my hand. I wasn't hungry, and we didn't need to eat, but the ritual of cooking calmed me, and I hadn't had the chance in a very long time. This wasn't how things were supposed to go. Mother was supposed to understand, even if she didn't like it. That's what she always did: she understood. And there was nothing wrong with me and Hermes. He made me happy, and if she was so worried about it hurting Hades, then he would never have to know. I certainly had no intention of telling him.

"Persephone." She set her hand on my shoulder, and I shrugged it off. "We all make mistakes—"

"This isn't a mistake."

"Rarely does a mistake feel like one at the time," she said. "All I'm asking is that you don't jump headfirst into something you can't stop. And by hurting Hades—"

"I already hurt him. Every second I'm down there, miserable and alone and hating it, I hurt him. At least this way I can be happy, and we both get what we want."

"And how does he get what he wants?" said Mother.

"By me not being so miserable, even if it's just for a while." I turned to face her. "Please, Mother. Just give me this. Let me be happy."

Her eyes locked on mine for the space of several heartbeats, and at last she sighed. "I cannot condone it, but I will not forbid it, either. If you insist on letting this happen, then I must also insist that when you return to the Underworld, you act as you should. You rule beside Hades without complaint, and you let this happiness bleed into your time down there, as well. Can you do that?"

I nodded. If it meant I could spend the summer with Hermes, then I would. "Thank you."

She pressed her lips to my forehead. "I want you to be

happy, too, my darling, but not at the expense of others. Just be careful. You're playing a dangerous game."

"I know." I let her hug me, resting my head on her shoulder as she ran her fingers through my hair. "But he makes me happy."

She sighed. "Then for your sake, I hope that is enough for us all."

That summer was the best of my life. Mother and I spent every day together, sometimes with Hermes, sometimes without; but he and I spent every night together, as well. We explored the forest, swam in the cool lakes, and never once did I feel an ounce of guilt about betraying Hades. How could I, when he was the one who wanted me to be happy?

But it couldn't last forever, and finally the autumnal equinox arrived. Hermes and I both agreed we would halt our affair while I was with Hades, though of course I would see him often in the Underworld as a friend. The prospect of getting to spend time with Hermes no matter what realm I was in made giving up the surface a little easier to bear.

Mother led me to the clearing where Hades had dropped me off the spring before, and he was there waiting for us, his hair shining in the morning light. He really was beautiful, in a way Hermes would never be, but Mother had been wrong. My time away hadn't made me any fonder of him, and the moment our eyes met, that unyielding bitterness returned. There was something new on my side now though—contentment, and not the sort I had to fake. We might never be able to break down the wall between us, but at least we could both accept our fate.

"Persephone," he said quietly, offering me his arm. I kissed Mother goodbye and took it. "You look well."

"I feel well," I said, and I did. Even the dark power that

surrounded him couldn't spoil my good mood. I felt lighter somehow, and Hades must have sensed it, because he gave me a small smile.

"I am glad."

The trip into the Underworld wasn't so bad this time, and the rock that surrounded us didn't feel quite so heavy now that I knew it wasn't permanent. Half a year, that was it; then I would be free to be with Hermes again. I could do that.

I expected the usual round of duties when we returned to his palace, but instead he stopped me in the antechamber that led into the throne room. For a moment he said nothing as he stared at the floor, his face stony. I frowned. What was going on?

"You are happy, yes?" he said. "With…"

My entire body went cold. Hermes. He knew. Had Hades been spying on me?

No, he wouldn't. He may have been many things, but a sneak wasn't one of them. Mother had told him—she must have. Why? To hurt him? To make me feel guilty? To make sure I couldn't play him like a fool?

But I didn't think of him as a fool, and neither did Hermes. I'd kept this a secret not to hurt him, but to make sure I didn't. And Mother had to go and ruin it all.

I swallowed, the words stuck in my throat. "Yes," I finally said. "I'm happy. And—that's just the summer, all right? Down here, you and I are…whatever we are. These seasons are yours."

He nodded, not quite meeting my eye. "Very well. So long as you are happy, that was all I wanted."

The pain behind his words coiled around my insides until it nearly suffocated me. Why had Mother done this? She must've known how much it would hurt him. "I'm sorry Mother told you," I said quietly. "I never meant for you to find out.

I knew it would hurt you, and we weren't going to continue it down here, and—"

He shook his head. "Your mother did not tell me."

I blinked. "Then who?" Who else knew?

Hades was silent, and he took my arm as the doors into the throne room opened. Rows of the dead turned to watch us, and at the end of the aisle, standing beside Hades's throne, was Hermes.

Of course. He was the only other person who knew. Why had he told? Absolution? To ease his guilt?

Whatever it was, I glared at him as Hades and I reached our thrones. *Did you really have to tell?*

Yes. His voice whispered through me, for my mind only. *I don't want us to be a secret, not from Hades.*

You hurt him. Badly.

We both did.

I sat down in my throne, tearing my eyes away from him and focusing instead on the faces of the dead awaiting judgment. The first one moved before us, her head bowed as Hades addressed her, but I was deaf to his words. *I wish you hadn't.*

I'm sorry. I respect him too much to go behind his back like that.

Yet you don't respect him enough to keep your hands off his wife in the first place?

You were free to do whatever you wanted then. But I won't keep it a secret from him, either. He deserves better than that.

He did, and I hated myself for agreeing. *He knows we aren't together while I'm down here?*

Yes.

And he's all right with that?

As all right as anyone could be. He loves you. He wants to see you happy as much as I do.

You have a strange way of showing it.

Hermes didn't reply. Between us, Hades sat stiffly, his eyes blank as the woman talked about her life. Slowly, as if it were the most casual thing in the world, I set my hand over his. I hadn't meant to hurt him, but I'd been a fool to think I never would. There were consequences for everything. Even happiness.

As much pain as it caused him though, that was a price I was willing to pay.

Despite that first day, Hades and I settled back into our old routine, this time with genuine friendship between us. I managed to carry the contentment of my summer into our time together, and as the years passed and I went back and forth between him and Hermes, I continued to do the same.

It wasn't simple, but the uneasy truce between the three of us became all but permanent. Years turned into decades and decades into centuries; before long, I'd lost all track of time, my only benchmarks the beginning of spring and the end of summer.

But we were happy. Even Hades eventually adjusted, and I no longer saw pain in his eyes when he met me in the meadow every autumn. Instead he seemed pleased to see me once more, and slowly I grew to be happy to see him, as well. I hated the Underworld, and that wall between us was as strong as ever, but his understanding made me more accepting of his world.

Nothing changed for a long time. But one day, as I lingered in the observatory after we'd finished our judgments, I closed my eyes and did something I'd done thousands of times before: I found Hermes. Summer was only a short time away, and I was anxious to be with him again.

He was in his chambers in Olympus, standing on his balcony as the sun reflected off his light hair. And he wasn't alone. That wasn't anything unusual—he was social by nature, the complete opposite of Hades, and he usually spent a great deal of time with our brothers and sisters. But this time it was Aphrodite who stood beside him.

And she was naked.

Not that *that* was anything unusual, either, but the way she hugged his arm to her chest, the way he touched her—

I was going to be sick.

Hermes and I had never talked about what he did during the winters. He knew I wasn't with Hades, not like that, and I'd always let myself believe that he waited for me. Maybe most of the time he did. But we didn't have any rules about our time apart, and I had no right to feel as furious as I did.

It was Aphrodite though—the goddess who had everything. Love, satisfaction, a perfect life, a happy marriage. And now she was taking the one thing I had that was mine, the one damn thing in the world that gave me any amount of real joy.

But Hermes certainly didn't seem to be complaining.

How dare you. I pushed the thought upward with every ounce of strength I had. It still took ages to reach Hermes, but when it did, his eyes widened, and he immediately moved away from Aphrodite. His cheeks turned red, and when she tried to rejoin him, he sidestepped her. So he knew he was doing something wrong, after all.

"Persephone, please—I'll explain everything later."

Like hell he would. Like hell I would let him. What would he say, that Aphrodite had accidentally slipped into his arms? That it was only a onetime thing? That he'd missed me and he was lonely, and he couldn't wait any longer?

This is over. Don't bother to come by this summer, because you and I are done.

"Persephone?" said Aphrodite, and she looked around. "She's watching?"

I didn't bother to wait for Hermes's response. I pulled myself back into the observatory so quickly that for the first time since mastering my powers, I grew dizzy. I sat there for a long moment, my head between my knees, and struggled not to break down.

What else had I expected? He was Zeus's son as surely as I was Zeus's daughter. Cheating was in our blood. But no matter how many times I'd done it to Hades, that slap in the face—that complete and utter betrayal—had never hit home for me before.

My face was hot, and tears prickled in my eyes, but I refused to let them go. Instead I forced myself to breathe in and out slowly, counting each breath. Hermes loved me; I was certain of that. But why had he gone to Aphrodite? Was half a year really so long to wait?

Or had she seduced him? Were Ares and Hephaestus and Poseidon not enough for her?

Of course not. This was Aphrodite. She could never have enough, and she took whatever she wanted without a second thought. Mother may have considered me selfish, but I was nothing compared to my sister.

The door to the observatory opened and shut, and I wiped my dry cheeks angrily. I wanted to hurt something. I wanted to wrap my hands around Hermes's neck and squeeze. It wouldn't kill him, but it would help me feel a hell of a lot better.

"Persephone?"

And now I might have my chance. I straightened, my eyes narrowing as I focused on Hermes. He looked as if he'd dressed in a hurry, his clothing rumpled and his hair a mess. At least he'd bothered at all. "I told you not to come."

"Actually, you didn't," he said, shuffling his feet. "You said we were over, but—"

"And we are, so you have no business here," I snapped. His expression crumpled.

"Persephone, come on. I'm sorry. It was just once—"

"And I happened to peek in at the exact wrong moment?"

"You never said I couldn't see anyone else during the winter."

"I never said you could, either."

He exhaled. "What's really bothering you? Did you have a fight with Hades?"

I stared at him. He really didn't get it, did he? "What's *bothering* me is the fact that out of all the girls and goddesses in the world, you had to sleep with Aphrodite."

"And what's wrong with her?"

"She's *Aphrodite*. She has Ares, she has Hephaestus, she has every damn person she wants. You're mine. You're the only person I have, and she—she steals you like it's no big deal—"

"Nobody stole me." He knelt down in front of my chair, careful not to touch me. "I'm still yours. I'll always be yours, and I'm sorry about being with Aphrodite. You're right, it wasn't fair to you, and I should've asked you first."

I took a deep, shaky breath. "It doesn't matter. We're over."

"Persephone—"

"No." I stood and moved around him, narrowly avoiding kneeing him in the chin. "I was happy because of you, and I can't be that happy ever again, not when I know what you did with her. You stole that from me—you *both* stole that from me, and I will never forgive you for it."

"Persephone, come on, don't be like this—"

"Don't be like what? Angry? Upset? Hurt?" I whirled around to face him. "Why did you do it? Out of all the girls you could've slept with, why her?"

He hesitated, looking to his left for a moment. "Because— I don't know, all right? It's Aphrodite. If she wants you, you can't say no."

I balled my hands into fists. "Wrong answer."

As I stormed toward the door, the sound of his footsteps scrambling behind me echoed through the long room. "I'm sorry, all right? She was there, you weren't, and it isn't fair, but it won't happen again. Ever. I love you."

"If you really loved me, you would've never touched her in the first place." I flung open the door. "Hades would've never done that to me."

I glanced over my shoulder in time to see the stunned look on his face. "Hades? You're really going to compare me to Hades now? You don't even love him. You don't even want to be with him."

"If you're my only other option, then maybe he isn't so bad after all," I snapped. "Leave, Hermes. I don't want you here anymore."

With as much dignity as I could muster, I walked out of the room and down the spiral staircase that led to the lower floors. My eyes brimmed with tears, but by the time I reached my destination, I'd blinked them away without shedding a single one. Hermes wasn't worth it. I would've given him everything, but if he couldn't spare me honesty or fidelity—

I was an idiot for expecting him to stick with me. No one ever did. Not even Mother had much love left for me anymore, not after my failed marriage and centuries of being with Hermes. The only constants in my life were the seasons and Hades. No matter what I did to him, no matter how I acted, he was there for me without complaint. Always.

I should have loved him. I should've loved him so much that I ached over the thought of having hurt him. I wanted to so badly that part of me did, but that wall was still there, preventing anything real.

I hated that wall, and if it were possible, I would've ripped it down with my bare hands. Loving Hades should've been the easiest thing I'd ever done. He was a good man. Better than me, better than Hermes, better than every god and goddess who dared to call themselves Olympians. In a pit of deceit and jealousy, he was the one thing that hadn't been tainted by time. And I'd hurt him again and again.

Without bothering to knock, I burst into Hades's chambers. He sat at his desk, shuffling through scrolls and parchment, and he looked up as I strode over to him. "Persephone?" he said, a hint of confusion in his voice. No wonder, either, since I hadn't stepped foot in his chambers since our wedding night. "To what do I owe—"

Before he could finish, I crawled into his lap and kissed him. Not the kind of hesitant kiss we'd shared few times before, but the burning kisses I'd shared with Hermes. The kind that filled me with fire, all-encompassing and eternal. The kind that begged for more no matter how much I'd already fed it. It was the kind of kiss that no one, not even Hades, could ignore.

And he didn't. For a long moment, he didn't move—he didn't touch me, he didn't kiss me back, he didn't react at all. But at last his hands found my hips, and his lips moved against mine with equal fervor.

That wall inside me loomed, as dark and resentful as before, but despite the way my entire body screamed for me to stop, I kept going. His touch burned my skin, and that hatred wrapped around me so completely that I could barely breathe. But I needed this. I needed to be loved, even if the only person who could do it was the man I couldn't stand.

"Bed," I whispered between kisses, leaving no room for negotiating. He lifted me up without protest, and I wrapped my legs around his waist as he carried me across the room. I'd sworn to myself I would never go back here, but as he laid me down amongst the silk, I steeled myself against my body's protests and pulled him down with me.

I don't know how long we kissed—long enough for both

of us to get undressed, long enough for us to be seconds away from doing something neither of us had thought we'd ever do again. But before we got that far, Hades broke the kiss, his eyes searching mine.

"You're sure?" he whispered, and after a split second, I forced myself to nod. He loved me—I could see it in the way he looked at me, feel it in the way he touched me, everything. He loved me in a way Hermes never would, and I was an idiot for throwing all of that away without even trying. I knew what love was supposed to feel like now, and I could have that with Hades if I tried. I just had to want it bad enough.

He kissed me again, gentler this time, but he still didn't close the gap between us. "Why now?" he murmured, brushing his lips against the curve of my neck. I let out a frustrated groan.

"Because—because," I said, my voice breaking. "Because I want to, and you love me, and—can't we at least try?"

Hades pulled away enough to look me in the eye. "And what about Hermes?"

I swallowed, and something must have flickered across my face, because Hades frowned. "It's over with him," I said. "Please, can't we just…?"

"Do you love me?" he whispered. I blinked.

"I—I want to." I ran my hand down his bare arm, feeling the muscle beneath his warm skin. "Please give me the chance to try."

He exhaled deeply, as if he'd been holding in a breath for eternity. "I made that mistake once." He kissed me again, this time with aching gentleness. "I will not make it again."

Suddenly the weight of his body was gone, and he turned away to put his clothes back on. I lay there, exposed and shivering in the open air, and the tears I'd been holding back all evening finally broke through. "Don't you love me?"

He flinched, staring at the floor. "I love you, Persephone. More than my own existence. But it is because I love you so much that I cannot do this. In time, if we were to take this slowly, I would be honored. Under these circumstances, when I am nothing but a release to you…" He shook his head. "I'm sorry."

I opened my mouth to tell him he was so much more than a release, but I couldn't force the lie out. If anything, he wasn't even that. He was a way for me to feel loved. A way to get back at Hermes. And I didn't care if it made things worse, so long as the pain of Hermes's betrayal disappeared.

But whether I wanted to admit it to myself or not, that wound was far too deep for anything to mask it, even sleeping with Hades. I *hurt* in a way I'd never hurt before, and Hermes had created a gaping hole in my chest that nothing could fill. I curled up in a ball, not caring that I was still naked, and I let out a choked sob. Hades must have been halfway to his desk by then, but instantly he touched my back. It was a comforting gesture, not a romantic one, and it was something I desperately needed.

"You're all right," he murmured, and he wrapped a blanket around me. "Everything will be okay."

He could say that as much as he wanted, but he didn't know. He couldn't. I buried my face in his pillow, making a mess of the deep blue silk, but he didn't seem to mind. Instead he lay down beside me and gathered me up in a gentle embrace. "It will get easier," he murmured. "It may not feel like it now, but it will."

That only made me cry harder. Of course he knew what this was like. I'd done this to him again and again throughout our marriage, and never, not once, had he broken down in front of me. He'd kept that pain bottled up, refusing to take it out on me no matter how much I may have deserved it. Between him and Hermes, there was no contest. Hades would've never been with Aphrodite. He would've never even thought about her that way. He would've been there for me every moment of every day—he *had* been there for me, and I'd just never seen it before.

And now that I did, now that my eyes were open and I finally understood, I couldn't be with him. I'd messed it all up. I'd hurt him too badly for us to ever move beyond it. And that wall of hatred and resentment—it would never disappear. Whatever was causing it, whatever had made me feel that way to begin with, we were long past the point of fixing it. That wall was as much a part of me as Hades's love for me was a part of him. There was no getting around it no matter how hard I tried. If sheer willpower alone could've made it crumble, I would've managed that a long time ago.

Eventually I fell asleep, and during the night, Hades never left my side. When I awoke, his arms were still wrapped around me, and his eyes were open. He'd spent the entire night holding me, knowing we could never be together the way he wanted, knowing I would almost certainly go out and hurt him again as soon as the pain from Hermes's betrayal healed.

No. I wouldn't. Not this time. Hades had already given up too much for me, and no matter how miserable I was, even if it meant an eternity alone, I would never let that wall—I would never let *myself*—hurt him again.

Centuries passed, and then eons. Every spring equinox, Hermes was there waiting for me when Hades dropped me off, and I walked past him without a word every single time. Eventually we began to exchange glances, and then smiles; after the first thousand years, he finally came to visit me one summer, and we spent the day tending the garden with my mother. Although we began to talk again, it was never as anything more than uneasy friends.

Without Hermes's companionship, my summers weren't much better than my winters anymore. Hades built me several homes scattered across the world, and while I visited each and admired them all, my summers always began and ended at my mother's cottage. But over time, she grew increasingly distant. Some summers she could pretend nothing was wrong, but I still felt the heat of her disappointment when she thought I wasn't paying attention. Every glance, every absent hug and kiss—I felt them all, and they wore me down faster than my winter tomb ever could.

Hades and I never became anything more than we were, though I kept my promise to myself: I didn't cheat on him again. And that faithfulness gave me what small amount of happiness I could find. I'd made mistakes, I'd been a terrible person, but I could at least give Hades my loyalty now. We ruled together, side by side, and we may not have been deliriously happy, but we were content. I grew better at appreciating the small things, finding joy in our routines, and eventually I accepted my fate. This was my life, and the time to change it had long since passed.

All of that shattered the day I saw him.

I was up in the observatory, but instead of watching the afterlives of the dead, I'd let my mind wander to the surface. Though I would've rather died than admit it to anyone, occasionally, when I was at my worst, I watched Aphrodite. While I languished in loneliness, she had lover after lover, a whole host of men who would have died for her—and some who really did. She had everything I wanted, and no matter how I tried to console myself, my hatred for her only grew.

But I never stopped watching her. Sometimes to live vicariously through her; sometimes to convince myself that I had it better. I didn't, of course, but once in a while I'd stumble across moments that let me fool myself into believing it, if only for a short while.

This wasn't one of those moments. As the last vestiges of sunset stretched across the horizon, Aphrodite splashed in the ocean with the most beautiful man I'd ever seen. He was tall and strong, his face perfectly proportioned and his coloring fair. His smile seemed brighter than the sun, and when he glanced in my direction—unable to see me, of course, but still—my heart pounded, and warmth filled me from head to toe. It was the way Hermes had made me feel so many lifetimes ago. The way I wanted Hades to make me feel.

I was instantly smitten, but I wasn't the only one. As I watched them together, Aphrodite couldn't take her eyes off him, either. Despite their games, she constantly kept a hand on him, as if she were afraid he would disappear. Maybe he would. Maybe he was some sort of illusion. There was no other explanation for how someone so handsome could exist and not be one of us.

He tackled her to the sand and tickled her, and her shrieks of delight made my head ache. So she'd won again. Another boy, this time the most perfect one I'd ever seen, and Hephaestus didn't seem to care. If anything, he'd love her more tomorrow than he did today, because that's the kind of man he was. Just like Hades.

"Adonis!" she cried, laughing. "Adonis, no, I have to get back. I'm already late as it is."

"Take me with you," he murmured, kissing her, and she melted against him. Usually this was my cue to look away or disappear, but something stopped me.

Adonis. That was his name. I whispered it to myself, feeling the syllables roll off my tongue, and I smiled. It was perfect. He was perfect. And I wanted him.

"Mmm, you know I would, but Daddy would kill me," said Aphrodite, stealing another kiss. "I mean it this time—I *really* have to go. I have a council meeting."

I blinked. Adonis knew she was a goddess? Not that men didn't usually suspect when it came to her, but to actually mention the council…

"Very well," he said, releasing her with one last kiss. "I will see you again shortly?"

"Soon," she promised. "I do have to spend some time with my husband, you know."

He grinned, and she blew him a kiss. A moment later, she disappeared, and Adonis stared at the spot where she'd last stood. He had a wistful look on his face, as if he were thinking about a future he could never have. And if he were really mortal, then he was right. He couldn't.

Before I could stop and think, I slipped through the barrier between us, and I arrived on the beach in exactly the spot where Aphrodite had stood. Adonis's eyes widened, and he blinked several times.

"Who are you?" he said, but he didn't step back. That was something.

"Persephone," I said. "I didn't mean to barge in—"

"Persephone? Queen of the Dead?" he said, and now he did stumble backward. Damn. "Am I dying? Am I to be punished for being with the goddess of love herself?"

I snorted. "Please. If every man she slept with died because of it, there'd be no men left in the world. I'm sorry, I didn't mean to scare you. I'm not here to carry you off to the Underworld or anything." Though he had the good sense to fear it, at least. "I just…"

What was I supposed to say? That I'd been spying on him and Aphrodite? That he was the most beautiful man I'd ever seen? That I saw my future in his smile, that light and warmth and heart—that I wanted a piece of that happiness, no matter how small?

Oh, please. Love at first sight was the sort of thing Aphrodite believed, not me. I should've never come.

But the thought of returning to the Underworld and leaving him behind made my shriveled heart twitch in protest. He was a stranger, but at the same time, when I looked at him, I saw the familiar. I saw everything I'd ever wanted in those blue eyes, and I couldn't tear myself away.

"You just what?" he said, his voice gentler now, as if he could feel whatever drew me toward him, as well. Maybe he could. Maybe this was another one of Aphrodite's tricks, designed to humiliate me in front of everyone.

I needed to go. Or come up with a better excuse that had nothing to do with the truth. I took a breath, weighing my options. Not much of a choice. I could no sooner leave him than I could throw myself into the bottomless pit of Tartarus. "You looked—lonely, that's all. I'm sorry. Please don't be scared."

He eyed me, and as the sky turned from rainbow to purple, he relaxed. "It takes loneliness in oneself to recognize it in another."

"Yes, well. I don't exactly have a whole host of people in the Underworld begging to come to my parties," I said wryly.

That got a smile out of him, and it was just as beautiful as the ones he'd given Aphrodite. Maybe even more so, now that this one was meant for me. "I am Adonis," he said, stepping forward. Though he hesitated, he took my hand and brushed his lips against my knuckles. "I am afraid I do not know the proper protocol for addressing royalty."

"This isn't my realm," I said, "and right now, I'm not the queen of anything. I'm just Persephone."

That was technically a lie; I still had a month to go before spring, but Adonis didn't need to know that. "Well, just Persephone, it is the greatest pleasure and honor of my humble existence to set eyes on a creature as beautiful as you."

I blushed. "Please. I know you've seen Aphrodite."

"And yet I speak the truth."

No wonder Aphrodite liked him. He could probably talk his way out of the Underworld. "Do you live here?" I said, and he nodded.

"Aphrodite brought me here to keep me safe," he said. "Though safe from what, I'm afraid I do not know."

I did. One look at Adonis, and it was obvious Aphrodite was worried someone else would claim him for their own. "What about your home? Your family?"

He shrugged and took my arm as if it were the most natural thing in the world. "I have none."

"Oh. I'm sorry."

Adonis shook his head, and his blond curls fell into his eyes. "Don't be. All the more time to spend with you. Do goddesses eat? Might I interest you in dinner?"

I should've said no. Hades would miss me before long, and I'd promised myself I would never betray him again. But Adonis made me feel as if I was flying—one look, one smile, and that was enough to wash all of the bad away. This was what I'd missed since Hermes. This was what I'd craved. And no matter how much I loved him, Hermes was nothing compared to Adonis.

"Yes," I said. "I think I have time for dinner."

He beamed and brushed his lips against my cheek. The spot where he'd touched me seemed to sear itself into my skin, and as he led me toward the edge of the woods, I hugged his arm. It wouldn't hurt to miss one evening with Hades. I'd make it up to him, stay an extra day after the spring equinox or something. But nothing, not even my soul-crushing guilt, could make me walk away from Adonis.

★ ★ ★

Each evening, after Hades and I finished our judgments, I visited Adonis. Sometimes I stayed for a few minutes, sometimes for hours, always timed to make sure Aphrodite would never find us. But she stayed away more and more, always grumbling about Ares or Hephaestus needing her attention. Adonis never complained, and she never asked why.

But I was that reason. The time I spent with Adonis was bliss, and from the way he lit up upon seeing me, I knew it wasn't just me. Together we explored the island hand in hand, and we talked about everything. My life, his, the role the council played in the lives of mortals—Aphrodite had told him far more than we were permitted to tell mortals, and that made the conversation much easier. I wasn't bending any rules she hadn't already broken, and Adonis seemed to enjoy hearing about what we did.

Mortals already told stories about my family—some true, some embellished, some outright ridiculous, and Adonis took great joy in relaying them to me. We made a game of it; he would remove or replace the names, and I would try to guess which member of my family he was talking about. I'd never laughed so hard in my entire existence.

I didn't kiss him though, and while we held hands, he never pressed for more. I couldn't give it to him, not while it was still winter. Not while I was still Hades's. Being here was enough betrayal on its own. I couldn't make things worse no matter how tempting Adonis was.

I ached for spring to come. We talked about Mother's cottage and how we might get one of our own; Adonis had never had a home before, not a proper one he'd chosen for himself, and he relished the idea of seeing the place that had become my summer retreat. As spring neared, I grew giddy with the thought of showing him my home and sharing my summer with him. He, in turn, was never too embarrassed to tell me exactly how excited he was, as well.

That was the best part about being with him—the honesty. The openness. After millennia of enduring the lies and secrets within my family, even down in the Underworld, it was a relief not to question every word he said. He was everything I'd ever wanted, and even if I could only have him as a friend, that would still be more than I'd ever thought I'd have.

But I did want more. I longed to kiss him, to touch him, to bask in his outer beauty as much as I enjoyed the beauty inside. We were perfect together in every way, and as soon as I could, I would steal him from Aphrodite and give him the life he wanted. The life he deserved. The life we both deserved.

Days before the spring equinox, he and I sat together on the beach, our hands clasped as we laughed over a story he'd told me about his childhood. I was oblivious to our surroundings, barely aware of time passing at all, and it was only the look on Adonis's face that alerted me to the fact that something was wrong.

I turned. Standing in the sand, her arms crossed and a scowl on her pretty little face, was Aphrodite.

Lovely.

"I wasn't aware it was spring already. What are you doing here?" she said in a sickeningly sweet voice.

"Talking to a friend," I said, not bothering to match her tone. Adonis knew exactly how I felt about her. "What are you doing here? Cheating on your dozen boyfriends?"

She scoffed. "Only a dozen? You severely underestimate me. Hi, love," she said to Adonis. "Is Persephone bothering you? I can make her leave, if you'd like."

I bristled. "Make me leave? How? By cooing at me?"

"Don't you have a husband to get back to?" she snapped.

"Don't you?"

She sniffed. "He knows exactly where I am, though I'm willing to bet Hades has absolutely no idea where you are. You *do* know who she is, don't you, Adonis? And who her husband is? He controls your afterlife, you know. Are you really willing to risk that?"

Adonis stared at our intertwined fingers. At least he wasn't trying to make me let go, but he didn't say anything, either. I squeezed his hand.

"Adonis and I are friends, nothing more." The urge to rip her hair out twisted inside me, and it took every ounce of my self-control to stay seated. "Though he will be coming to stay with me on the spring equinox."

"Is that so?" Aphrodite raised an eyebrow. "And who decided that?"

"Adonis did."

She huffed. "You have no right to come here and steal him like—"

"Like what? Like you stole Hermes?"

She let out a bitter, empty laugh. "Is that why you're doing this? Because of Hermes? That was *eons* ago."

"I'm doing this because Adonis is my friend, and I love him," I said with as much dignity as I could muster. "It's his life, and you don't get a say in it."

"Adonis, tell her," demanded Aphrodite, not taking her eyes off me. I glared back. *"Adonis."*

To my immense satisfaction, Adonis said nothing. I smirked, even though it was petty, and Aphrodite let out a frustrated screech that startled the seagulls.

"Daddy!" she shrieked, and even though the sky was blue and clear, thunder rumbled through the air. Adonis's eyes widened, and he started to stand, but I gently tugged on his hand.

"It's fine," I said quietly. "He won't hurt you." I hoped.

Lightning sizzled on the beach, and in the blink of an

eye, Zeus arrived. No chance in hell he would've come that quickly if I'd been the one to call. Standing an even distance away from us, he frowned and crossed his arms over his broad chest. "Dare I even ask?"

Aphrodite was in tears now, and of course she looked beautiful when she cried. I hated her. "Per-Persephone is trying to steal Adonis from me."

My mouth dropped open. "Excuse me? He *wants* to stay with me, and he has every right to choose his own life."

"He already chose me long before you showed up, you cow."

"*Cow?* You vain little—"

"Enough, girls." Zeus sighed and pinched the bridge of his nose. "Aphrodite, start at the beginning."

She sniffed and straightened her shoulders, looking down her nose at me. "Adonis and I've been together for ages. We love each other, and we're perfect together, naturally."

"If you're so perfect together, then why do you keep him trapped on this island?" I said.

"I'm not trapping him. I'm protecting him."

"From what? Other girls who might actually be able to devote themselves to him completely?" I snapped.

"Persephone," said Zeus in a warning tone, and I huffed. This was completely unfair. Not just for me, but for Adonis, too. It was obvious he wasn't going to speak up in his own defense, though. Not that I blamed him, of course—my father could be intimidating at the best of times, and I was a goddess. I couldn't imagine what being in his presence was like for a mortal.

"I keep him here to protect him from Ares," said Aphrodite. "He's been acting a little jealous lately, and there's no point in causing a skirmish."

As if she hadn't caused a million of those in her existence.

I sandwiched Adonis's hand in both of mine. Screw Zeus's commands. I wasn't going to stay quiet, not about this. "So not only are you keeping him here like some kind of pet, but you're endangering his life, too. What sort of love is that?"

Aphrodite's face turned red. "How dare you—"

"Silence, both of you," said Zeus in a voice that rolled like thunder, and even Aphrodite obeyed. "Adonis—that is your name, yes?"

He swallowed and nodded, averting his eyes. His grip would've likely broken my bones if I hadn't been immortal.

"What is it you choose to do, Adonis?"

I exhaled. A choice. At least Adonis would have that much. I patted his hand. "It's all right," I whispered, and across from me, Aphrodite stomped her foot in protest. Too bad.

"I…" He stopped and shook his head, staring at the sand. Why, because he thought Aphrodite would curse him if he didn't choose her?

Probably. And I wouldn't put it past her, either. "It's your life," I whispered. "Remember that."

But he still said nothing. At last Zeus ran out of patience. "Very well, then I will decide. In the absence of the young man's opinion, I will split his time equally between both of you. He will spend one third of the year with Aphrodite, one third of the year with Persephone and for the final third, he will do what he pleases. Is everyone happy?"

No, not in the least, and judging by the pinched look on Aphrodite's face, she wasn't, either. But we both nodded, and Adonis didn't protest. He barely even blinked.

"So be it. Now, if my beloved daughters do not mind, I have matters much more important than this to attend to." Without another word, he disappeared, and instantly Adonis relaxed.

I turned to Aphrodite. I could've said a million things to

her, but instead I blurted, "Why wasn't Zeus mad that you told Adonis who you are?"

Aphrodite shrugged, clearly put out over having to share him. "Because I've been lobbying Daddy to let Adonis join us, of course. But now you had to go and ruin it, didn't you?"

I snorted. "And how did I ruin it? You're the one who wouldn't let him make up his own damn mind."

"Persephone." Adonis's voice was hoarse, but at least his grip on my hand wasn't quite so tight anymore. "I apologize to you both for not speaking up. It is just…"

"No need. We both know Daddy's a little intimidating sometimes," said Aphrodite cheerfully, though there was a glint in her eyes as she looked at me. "But now that Daddy's made a decision, we have to figure out who gets what third."

I scowled. No doubt she'd try to make me take the winter months. "I want him starting on the spring equinox. The entire spring and first month of summer."

She eyed me, and I steeled myself for the fight I knew was coming. Instead of objecting, however, she nodded. "Yes, I think that's an excellent idea. I'll take the next four months, and then Adonis can do whatever he pleases with the final four."

I blinked. That was it? Not even a hint of protest? "What's your game, Aphrodite?"

"Game?" she said, her eyes widening innocently. A sure sign she was lying through her teeth. "Is it so terrible to give my sister a chance at happiness?"

There wasn't much I could say to that, not without looking like a monster in front of Adonis. I would figure it out eventually though, and when I did, I would rip her apart. "Fine. At the start of the spring equinox, you and I will go to my cottage," I said to Adonis. "And Aphrodite will stay very, very far away."

She sniffed. "Fine, as long as you promise to never come back here, either. This is my island, not yours."

"Fine."

"Fine."

We glared at each other. This war wasn't over, but for now, we had no choice but to call a ceasefire. I would discover her game soon enough, and until then, I wasn't about to let her or Zeus or anyone ruin my time with Adonis.

On the morning of the spring equinox, Hades dropped me off in the meadow as he'd done thousands of times before. I leaned in to give him a kiss on the cheek goodbye, nothing more than what it was, but he stiffened.

I frowned and looked behind me. Standing in the clearing, as promised, was Adonis. And Hermes. And Mother.

Terrific.

"And that, I take it, is Adonis?" said Hades quietly, and I blanched.

"Yes." Who had told him? Aphrodite or Zeus? Did it even matter? "We're just friends."

"For now," he said softly, and I gave him that peck on the cheek.

"I'll see you on the autumnal equinox. Take care of yourself."

He remained stoic as I walked across the meadow, and a knot of guilt formed in the pit of my stomach. I should've told him, but these seasons were mine, and telling him before anything had happened wouldn't have made it any easier. It wouldn't have made him hurt any less.

I ignored Hermes completely. He frowned as I passed, but to my relief, he didn't say anything. The situation was awkward enough as it was without his getting involved. Instead I headed toward Adonis first, taking his hand and giving him a smile. He returned it, albeit nervously, and he glanced over my shoulder. At Hades, no doubt. "It's fine," I said, and I led him toward Mother. "I want you to meet my mother, Demeter. Mother, this is—"

"I know who he is," said Mother quietly. Instead of welcoming him like I expected, as Adonis bowed in greeting, her lips curled back with contempt. "I thought you were past this, Persephone."

"Past what?" I said. "Past making friends? Past wanting to be happy?"

"Past causing your husband pain in the most deplorable way possible," said Mother. Beside me, Adonis straightened, and I touched his elbow. No need for him to waste effort if she was going to be cruel about it.

"You're the reason that me finding a bit of happiness is so *deplorable* in the first place," I said. "If you can't support me, then fine, I don't need your support. And I don't need you here, either."

I didn't know what I expected—an angry retort, a sneer, Mother to break down and beg my forgiveness. Either way, I didn't expect her to fold her hands, give Adonis a slight nod and disappear completely.

All the air left my lungs, and I stared at the empty space where she'd stood moments before. She'd gotten mad at me before, of course, and her disappointment over the years had become impossible to bear. But never had she turned her back on me. Not like this.

"I am sorry," whispered Adonis, his lips brushing against my temple. The regret in his voice only made the ache inside me grow.

"Don't be. Please." He shouldn't have had to suffer for my mistakes. "Let's just go."

"All right," murmured Adonis, leading me down the path

I'd traveled thousands of times before. I trailed after him, heartbroken and empty, and not even the warm weight of his hand in mine brought me comfort.

I thought I'd known what loneliness felt like, but it wasn't until I walked that trail without Mother that I finally understood. Even in my darkest hour, Mother had been there for me. She'd loved and supported me no matter how often or hard we fought. And now—

Now the one person I'd always needed, the one person I'd thought would always be there for me, was gone.

That summer was simultaneously the best and worst of my life.

The hole Mother had left inside me only grew as it became clear she had no intention of returning. But at the same time, those four months with Adonis filled me in a way nothing ever had before. Every moment was an adventure—I'd explored the forest around the cottage countless times, but somehow every day he managed to find something new, something small but beautiful that I'd overlooked. A wild garden full of exotic flowers that tangled together in chaos. A tree so ancient and gnarled that I suspected it outdated Zeus. He reintroduced me to things I'd long since lost—the warmth of the sun on my skin, the shiver down my spine as I stepped into a cool river. He gave me back pieces of my life I'd never realized I missed.

No one could deny Adonis was gorgeous, but the more I got to know him, the more I realized that his appearance was little more than a taste of his inner beauty. He was kind, generous, honest and, despite the fact that Aphrodite had gotten to him, he was innocent in a way I hadn't been since my marriage eons ago. He had nothing but love inside him, and he radiated it every waking hour. I drank it in, letting it fill me until all of the negativity washed away, and by the time four months was up, I'd never been more content with my lot in life. All of it, every last terrible moment, was worth it now that I knew it had led me to Adonis.

In the middle of summer, Aphrodite came to claim him. To her credit, she was mostly polite about it, only giving me a small smirk when Adonis turned his back. But the instant they left, that hole in my heart opened up, hemorrhaging all of the happiness I'd collected during our four months together.

I cried harder than I ever had before. Now that Adonis was no longer there to act as a buffer, for days I did nothing but curl up in bed and stare at the wall as reality set in.

Mother hated me. I'd cheated on Hades again. Hermes was barely talking to me, and the one light in my life was currently with a blonde whore who couldn't possibly love him the way I did. He was just another toy to her, and the thought of him going through that, having no say in his time with Aphrodite the way I'd had no say in my time with Hades—

It wasn't fair, but there was nothing I could do about it, either. Zeus had made up his mind, and if Adonis wasn't willing to speak up on his own behalf, then so be it.

Though I wasn't proud of it, I spied on them. He didn't kiss her the way he kissed me; he didn't watch her the way he watched me. And every time Aphrodite laughed, I swore I saw him flinch.

That should've given me some amount of satisfaction, but it only made me more miserable. Adonis should've had what I didn't—freedom. And instead, in my quest to find happiness, I'd stolen that from him. Did that make me as bad as Hades? As bad as Mother and Zeus?

Eventually summer turned into autumn, and it was time for me to return to the Underworld. Hades greeted me in the meadow as always, but rather than a smile and a kiss on the cheek, he simply nodded coldly and took my hand without a word. Whatever he'd gone through in those six months, whatever thoughts and questions had haunted him, had also ruined every step of progress we'd made in the thousands of years since Hermes and I had broken up. And more than ever, self-loathing snaked through me, doing nothing but compounding my despair. I didn't deserve Hades's friendship. I didn't deserve Adonis, not after doing this to him. I didn't deserve any of it.

Those six months in the Underworld were blank. I went through the motions of existing, but some integral part of who I was had given up entirely. Hades stopped spending the evening with me. He no longer brought me breakfast. He could barely stand to look at me even when we had to, even when a mortal's eternity depended on our communication. And rather than take steps to fix it, all I could do was drown in the darkness that was my life. Not even the promise of four months with Adonis in the spring made it better.

After several weeks of spying on Adonis and Aphrodite, I stopped, unable to stomach seeing him so upset any longer. But eventually her time with him passed as well, and shortly before the spring equinox, I couldn't resist checking in on Adonis once more.

He stood in a stream I didn't recognize, using a net to capture fish. I watched him, invisible to his eyes, and just seeing him like this—free and happy—was enough to make me smile. Four months wasn't forever, and one day Aphrodite would grow bored of him. I never would though, and eventually, when mortality claimed him, I would have him entirely to myself. Aphrodite wouldn't be able to touch him in the Underworld.

Behind me, someone giggled, and a cold wave of dread crashed through me, washing away what little warmth had blossomed. Even though it was his four months of freedom, even though everything I'd witnessed made it clear he didn't love her, Aphrodite skipped out of the trees, a flower tucked behind her ear.

"Adonis! There you are." She stepped into the stream with him and set a hand on his bare back. "Any luck?"

He shook his head. "A few close calls."

"Well, I'll just ask the nymphs to make us dinner then," she murmured. "I'm *starving.*"

Standing on her tiptoes, she kissed him on the mouth, her hand dancing downward toward his waist. She wasn't hungry for food, that was for damn sure.

I was going to kill her.

This was supposed to be Adonis's time alone, not an extra third of a year for her. And why was he going along with this? Why hadn't he refused her and walked away?

The same reason he hadn't spoken up when Zeus had asked him, more than likely. Mortals with any sense of self-preservation didn't question a god. Even one as feeble as Aphrodite.

I didn't hesitate. I pulled my body through the space between us as I'd done almost exactly a year ago, and this time Aphrodite didn't seem the least bit surprised to see me.

"I was wondering when you'd stick your nose where it doesn't belong," she chirped, sliding her arm around Adonis's torso. He paled at the sight of me, and though he tried to step back from Aphrodite, she held on. Naturally. Couldn't risk letting her trophy think for himself, else her precious ego might be bruised.

"You don't have to spend these months with her," I said to Adonis, keeping my voice as steady as I could. "You know that, don't you?"

He nodded and averted his eyes, his fishing net all but forgotten. "I'm sorry."

"Don't be," I said, glaring at Aphrodite. "I'm sure this wasn't your idea. Why are you here with her?"

"I couldn't just turn him away in the middle of winter, now, could I?" said Aphrodite, her eyes wide.

"He spends those four months alone. That was our deal," I said.

She tilted her head and gave me the perfect imitation of a smile. "Oh? I recall Daddy saying he could spend this third doing whatever he wanted. And rather than starving to death, he chose to remain with me."

That conniving bitch. I raised my hand to slap her, but what was the point when she couldn't feel pain? "So that's why you let me have the first four months with him—so you could trick him into spending his free four with you."

She laughed. "Of course. Honestly, it's not like he could go to you anyway, so why shouldn't he spend them with me? He loves me."

"Not the way he loves me," I snarled.

"Is that so? Adonis, tell Persephone how much you love me."

He grimaced, not meeting either of our stares. At last he slipped from Aphrodite's grip, and taking his net, he splashed toward shore without a word.

Fine. If he wouldn't defend himself, then I would.

"See? He can't even answer you," I said, drawing myself up to my full height. "He loves me without trickery, and if I were here to spend time with him—"

"But you aren't," said Aphrodite. "Don't you see that? Hephaestus knows about my affairs—he knows this is something I need in order to be myself, and he accepted that long before we married. But Hades didn't. Despite everything you've done to him, he loves you. He's loved you for so long that it's as much a part of him as the Underworld is now. And even though you have his unconditional, endless love, you have no problem turning your back on him and hurting him in the worst ways possible."

I opened my mouth to speak, fury building inside me faster than I could release it, but she kept going. She stood only inches in front of me now, her nose practically touching mine, and it took everything I had not to throttle her.

"You're selfish, Persephone. You're the most selfish person I've ever met. You hurt Demeter. You hurt Hermes. You hurt Hades so badly that he's nothing more than a ghost of who he was before you ripped his heart out and fed it to the dogs. You hurt people again and again, and the worst part about it is that you don't care. You can claim to love Adonis all you want, but he'll never have all of you. And one day, you're going to hurt him the way you've hurt everyone else in your life, and I won't let that happen."

I stared at her, every word I'd planned to fling back in her face dissolving on my tongue. In spite of her many flaws, Aphrodite knew love, and she knew people. She could see the good side and the bad, and she, more than any of us, could weigh them against each other rather than rushing to judgment. And if that's how the most understanding of us saw me—

Maybe it was our battle over Adonis. Maybe it was my constant jealousy. Maybe she just wanted to win. But even so, she still wouldn't say those things if she didn't believe them.

The weight of her words crashed down around me, leaving me shaking and exposed and vulnerable in a way I'd never been before. Was that what the entire council thought of me? Was that how Hades saw me? And Mother—did she believe it, too?

Were they right?

"I—" I swallowed. "I need to go." Stepping back, I mustered what little strength I had left and said, "Cut him loose,

Aphrodite. Give him his freedom. If you really love him…"
I shook my head, and without giving her the chance to rub
salt in my already gaping wound, I disappeared back to the
Underworld. Back to Hades.

Back where I belonged.

I stayed in the observatory for the rest of the night, not
bothering to go to my chambers. Hades wouldn't notice, and
on the remote chance he did decide to come visit me, I needed
to be alone.

I turned Aphrodite's words over in my mind again and
again without reprieve. She was right, and I hated myself for
it. I hated myself for every bit of it. But at the same time, she
didn't understand—she didn't see the whole picture, the life I'd
lived and the things I'd missed, things she'd never wanted for.
She was loved wherever she went by everyone who set eyes on
her. Me—I was the dreaded Queen of the Underworld. I was
the person no one wanted to see, and when I did run across
the rare mortal on the surface, they all fled. Except Adonis.

To Aphrodite, he was nothing more than an exceptionally
beautiful toy, but to me, he was everything I'd never had before. She didn't understand that—how could she, when her
world was saturated with love? She would never be alone. She
would never face an eternity of loneliness and heartache. But
that was my reality, and no matter how good a judge of charac-
ter she was, it simply wasn't in her capacity to understand that.

By the time morning came, I itched with the need to defend
myself. For a few minutes, I debated going up to the surface
and giving her a piece of my mind, but it wouldn't do any
good right now. I needed her to understand, and in order to
make that happen, my argument had to be perfect.

I dragged myself to the throne room at the appointed time,
and when Hades trudged down the aisle, I was already seated

in my throne. The way he eyed me confirmed he knew I hadn't spent the night in my chambers, and I made a mental note to straighten that out later. He deserved the truth. And an apology.

At last the judgments got under way. They were routine, for the most part—mortals who hadn't believed in the afterlife, or mortals who had believed, but had never anticipated what it might be like. A few children mixed in with the adults as well, and those judgments always hurt the most, seeing their young lives over before they'd begun. Hades and I had agreed long ago that they would always be granted their happiest memories regardless of whatever hell a handful of them thought they deserved.

The throne room was full that day, and by the time evening came, we'd barely made it through half. Hades and I had other duties as well, of course, but neither of us halted the proceedings. I stole a glance at him, searching for signs of fatigue, but he was as stoic as ever. And I was too keyed up from my fight with Aphrodite to stop, either.

A woman moved to the spot before us where countless other souls had stood. Her hair was long and stringy, and her hands shook as she regarded us with a wavering gaze.

"I know that because of my misdeeds, I am to be banished to an eternity of fire and brimstone to dance with the devil himself," she said, her voice shaking as much as her hands. "But I beg of you—I only acted out of love."

"And what are these acts of which you speak?" said Hades in a low voice. The woman winced.

"I—betrayed my husband. But he wasn't good to me, your majesty. He had little love for me, and after a time, I could no longer love someone who didn't love me back. I cherished my vow to him for as long as I could, but—when I met someone else, someone who loved and appreciated me..."

She broke down, and I glanced at Hades. Was this his idea of a joke? His brow was knitted, however, and he clutched the arms of his black-diamond throne. No way he'd planned this.

Our eyes met, and he quickly looked away. So he was aware of the irony, as well. Not that adulteresses were all that uncommon, but this woman's story tugged at me in a way none of the others before her had. Maybe it was because of Aphrodite, or maybe Adonis—whatever it was, I ached for her.

"This other man," I said, and the woman focused on me, wringing her hands desperately. "He made your life worthwhile?"

"Yes," she whispered. "He made me content. He made me feel as if I were loved."

"Yet you took a vow to remain faithful to your husband," said Hades. "Did you believe your affair to be wrong, despite how it made you feel?"

Her eyes watered. "Y-yes."

"But what good was her vow when it was choking the life out of her?" I said, turning toward Hades. "What's more important—a few words in front of family and friends, or her entire life's happiness?"

"Yes, what *is* more important, Persephone?" he said. "Her virtue or her own selfish desires?"

I clenched my jaw. There was that word again—*selfish*. So that was how he saw me, as well. "How can you call her selfish when all she was trying to do was find some small joy in her life?"

"And how can you not see the pain and humiliation she must have brought upon her husband?"

"Maybe if he'd listened to what she wanted, she would've never had to stray."

"Perhaps if she gave him a chance to prove himself, she

would have never felt the need to break her vows to begin with."

I slammed my hand onto my armrest. "And maybe if she'd had a choice in the first place—"

The doors to the antechamber opened suddenly, and Hades and I both looked up, along with every soul in the throne room. Hermes stood in the doorway, and upon seeing everyone staring at him, he turned pink and hurried down the aisle.

Hades sighed and leaned back in his throne. "What is it, Hermes?"

Hermes glanced at me, his lips pressed together, and he hesitated. "I'm sorry for interrupting—"

"Then get on with it," said Hades. I glared at him, but he stared straight ahead. Bastard.

Hermes shuffled his feet, his brow furrowed and his eyes glued to the marble floor. All my pent-up anger drained away, and my heart sank. Whatever it was couldn't be good.

"It's Adonis," he said. "He's dead."

PART THREE

Naturally Aphrodite was responsible.

Not directly, of course, but close enough. Ares, who we all knew was the jealous type, had sicced a wild boar on Adonis the moment Aphrodite had left his side. Why she hadn't seen that coming, I didn't know—more important, why she'd put Adonis in that sort of danger, knowing Ares might try to take revenge…

It didn't matter. Adonis was a citizen of my realm now, and I sat frozen in my throne as Hermes explained what had happened. Hades dismissed the remaining dead, leaving the three of us alone, and the tension was as high as ever between us. I'd searched the faces of the departing souls, but Adonis wasn't among them. No surprise there, really. Only a small percentage of our subjects needed to be judged.

"I'm sorry," said Hermes once he'd finished his horrific story. Adonis had bled to death on the bank of a river, and nausea rolled through me as I imagined his blood mixing with the water. How long had it taken him to die? How badly had it hurt? Had Ares stood there, watching the life drain out of him?

"Do not apologize," said Hades. "For once, this is not your doing. Persephone?"

It was the first time he'd addressed me all winter. I looked up, blinking away my tears. There was no point in crying. I couldn't change the pain Adonis had gone through, and at least now he was safe from Aphrodite's games. "I'm all right," I whispered. "I need to go."

His lips thinned, but even though he must've known exactly where I was going, he nodded. "Very well. Make it quick."

I stood, and without bidding them goodbye, I pushed myself through the space between myself and Adonis's new eternity. In that split second, a barrage of images flashed through my mind—possibilities of his afterlife. The shore where we'd first met. Mother's cottage. Even his childhood home, which I'd never seen, but he'd told me about in passing. What were Adonis's favorite memories? Which ones would he want to surround himself with for the rest of forever?

I held my breath as my feet landed on solid ground once more. Instead of the green forest I'd expected, however, swirls of white surrounded me, and something soft and cold brushed my cheek. Snow.

My feet were buried in several inches of it, and it fell heavily from the gray sky, thick enough that I couldn't see my hands. This couldn't possibly be right.

"Adonis?" I called. I must've managed to land on the edge of another soul's afterlife. One step in the right direction, and this would melt away, returning me to the familiar. "It's me—where are you?"

A groan cut through the silence, and my heart leaped into my throat. I scrambled through the drifts of snow, unused to moving around in it. We didn't exactly get any at Mother's cottage during the summer.

My foot caught on something, and I flew forward, landing on my hands and knees. With my nose to the ground, I saw a patch of crimson leading to a soft mound only a few feet away. And visible through the snow were several locks of familiar blond hair.

No. Not possible. My body turned to ice, and I forced myself to move toward him. Brushing the snow away, I found the mangled remains of a torso slowly healing itself, and my stomach convulsed.

"Adonis," I whispered, brushing away the rest of the snow to reveal his face. His cheeks were as white as the world around us, and his eyes were dull and his lips blue. He blinked slowly, as if every effort to move was a war, and I gently gathered him up.

"Per-Persephone?" he whispered, hoarse.

"Yes, of course." I brushed a few flakes from his forehead. "Come. We're going to get you out of here."

"No." A drop of strength returned, and gritting his teeth, he tried to move from my grip. But he was too weak and I was too determined to never let him go again. "You—you have to—"

"I have to what? Let you suffer like this?"

"I deserve it." He slumped against me. "Please."

"You don't deserve this. No one deserves this."

"I do. For…for hurting you. Aphrodite. Your families." He took a great shuddering breath, and a river of blood flowed from his healing body. What had done this to him? "I saw the look on Hades's face—"

A roar ripped through the quiet, and a great white bear appeared through the veil of snow. It bared its teeth, its muzzle stained with red, and its paw lashed out at me. Sharp claws clashed against my skin, but it did no damage. And I wasn't going to let it hurt Adonis again, either.

"Be gone," I ordered. "I am your queen, and you will obey me."

It let out another roar, standing tall on its hind legs. "Please, let me…" whispered Adonis, and I held him closer.

"No," I said desperately. "You don't deserve this. It was never your battle, all right? Please—you can make this better for yourself. You can control it."

The bear struck again, and as its claws caught my face, I screamed. Not in pain, not in fear, but with unadulterated fury. At myself, at Aphrodite, at this damned and miserable place—this couldn't be Adonis's eternity. It couldn't.

With a thought, I dragged him through the space between his section of the Underworld and the palace, leaving the bear behind. A swirl of snow puffed around us as we landed in the throne room, and in my arms, Adonis groaned. His wounds healed instantly, and his color returned far faster than it would have if he were still alive, but his face still pinched in pain.

"Persephone." Hades stood. "What are you doing?"

"He was torturing himself," I said, helping Adonis sit up. His expression was blank, and he showed no surprise at suddenly appearing in a palace. Not many souls realized where they were, but Adonis should've known.

"So you removed him from his afterlife?"

I wrapped my arms around Adonis. "I had no choice."

"But it was not your choice to make."

"A bear was eating him alive in the middle of a blizzard," I snapped. "I don't care what his religion or beliefs dictate. What did he ever do to deserve that?"

Hades's expression remained painfully neutral. "Some might say that having an affair with not one, but two married goddesses might very well be enough of a catalyst to make him believe he deserved eternal torture."

"He makes me *happy*." My words were thick, and I clung

to Adonis. Hades wouldn't have his way, not this time. "We have to fix this."

"You know the rules. If a mortal does not ask for our guidance, we do not tamper with their afterlife."

"I don't care about your damn rules. I care about Adonis."

"And what of me?" said Hades softly. The pain that had faded during those eons of peace between us flickered across his face, the first hint of emotion I'd seen from him in months. "You are asking me to go against my own laws and condone your affairs."

"I'm asking you to do the right thing. You once told me that all you wanted was for me to be happy. Is that still true?"

Silence, and at last he nodded.

"Adonis makes me happy. He makes me happier than you or Hermes or anyone ever has. Not because he's beautiful, but because we're two halves of the same whole. I found my person, Hades. And I am so sorry—sorrier than I can ever possibly tell you—that it isn't you. But it's Adonis. And I would give up everything to make sure he's all right, even if it meant I could never see him again. It would hurt like hell, but I would do it if it meant getting him out of there." I shifted. "Please. I am begging you—do something."

Hades closed his eyes, his face crumpling. It was the closest I'd ever seen him come to crying. For a long moment he said nothing, and Hermes looked back and forth between us as if deciding whether or not to speak.

"I am sorry," said Hades, his voice nothing but feeble words and anguish. "You know as well as I that there is nothing. The only person who can change his afterlife is Adonis himself."

"Then—then what could make him change it?" I said. "Could we reason with him? Make him see that it's my fault, not his? Could you—forgive him or—"

Hades looked away, the firelight reflecting in his watery

eyes. No, he would not forgive him, and my face burned with shame for even asking. Besides, Adonis wasn't the one he had to forgive. I was.

I buried my face in the crook of Adonis's neck, rocking him back and forth. He couldn't go back there. I would've given anything—my freedom, my love, my entire existence to make sure he didn't, but what did I have that could possibly change his mind?

"I'm sorry," I whispered. "I'm so sorry I wasn't there for you. Please don't do this. Please—isn't there something you want more than to torture yourself?"

He took my hand and brushed his thumb against my palm. Me. He wanted me. Even in the blizzard, he'd called out to me, letting me save him well past the point it should've been possible.

An idea formed in my mind, something so crazy and preposterous that I discarded it immediately. But it cropped up again before I could move on, burrowing itself into my thoughts, refusing to let go.

It was mad. Beyond words. Even as I struggled to find something real, however, it persisted.

I could do it with the council's permission. It would shatter everything, and there would be no going back, but if I did— if Adonis really loved me the way I loved him—it might be crazy enough to work.

"Hermes," I said in as steady a voice as I could muster. "Would you please help Adonis into one of the guest rooms and keep him company? I need to speak with my husband alone."

"Of course," mumbled Hermes, and he helped Adonis to his feet. Adonis stumbled, but he managed to right himself, and at last he let go of my hand. But even as the pair of them walked up the aisle, his touch still lingered on my skin.

Yes. It was mad. It was insane. But I loved him too much not to try.

Once they were gone, I stood and smoothed my dress. "Sit down," I said softly, and though Hades frowned, he obeyed. I took a deep breath. Now or never. "I want to give up my immortality."

His silver eyes widened, and his jaw went lax. Before he could object, I continued.

"The way you feel for me—that's how I feel for Adonis. I love him. He breathed life back into me, and I want nothing more than to spend eternity with him. You would give up your immortality for me. I know you would. And I cannot tell you how much that means to me—how much *you* mean to me, even if I can't show you the way you want me to. But I want to do the same for Adonis. And I need your help."

Hades stared at me for the longest minutes of my life. He didn't blink, he didn't breathe, and even his heart stopped beating. The silence grew around us, heavy with everything we both couldn't say, and at last I reached forward to touch his hand.

"This is the greatest gift you could ever give me," I said softly. "I've spent my existence living a life I never wanted. I couldn't be more grateful for all you've done for me, but we will never be happy together. Not the way I am with Adonis, and not the way you deserve to be. I've done terrible things to you, things I can never make up for, and I've broken more promises than I can count. But if you do this for me, if you support me in front of the council and give me your permission to step down from my throne, I promise I will love you until the sun fades and there is nothing left of me."

A single tear escaped the corner of his eye, trickling down his cheek and pooling at the corner of his mouth. The shadows in the throne room danced with the torches' flames, and for an eternity, our eyes locked together as he searched for something he would never find.

Hades set his free hand over mine, and at last he whispered, "Very well. If it means your happiness, then you may be free."

I touched his cheek, brushing away the glistening trail on his skin. "Thank you."

He nodded once and stood, brushing past me without a word. In his measured gait, he walked up the aisle, and before he could reach the door, he was gone.

The council convened less than an hour later. Whatever Hades had said to get them all to appear must have been something, but then again, no one had tried to give up their immortality before.

I stood in the center of the Olympic throne room, surrounded by the fourteen members of the council. My own throne was gone. Zeus rose as Mother, the final member to join us, took her seat, and my heart hammered. She refused to look at me.

"Daughter," said Zeus, and I inclined my head with as much respect as I could bear to show him. He was the reason I was in this situation to begin with, after all. "Our brother has informed us that you desire to step down from your role as Queen of the Underworld and shed your immortality, all to be with a mortal."

"Yes," I said, glancing at Aphrodite. Her eyes were thin as slits, and she gripped the arms of her throne so tightly that her knuckles were white. Good. "While it pains me deeply to think of leaving all of you, I ask for you to allow me to step away in order to die. Adonis, the mortal I love, is trapped in eternal torture in the Underworld, and the only way I can help him is to give him an afterlife he wants more."

"You are certain this will work?" said Athena.

I shook my head. "I'm afraid it's impossible to say for sure, but I believe it's probable enough to take that chance."

"And what if it doesn't work out?" said Artemis, leaning back in her throne and giving me a look I knew all too well. It was the same look she'd given Aphrodite every time she went on and on about one of her new *friends*.

I hesitated. What if it didn't? What if I were doing this for nothing? There would be no going back. Once I was mortal and dead, I would be another one of Hades's subjects, nothing more. I would be powerless and alone, trapped in the Under-world for eternity—

And how was that any different from my life now?

I squared my shoulders. "I love Adonis. I love him more than my own existence, and I believe he feels the same for me. I understand the consequences if I'm wrong. I understand what I'm giving up regardless, and I'm willing to take that chance."

"You would leave us?"

Mother's voice cut through my skin, burrowing into a part of me no one else could touch. Not Adonis, not Hades, no one. I looked at her, and the agony I saw in place of Mother—

A lump formed in my throat. I hadn't thought it possible for this to hurt anyone more than Hades, but it had never occurred to me that Mother might still care. She'd walked away from me. She'd never listened when I'd told her how miserable I was, and again and again and again she'd insisted things would get better. They never had though, not the way she wanted them to, and because of that, I was sure I'd lost her.

Maybe I hadn't lost her before, but as I watched her shatter into infinite pieces, I knew I had now.

"If the council grants me my request, I would like nothing more than to see all of you as often as you'd be willing to visit me," I said unsteadily. "I would still be eternal, just in another form, and it wouldn't have to be goodbye unless you wanted it to be."

Mother said nothing to that, and beside Zeus, Hera cleared her throat. "Do you love him more than Hades?" she said in her girlish voice.

I frowned. Did Hera not understand what had happened between me and Hades? Or was she just searching for affirmation? "Hades is my friend. He will always be my friend, but we never fit. We've tried for thousands of miserable years. I can't love him the way he wants me to, and the way I'm forced to linger just out of his reach is torture for him. I don't want to hurt him more than I already have, and the only way I trust myself to do that is to step down and leave him completely."

The council members all turned to look at Hades, who remained stoic as ever in his throne. Hera pressed her lips together, and I could've sworn I saw a hint of a smile. Why? Because someone was finally as miserable as she was?

It didn't matter. She could think whatever she wanted as long as she let me go. "This isn't an easy decision for me, and I'm more terrified than I've ever been in my life," I said. "But Adonis needs this. Whatever I'm feeling is nothing compared to ensuring his eternity. Please—I know this is unprecedented. I know it'll throw everything into chaos for a while. But if you allow this, eventually the wounds will heal. If you do not, they'll fester until Hades and I both shrivel into ash."

"And you are all right with this, brother?" said Zeus.

"I am," said Hades hollowly. "I have seen enough to know that she speaks the truth, and I wish nothing more for her than eternal happiness. I ask the same of you all, as well."

A murmur rippled through the council, and Zeus raised his hand, silencing them. "Very well. We will take a vote. Given the weight of the matter at hand, I ask that we all be unanimous in our decision." He cast his gaze around the circle, focusing on each of us individually. "Those who agree to grant Persephone's request?"

I held my breath, and one by one, the members of the council nodded. Hera first, then Ares, then Hephaestus—Artemis, Apollo, Athena, Hestia, Poseidon, Dionysus, even Hermes. Even Hades.

And though her eyes shined with unshed tears, even Mother.

But despite the others' consent, Aphrodite remained still. Seconds passed in silence, and finally Zeus said, "And you, my daughter?"

"No." She clenched her jaw so tightly that the cords in her neck stood out. "I won't agree. She barely knows Adonis—she stole him from me, and she's betrayed Hades and the council's wishes repeatedly. I don't see any reason to reward her for it."

I opened my mouth to retort, but Zeus raised a hand again, and I fell silent. "Are those your only objections, Aphrodite?"

"Do you really need more? Because I have them."

In a gentle voice he only used with her, he murmured, "Is it possible you feel this way out of jealousy and grief? He did only die this evening."

"He did," she said, her voice shaking. "And the only reason he did is because she insisted I leave him. She couldn't stand the thought that he might love me more."

Fury coiled in the pit of my stomach, hot and unyielding. If that was the kind of game she was going to play, then forget silence. "I don't *care* if he loves you more," I said. "Don't you get that? It has nothing to do with you, and it never did. He's suffering. He's torturing himself because of what we did to him, and I don't care if he hates me. I love him too much to let him go through that, and I will do whatever I can to make sure he doesn't have to, even if it means giving this up. Even if it means spending the rest of my existence alone."

Aphrodite said nothing, and her entire being seemed to burn with vehemence. Rather than wearing her down, as I'd hoped, my words only seemed to reinforce her hatred. Terrific.

Zeus sighed. "Aphrodite, I will give you one more chance. Yay or nay?"

"Nay," she said. "And it will be nay no matter how many times you ask or how often she begs. I will not allow her to win."

I let out a frustrated noise in the back of my throat. Didn't she get it? It wasn't about winning. It was about Adonis and his well-being and making sure he didn't spend eternity in the cold, being eaten alive by a bear. But she didn't care—all Aphrodite could see was the fact that I would be with him and she wouldn't.

I may have been selfish for hurting Hades the way I did, but in that moment, Aphrodite was more selfish than any of us. Because of pride or lust or envy or all three, she would stop Adonis from having the afterlife he deserved, and I hated her. I hated her more than I'd hated anyone, even myself.

Zeus straightened, a flicker of regret passing over his face, and he let out another weary sigh. "So be it. As you have made it clear you are incapable of ruling without bias, I am forced to overturn your vote."

Both my mouth and Aphrodite's dropped open simultaneously. *"What?"* she screeched. "Daddy, you can't—"

"I can, and as you have given me no choice, I will," he said. "Persephone, your request is granted. When you return to the surface, you will be mortal. Take a moment to say your goodbyes. Aphrodite, if you would follow me."

She sputtered in protest, and as he made his way into one of the hallways, she stormed after him. Once she was gone and silence filled the throne room, I looked around at the members of my family, growing dizzy as reality set in.

I was going to be mortal. I was going to die.

And I would never come back here again.

But even as I thought it, I pictured Adonis's face in the snow and the bear that loomed over him. Even if it didn't work and he remained in his frozen hell forever, at least I would have the satisfaction of knowing I'd tried. I would find him no matter how long it took me to scour the Underworld. And even if all I could do was hold his hand as he suffered, then at least I would be there for him for eternity.

One by one, the members of the council said goodbye. My brothers and sisters hugged me, even Ares, and Hestia and Poseidon kissed my cheeks. Hera smiled as she embraced me, and as her lips brushed against the shell of my ear, she murmured, "You made the right decision. You deserve the future you want, and you would have never been happy with Hades."

Something about the way she said it sent a shiver down my spine, reinforcing the wall that had stood between Hades and me since our wedding. That war was over now though, and neither Hades nor I had won. But at least we wouldn't end up like Hera and Zeus.

Finally it was Hermes's turn. He gave me a small smile that didn't reach his eyes, and despite everything between us, he trapped me in a giant bear hug. "I'll miss you," he said. "Things won't be the same without you."

"You'll know where to find me if you ever get bored," I said, but even if he did make the trek, he was right—things would never be the same. "Take care. And do yourself a favor and stay away from Aphrodite, would you?"

He snorted, but a cloud passed over his face, as well. I didn't understand what it meant—then again, maybe I wasn't supposed to. We all had our demons, and Hermes would have the chance to face his when he was ready.

Once he let me go, I turned toward Mother, who stood

stiffly beside her throne. Her eyes were trained on the floor, her hands clasped tightly together, and as I took a step toward her, she backed away. With that one movement, my heart broke completely.

"I hope you are happy," she said in a strange, almost formal voice. "I will come see you when I can."

"Thank you," I whispered, though we both knew that if she did come, it wouldn't be for a very long time. We'd both made mistakes, and it would take a lot more than this to fix the rift between us. But despite everything that had happened, I ached for the certainty that one day, things would be okay again. No matter how long it took.

Hermes slipped his arm into hers, and as he led her from the throne room, he glanced over his shoulder to give me one more smile. Mother didn't look back.

I took a deep, shuddering breath. Hades and I were alone now, standing face-to-face, and I had no idea what to say. I should've apologized. I should've thanked him. I should've said a million things, but nothing came out.

"Are you ready?" he said quietly, and I nodded. He took my hand, and as I gazed around Olympus one last time, the sky-blue ceiling and sunset floor faded. This was it, the moment I'd been racing toward ever since Adonis had taken his last breath. But no matter how frightened I was of mortality, of what it would be like to need to breathe, of what it would be like to feel pain and the world around me as a mortal, a sense of calm washed over me, as well. I'd made the right decision. That was all I needed.

When we landed, a sharp pinch jolted through the bottom of my foot, and I opened my eyes. We stood in Mother's cottage, and the moonlight seemed to light up every corner. I shifted my weight, and underneath my foot I found the source of that jabbing sensation: a pebble.

So this was what it was like to be mortal. I set my hand over my chest, feeling my heart beat, and I drew in each breath with care. Everything felt like it was *more* somehow—smoother, rougher, hotter, colder, all of it. It was as if I'd woken up from a deep sleep, and I was only now aware of the world around me.

"Are you all right?" said Hades, and I nodded.

"It's just…odd."

He smiled sadly. "I cannot imagine."

We stood there side by side for a long moment, and all I did was breathe. In and out, in and out, memorizing the awareness of mortality. How was it possible to feel so alive every day and not burst?

But as much as I enjoyed it, it couldn't last forever, and I didn't want it to. I sat down on the edge of the bed and shoved my trembling hands between my knees. "I'm ready. How…?"

"Leave that to me," he said quietly. "Make yourself comfortable."

I lay down in the bed, my heart pounding so hard that it actually hurt. "I'm scared," I whispered, and Hades took my hand. I'd never realized how soft and smooth his skin was.

"Do not be," he said. "I promise everything will be all right."

For once, I believed him. "Thank you," I whispered. "I know I was never very good at showing it, but you're my best friend. Even when things were rotten, you were always there no matter what I did to you. I'm so sorry for everything."

"What's done is done," he said quietly. "All I have ever wanted was for you to be happy, and if this is the way…"

"It is." I propped myself up on my elbow. "This is exactly what I want."

He stared down at our joined hands, his expression forlorn, and he said nothing. He really had been so damn wonderful to me—maybe I hadn't seen it at the time, but I did now. He deserved so much better than what I'd given him, and in that moment, I wanted nothing more than for him to find it. I was only sorry it'd taken me so long to realize it.

Before I could stop myself, I leaned in and touched my mouth to his. It was a gentle, tender kiss, the kind he'd given me the night we'd nearly slept together a second time. Now I was glad he'd stopped me. Between us, we had enough regrets without inviting more.

Warmth spread through me as I moved my lips against his, and all too soon, he pulled away. For several seconds, neither of us said anything, and my heartbeat resonated in my ears. How was I supposed to say goodbye when I'd spent my life thinking I would never have to?

"I will be there for you whenever you need me," he whispered. "All you need to do is ask."

A lump formed in my throat. "Thank you. Come visit me sometime, yeah?"

But even as he nodded, I knew he never would, and asking him was cruel. He deserved the chance to move on. We both did.

"Lie back," he murmured, and I obeyed. His silver eyes met mine, and as the weight of sleep pressed down upon me, he gave me one final smile. I returned it.

"I love you," I whispered, and he was silent. At last my eyelids grew heavy, and darkness closed in around me as eternity claimed me as her own. It was painless, peaceful, everything death should have been, and I went quietly. I went gladly.

The last thing I saw was him.

The sun in my afterlife wasn't as warm or as bright as the real thing, but it was enough to wake me.

I shielded my eyes, squinting at my surroundings. I lay in the bed that I'd died in, but it was daylight now. Somewhere in the distance, birds chirped and a strong breeze rustled the trees, and the flowers hanging from the rafters of Mother's cottage filled the room with the most incredible scent.

So this was what my afterlife would be.

My afterlife. Adonis. I scrambled to my feet and looked around the one-room home, but he wasn't there. My heart sank. He had to be here. After everything that had happened, he deserved peace.

I pushed open the door and stepped into the artificial sun. It wasn't the real thing—beyond the illusion of my afterlife, I was among the dead in the caverns of the Underworld, surrounded by the very rock I'd hated for eternity. The unbearable weight was gone though, along with the wall that had haunted me for eons. Apparently they'd died with my mortal body, leaving my soul free. Finally.

Inhaling deeply, I looked around my afterlife. Flowers bloomed in the garden, a rainbow of colors and as fresh and new as the spring, and the scent of a summer day wafted through the air. It was beautiful, but it couldn't be perfect, not without—

A figure appeared on the path, shaded by the trees, and warmth filled every inch of me. As he stepped into the sunlight, I grinned and launched myself down the path.

Adonis.

He caught me in an embrace, his strong arms lifting me into the air, and he kissed me with the same love and passion and happiness that coursed through my body. Every doubt and regret I'd entertained in those few seconds without him vanished, and in that moment, I saw our eternity.

He was here. We were together.

And at long last, I was home.

★ ★ ★ ★ ★

GOD
OF
THIƐVƐS

There's a rumor going around that I stole my big brother's cattle the day I was born. That hours into my life, I not only managed to wrangle fifty prized cows and hide them from Apollo, but I invented the lute, as well.

Hours into my life. Not days, not years, but *hours*.

Come on. I'm good, but I'm not that good.

So let's set the record straight: I was seven when I invented the lute, and Apollo spent the next four years trying to steal it from me. But since he's not me, he failed time and time again, and that's when I stole his cattle to see if I could—when I was eleven.

Eleven years old, not eleven hours old. I guess it sounds better to say that a newborn did all those things, somehow making me more godlike or powerful, but I've never met a newborn who could sit up, let alone herd cattle.

It'd be pretty cool though, I have to admit.

But it did get one thing right: Apollo was pissed. And I did have to give him my favorite lute in return for not getting thrown off Olympus. So there's that.

Ever since, it feels like I've been living that down. Every

time I do something the council doesn't like, Zeus rolls his eyes and brings it up again, while Apollo sits there smugly. I don't know what they expect—I'm just doing my job, exactly like all the others. No need for them to act all high and mighty and ignore me.

But this time, I admit I deserved it. I sat in the otherwise empty throne room of Olympus, throwing a ball against the wall and catching it as it flew past me. Nothing much happened in the throne room without the council present, but it was never completely abandoned for this long, and I knew exactly why.

Me.

Ever since Persephone had given up her immortality and single-handedly thrown the council into chaos three decades ago, I'd been persona non grata. No one spoke to me. My suggestions during meetings were completely ignored. Even the minor gods and goddesses gave me the cold shoulder, as if being a pariah was contagious or something. For all I knew, it was. One touch and they'd never have a decent conversation again.

Normally it wouldn't have bothered me as much as it did. Wasn't the first time I'd been shoved into social exile, after all. But this time Zeus hadn't brought up cattle even once. And when Zeus missed an opportunity like that, clearly it was serious.

Funny thing is, none of this was my fault. If they were going to blame someone, they should've blamed Aphrodite or Ares. She was the one who'd messed things up so badly with Adonis, after all, and Ares had been the one to kill him. I'd just had an affair with Persephone eons ago.

That was it. That was my entire involvement—falling in love with my best friend and giving her some freedom when everyone else had been trying to keep her in chains. Not exactly a capital crime if you ask me, but no one ever does.

The council needed a scapegoat though, and I was convenient. No way Zeus would ever punish Aphrodite for anything, or Ares, Hera's favorite son. So I, the screwup, was forced to take the blame even though I'd never said a single word to Adonis.

Not fair, not at all, but the council doesn't exactly run on fairness.

Scowling, I threw the ball hard against the wall, and it bounced off at an angle, heading directly toward the circle of thrones in the center of the room. With a muttered curse, I stood. Couldn't give Zeus any more of a reason to get pissed off at me. I was already way over the line as it was, at least as far as he saw it. And on the council, that was all that mattered.

"Looking for this?"

At the sound of that familiar voice, I grinned and turned around. Apparently not everyone had completely given up on me. Just almost everyone. "Iris. Haven't seen you for a few decades."

"Zeus sent me on a scouting trip." She examined the rubber ball and gave it a tentative bounce. "It wasn't pleasant. Besides the fact that it took half a damn century, a lion tried to eat me, and he looked awfully confused when his teeth and claws seemed to stop working."

"Shame he didn't succeed." I leaned up against the wall, crossing my arms. "I could use a new job."

"As if you could do a tenth of what I do."

I snorted. "Please. Zeus only lets you be his messenger because no one else wants the job. And you don't snitch on him to Hera. Or gossip about his affairs. That's more than just about any other minor god or goddess out there, you know."

A dimple appeared on her cheek, one that only showed up

when she was annoyed. Usually with me. "I am *anything* but minor. What's wrong with the job you have now?"

"You mean you haven't heard?" I said, raising my eyebrow. Then again, she *was* talking to me. Couldn't have known much. "Persephone gave up her immortality. Rather than everyone blaming someone who actually had something to do with it, they all decided to gang up on me instead."

Iris's eyes widened, and she seemed to forget about the ball in midair. With a dull thump, it hit her on the head, right in the middle of her coppery curls. "Wait—you mean that actually happened?"

I eyed her. Was she pretending to be clueless to get my side of the story, or did she really not know? "What have you heard? Kick the ball my way, would you?"

She made a halfhearted attempt, but the ball only rolled three-quarters of the way back to me. Figured. "I heard whispers. Nothing confirmed. Then again, I haven't exactly been in the center of things lately."

No, she hadn't, which was a damn good thing for me. "Persephone fell in love with a mortal. Unfortunately for her, Aphrodite was already sleeping with him—"

"Who isn't Aphrodite sleeping with?" muttered Iris, and I smirked.

"Ares was his usual violent self and decided to take out the competition. Wild boar," I added when her mouth opened. She winced and touched her stomach in sympathy. "Apparently the mortal's afterlife wasn't so great, so Persephone decided to sacrifice her immortality and die in order to give him an incentive to leave his own personal hell for something better."

"Oh." Iris let out a romantic little sigh, and now it was my turn to make a face. "Did it work?"

I shrugged and averted my eyes under the guise of fetching the ball. "No idea."

"You mean Hades hasn't mentioned it?"

"We're not exactly on speaking terms."

"No surprise there. But none of the others brought it up?"

"We're not exactly on speaking terms, either."

Her eyebrows arched. "They're taking this whole ganging up thing seriously, aren't they?"

"You're telling me," I muttered.

She crossed the space between us and set her hand on my cheek. Against my better judgment, I tilted my head into her touch. First time anyone had bothered in months. For a second, our gazes met, and her weird purple irises seemed to turn an even darker shade of violet.

"Your eyes are the shade of ripe grapes," I said. "What does that mean?"

She dropped her hand and gave me a look, and her eyes reverted to their normal purple. Or at least it was normal around me. They changed color with her mood, I knew that much—sort of like Persephone's hair with the seasons—but what those colors meant, she refused to tell me. Not that I blamed her, but still. The few clues I had weren't much to go on. When I wasn't public enemy number one, Ares had informed me in no uncertain terms that her eyes were blue, and Aphrodite swore up and down they were green.

Didn't matter anyway. Eyes were eyes, and Iris didn't deserve to have her emotions splashed all over the place. We might not have been big on privacy, but even that was crossing the line.

"I'm sorry," she said. "It's terrible of them to put you through that. Not even you deserve the cold shoulder from your whole family, even if you are an ass."

"I think that's about the sweetest thing you've ever said to me."

"Yeah, well, don't get used to it." She touched my hand

this time, barely a brush, but again it was more affection than anyone else had shown me. "I'm afraid I don't exactly have the best news, either. You might want to stick around—there's a good chance Zeus is going to call a meeting as soon as I find him."

Fantastic. Another opportunity for the rest of the council to pretend I didn't exist. "What sort of news?"

"The kind they'll need Hades for," she said, and I grimaced. Definitely not good. Hades normally avoided coming up here, only bothering for the big stuff that would affect his realm, too. And the things that affected the Underworld were never warm and fuzzy. Or easy to work out.

So much for having a halfway decent day, relatively speaking. And with Iris back, it would have been.

Sure enough, shortly after she ran off to track down Zeus, a booming voice filled my head. *The council will convene in five minutes. Everyone is required to attend.*

Apparently Iris hadn't been overreacting. I couldn't remember the last time I'd been *required* to attend a council meeting. Generally everyone came because if we didn't, we'd risk getting kicked off, and going from kings to paupers wasn't exactly the greatest feeling in the world. But being required to come was definitely something new.

I reached my throne first, of course, considering I was in the room anyway. Everyone else arrived promptly, and even Hades made it in under the wire, appearing right as Zeus took his seat. I eyed my father's face. Brow knit, prominent frown. His usual cheery self.

"I am afraid Iris has brought news of Helios and Selene," he said quietly. That was odd. No formal announcement that the meeting had started, no showing off and making sure everyone knew he was the one in charge. Just this. Dread settled over me. This wouldn't be good.

"What about them?" said Demeter, her frown matching Zeus's. At least I wasn't the only one who had no idea what was going on. Why was Zeus worrying about Helios and Selene anyway? They were ancient gods, older than Athena, and while they weren't part of the original six siblings that formed the council, they were powerful in their own right. God of the Sun and Goddess of the Moon, at least until Apollo and Artemis had more or less hijacked their roles. No doubt they could take care of themselves without Zeus's so-called help.

He hesitated, focusing on the portal in the middle of our circle. "They're gone."

A murmur rippled through the council, and I sat up straighter. "What do you mean, gone?"

But of course Zeus didn't respond. After ignoring me for so long, it was entirely possible he'd trained himself to tune me out. Wouldn't put it past him. Across from me, however, Ares jumped to his feet, already reaching for his sheathed sword. Typical.

"We will scour the world until we find them, and we will show their captors what happens when one dares to kidnap a god," he growled. "Hermes! Where are they?"

So now they wanted to talk to me, when I was the only one who could help them. But I wasn't exactly in a position to demand any niceties, so with a sigh, I closed my eyes and dived down, focusing on the one clear memory I had of Helios. When I was six, he took me for a ride in his chariot— which, contrary to popular belief at that point in time, was not actually the sun. Just a representation of it, more or less. And that was when I spotted Apollo's cattle, and the plotting started from there.

I focused on Helios's face. Tan, with deep-set pale eyes and a narrow nose. The details were important; names sometimes weren't enough, and the more I could picture who or what I wanted to find, the easier it was. Though I didn't actually go anywhere, I felt as if I was flying above the earth, scouring the land for any sign of him. He'd be easy enough to spot—whatever I wanted to find stood out like sunshine against the greens and browns of earth.

But I couldn't find him. I mentally circled the world three times, but nothing jumped out at me.

Great. I repeated the process again, this time picturing Selene's pale, oval face and her doe eyes. I'd never met anyone who looked like her before, and it should've been easy to spot that unique glow.

Three times around again, and still nothing. I huffed with frustration. This never happened. I always found what I was looking for.

I opened my eyes, and everyone—even Demeter and Hades—was staring at me. My lips thinned. This wasn't exactly the break I needed to get back on their good side. "I couldn't find them."

"What do you mean—" started Ares, but I cut him off.

"I mean, I couldn't find them," I snapped.

"Did you check the cold lands?" said Ares, and I nodded. "What about the Underworld?"

"Of course." I wasn't stupid. "They aren't anywhere."

Silence. Ares sat back down slowly, while everyone else glanced at one another, too afraid to say anything.

"You are sure?" said Zeus in a low voice, glaring at me as if this was my fault.

"I'm sure," I said. "I checked three times. It's like they don't exist anymore."

"Cronus warned us this might happen," said Hera. "He said we would not last forever, dependent as we are on mortals. Our purpose is so wrapped up in them that when we are no longer needed—"

"But who among us is more necessary to mortal life than the sun and the moon?" said Demeter. The two of them glared at each other, and while normally I would've been on the edge of my seat in anticipation of a catfight, somehow now didn't seem like the time.

Hera raised her chin half an inch so she could look down her nose at Demeter. Not that I was judging—I wasn't Demeter's biggest fan right now, either, after the way she'd treated Persephone. But still. Life and death, people. "I hardly see their importance now that Apollo and Artemis have usurped their roles."

"We didn't usurp anything," said Artemis, bristling. On the other hand, maybe a catfight would help take our minds off this. "We apprenticed with them. We didn't steal their jobs."

"And yet here we are, with every shred of evidence pointing to Helios and Selene having faded," said Hera. "Tell me, do you have any other explanation?"

Artemis clenched her hands. "I don't know. Maybe Rhea went rogue."

"And decided to kill them instead of us? I highly doubt it."

Poseidon cleared his throat. He never spoke up much during meetings, since we mostly dealt with mortal problems, and the sea was his realm. But when he did, everyone paid attention. "If Hermes believes they are no longer present in any of the realms, then we have no reason to question it. His judgment is as sound as each of ours."

Across from me, Hades hissed, but he said nothing. Coward. If he had something to say to me, he should've said it to my face.

"Hermes, do you believe they are gone?" said Zeus, and I nodded. Had to focus on the big picture here. Hades was never going to like me again no matter what I did—no point in wasting energy trying to win him over.

"If I can't find them, then they're nowhere at all. And the only explanation is that they've faded."

A hush settled over the council again, and in the throne beside Ares, Aphrodite dabbed her eyes. "Are we next?"

"No." Hephaestus set his hand over hers, ignoring Ares's glares. "We are simply too important to fade like that."

"So were Helios and Selene and who knows how many others," said Athena. "How can we possibly be sure this isn't the end of the age of gods?"

"How could it be?" said Hera. "Perhaps some minor gods may be facing the end, but we are indispensable. Mortals still need us."

"For how long?" said Athena. "For another century? Millennia? How long until they have moved beyond us? Whether we want to acknowledge it or not, we are in danger, and we cannot continue to revel in ignorance. We must figure out why this is happening. If Helios and Selene are missing, there may be others, and our best shot is to find out who is gone and discover a common link."

"I can help with that," I said. It would take a while, tracking down every single god and goddess, but if it meant they would start treating me like family instead of a fungus, the time and effort had to be worth it. "And maybe I could go down to the surface as well, see what I can find."

"Are you sure that is wise?" Hades's voice seemed to fill the throne room, even though he was practically whispering. "May I remind the council what happened the last time Hermes offered his help where it was not welcome?"

My face grew hot. Who the hell did he think he was, talking to me like that? "Persephone has nothing to do with this," I said.

"On the contrary. Perhaps if you had not been so engrossed

in your affair, you would have done your duties and realized Helios's and Selene's absences sooner."

So we were back to this again. "That was thousands of years ago," I said through gritted teeth. "I am not Adonis. She did not die for me. Get over it already."

"I will get over it when we are even," he said, and a rumble of thunder interrupted my retort.

"Enough," said Zeus quietly. "Bicker in your own time. Hermes, we will need to know who is still among us and who else has faded as soon as possible. But I do not see what mingling with mortals will accomplish."

"But Athena just said—"

"Let Athena and the others deal with that," he said. "You have your orders. Now, for once, do as you are told."

Yes, I did have my orders: be mindlessly obedient when they needed me, and when they didn't, shut up and be invisible, because no one wanted me there anyway. I'd been in trouble before—who hasn't?—but this was a whole new level of punishment. I would've taken being banished from Olympus any day over being pushed out of my family.

But I didn't protest, because it wouldn't have changed things anyway, and I'd need my strength for this job. Social exile was exhausting enough as it was, and lethargy wasn't a good look on me.

Zeus handed out a few more jobs, none of which consisted of going down to the surface and actually talking to mortals to see where we stood, and the council adjourned. Seconds later, Zeus floated a scroll toward me. Apparently not even my father wanted to get close enough to touch me.

"A list of every god and goddess we know of," he said. "If you value your place on the council, you will have your report to me this time tomorrow."

If I— Was he serious? Was he really going to strip me of my throne if I didn't get this to him in time?

No, it had to be some kind of mind game. A way to scare me into submission, nothing more. Zeus had worked far too hard to ensure that the council was under his thumb, and if he upset the balance by removing me, Hera would be one vote away from taking the crown.

Then again, maybe he'd use me as an example. Show that anyone who dared to defy him was one swift kick in the ass away from joining Helios and Selene in the unknown. Either way, I didn't have much time.

I uncurled the scroll, and my eyes nearly popped out of my head. The list was endless. "You want me to find every single person on this list by tomorrow?"

No reply. I looked up, and Zeus's throne was empty. Perfect. I glanced down at the scroll again and scowled. One day. Countless names. And no one to help me, because the entire council thought I was the plague.

Maybe that's what Zeus was counting on—I'd fail, and he'd have a valid reason to remove me from Olympus. And if that were the case, maybe I'd be better off a drifter anyway. If I didn't fade completely.

I wouldn't go down without a fight, though. Not now, not ever, which meant I had one option in the next twenty-four hours: prove Zeus wrong, no matter how impossible.

Usually I didn't need sleep. I could go weeks, if not months without it when I wasn't using my powers—all of us could. But before I was halfway done with that list, I needed sleep more desperately than I'd ever needed anything in my entire life.

I leaned against the golden wall of the throne room, struggling to keep my eyes open. I couldn't fall asleep. Time was precious enough as it was, and if Zeus knew I'd been sleep-ing on the job, too—

Right. I liked my ass right where it was, thank you. I leaned forward and forced myself to focus on the list of names. Next up was Pollux. Not too hard to find him and Castor, even though they were on the run, so at least this wouldn't take much effort.

"How're you holding up?" Iris crossed the throne room, balancing a tray in her hands.

"I'm seriously considering running away and spending the rest of eternity holed up in the woods," I said. "What's that?"

"I brought you some tea. Figured you might need it."

That was oddly nice of her. Maybe Zeus had laid into her, too. "Thanks," I said, stretching. She sat beside me, and I picked up the cup and sipped. It wasn't a solid night's sleep, but it would do. "I mean it, though. There's no way I'm finish-ing this list. Ten hours left, and I'm not even halfway done."

She smirked, but there was a hint of sympathy behind it, too. "When Zeus fires you, make sure to put in a good word for me, would you?"

It would've been funny if it hadn't been so true, and I glow-ered into my tea. "Zeus said if I don't finish in time, I really will be kicked off the council."

"Zeus likes to say a lot of things. Most of them aren't true."

"This is, though." I nudged the list in her direction. "You didn't happen to run into any of these gods on your trip, did you?"

She examined the names, and with a wave of her hand, she crossed off well over two dozen. "I know where to find loads more. If you want, I can check out a few places. That'll cut your list down, as well."

"You'd really do that for me?" I said. "What about want-ing my job?"

Iris shrugged, and a curl escaped from behind her ear. "I'll take pity on you just this once. Are you serious about running away?"

I leaned my head against the wall. If it were possible for immortals to have headaches, I would've had a raging one right about now. "Hermit jokes aside, someone needs to figure out what's causing all of this. None of the others have spent time with mortals like I have."

"And yet Zeus won't let you go?"

"You know how he is. Can't handle someone else having a better grip on things than he does."

Iris gave me a look. "So while gods and goddesses are mysteriously dying for reasons the council can't possibly be sure of, you're going to listen to Zeus for the first time in your life."

"He'd track me down the instant he knew I was gone. You know that."

"Unless..." Her fingers danced over the parchment, an inch from my knee. "Someone kind, generous, thoughtful and extremely beautiful covered for you."

I raised an eyebrow. "Do you think someone like that actually exists?"

She punched me in the arm. "You're a jerk. Maybe I won't help you. Bet I could do your job with both hands tied behind my back."

"Right now I'm not sure *I* can do my job, not if Hades keeps acting like this. And not if Zeus keeps giving me impossible tasks."

"Hades will come around eventually, and we'll work together on this list," she said. "I'll go down to the surface and check things out. You focus on the names I've circled, all right? But on one condition—after you finish this, you're going to sneak off and mingle with mortals. I'll cover for you."

I glanced down at the list. Somehow she'd narrowed it down to a manageable number. "Really?"

"Really." She squeezed my arm. "Some things are more important than kissing Zeus's ass."

Coming from Iris, that meant loads. "If we get through this, remind me to tell you I love you."

She snorted, though her cheeks turned pink. "Please. I know you love me. It practically oozes out of you." Giving me a pat on the hand, she stood. "Don't fall asleep, lazy, else I really will have no choice but to replace you, bloodlines be damned."

"Whatever you say," I said with a tired grin. But the tea helped, and if she stuck to her word, this might be doable, after all. "And Iris?"

She stopped, inches from the portal. "Yeah?"

"Thanks. You're not nearly as heinous as everyone says you are."

Rolling her eyes, she stepped into the crystal circle and grinned. "You really are such a jerk."

Together, Iris and I finished the list by the time the council reconvened. No idea how we managed it—magic, probably, or some sort of tear in time—but we did.

Six names were unaccounted for. Older gods and goddesses whose roles had been taken over by newer ones. I'd triple-checked those to make sure, but it wasn't good news. Neither of us could find them. I should've stayed to tell the council; someone had to, after all, but by the time we finished, Iris was practically pushing me toward the portal.

"Go," she said. "I mean it. I'll give the list to Zeus."

"He'll smite you if he finds out you're covering for me. Sure it's worth it?" I said.

"Yes, I'm sure. Besides, if you figure this out, maybe they'll forgive you for the whole Persephone thing."

I frowned. Right. I didn't need another reminder, but it was a possibility. Maybe they *would* forgive me. Maybe this would be enough to get me back on the council's good side. Doubtful, but worth a shot.

Iris sighed dramatically and gave me a little shove. "Why do you always have to be so difficult? Get your ass down there before I have to drag you to the balcony and throw you."

"Fine, fine, I'm going. Be safe, all right? Don't disappear in a puff of smoke or whatever."

"You, too," she said. "And don't come back until you've figured this thing out."

"Which might be never."

"By then, we'll all be gone, so it won't matter." She stood on her tiptoes and brushed her lips against my cheek. Unexpected, and my face grew hot. Iris laughed. "For luck, not to feed your fantasies. Now get out of here."

Footsteps sounded from one of the hallways, and I didn't need any more encouragement. I hopped onto the portal and gave Iris a halfhearted wave. This wasn't one of our better ideas, but we didn't have much choice. The gods were dying off. Even if we had several eons before the council faded, that wasn't a chance any of us could take. Zeus was an idiot for playing it safe.

I slid through the portal with ease, and in the midst of dropping to the surface, I closed my eyes and relaxed. The solution had to be somewhere on the surface. A book, a town, some kind of religious theory—whatever it was that would bring me closer to understanding why we were dying.

That sort of hazy thought didn't always work, and when I landed in the trees, I cursed. I'd expected to wind up in Rome or a library or something—somewhere with books and knowledge and answers, the kind Athena always seemed so good at finding. I didn't have a chance of unearthing anything like that in the middle of a forest.

But when I started a more focused sweep of the surface, something twanged in my core, pulling me south. Not the kind of connection I usually got whenever something I was looking for was within reach—instead, it was a vague feeling that made me want to kick a tree. Vague wouldn't solve this problem. It wouldn't give me answers. And it sure as hell wouldn't save my family.

Not as if I had a lot of leads though, and I needed time to cool down before I tried again. With Iris helping me with the list, I'd had time for a short nap, but exhaustion did nothing for my temper. And I'd be no good to the council pissed off.

I took a deep breath. It wasn't my fault Hades was acting like an ass, and it wasn't my fault Persephone had chosen to give up her immortality. Everyone liked to pretend it was, but it wasn't, and I forced that one simple truth down my own throat. I was a scapegoat. And the only way I could make them see it was by finding a solution.

So I kept walking. The forest grew dim as the sun dipped below the horizon, and owls began to call to one another. Most mortals feared night, but I loved it. Quiet, dark, gave me time to think, and nothing seemed as bad as it did when the sun was out. I relaxed soon enough, letting my anger drain away, replaced by determination. I would figure this out, my family would accept me again and no one else would fade. I'd be a hero, and not even Hades would be able to treat me like the villain anymore. Everything would go back to normal, and that's all I wanted. To act like none of this Persephone drama had ever happened.

Soon enough, I stumbled onto a trail. It wasn't much— mostly a path that looked wide enough to fit a horse, but that was about it. It looked well traveled though, and that tug in my stomach grew stronger with each step. Maybe all of this self-loathing had thrown my powers out of whack. I didn't see how the secret to our immortal existence could possibly be hidden here.

But I had to find whatever it was that pulled me in this direction. Whether or not my inner compass was broken, something was going on in these trees, and I needed a bit of fun right about now.

I'd been on the trail for five minutes when I heard it—a faint crackle, as if someone with loads of experience sneaking up on people was walking on dead leaves. Excellent. Things were about to get interesting.

The first one appeared seconds later. He couldn't have been older than nine, and he cried out at the top of his lungs as he ran toward me, brandishing a stick like a sword. I stopped, bemused. Did he really think he could hurt me?

To my surprise, he skidded to a stop a few feet away, his eyes wide. "What're you gonna do, just stand there and stare?"

"Was there something else you wanted me to do?" I said. Another set of footsteps behind me; a third pair to my left, and a fourth to my right. It didn't take an idiot to figure out I was being ambushed. By children, apparently.

"Yeah," he said, puffing out his chest. "Hand over your things."

"What things?" I held out my arms. I wore a simple tunic, not unlike the one he had on, and a pair of trousers. Judging by the style, I was in…England. Probably. "My clothes?"

"Your valuables," said a second voice to my left, deeper than the first. "Jewelry. Food."

"Does it look like I have any on me?"

"Then where did you set up camp?"

"Nowhere." At least that was the truth, even if the look

on the first boy's face told me he didn't believe it. "I'm just walking."

"Where?" said the same deep voice.

"Well, that's none of your business, isn't it?"

"We just made it our business."

The thief behind me shoved me hard, and I landed at the first boy's feet. "Are you sure you want to do this?" I said calmly, making no move to stand. They'd just push me down again anyway.

The second boy's answer was a swift kick to my ribs. Perfect. Now I was going to have to either fight or run like hell, and I wasn't in the mood to take off like that.

Instead I fell over as any mortal would, clutching my ribs halfheartedly. It wasn't much of a ruse, but the second boy continued to kick me, while the first screeched, "Your gold or your life!"

Good grief. Talk about overkill. "Since—I don't have any gold—guess it'll be my life," I said between kicks. Wasn't doing that great of a job imitating wheezing, but I didn't care too much right now.

Behind the second boy, a third joined, this one much bigger than the other two. He had a baby face though, and he held his weight awkwardly, as if he wasn't used to being so large. Even though he had to be the strongest, he didn't join in, and I liked him instantly. Unless he was the brains of the operation, but he didn't hold himself like an authority figure, either.

The second boy knelt down in the dirt and began to pummel me, and I sighed inwardly. They really weren't going to give it up, were they?

"Stop."

A fourth person, and a voice that was definitely not male. I raised an eyebrow, and despite the beating I was supposedly enduring, I lifted my head. A girl around seventeen stepped onto the trail, wearing the same tunic as the boys. But unlike them, her bright blue eyes sparkled with intelligence and cunning, and as the second boy reluctantly stopped hitting me, she began to circle us.

"Notice anything unusual, Sprout?" she said, and the hitter pulled back enough to eye me.

"He's not bleedin'. They always bleed when I get to 'em."

"The small ones, anyway," said the leader, and she bent down. "Why aren't you bleeding?"

I sat up. She was pretty for a mortal, even with dirt smudged on her cheek and her black hair pulled back into a braid. But pretty didn't mean much when she was the sort to sic her goons on unsuspecting travelers, especially when they weren't carrying anything of value.

Then again, she had stopped him, so there was that. Though had I been mortal, I would've been unconscious for sure by now.

"My secret," I said. "Mind if I go?"

"Not yet." She leaned toward me, scrunching her nose. "You don't smell bad, either. And you're clean."

"Is that a crime?" I said.

"No, but it means you're not what you look like," she said. "Where are you going? Tell me, or I'll let Mac have a go at you."

The big guy with the baby face cracked his knuckles. Mac, then. "I don't know where I'm going," I said. "That's the truth. I don't even know where this path leads."

"So you're a drifter," she said. "Fair enough. But where are your things?"

"I live off the land. I figure if humans did it for ages before us, I can, too."

"But no tools? No water pouches?"

I shrugged. "I have good luck."

The girl leaned toward me, her face an inch from mine. The tug in the pit of my stomach urged me forward, almost painfully insistent. I had to get going before anyone else disappeared.

Before I could move, however, the girl touched my chin. A familiar sizzle jolted through me, and as it always did when I found what I was looking for, that tug instantly vanished.

She was the answer? Now I was damn sure my powers were messed up. She probably couldn't even read—had likely never held a book in her life. And she certainly didn't have the secret to our eternity locked in her head. That just wasn't something a single mortal could know.

But I stayed put, allowing her to tilt my head from one side to the other as she examined me. She was entrancing. No surprise that she'd managed to rope three boys into doing her bidding. And not everything was what it seemed. Maybe there was something special about her. Maybe she was one of Zeus's many bastards. The possibilities were endless, and as I stared at her, I gave her a grin. Whatever it was I was looking for could wait a little while longer.

"You really aren't hurt at all," she said, stunned, and she stood abruptly, exchanging looks with the three boys. I expected amusement or curiosity, but all I saw was fear. "All right, so—you can go, then,"

I stood, brushing off my tunic. "Finally decided I don't have anything worth stealing, did you?"

"Just go," she said, paling as she took a step away from me. "Before I change my mind."

That was a new one. Usually mortals didn't try to push me away. Even when I didn't admit who I was, there was a natural connection between gods and mortals. Sort of like the food chain. We're dependent on them, they're dependent on us—

So why were we dying off when they were still here?

As the girl started down the trail, flanked by her three henchmen, my stomach grew hollow. I'd known her for all of two minutes, and seeing her walk away made me ache. So maybe my powers weren't completely out of whack. Maybe she did know something.

"Wait," I called, trotting toward them. "Could I join you?"

"No," she said flatly without turning around. "We have trouble finding enough food for all of us as it is."

"I can get my own," I said. "Hell, I can get yours, too."

Her steps grew uneven, as if something was holding her back. "I don't believe you."

"Then let me prove it." I nodded to the trail. "Meet me back here in ten minutes."

"You can get enough food to feed all five of us in ten minutes?" She turned to face me, smirking now, though there was still a hint of fear in her eyes. "All right, we'll wait. And if you don't show up with enough to feed us, then we're leaving, and you're on your own. And we take whatever food you do bring."

"Deal." I gave her a slight bow. "Don't move."

"Wasn't planning on it."

She sounded confident enough, but one wrong move, and I knew she'd be gone. So I walked into the woods with as much purpose as I could muster. If robbery was a matter of survival for them, then no wonder they were practically drooling at the thought of a full meal. From the looks of the youngest kid, they'd probably been hungry for most of their lives.

Once I was completely out of sight and earshot, I created five dead rabbits and three quail, along with a pouch full of berries. She already knew something wasn't right about me, so no harm in exacerbating it. With luck she'd be willing to excuse it if it meant her belly was full.

"Dinner," I called as I stepped back onto the trail. "Couldn't find any greens, but I figured you've all had enough of…"

I trailed off. The path was empty. Was this the right spot? Of course it was. I never got lost. Where the hell were they?

I sighed. I could take off. Figure out another way to find this solution. The universe had a sense of humor sometimes, sure, but that didn't mean I had to put up with it. There had to be a better way.

As soon as I closed my eyes, however, a bolt of lightning lit up the sky, followed by the dangerous clash of thunder. Perfect. If Zeus knew I was here, it'd only be a matter of time before he found me. He didn't have my abilities, but he *was* Zeus.

I took off as fast as I could without dropping the game. No idea where I was going—I just ran. The deeper into the woods I was, the less chance Zeus would have of spotting me, and right now I really did not want to go back to Olympus.

I stumbled across their camp without realizing that's where I'd been heading the whole time. The four of them sat around a pitiful fire, and though they'd been talking in low voices before, the moment I appeared, they all fell silent. The little kid—the one who'd stopped me on the trail—fell off his stump.

"Devil be gone!" he cried, while the girl stood abruptly.

"What are you doing here? How did you find us? And what—" Her eyes narrowed. "What is all that?"

"This?" I held up the game. "Your dinner. Or it would've been if you hadn't ditched me."

Her eyes went huge, and she moved toward me, holding out her hand. I stepped back.

"Nope," I said. "Not until you let me join you."

"We're full up, sorry," she said, making another grab for the food, but I shifted away from her.

"Then it looks like I'm going to be gorging on rabbit and quail tonight."

"C'mon, Tuck," said the boy. "Just for tonight. I'm really hungry."

"Please, Tuck," said Sprout, whose hands were wrapped in cloth. Apparently someone had been injured in our little fight, after all. "We're starving."

The girl—Tuck, I assumed—scowled. "Fine. One night."

The two boys erupted in cheers, while Mac grinned on the other side of the fire. I offered her the string of rabbits, and she snatched it from me. "Thank you," I said.

"Don't thank me. You're gone by morning."

"And what if I don't want to leave?"

"Then we'll just ditch you again. Mac, here." She handed the rabbits to him, and Sprout leaped forward to take the quail from me, too. "Perry, do something about this fire. It's pathetic."

The little boy darted forward to tend to the flames, and I made myself comfortable on a log. After Perry spent a few minutes unsuccessfully poking the embers with a stick, I *encouraged* the fire to burn a little warmer. No harm in helping out. They didn't need to know.

When the flames grew without any real help from Perry, however, Tuck gave me a look. I returned it with a vague smile. She might've suspected, but after the way she'd run away, I wasn't about to give up my secrets. Not until she gave up hers.

Soon enough, a delicious scent wafted through the air, and even my mouth started to water. I'd used my powers too much today—I needed food, and I needed sleep. Desperately. Rabbit and quail weren't usually my thing, but they'd have to do tonight.

Mac offered the first rabbit to Tuck, who waited until we

all had one before she started to eat. Polite to her own, at least, even if she couldn't spare some of that grace for me.

"So how do you all know each other?" I said. They were all so engrossed in eating their rabbits that for a moment, no one spoke. At last Tuck stuck a bone in her mouth, sucking off the juices.

"Luck," she said. "Our parents were killed in the war, so we all banded together. Only way we can survive."

"Doesn't seem like you're doing a great job of it," I said, and the moment the words left my mouth, I regretted them. Stupid, stupid, stupid thing to say, insulting her like that in front of everyone, and I quickly added, "I mean—can't be that easy, living in the woods by yourself."

Tuck's expression hardened, and she threw the bone into the fire. "We can't all be a hunting prodigy like you," she muttered, refusing to look at me. Didn't blame her. Why couldn't I keep my mouth shut for once?

"Tuck's brilliant," said Perry through a mouthful of rabbit. "She's the smartest person I know."

"That's because the only other people you know are Sprout and Mac," said Tuck, but she blushed at the compliment anyway.

"Is that why you won't let me join you?" I said. "Because you're afraid I'll replace you as leader?"

She looked at me sharply, her blue eyes guarded. So I was right, then, "I won't let you join us because I don't trust you."

"But I could feed you," I said. "And I could never take your place, you know."

"Doesn't matter. I still don't trust you. I don't even know your name."

I sighed. "If I tell you my name, will you let me into your group?"

"If you tell me your name, I'll consider letting you prove yourself to us," she said. "No promises."

Clearly that was the best I was going to do, so I shrugged. I could lie, but if she really held the answer to what was happening to my family, then I couldn't risk destroying the shaky ground we were already on. Besides, it wasn't as if I hadn't revealed myself to mortals before. It'd gone well in the past. Most of the time. And between the lack of bleeding and the quick turnaround on a feast, I'd already shown them my abilities. They had no reason to question me.

That was the worst, when mortals went on and on, quizzing me, testing me, demanding to see my powers in action—as if my word wasn't enough. Which, all right, to be fair, it probably wasn't. Otherwise any crazy mortal could go around acting like they were one of us.

So I squared my shoulders, looked her straight in the eye, and said, "My name is Hermes."

I expected her to gape at me, to gasp, to demand proof—any one of the same reactions I'd gotten time and time again. Instead she stared at me.

And—that was it. She just sat there. And blinked. And finally said, "That's the dumbest name I've ever heard."

Now it was my turn to stare. She'd never heard of me? "Sometimes I go by Mercury," I said cautiously. The Roman Empire was still around, after all.

"That's even worse," she said. "I mean, really. If you're going to give yourself a nickname, at least let it be a good one."

She really had no idea. Normally that wouldn't have been any big deal, but we weren't that far from Greece, and this island had once been part of the Roman Empire. Yet she didn't have a clue. None of them did.

We were their gods, their rulers—our word was absolute,

or at least it was to them. How was it possible they didn't even realize we existed?

"So," she said, interrupting my thoughts. "Since Hermes and Mercury won't do, what are we going to call you?"

I bit my tongue. The last thing I needed was for her to take a sarcastic response seriously. "I don't know. What do you consider to be a *proper* name?"

Tuck drummed her fingers on her thigh. Even when she was sitting there, doing nothing but thinking, there was something incredibly intriguing about her. Something didn't fit. The way she held herself, the way she spoke—she was too cultured for this life. And for a girl to take the lead of a pack of boys, all of whom would be stronger than her in a few short years, if they weren't already...

Across the fire, Sprout cleared his throat. "If you two lovebirds need a minute alone..."

Another bone went flying through the air, bouncing off his head with surprising grace. Tuck glared. "Don't even, Sprout."

He cowered and held up his hands in defeat. "All right, I'm sorry!"

"You'd better be. One more wisecrack, and Perry gets your blanket tonight. Now." She turned back to me. "Your name. This is important, you know. You don't have to look like you're about to burst out laughing."

I wasn't, but for her sake, I made my expression go neutral. "Why is this important?"

"Because your name is your destiny. It's your identity— it's everything you are. Once you have your name, that's it. That's all you'll ever be."

"And yet you're giving me a new one," I said, and she shrugged.

"Sure, because once you have a new name, you'll be a new person. Not literally, obviously," she said when I opened my mouth to protest. "But in the eyes of everyone else, you're fresh. You're unknown, a blank slate, and your name decides whether you stand out, blend in—you can fool yourself into thinking you're more than your name, but you never will be. Not until you start over and make another one for yourself."

Something pinged in the back of my mind, but I was too caught up in the way her lips moved to pay any attention. "So who am I then?"

She tapped her chin, and I held my breath. I understood what she was saying far better than she probably thought I did; I'd had plenty of names before, after all, but for some reason, this seemed monumentally more important than all the rest. "James," she said. "Definitely a James."

I raised an eyebrow. So much for monumental. "James? Really?"

"Yes, really. What's wrong with James?"

"Nothing, I just—"

"You just what?"

I watched her for a long moment, and she didn't so much as blink. "It'll do," I finally said, and she grinned.

"Of course it will. You don't look like much, but a lot is happening underneath the surface. That's the kind of name James is." Popping a few berries into her mouth, she chewed slowly, her eyes fluttering shut as if she were savoring them. "Mmm. I've never had these before. You're sure they're not poisonous?"

"Positive. Despite your strange taste in names, I wouldn't do that to you."

"I'm not so sure." She opened her eyes again and glanced around the circle, as if she was sizing everyone up. "All right, James. You really want the chance to prove yourself to us?"

They weren't getting rid of me, but I might as well be polite about it. "Yes."

"If you're going to run with us, you're going to have to steal. You think you can do that?"

"I think I can manage."

"Tomorrow the earl who owns this land is going to be coming down that trail—"

"Tuck!" cried Perry, but Sprout clapped his hand over his mouth.

"—and you have to rob him."

Perry squirmed in Sprout's grip, but I held Tuck's gaze. A robbery. Easy enough. I'd done plenty of those in my lifetime. "Anything in particular you want me to take?"

She toyed with the end of her braid, but there was something in the way she watched me that made it clear this was more than just some robbery to her. A hunger that hadn't been there before. "Let's make it interesting. Steal the pendant from around his neck, along with any other valuables you find."

"And if I can do it?"

"Then you'll be one of us."

"And if I don't?"

"You show us how you hunt, and then you leave us alone. Forever."

Forever was much, much longer than she realized. I stuck my hand out, and she grasped my fingers, her grip surprisingly strong. "Deal," I said.

She smirked, and my stomach did a flip-flop. "Deal."

The convoy approached our section of the trail shortly after dawn. Six men, all riding stallions that pranced too much to be completely broken. Good. That would work in my favor.

It was easy enough to tell who the leader was—not the man at point who wore a cape with an insignia on it. Judging by the way he tilted slightly to his left, toward an older man who sat up straighter than the others and stuck his nose in the air, the first was a decoy. The other man was the real earl.

Tuck, Sprout, Perry and Mac—who still hadn't said a single word to me—all waited in the trees, shielded by the thick foliage. Even if someone did spot them, they'd have the advantage, and that calmed my nerves. The last thing I wanted was to have to escort one of them down into the Underworld. Judging by the way Perry had deftly avoided me that morning, however, I figured they all expected me to be the one who bit the dust.

I sat in a tree as well, much lower than the others, and I waited. The procession had to squeeze through the narrow pathway, the horses bumping one another and spooking, but there wasn't anywhere to go. They were trapped. I held my breath and slowly counted. Three, two, one…

Leaping from the tree, I landed squarely on the back of the earl's horse, and I held a piece of sharp rock to the old man's neck. The other men shouted, and their horses reared. But despite flying hooves and the screech of metal against metal as they unsheathed their swords, I held on tight. This was the easy part.

"Can't run me through, not without hurting your master, as well," I said, snatching the pendant that hung around the earl's neck. Whatever it was, it meant more to Tuck than my life—not that that was saying much, but still.

"Let me be," he wheezed. "Take whatever you wish."

"I already have." I nodded to the other horsemen. "Unload your packs on the side of the trail. Don't hold anything back."

The earl waved a trembling hand, and one by one, the others dumped the contents of their packs into a pile. Even though they were armed and far bigger physically than I was, they sensed what Tuck clearly hadn't—my godhood. My immortality. The natural fact that I was *more* than they were.

Maybe Tuck did realize it. Maybe she just clung to her leadership so tightly that she couldn't yield to anything, even instinct. Didn't matter, really. I didn't want her job. I wanted the answers she didn't know she had.

"Good," I said once they'd finished. "The rest of you, go up the trail. Once you're gone, I'll let your leader go."

The guards did as I said, disappearing as fast as they could spur their skittish horses into submission. I held on to the earl until they were out of sight, and after I waited half a minute, I loosened my grip on him. "Leave. And if I receive any word of retaliation, your neck will be the least of your worries."

The moment I jumped off his horse, they took off, the old man clinging to the beast for dear life. I should've felt sorry for him, and part of me did, I suppose—it'd hardly been a fair fight. But whoever he was, he was clearly much better off than Tuck and her gang. And I couldn't muster up an apology for helping them.

"That was brilliant!" cried Perry from far above me, and he slid down the trunk of the tree and scampered toward me. "How did you do that?"

"I think we'd all like to know," said Tuck, and she swung down from the lowest branch, landing on her feet. "How did you manage to convince the most fearsome earl in the land to give up his most prized possession?"

"What, this?" I said, holding up the pendant. She made a grab for it, but I pulled it back, far out of her reach.

"Give it," she growled, and I grinned.

"You said I had to steal it. You never said I had to give it to you."

"Mac!" she said. "A little help?"

Mac, who was busy rummaging through the pile the guards had left behind, raised his head and blinked. And without saying a word, he ducked back down to examine a bag of beans. My grin grew wider.

"Tell me why you want it, and I'll give it to you," I said.

"It's worth your weight in gold, that's why."

But the cautious way she watched the pendant didn't make sense. She didn't act greedy about it—instead she reeked of desperation. Like this meant more to her than air. "I don't believe you."

"I don't care," she snapped. "Hand it over, or I'll change my mind about you joining us."

She wasn't getting rid of me no matter what she wanted to think, but I needed her cooperation. And she didn't handle teasing very well. Dangerous combination.

"All right, you win," I said, and I offered her the pendant. She snatched it from me, cradling it as if she was holding her heart in her hand. What could possibly be so important about a necklace? "Just do me a favor from here on out."

"What?" she mumbled, turning the pendant over in her hands. She wasn't admiring it or appraising its worth—she was inspecting it for damage.

"Trust me. Or at least try. I'm on your side."

"No one's on our side but us," she said, and she finally looked up, her fingers clutching the pendant. "No one."

"Then let me be one of you. I can help hunt, I can gather, I can do whatever you need me to do, and I *will* be your subject, not the other way around. I promise."

"Yeah? What's in it for you?" said Tuck. By now the boys had finished packing up the loot, and Mac lumbered toward us, carrying a good two-thirds of our take. "You could survive in these woods for the rest of your life without any help from us. So why bother sharing?"

I hesitated. Not because I didn't know what to say, but because my answer was too close to the truth for me to swallow.

But it was either that or lose everything. "I've been alone for a long time, and I'm sick of it. I won't take advantage of you or rob you blind or ditch you, I promise. I help you, and in return, the lot of you won't give me the cold shoulder whenever I do something wrong. Which will be as infrequent as I can manage," I added. "That's all I want. Friends. A family. Somewhere to belong."

Tuck's expression softened, and her grip on the necklace loosened a bit. Silence hung between us, but before things got too awkward, Perry moved beside me and slipped his hand into mine. "We're all family," he said in a shy voice. "You can be part of it, too, as long as you don't eat too much."

I managed a chuckle. "I'll do my best to gather enough game so none of you will ever have to worry about portions again."

He beamed, and all four of us looked at Tuck. For a long moment, no one said a word, and at last she sighed. "Oh, fine. As long as you hold up your end of the deal, you can stay."

The boys burst into cheers, and I gave her a pat on the shoulder. "You won't regret it."

"I better not." She slipped into the woods, leaving the four of us to trail after her. I grinned. No matter what she wanted me to think of her, I knew the truth: she wasn't nearly as bad as she pretended to be.

We spent the rest of the day in camp. I showed Mac how to make sure a cooked rabbit stayed juicy; Perry and Sprout tidied up in between wrestling matches; and Tuck examined our bounty, though her hand was never far from that pendant.

It was nice—almost domestic, something I'd never had before. The council rarely spent time together in groups of more than two or three, and the way the boys laughed and played—it really was a family. Tuck was more an older sister than a mother, but they all deferred to her regardless, and while Perry occasionally called for her to join them, she stubbornly remained sitting.

There was something different about the way she held herself, too. A secretive smile danced across her lips, and she was more relaxed, more confident, not as nervous as she'd been before. Almost as if she'd conquered the unconquerable. I slid closer to her.

"You look happy," I said, and her smile vanished. "So how do you know that earl?"

"What's it to you?" she said.

I shrugged. "Just curious. You don't seem to like him much."

"Not many people do."

"So what's your reason?"

She sighed. "You're obnoxious, you know that?"

"So I've been told. You still haven't answered my question."

She tugged on her braid, staring into the fire. It was twilight now, and if I'd wanted to, I could've gone back to Olympus. But as far as I was concerned, I was staying right here for the foreseeable future.

"He killed my mother," she finally said. "And he's the reason their fathers are dead." She nodded to the boys, who either were ignoring us or couldn't hear her soft voice over their own laughter. "That's why we all banded together."

"How did he do all that?" I said, and she gave me an odd look.

"The war? Weren't the men of your village recruited? Weren't *you?*"

I frowned. "Why do you assume I lived in a village?"

"Well, you weren't raised by wolves, were you?"

In a manner of speaking. "So this man—this earl, he sent all of your fathers off to war?"

"And killed my mother," she added. "That's important."

"So what does the pendant have to do with it?"

She stared down at the necklace, brushing her thumb almost wistfully against the blue jewel. "I already told you. It's—"

"Worth more than I could possibly imagine," I finished. "I still don't believe you."

"Too bad." She glanced into the purple sky. The stars were just beginning to appear. "Can you keep an eye on the boys? I have somewhere I need to be."

"Yeah? Where's that?"

"I know a guy who will buy the loot we can't use."

"Like your pendant?"

Her fingers tightened around it. No way was she letting that go anytime soon. "Yeah, like the pendant."

"Let me come with you. You shouldn't go on your own."

Her eyes flashed. "Why? Because I'm a girl, and I need your protection?"

I snorted. "The day you need my protection is the day the sun rises in the west. I'm good with trade, that's all. I could make sure you're getting your money's worth."

She mumbled a curse under her breath. "If I let you come, will you stop asking stupid questions?"

"Only if you promise to be honest with me from here on out."

"When have I not been honest with you?" she said. I nodded to the pendant.

"Right there."

Tuck stood. "I'll think about it. Are you coming or what?"

Leaping effortlessly to my feet, I gave her a grin. "You won't regret this."

"I already do. Mac, you're in charge," she called, trudging into the woods. I gave the three boys a wink and followed.

For most of the journey, silence hung between us. Tuck

looked about as willing to talk as Hades did most of the time, and I tried to come up with a way to ease her into it. There was a reason I'd wound up here with her, and if she wasn't willing to talk to me, then I might as well accept the imminent death of my entire family.

Right. Not gonna happen.

I cleared my throat as we worked our way over a fallen tree. "It's great of you to take care of the boys like you do."

She shrugged. "We take care of each other."

"What's your plan?" I said. "I mean, are you going to be robbing the wealthy when you're eighty?"

Tuck let out a hoarse, almost violent laugh. "Please. At this rate I'll be lucky to see twenty. In three years," she added before I could ask.

"How long have you been out here on your own?" I said.

"Six months. We make do."

Six months—so the spring and summer. Persephone's seasons. "What about the cold months?"

She slipped in the narrow space between two trees and said nothing. I walked around them to rejoin her.

"Have you thought that far ahead yet?"

"I've let you join us, haven't I?" she snapped. "How do you survive the winter?"

I shrugged. I'd never actually spent one this far north. "Guess we'll see."

Without warning, she grabbed my elbow and spun me around to face her. "If you turn us in or abandon us or do anything to hurt them, I will hunt you down, carve out your eyeballs, feed them to the dogs and flay you. Got it?"

"Is that all?" I said lightly, and she glared at me. "Tuck, I'm on your side. Believe me. I meant what I said this morning, about family and all."

"Yeah? What's someone with your skills doing anyway, running away from yours? Aren't they starving without you?"

"Hardly." The idea of Zeus wanting for anything was laughable. "They know how to take care of themselves."

"I bet," she muttered. "Still, you know why I ran. Why did you?"

I didn't know her reason why, actually, but it didn't seem like the time to correct her. Not when she was finally talking. "How do you know I'm running from anything?" I said, and she rolled her eyes.

"You're not nearly as mysterious as you think you are."

I set my hand over my heart. "You wound me."

"Not as badly as I will if I find out you're a spy. No one walks around in the middle of these woods without so much as a satchel or a skin of water."

"I've already promised to show you how I do it," I said. "This would all be a whole lot easier if you at least tried to trust me."

"The last time I trusted someone I didn't know well, my mother wound up dead."

I was quiet for a long moment. "How did it happen?"

Tuck shook her head, her gaze distant. "It doesn't matter anymore. Come on, it's just up ahead."

She changed her angle, as if she was circling around something, and I followed. Right—she didn't want anyone to know which direction she was coming from. She was smart, smarter than the rest of the council would give her credit for, but I still had no idea what answers she was supposed to give me. And it wasn't as if I could come right out and ask. She'd think I was crazy.

So for now, all I could do was watch her. Not that that was the worst job in the world—there was something inherently pure about her, despite her sharp edges. She cared for those boys more than Zeus had ever cared for me, and the thought of staying here with them in the woods sounded a hell of a lot better than returning to Olympus.

I still had to find the answers—no matter how my family treated me, I couldn't walk away from them. But in the meantime, I could enjoy this life, too. I could enjoy being part of something, being appreciated, being needed. Being more than the one who constantly made mistakes everyone else had to clean up.

We arrived in a clearing alive with chirping crickets. Tuck lingered on the edge, cloaked in darkness, and I remained behind her. Together we waited, letting the forest drown out the sounds of our breathing.

At last something rustled in the trees, and a weedy young man stepped out from the other side of the clearing. He was older than Tuck, but still gangly, as if he hadn't adjusted to his long limbs yet. Or maybe he was just too thin.

"I know you're here," he said. "I haven't got all night."

Tuck held her finger to her lips, and we remained still. The young man paced up and down the length of the clearing, sighing often and dramatically.

"I heard 'bout your job this morning. The whole bloody village has. I've got buyers, so how about we stop all these games and get down to business?"

Even in the darkness, I saw Tuck's posture change. Crooking her finger at me, she stepped into the clearing, her shoulders square and her blue eyes bright in the moonlight.

"What kind of buyers?" she said, and I followed a few paces behind.

"The kind that pay with anything you want," said the young man with a gap-toothed grin, and he trained his focus on me. "You must be the thief I've heard so much about. Seems you gave our dear earl a right scare. I don't see it, personally."

"Yeah, well, wait until he has a knife to your throat, Barry," said Tuck. "Now let's talk price."

I stayed quiet as the two of them bartered. Tuck only accepted food that would keep and things we would need to survive in the forest—clothes, weapons, the essentials. Anytime the young man, Barry, mentioned gold or silver, Tuck shook her head and steered him back toward useful trades.

There had to be something I was missing—something the Fates needed me to see—but what was it? A thought nagged in the back of my mind, but every time I tried to get closer, it moved just out of reach.

Perfect. Wasn't as if the entire fate of my family was on the line or anything.

At last they seemed to reach an agreement, and Tuck moved back toward the trees. "Meet me back here at dawn with the goods. I'll bring the loot. If anyone follows you, I'll hang you from a tree using your own innards."

Barry grinned, and there was something unnerving about it. "Couldn't possibly turn you in, m'lady. That wouldn't be at all chivalrous."

He slipped back into the darkness, and as Tuck and I headed through the trees—a hundred and twenty degrees in the wrong direction—I realized what felt so wrong about this whole thing.

"He didn't mention the pendant," I said as we started to turn back toward camp. "He knew exactly what was taken, down to the bean, but not a word about the earl's most prized possession."

A line formed between Tuck's eyebrows. "Because he knows I'd never give it up," she said, but there was doubt in her voice.

We walked the rest of the way in tense silence, both undoubtedly contemplating the same thing. Did Barry know she wouldn't give the pendant up? Or was there another reason?

I should've known—mortals weren't that difficult to figure out most of the time, but when Tuck wasn't willing to give me all of the information, I didn't have a chance. Hard to put the pieces together when they weren't all there.

Less than fifty paces from camp, I heard it—the faint sounds of rustling behind us. I froze and held up a hand to Tuck, and she stopped midstep.

Climb a tree. Never in a million years should I have talked to a mortal like this, but we didn't have much choice. Her eyes widened, and all the color drained from her face. *Do it. We're being followed. I'll explain later.*

To her credit, she only hesitated for a split second before she soundlessly climbed the nearest tree. I didn't have time to admire her skills—I scampered up after her, and together we balanced precariously on the highest branch that could hold us. She clung to the tree, her nails digging into the bark, and I wasn't sure which she was more afraid of: me or the people following us.

Four men emerged from the trees within seconds. They wore the same black as the guards from that morning, which helped them blend into the night, and the one on point held up his hand. Beside me, Tuck stiffened. And we waited.

And waited.

And waited.

"They're gone," whispered one of the guards, and another one nodded in agreement. The leader grumbled.

"Gotta keep looking. I'd rather not be flayed, if it's all the same to you lot."

"We'll have no chance," said the first guard. "Not without a trail."

"Couldn't have gone far. If we split up, we'll have a better chance of—"

He stopped cold, and in the distance, the sound of Perry's laughter filtered through the night.

The boys. They were sitting ducks.

Except for the fact that I was a god and had plenty of options. I took a breath, ready to divert their attention and send them in the opposite direction, but before I could tell Tuck I had it handled, she screamed.

It was an earsplitting scream, the sort that would be heard for miles, and I grimaced. There went our chances of getting out of this. The guards shouted and pointed upward, but all I saw on Tuck's face was grim determination. The scream wasn't out of fear; she was trying to warn the boys.

But naturally, as Tuck jumped from the branch and landed on one of the guards, the boys came running toward us. Even if Tuck had planned some sort of signal ahead of time, she severely underestimated what they were willing to do to help her.

Sprout charged through the trees, brandishing a club, with Perry and Mac close behind. He caught the first guard by surprise, bashing his kneecaps, while Perry launched himself at the second. Mac sent his elbow flying into the face of the third, and Tuck continued to wrestle with the leader.

I dropped to the ground. It was chaos—limbs flying, shouts echoing through the night, and the screech of metal against metal as the guards unsheathed their swords. Fists and knees were one thing, but they didn't stand a chance against weapons.

"Stop!" I called, and at the same time, I pushed the thought into each of their heads. Two of the guards fumbled their weapons, while Tuck's guard was too busy fending off a choke hold to do much. But the fourth—

The cliché about time moving in slow motion isn't a cliché for no reason. I'd lived for thousands of years, but that moment was the first time I'd experienced it firsthand. Too stunned to react, I watched in horror as the sword sliced through Perry's stomach, blossoming from his back. As the guard yanked it out, everyone went still, and Perry looked down at his torso.

Blood soaked through his tunic on both sides, and he fell to his knees, his eyes wide. "Tuck?" he whispered, looking to her for help. But Tuck remained frozen.

I darted to his side. Healing wasn't my thing—Apollo was better at it than I'd ever be, but I didn't have much choice. I set my hands on his chest, closing my eyes and willing his wounds to heal. Life drained out of him quicker than I could stop it though, and I cursed. Not now. Not tonight. Not with Tuck watching.

"Stay with me," I commanded. I didn't exactly have the pull Zeus did, but to a mortal, it was enough. Perry groaned, tearing up in pain, and I poured everything I had into healing him.

Apollo. I pushed the thought as hard as I could. *I need your help.*

Whether he heard me or not, I couldn't tell. Thoughts took time to travel through space, and I willed myself to keep healing. There was only so much I could do with a mortal wound though—I wasn't Apollo or one of the original six siblings, and my powers were limited.

"Keep breathing." Another command, but this time much gentler. "You will be all right. Just keep breathing. One breath in, one breath out."

The space between my hands and Perry's wound glowed with golden light, and that was enough to stop the guards cold. For now, at least.

Soon enough, however, a dozen more men surrounded

us, each stopping as he saw what I was doing. I didn't care—whether they knew who I was or not, whether they believed in me or not, it didn't matter. The only thing that did was keeping Perry alive.

At last the biggest, burliest guard stepped forward, his sword drawn and pointed directly at me. "What sorcery is this?"

Several others drew their weapons and surrounded us. I didn't move. Somewhere nearby, Sprout was sobbing, and the remaining guards took the others into custody. Including Tuck.

But I couldn't move, not if I wanted Perry to stand a chance. One by one, the guards wrapped rope around their hands, and they dragged them off into the woods. Sprout's sobs faded, and Mac was silent as ever; Tuck, however, shouted as they carried her away, "James, don't let him die!"

I gritted my teeth. *Apollo—please. I'll do whatever you want.* A dangerous proposition, all things considered, but I was desperate.

Anything I want, all for a mortal?

Apollo's voice filtered into my mind, much faster than I'd expected. I craned my neck, searching for him in the trees, but of course I didn't see him. We may not have had powers of invisibility, but no one saw us without our permission.

Yes, anything. Just heal him.

A pause, and then, *Fine. Get rid of the other mortals. I can't do this with them watching. Zeus is going to kill you, you know.*

Yes, I know, I snapped. *If I get myself captured, do you promise to do everything in your power to save him?*

I could practically feel his indignation from here. *I've already said I would. Now get out of here before I change my mind.*

Pushing the last of what energy I had left into Perry, and hoping against hope it would hold him until Apollo reached him, I held up my hands and stood. "All right, you have me. Let's go."

For the longest ten seconds of my existence, no one said a word. At my feet, Perry grew weaker, and I let out a frustrated growl. Obviously they were scared, but did they have to be cowards about it?

"Listen, either you can arrest me right now, or I can kill all of you and walk out of here without a scratch," I said. It wasn't an empty threat. Perry's life was at stake, and I wasn't playing around. Not anymore.

A few guards shuffled forward, still holding their swords, though their fear damn near smothered me. I held out my hands, and the bravest of the lot quickly bound them. Nothing I couldn't get out of, but I'd drained myself trying to save Perry, and my legs were unsteady and the edges of my vision fuzzy. I could still take them, though. Probably.

"Come on," I said, stumbling forward in the direction the guards had led the others. In the distance, I sensed some sort of village, along with a castle and a sizable farming community. That must've been where Tuck and the others had come from and where the guards were taking them now. Sure enough, I could feel Tuck's trail, warm and red with panic.

I led the way, and none of the guards questioned me. Despite the binds on my hands and the weapons in theirs, they kept their distance, muttering things to one another that they thought I couldn't hear. I could, but it didn't matter. I had to find Tuck.

Apollo? Is he all right? I said once the outskirts of a small village came into view, mostly made up of wooden shacks and dirt. He didn't answer. Emaciated horses stood at their posts, their heads hanging low. Regardless of the late hour, serfs were scattered throughout the roads, packing or hauling carts filled with food they would likely never get to eat, and they raised their heads to watch us as we passed. No one looked well fed or clean.

Apollo? Still no response. I tried again, but all I heard was silence. Perfect. Either he was ignoring me or Perry had died, and he wasn't in the mood to tell me. I clenched my fists and pushed onward. He'd healed him. This was a game—Apollo's idea of a joke. He'd tell me eventually. Everything would be fine.

Despite the rampant poverty the serfs lived in, the walls around the village were staffed by several dozen clean-cut guards dressed in the same black uniforms as the ones who trailed me. All of them looked as if they'd had three square meals a day for the majority of their lives. And inside the stone walls, the homes became better somehow—slightly larger, cleaner, sturdier, infinitely more habitable. The horses in the street were plump and groomed, and the few people still outside after dark wore clean clothes and smiles. Until I passed, of course.

Looming in the distance was our ultimate destination: a castle. Nothing that would ever compare to Olympus, but against the backdrop of menial living, it looked luxurious and much better than it was. The guards took it from here, though they all hesitated before surrounding me. Still, it wouldn't look good to have a prisoner lead himself in, so the leader took point while the rest of them tried not to get too close.

The inside of the castle was dark and dank, with torches lighting the way. Definitely nothing like Olympus. I followed the guards, who led me straight down Tuck's trail. She wasn't far—I could practically see her glow through the stone walls, and I grew more and more anxious the closer we got. What if Apollo hadn't saved Perry? What if he gave up as soon as he saw how badly he was hurt?

It didn't matter. I couldn't tell Tuck the truth.

We entered what must've been some kind of great hall, complete with two long tables flanking a shorter one on a raised platform. Sort of like a throne room, except this man—this earl—wasn't a king. With the way he sat in his gilded chair, however, his head held high as he stared down his nose at the three hunched figures kneeling in front of him, he seemed to think he was.

Tuck. Mac. Sprout. Even from the entranceway, I could sense their pain and terror. Sprout was practically vibrating, he was trembling so hard; Mac was a sickly shade of green; and Tuck...

I'd never sensed such a weird combination of fear, anger and hatred in someone before. Terror rolled off her, filling the room with an odd chill. But she stared up at the earl, her head raised when everyone else's was bent. That was my Tuck.

"My lord," said the lead guard, and the others ushered me forward. "We have found the scoundrel who led the attack this morning."

The earl paled. "And you have brought him here bound by nothing more than rope?"

The guard hesitated. "That was all we had, my lord. We subdued him, and he is compliant."

"Are you willing to stake your life on it?" growled the earl, and the guard said nothing. "Come closer into the light, boy. You are a boy, are you not? Certainly not old enough to yet be considered a man."

Please. I looked Tuck's age or older. This was some sort of game, something to unsteady me, but he wasn't going to win. I was older than the wood he sat on. Older than the rock his castle was built with. But I moved forward anyway, eager to get closer to Tuck. The guards sidestepped me, clearly still afraid despite their earl's show of bravery. Smart.

"What are you called?" said the earl, peering down at me. I glanced at Tuck, who was watching me with red-rimmed eyes.

I did my best. I pushed the thought silently into her mind, and she leaned away from me. Damn. "I'm called James. And you?"

He scoffed, but I held his stare, and slowly the amusement drained from his face. "I am your lord and ruler of this land. That is all you must concern yourself with. How did you fall in with these children?"

"According to you, I'm a child myself," I said with as much mock innocence as I could muster. Living with Aphrodite for eons came in handy, after all. "Clearly it's natural for children to band together when no one else will help them."

"Do not be smart with me, boy," he snarled. "You will answer my questions, or I will assume your guilt and have you hanged by morning. Is that what you want?"

I shrugged. "I don't really care."

The earl's face turned a strange shade of purple I'd never seen on a human being before. "And your friends? Do you care if they are hanged?"

"I care enough to promise you that if any harm comes to them because of something you do, I will make sure you regret it for the rest of your short life."

He gripped the arms of his so-called throne. "Guards! Search them for my pendant."

As soon as the nearest guard put his hands on Tuck, she let out a sound I'd only ever heard from a wild animal. Her elbow connected with the guard's face, and he hollered, blood gushing from his nose.

Half a dozen guards drew their swords, and Tuck stilled. She glared up at the earl though, and he clapped his hands together with glee.

"Dear, dear Laurel, you always did have a flair for the dramatic," he said with a chuckle, and I blinked. Who was Laurel?

Tuck tensed, her eyes narrowing into slits. "Don't call me that."

"And why not?" said the earl with a twisted smile. Clearly he was enjoying this. "It is your name. I remember giving it to you."

Wait. I glanced at Tuck, who kept her focus glued to the earl, even though she had to know I was watching her. Unless earls had a habit of naming every child in their village…

He's your father?

The corners of Tuck's mouth turned downward, and she gave a slight, barely perceptible nod. Perfect. Could've known that sooner, but at least now I knew he wouldn't actually carry out his threat to execute them. Or Tuck, at least. Abhorrent as he was, he wouldn't kill his own daughter.

"You will stand still while the guards search you," said the earl, and he gestured toward the boys. "Or my guards will run your friends through with a sword. Is that understood?"

Tuck didn't move. She had to have the pendant on her—she might have let it drop in the woods, knowing the earl would never be able to find it, but I doubted it. Not when the pendant meant so much to her.

Where was it? Closing my eyes, I reached out for it, and—

In her shoe. How the hell had she managed to get it in there without me noticing? Didn't matter. As the guards approached her, warier this time, I mentally took hold of it. It was strangely warm, connected to Tuck as it was, and while one brave guard with trembling hands patted me down, I vanished it.

Not an easy trick, and not something I did lightly. But as mad as the earl would be when his search turned up nothing, Tuck would be even worse off if the pendant returned to her father.

She must have felt the pendant disappear, because she finally looked at me, a question in her eyes. If she couldn't give me the truth, then I didn't owe it to her, either. At least not yet.

When the guards turned up empty-handed, having searched all of us, the earl stood. "I *will* find it," he growled.

"Are you sure about that?" said Tuck with more sass than was wise, all things considered. The earl's face turned red again, and he slammed his fist down on the table.

"I am sure enough that if you do not produce the pendant or give us adequate information to find it by sunup, I will kill each of your friends. And if you do not tell me by sundown, I will kill you."

She scoffed, but there was fear in her voice, as well. "You wouldn't."

"Try me."

"You won't," I interjected. "Else you'll be the next to die."

Silence. The earl leaned forward against the table, and if he could've set me on fire through hatred alone, I was pretty damn sure I would've been ash by now. "And you," he murmured in a poisonous voice. "You will be the first to die."

"You can kill me as many times as you'd like," I said. "Right now, if you don't mind, I'm tired."

If it were possible for steam to pour out his ears, I was absolutely positive it would happen right about now. "Guards!" he barked. "Take them to the dungeons."

"The dungeons? But—" Before Tuck could finish, a guard yanked her backward, half carrying her twisting form toward the door. "You can't do this to them! I don't know where the pendant is—I dropped it!"

"Perhaps your mother would have believed your lies, but I'm not soft like she was. Take them away," the earl said again, and the guards marched the rest of us out of the hall. Sprout and Mac look scared out of their minds, their eyes wide as they wore identical masks of terror, but there wasn't much I could do to reassure them.

Tuck continued to kick and scream the entire way into the dungeons, but the guards didn't pay her much attention as they artfully dodged her flailing limbs. Somehow I got the feeling this wasn't exactly the first time she'd been down here, and that only made my hatred for the earl burn hotter. Who locked his own daughter up? No wonder she'd run away.

The guards shoved Mac and Sprout into a cell near the stairs, but they led Tuck and me deep into the darkness, with only torches to light our way. It felt unnatural down here, almost like the Underworld—but unlike the Underworld, my powers worked just fine in the earl's dungeon. It was a maze to the center, where a high-security cell awaited us, complete with four guards and a stone door operated by some sort of pulley system. No way anyone mortal could knock them in.

The lead guard pushed me into the cell first, and the others threw Tuck down onto a pile of hay before the door dropped, shaking the walls around us and effectively sealing us inside.

"Well," I said, leaning up against the nearest wall. "This is inconvenient."

Without warning, Tuck launched herself at me, pounding her fists into my chest. "Who—the hell—*are you?*"

I stood still, letting her get out her anger and frustration and worry and whatever else she was feeling. Didn't hurt me one bit, and if it made her feel better, brilliant. "I already told you. I'm Hermes. Sometimes called Mercury, especially in Rome."

"I don't know who that *is.*" With one final punch, she went limp, barely able to keep standing. I wrapped my arms around her before she could fall.

"I'm a god," I said. No need to dance around it. "One of the twelve Olympians. Well, er, fifteen now. Bit of a long story."

She shook her head wearily, and I lowered her down onto

the ground. "I don't understand," she whispered. "There's only one god."

Only one? I frowned. "No, there's definitely more. Zeus, my father, he's head of the council, but—"

"There's only one. Or are you pagan?"

I blinked. Was she serious? "You really have no idea who I am or how many gods there are?"

"I rather thought it was all just a matter of opinion," she said. "I mean, here you have one god. Some people say more than one. Some people say there isn't any god, though how they could possibly believe that and live in this world…" She shook her head. "Do you really think you're a god?"

"I really *am* a god." This was going to get very old very fast if she kept it up. "I've been to plenty of places where the people don't know who I am, but we're not that far from Greece, where the religion centered around our best-known identities started."

"Greece?" She frowned. Did she even know where—or what—Greece was? Before I could ask, she changed the subject, confirming my suspicions. "How can you possibly be a god and look so—*normal?*"

I shrugged. "We can change our appearance at will, and I like blending in, I suppose. Let me prove it to you. Hold out your hand."

She immediately clasped them behind her back. "If you're going to show me magic or—something—"

"You've already seen what I can do," I said with a small smile. "I won't hurt you. The opposite, I promise. Just hold out your hand."

Tuck eyed me for a long moment, and even though we were in a darkened cell with only a single torch for light, her eyes were as blue as ever. Reluctantly she offered me her palm, and I set my hand over hers. My skin tingled where we touched, and exhaling slowly, I willed the pendant back from nothing. It arrived in her hand, heavy and warm, and she gasped.

"How did you…?" She stared at me, stunned, and without warning, she kissed me on the mouth. *"James."*

My entire body grew hot. "It's nothing," I mumbled. "Just a trick. I'm sorry I didn't tell you the truth sooner. It's sort of… you know. Not something you go around bragging about."

She snorted, her lips still half an inch in front of mine. "If I were a goddess, I'd run around the world telling everyone I met. To have that kind of power…"

"It isn't all it's cracked up to be, you know. I might be powerful, but there are loads of others even more powerful than I am."

"A frightening thought," she said with a small, distant smile. "Still, for even a fraction of that…for some sort of control…"

I hesitated. It clearly wasn't something she wanted to talk about, but I had to know. "Why did you run away?"

"Isn't it obvious?" She made a vague gesture that reminded me all too much of the earl. Her father. "I was trapped here. Never had any freedom. My only friend was my mother, and when she died, I didn't want to stay here anymore. I didn't want to be under his thumb. He tried to marry me off, you know, to a neighboring lord. In exchange for land. *Land.*" She shook her head, as if that were the most insulting, preposterous thing she'd ever heard. "Like he doesn't have enough of it already. So I ran. Met the others in the village, and the four of us took off together."

"I'm sorry," I said. "Most of us are tied to our lives one way or the other. You're lucky you had the option of running."

"We all have the option of running," she said. "It's just a matter of whether or not you're brave enough to do it. It isn't just running, you know. You have to change yourself completely. Become the person you need to be in order to survive. It isn't easy, but it has to be done. That's the only way you can choose your own life, you know?"

I did know, and I nodded, running my fingers through the ends of her tangled hair. Somehow her braid had come undone. "I won't let anything happen to you or the life you want," I said quietly. "I promise."

"Don't make promises you can't keep," she said, and she stared at the pendant in her hand, a hint of sadness flashing across her face. "I knew what would happen when I asked you to steal this. Well, actually, I figured the guards would kill you. Sorry."

She gave me the tiniest of smiles, and I grinned back. I'd already guessed as much.

"I just...I'm prepared. I knew this might happen, and I was willing to swallow the consequences. But for Mac and Sprout and Perry..." She bit her lip. "Is he okay? Do you know anything?"

I hesitated. "I know he's in good hands. The best there is in literally the entire world. If anyone can save Perry, it's him."

"Thanks," she whispered. "You didn't have to do that. You didn't have to do any of it, yet you did anyway."

I pulled her in toward me. She rested her head on my shoulder, her breaths coming in deep and uneven. "I did, though. Chosen family and all."

"Even if you'll outlive us all?"

My chuckle was void of all humor. She had no idea how much that reminder twisted the knife already buried deep inside me. "There's an afterlife, you know. My uncle runs it, and sometimes I help escort lost souls there. What do you think will happen when you die?"

She hesitated. "I don't know. Hell, I guess. Eternal fire and torture for everything I've stolen and done and...right."

"No, it's nothing like that." Or at least it wouldn't be for her—I refused to let her think that way. "It's the best place you can imagine. The happiest moment, the people you love most—it's whatever you want. Whatever you believe deep inside of you."

Tuck didn't move for a long moment, and at last she whispered, "I don't want to die. And I don't want Mac and Sprout and Perry to die, either."

"I won't let that happen," I said firmly. "Just trust me, all right? Hard as it might be, I won't let anything happen to you. We can leave now, you know, if you want."

She peered up at me. "We can?"

"Sure. Just say the word, and you and I will walk out of here without a care in the world."

"But—Mac and Sprout—"

"I'll come back for them, of course," I said. "I wouldn't leave them behind."

Tuck shook her head fiercely. "No. If you can really get us out of here, then they need to go first. The moment my father discovers I'm missing, he'll have them killed. I can't let that happen."

I laced my fingers with hers. They were cold and much smaller than I thought they'd be. "All right. Mac and Sprout first. I'll bring them to a safe place in the woods, and then I'll come back for you. Deal?"

"Deal. Wait a little bit before you go, though."

"Why?" I said, tightening my grip on her hand. "Like spending time with me after all?"

Tuck snorted. "Yeah, right. The later it is, the less likely you'll be spotted, that's all. Sorry to shatter your hopes and dreams."

I gazed down at her in the flickering torchlight. She was practically a kid—a mortal kid, no less. But there was something about her that made me want to stay in this cell forever with her. Just the two of us curled up together in the hay, waiting for morning to come. Despite everything that had happened, I hadn't felt this sort of warmth in eons, not since Persephone.

Lives with mortals weren't impossible—they weren't exactly encouraged, of course, but several council members had mortal spouses and children they visited often, Zeus included. It was a leap, since twenty-four hours ago, Tuck could barely stand me, but in that moment, I saw a future. A real possibility of happiness, even if it would eventually end with her death. But a little happiness, no matter how temporary, was better than none at all.

"Hey," I said as the minutes ticked by. "When we get out of here, why don't we build a cottage somewhere as far away from this place as we can get?"

She peered up at me, her brow furrowing in confusion. "Like a home?"

"A home. A place in the woods where no one will bother us, but close enough to travel if we need to. We can take care of the boys until they're old enough to decide what they want to do. If they want to stay, brilliant—if they want to venture out on their own, they can always come back. And you'll never want for anything, I promise."

Tuck's expression softened, and finally she said, "That sounds perfect."

I kissed her temple. "Then that's what we'll do. And you'll never have to worry about any of this again."

"That'd be really nice." She sighed. "Thanks for—you know. Not being terrible. Even if I still don't believe you about the whole god thing."

"No problem," I said. "Now sleep. I'll wake you before I leave."

She snuggled against me, wrapping her arms around my

torso as if I was a pillow. Soon enough her chest rose and fell evenly, and her heart beat slowly but steadily.

I would give that to her no matter what it took. Even if I had to walk away from the council, even if I could never see my family again—I would have a new family with her and the boys. I *did* have that new family. And I wasn't going to give them up for anything.

Iris arrived shortly after midnight, appearing in the cell with a burst of rainbow. Her red hair hung in waves, and she wore one of her fancier outfits, as if she'd taken time getting ready.

"Hey," I whispered. "Thanks for coming."

"Sure thing." She eyed Tuck, who had shifted sometime in the past hour or so. Her head was in my lap, and she snorted softly. "Who's this?"

"A friend. Her name's Tuck. I need your help."

"Of course." But Iris didn't tear her eyes away from her. "What sort of help? I don't have much time before Zeus figures out I'm gone."

"I need your help getting a few kids out of here. They're in a cell a little ways down—I can show you where. They need to be brought to a safe spot in the woods where no one except us can find them. Go through the walls if you have to."

"But—"

"No buts," I said. "I've already shown them my powers. They'll be surprised, but they'll go along with you. I need you to do this fast, Iris. As fast as you possibly can. And as soon as you're done—"

"Let you know," she said. "I'm not an idiot."

"No, you aren't. Just—please. This is important. Life-or-death for them."

"Right." She eyed Tuck again. "And what about her?"

"As soon as we find the kids, I'm coming back to get her."

Iris twirled a curl around her fingers, and finally she nodded. "I'm always in the mood for a little trouble. Let's do this."

Reluctantly I shifted Tuck's head out of my lap, running my fingers through her dark hair one more time. "I'll be back soon," I whispered, and once I could stand, I offered Iris my hand. "Walk right on through. The more scared they are of us, the more likely they'll be to leave us alone."

"Can't imagine anyone ever being scared of you." A split second later, we walked together through the thick stone wall opposite the door, arriving in the passageway. It was almost completely dark in here, but I guided Iris through the cells, careful to avoid the ones that were occupied. Much as I wanted to release them all, now wasn't the time.

At last we arrived in the cell the boys shared. Sprout leaned against Mac, twitching every few seconds in his sleep. Mac, however, was wide-awake, and he didn't so much as blink when we walked straight through the rock.

"You're all right," I said, relieved. Mac nudged Sprout awake, and the moment he opened his eyes, he sprang to his feet.

"James! You came!" cried Sprout, catching me in a bear hug. "See, Mac, I told you he would. Is Tuck all right? And Perry?"

"Tuck's fine. Perry—" I hesitated. "I don't know. But we're going to find out, all right? This is my friend Iris. She's going to get you out of here."

Sprout turned toward her as if he'd only just realized she was there. And upon seeing her, his mouth dropped open. "You're pretty."

"And you're very handsome," she murmured, taking his hand and offering her other one to Mac. "Come on. This will be quick, I promise, but we're going to walk through walls, so it might be a bit odd."

Sprout gasped, and while Mac looked dubious, he took

Iris's hand anyway. Before she led them off, however, Mac clapped me on the shoulder and looked me in the eye properly for the first time.

"Thanks," he rumbled, his voice hoarse with disuse. But that was more than I'd ever expected to hear, and I patted him on the arm.

"Any time. I'll see you both soon." All three of them, if Apollo had done his job, but I wouldn't find out until Tuck was safe. Wasn't sure I wanted to know until then anyway.

I watched as Iris guided them through the stone wall. It wasn't far to the edge of the castle; they'd make it in under a minute, even at such a slow pace. Which meant it was my turn to get Tuck out of here.

Taking a deep breath, I turned to open the cell door—and walked straight into a solid wall of immortal. Dazed, I shook my head and stepped back, my eyes widening when I saw who it was.

Zeus.

"I thought I told you to remain in Olympus," he said, and before I could protest—before I could so much as utter a single syllable in my defense—he gripped my hand, and we disappeared.

"You can't *do* this to me," I howled, pacing up and down Zeus's office. "She's relying on me to get her out of there, and the moment that damn earl finds out the others are gone—"

"I have no idea what you're going on about, nor do I care," said Zeus mildly, sitting at his desk. "Mortals are none of our concern. Forcing Apollo to save the life of that boy was foolish and wasteful. He is just a mortal."

"That's exactly the kind of attitude that's making us go extinct."

"That's quite easy for you to say. You are not the one who must explain to the Fates why he is still among the living."

Despite my anger, a bubble of hope formed inside my chest. Perry was alive. But if I couldn't convince Zeus to let me go back down to the surface, Tuck wouldn't be, not for long. "Please. Ten minutes, that's all I need. If you don't let me go, she'll die."

"You should've thought about that before you disobeyed me," said Zeus. "You will remain here in Olympus, as I have ordered. Do you have any idea what you've done to your mother and me? We thought you were dead."

"Like you've talked to my mother in the past thousand years," I said. "If you don't let me out of here, I'll—"

"Leave anyway?" said Zeus calmly. "Run away, as you've already done? So be it. If you leave Olympus, I will see to it that you are permanently removed from the council and banned from ever setting foot here again. Your duties to the Underworld will be revoked, you will be replaced, and I suspect that soon enough, you will fade completely. Is that what you want?"

I swallowed. "I want to keep my promises."

"And is your promise to the rest of the council no longer a priority?"

"Not when my friend's life is on the line."

"Then it is your choice. But I hardly think you'll have any chance of reaching her in time, so do choose wisely. Mortals have an afterlife, and even if she does unfortunately die before her time, she will live on in Hades's realm. But if you go... well, I would rather not see that happen."

"That's a comfort," I snapped, and he stood.

"Do not blame me for this mess, Hermes. I am only doing what I must to keep this council intact."

"Until we all fade because no one's doing a damn thing."

"We are doing all we can. Just because you are not privy to everything that happens does not mean we are doing nothing." He waved his hand dismissively. "Go to your chambers. Tomorrow I will come up with an appropriate punishment for what you have done."

"You mean practically killing the only friend I've had in centuries isn't enough?" I said, but he wasn't listening anymore. Instead Zeus flipped through several sheets of parchment, and the office melted away, replaced by my chambers.

Perfect. Now I really was trapped.

I slammed my hand against the golden wall, and the room trembled. Not all of Olympus shook though, as it would have if my father had done it instead. Another reminder that I was replaceable. Next to nothing compared to the original six. And Zeus's neutrality to whether I lived or died—

I should've protected Tuck. I should've done more somehow. They were my real family, not this, and even if I outlived them all, at least I would've had them for a moment. It couldn't end like this. Not for Tuck, not for the boys, not for anyone.

But even if I did drop from Olympus, I'd be stuck on the other side of the world. I didn't have the ability to travel in the blink of an eye like the original six—I relied on that drop-off point, and the best I could do was go down at sunset and hope to hell they hadn't hanged Tuck early. It wasn't enough to guarantee her life, and I couldn't settle for anything less than that now.

I paced. And paced. And paced some more. I practically wore a path in the floor of my chambers as the hours passed and Tuck's sunset grew closer and closer. She had to be awake by now and wondering where I was, and the thought of her fear only made my anger boil over. I couldn't let this happen no matter what it cost me. I couldn't live with myself otherwise.

At last I cursed and headed for the door. I didn't have a choice—dropping down at sunset was the only way I could hope to get to her in time. It had to be enough. Any other possibility was unacceptable.

Before I could cross the room, however, a soft knock sounded on my door. I threw it open, prepared for a fight, but instead Iris stood on the other side, looking pale and disheveled.

"Iris? Are you all right?" I stepped aside for her to come in, and she slipped past me, hugging her arms.

"I'm fine," she said with a weak smile that didn't reach her eyes. "Or I will be soon enough. Zeus wasn't too happy with me helping you out."

I touched her elbow. She set her hand over mine, holding it as if it was the only thing keeping her grounded. "I'm sorry," I said. "I should've never asked—"

"Don't be ridiculous. If I hadn't wanted to help, I wouldn't have," she said. "Did you get the girl out of there?"

I shook my head, the pressure of Tuck's impending fate weighing heavily on my chest. "She's going to be executed in a few minutes. If I don't get to her—"

"Don't worry about that. I've got it covered."

I blinked. "Iris, you can't—you're already in hot water, and if Zeus finds out—"

"I don't care." But there was a tremor in her voice that said otherwise. "It'll be worth it if we can save her life. I know Zeus doesn't care about that kind of stuff, but I do. I've met countless mortals, and while some of them aren't exactly savory, she doesn't deserve to be executed. And those boys love her so damn much." She shook her head, her eyes watering. "Don't bother arguing with me. I've already made up my mind. Like you said, I'm the only goddess who puts up with Zeus's antics, and even if he fires me, he'll hire me back soon enough."

I opened my mouth to protest. With the gods fading, even temporary unemployment wasn't safe. But before I could say a word, the sky-blue ceiling and sunset floor dissolved, replaced by clouds and rain and the smell of wet dirt.

The forest. And just beyond it, the serfs, the walls, the village—

Without giving it a second thought, I kissed Iris on the cheek and bolted down the path. I felt the tug of Mac and Sprout and Perry behind me, but I didn't have time to celebrate. I pushed my mind forward, searching for any sign of Tuck, and my heart skipped a beat. She was in the town square, by the gallows.

I raced through the gates and across the dirt road. The square wasn't very big, with only a few shops surrounding it. Maybe a quarter of the village's population could fit inside, but I didn't care about them. I'd blast them aside if I had to, if that's what it took to save Tuck's life.

When I burst into the square, however, it was empty. No sign of onlookers, no executioner—just a stout man dragging a wagon from underneath the gallows.

I knew what was happening. I knew what the tug that led me to that wagon meant. But even as I shattered into infinite pieces, I ran up to the man and pulled the crude canvas from his load.

Tuck's body, pale and still, lay underneath. Someone had mercifully closed her eyes, but I could see them in my mind, glaring at me for something I'd said or done. It would've been easy to pretend she was sleeping, if it hadn't been for the ring of deep purple-and-blue around her broken neck.

My own body seized, and anger and hurt and grief beyond words ripped out of me. The stout man took one look at me, glowing with fire and the screams of a thousand dead souls, and he ran.

Tuck. My poor Tuck. How could this have happened? It wasn't sunset yet. We should've had time—it wasn't supposed to be over yet. I was supposed to have time to save her.

A shuddering sob escaped me, and I gently cradled her body. I'd failed her. Because of me, she was dead, and I'd lost the one friend I'd had in a very, very long time. That agony and guilt swirled around inside me, compounding my grief for a girl I'd barely known two days. But time didn't mean a damn thing when it came to love, and as I stood there, rocking back and forth and trying to force the world to right itself, any last ounce of hope I'd had disappeared.

I don't know how long I stood there—long enough for shutters to be drawn and the villagers to escape into their homes. They weren't my targets though, and their fear only made my fury worse.

"Hermes?"

Iris's soft voice brought me crashing back down into myself, and I turned to her. Her face swam in front of me, but even through the tears I could see her concern. "She's gone," I choked. "He killed her."

Iris wilted, and her eyes grew red. "Oh, Hermes. I'm so sorry."

"Can you—" My voice shook. "Can you take her body back to the boys? She deserves a proper burial. I'll be there as soon as I can. I have something I need to do."

Iris reached for my hand. "Hermes…"

I jerked away from her—an instinct, not because I didn't want her to touch me. But I was too far gone to apologize, and instead I managed to force out, "Please. I'll join you in a little while. Just make sure the boys are all right."

Wordlessly she nodded, stepping back to give me a moment of privacy. I pressed my lips to Tuck's cold forehead. "I'm sorry," I whispered. "I hope you've found your happiness, and I swear to you, I will make sure the boys are all right. And I'll come visit you as soon as I can."

But even if I could get away long enough to hunt her down in the seemingly infinite Underworld, mortals weren't completely there. They didn't have a sense of time or place, as they did while they were alive, and even if Tuck recognized me, it wouldn't be the same.

Didn't have much of a choice now, and even half a Tuck was better than no Tuck at all.

After one more gentle hug, I relinquished Tuck's body to Iris, who lifted her up and started to walk toward the gates. She would protect Tuck better than I had, and she would see to it that Tuck wasn't buried in the very place she hated. That was all I could ask for now.

As soon as they were out of sight, I turned toward the castle. I don't remember walking up to it—one moment I was in the dirt square, and the next I stood in the great hall, glowing with that same fire. A dozen guards surrounded me, but I brushed them aside, storming up to the earl without an ounce of remorse. If they wanted to protect a murderer, then that was their choice. This was mine.

"You killed her." My voice was thunderous even to my ears, and the earl's face drained of all color.

"You—you ran away, and she wouldn't give up your location—"

I grabbed him around the neck, where the pendant that had started this all hung. That bastard. "You killed your own daughter. Do you know what Hades does to people like you in the Underworld?"

The earl was shaking too hard to reply, and I tore the pendant from his neck.

"This doesn't belong to you," I said. "And neither does this castle."

"Y-you—you can't—" He gulped. "Are you going to kill me?"

It was tempting. Very, very tempting. But death would be an escape for him, a way to weasel out of his crimes even if Hades did pass judgment against him. He would never be fully aware of what was going on, never feel the guilt and pain of his actions. And I wasn't feeling very merciful at the moment.

"Worse," I said. "I hereby strip you of your title and all your land and property. You are banished from this place, and rather than kill you, I promise you will live for a very long time. But you will not live here, nor will you live anywhere. I curse you to wander for the rest of your miserable life. You will never stay in one place more than a night, you will hunt only enough to survive, and you will never raise a hand against another innocent again. You are no one, nothing, and you will be forgotten by all who know of you."

The earl's eyes nearly popped out of his head. "You can't do that to me! I'm an earl, appointed by the king himself!"

"Does it look like I care about your king?" I said. "I am a god, and my word is law. You cannot break it, and it is already done. Now go."

I dropped him hard into his chair, and he winced, rubbing the red marks on his neck. They were nothing compared to the marks on Tuck's. "You think you can come in here and bully me in my own castle?" he muttered, his voice hoarse. "Guards!"

The guards who had previously surrounded me glanced at each other, confused and still pointing their swords. Instead of focusing on me, however, they all turned toward the former earl.

"Who are you?" said the head guard. "What business do you have in this court?"

"What are you talking about?" said the earl, dumbfounded. "I am your lord!"

I touched the guard's shoulder. "He is nothing—no one, a confused old man who doesn't know himself. Send him out of the village and on his way with enough food to get him through the night."

"Of course," said the guard, and while the others surrounded the babbling former earl, I turned and walked out of the hall. It wasn't much, and it certainly wouldn't bring Tuck back, but it was all I could give her now.

I met up with Iris and the boys shortly after. My feet felt heavy, and every step was a battle, but I clutched Tuck's pendant, allowing it to spur me on. By the time I arrived, Sprout and Perry were crying over Tuck's body, now wrapped neatly in silk that Iris must have created, and Mac had finished digging a grave between two trees.

"Do you think she'd like it here?" said Sprout, his cheeks stained with tears. I knelt beside him and nodded.

"I'm sorry," I whispered. "I never meant for this to happen."

He hesitated, and just as I was beginning to wonder if he'd hit me, he threw his arms around my neck and hugged me tight. "Don't be sorry. Iris told us what happened. You did everything you could."

I embraced him, and beside us, Perry joined in, as well. He felt even more fragile than usual, and his body radiated heat, but he was alive, and he would be okay. "Thanks for saving me," he said, resting his head on my shoulder. "I know Tuck would'a been really happy about it, too."

"She would have," I said quietly, and I swallowed. "I won't always be able to stay with you, but when I can, I'll be there every second. You're my family now, and I'll never let you down again."

"We know," whispered Perry, and the three of us knelt there, simply holding each other.

At last Mac set his hand on my shoulder, and I released the boys, forcing myself to my feet. "Take care of them," I said. "And when you're ready, go back to the village."

Mac's brow furrowed, and though he said nothing, I knew exactly what he was asking.

"The earl's gone. You're in charge now, when you're ready.

I know you'll be fair to your people, and they deserve a good ruler."

His baby face went white, and his mouth opened, but he didn't say a thing.

"You listen, and you watch," I said. "That's more than most rulers. Always remember who you are and who your people are. Never forget they're not pawns for your enjoyment. If you do that, you'll be just fine."

He continued to stare at me wordlessly, but I patted him on the back and knelt down beside Tuck. "Come on," I said, touching her cold hand over the silk. "It's time to say good-bye."

Shortly after midnight, Iris and I returned to Olympus. The moment our feet hit the floor, she squeaked and let go of my hand, hurrying off into a hallway. And once my eyes adjusted, I realized why.

The council was in full session. Perfect.

"Hermes," said Zeus dryly. "So glad you could join us as we decide your fate. Please, remain standing."

I'd been halfway to my throne when he said that, and I stopped and turned to face the others. They all watched me, some smug, some furious, some indifferent. But none of them looked at me the way Tuck had.

"Do I get the chance to speak in my own defense?" I said.

"I hardly see why he should," said Apollo. "He knew the consequences when he left."

And there went all of the goodwill we'd built up in the past day. "Yes, but I know something you don't," I said. "I know how to stop everyone from dying."

Instantly what few murmurs had been going around the circle stopped. Zeus stood, and even though he tried to hide it, I saw hunger in his gaze. "And how is it you came across this?" he said slowly.

"That girl you let die—she's the one I was searching for when I left," I said. "The Fates guided me to her. I wanted answers, and she's the one who gave them to me. Not directly, of course, but the things she said...I put them together."

Silence. "And?" said Zeus after a long moment.

"*And* if I tell you, I want two things."

"You will tell us because you are a member of this family, not because we have bribed you," he growled. It was the first time I'd heard anything other than a neutral tone from him in ages.

"That's where you're wrong," I said. "Family doesn't treat their own the way you've been treating me since Persephone faded."

Across from me, Hades flinched, but I kept going. Couldn't spare his feelings now, not when it was this important.

"I made a mistake, a huge one, and I've done everything I can to repent. But even though I'm still me, you've all treated me like scum ever since, and I'm sick of it. I don't treat any of you that way—except maybe you, Apollo, but only because I'm jealous of your teeth."

No one laughed. I took a breath.

"Listen. I don't want any of you to die. I just want to be part of the family again—a real part, not a 'let's pretend until we know everything's fine, then kick him out' part. I don't want to be forced to leave you, and I don't want any harm to come to Iris for helping me. And—that's about it," I said, uncertain now that I'd come to the end of my list. "Just treat me better, don't punish Iris, and we can all figure this thing out together."

Zeus stood in silence for the better part of a minute, obviously communicating with the rest of the council silently. I didn't care. As long as they did the right thing, they could be as petty about getting there as they needed to be.

At last he cleared his throat. "Very well," he said slowly.

"We accept your bargain and your conditions, but we have one of our own—if your advice does not live up to your promise, you will be immediately banned from the council and stripped of your role as an Olympian and all it entails. Do you understand?"

I nodded, swallowing the lump in my throat. Not as if I'd expected anything less from them anyway. "I understand, and I agree. As long as nothing happens to Iris."

"Very well, Iris is cleared of all wrongdoing," said Zeus. "Now, tell us what you've learned."

This was the hard part. I stood in front of my throne, not yet daring to sit, and I focused on each and every face. No matter how they felt about me, I loved them, and I couldn't stand the thought of something happening to one of them. Even if they'd denied me, I would've told them.

"You're going to object," I said. "It's different, and you're all going to resist. But before you dismiss it, give it a try, and remember the Fates themselves sent me to her." I hesitated. "We need to change who we are."

A confused murmur echoed through the room, and Zeus raised a hand. Everyone fell silent. "Explain, Hermes."

I launched into Tuck's story—everything she'd gone through and why she'd done it. How she'd adapted. What her real name was, how her self-chosen nickname had been a way for her to recreate herself and become the person she needed to be. How she'd changed who she was and what she'd believed and how she'd acted, all for the sake of her new life. And how much that new life had meant to her.

"So you're saying we need to change our names?" said Aphrodite, clutching Ares's hand. I nodded.

"But it's not just that. It's changing who we are to the world. We depend on mortals, and they depend on us, but they don't realize that. Most of them are completely unaware. People used to know who we were and what we were doing, and they believed in us. They think we're myths now though—stories to tell around a fire, not real people. And we need that belief."

"Then how do you propose we do that?" said Poseidon.

"We need to become more than what we are. More than gods and goddesses. More than Olympians. Yet at the same time, we need to become one of them, as well. Live among them, understand them, help them. Stop needing recognition. We need to integrate ourselves and stop being these great deities who are so far above humanity. Yes, we're immortal, but we feel the same emotions they do. We're happy, sad, angry, excited—we need to do away with that divide. We need to bleed blood instead of ichor. We need to adapt."

"I do not understand," said Hades quietly. "How would living among them benefit me?"

"It wouldn't, not you," I said. "Your subjects will always be there. They know who you are, at least to an extent. But ours—they believe in other gods now, or only one of us at a time, or whatever the case may be. We need to become those gods. To become these ideas in their minds." I shook my head. "I know it sounds crazy, but the core of the problem is that they don't know who we are. And short of exposing ourselves and ruling like kings, we can't change that. But we can live like—like Rhea."

At last a few faces seemed to light up with understanding.

"She lives among the people. I don't mean we have to abandon Olympus. We just need to join together with the mortal world and understand it. As long as there are mortals, there will always be love and music and travel, and in order to stay tied to those things as we are now, we must go down to earth and represent them. Everyone we meet will know who we are, even if they don't know our names, and we'll ingrain ourselves among them. Bottom line—we cannot hold ourselves above them anymore. We are not better than them, and we must remember that. We depend on them as they depend on us, and it's time to start acting like it."

"We have lost touch," said Athena, glancing around at the others. "It couldn't hurt to try."

Nearly a minute passed as everyone seemed to absorb this. A few whispered amongst themselves, but it wasn't until Zeus sank back down into his throne that everyone seemed to relax.

"We will try," he said. "Abstract as that is. Do you have any solid suggestions for what we might do to implement these... *ideas* of yours?"

"Yes," I said frankly. "We need to change our names. Right now. We need to cast aside our old identities, and we need to become the people we have to be in order to adapt and survive. The name's just the start of it, but it's as good a start as any."

No one looked happy about it, not even Hephaestus, who hadn't exactly won the name lottery. "What sort of names?" said Aphrodite, frowning.

"I don't know. Names that will stick around for centuries, though I suspect we can change them again if we have to," I said. "We'll do whatever we have to do to survive."

"Very well," said Zeus. "Then why don't you start us off? What is your new name, son?"

Son. It may have been a single word to him, but to me, it was a moment of acceptance—a moment when we moved beyond the struggles of the past eons and stepped into a new era where the slate was wiped clean.

It was exactly the kind of life Tuck wanted. And it was the life I would live when she couldn't.

"James," I said. "My name is James."

Three years later, we all still existed.

Couldn't lie and say it was easy—none of it was going to happen overnight, but to the council's credit, they each tried. Only Hera kept a Greek name, refusing to budge from the roots she held so dear, though at least we were able to persuade her to change her name to the lesser-known Calliope. Even Zeus found a name powerful enough to satisfy his ego.

Slowly but surely, the council changed. Instead of deities lording over a world that didn't know we existed, each of us began to spend time on the surface, interacting with mortals in a way few of us had in millennia. It wasn't painless—more than a few attempts resulted in varying disasters, mostly revolving around Aphrodite and her new set of mortal conquests. Apparently the world had changed since she'd last waltzed into the middle of a village and announced herself. But soon enough, we all adapted. We all started down the road of becoming the people we needed to be in order to survive.

In those three years, I visited Mac, Sprout and Perry often, occasionally bringing Iris along with me. The three boys moved into the castle soon enough, and Mac slipped seamlessly into his role as the new earl. He was a kind, fair leader, exactly as I'd hoped, and as time passed, my concern for them lessened. They'd be all right. They already were.

But despite that, I could never escape the guilt that surrounded me over Tuck's death. Even though the boys had long since mourned her, I'd never fully recovered, and that was why it took so long before I finally made the trip I'd been dreading.

I approached Hades's throne with my head bowed—partially to show respect, but mostly to avoid looking at Persephone's empty throne. He hadn't chosen a name yet, the last of us to do so, but there was no hurry. If he chose to remain Hades, his existence was secure. Even after the last mortal died and the rest of us faded, he would live forever. But if he didn't fill Persephone's throne, it would be a very, very long forever. And I didn't like the reminder of what I'd done to him.

"Hermes," he said in a deadened voice, and he paused. "James. Is there a problem with the souls you've transported?"

"No," I said.

"Then why are you here?"

It'd been an unspoken rule between us that I went out of my way to avoid seeing him while doing my duties in the Underworld. Despite a few awkward run-ins, most of the time we managed to keep our distance. "I have a request."

Silence hung between us, and at last Hades sighed. "You want to see the girl."

"I—" I clamped my mouth shut. Of course he knew. "Yes. I won't stay long. I just want to make sure she's doing all right, and I have something to give her—"

"No." The word echoed through the throne room, even though he hadn't spoken above a quiet murmur. "I cannot allow you to see her."

I gaped at him. Was he serious? "Why not? You've allowed others to visit mortals in the Underworld before. Why can't I see Tuck?"

But even as I said it, I knew. This was his revenge for what I'd done with Persephone. All these thousands of years of dancing around each other, pretending to be neutral—now that she was gone, now that he thought I'd played an integral role in stealing her from him, he was stealing Tuck from me. An eye for an eye.

"You can't do this," I said. "She hasn't done anything wrong."

"But you have." He leaned forward, his silver eyes locked on me. "You are the one who wants to see her, not the other way around."

"You don't know that."

"I do." He straightened again. "I will not allow it, and if you try to sneak away to find her, I will have her moved around the Underworld as many times as I must to keep her from you. You will never see her again, not as long as I am King of the Underworld."

He may as well have reached inside me and ripped out every

piece of me that had ever mattered. I stood there, trembling, trying to think of a way around it, but I'd already apologized a thousand times over. I'd already done everything I could to make it up to him. His pride and his fury stopped him from moving beyond this, and now, because of that, we were both stuck.

My hands tightened into fists. I could hit him. I *wanted* to hit him more than I wanted to live, but I'd worked too hard to get back on even footing with the rest of the council. Any attack on Hades would only send me spiraling again.

I couldn't do a damn thing, and he knew it.

"Then—could you give her something for me?" I said, slipping my shaking hand into my pocket. The moment my fingertips touched the pendant, however, Hades shook his head.

"No."

Of course. Of bloody course. I raked my free hand through my hair, my vision growing red. "It isn't my fault, what happened to Persephone," I blurted. "She's the one who made those decisions. I just pointed out the fact that she had a choice."

"She did have a choice," said Hades. "But so did you. I am not holding you accountable for Persephone's actions. I am holding you accountable for your own."

I turned away. He was right, even if his methods were despicable, even if he wasn't being fair. I'd made my choices, and I'd suffered the consequences for them time and time again. This was just the final one.

"All right," I said shakily as I turned back to face him. "Fine. I accept your ruling, under the condition that this is it. You can hate me as much as you want, but this is the last time you hold this over me. Period."

He tilted his head almost curiously. For one of us to talk to the original six like this—it was crazy, especially when he already couldn't stand me. But I didn't care. Enough was enough.

"We're even. I took Persephone from you, and you took Tuck from me. End of story."

I brushed my thumb against the pendant as I spoke. I'd never see her again. Not easy to swallow, not by any means, but I refused to break down in front of Hades. I was stronger than this. Tuck had made me stronger than this, and to accept this with anything but bitter grace would be dishonoring her memory. And I wouldn't do that.

"Very well," said Hades after a long moment, touching the empty throne beside him. "We are even. Now go."

I made my way past the pews, aware of the souls who'd witnessed every moment of our conversation. None of them mattered, though. The only soul I wanted to see was one I would never meet again. Hades had seen to that.

Halfway down the aisle, however, I stopped and faced him once more. An invisible fist squeezed my heart. "Is she happy?"

Even from a distance, I could feel Hades's stare burning into me. "Does it matter, when you cannot do anything to change it?"

"Yes," I said. It mattered.

He pursed his lips, and at last he sighed. "Yes, she is happy."

That was all I needed to know. It would never change the past, it would never get me there in time to save her, but at least I could rest knowing she wasn't in any pain. That was one small amount of comfort Hades could never take from me.

"Thank you," I said, and without another word, I turned and walked away.

★ ★ ★ ★ ★

GOD
OF
DARKNESS

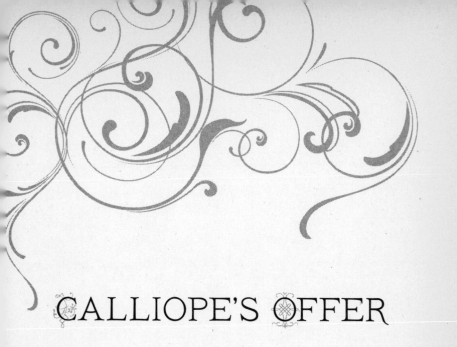

CALLIOPE'S OFFER

As Lord of the Underworld, Hades was feared by the living and revered by the dead. A member of the eternal council of gods, he had unimaginable power at his fingertips, ready to do whatever he must to uphold his duties and laws. And as the ruler of the souls who died, he would live forever, guaranteed true immortality through his duties to them.

But he would have traded it all if it meant he could be mortal.

In his existence, Hades had seen more faces and heard more stories than the rest of the council combined. Eventually every mortal entered his kingdom, and while he only came face-to-face with a fraction of them, he felt each and every presence. He felt each and every moment of their lost lives.

And that was why he envied them their mortality. To have a set period of time to live—to know there would be an end instead of an endless sea of time… It would have been a wonderful thing. That way, even if he wound up alone, he would know it would end someday. Being a god granted him no such relief.

He sat in his throne after a long day of judgment, the silence heavy around him. The number of souls had seemed to grow exponentially over the past few centuries, or perhaps it had only seemed so as he no longer had Persephone. His wife, his friend, his partner—he had depended on her far more than he'd realized. Even knowing she would never love him the way he loved her, he held on to her memory, treasuring it as one would a lifetime of happiness.

He'd kept his promise to himself, however, and had never gone to see her. It was agonizing, knowing she was so close yet so in love with someone else, and he couldn't allow himself that kind of pain. The wounds had only begun to heal, and while scars were inevitable, to rip them open again would only ensure they would never close.

Instead he allowed himself to dream about her during what little time he did sleep. He allowed himself to dream about a life they could have had if he had not been so wrong in his actions—if he had done what she wanted, said the right thing, never allowed Demeter to talk him into marriage in the first place. If he had asked Persephone herself what she had wanted all those eons ago, before they'd both done irreparable harm to each other. And during those brief hours, he was happy.

Leaning against his throne, he exhaled, his eyes falling shut. Five hundred years today. That was how long it had been since he'd let her go, and it still felt as agonizing as the day he'd watched her die. Forget scars. At that moment he was convinced it would never get better no matter how much time passed.

The doors of the throne room opened, and with a sigh, he stirred. The next batch of souls weren't due until morning, and James knew better than to bother him. But even though he hadn't anticipated anyone in particular, he certainly hadn't expected the girl standing in the archway at the end of the aisle.

"Hera. Calliope," he said, correcting himself as he stood. "It is good to see you."

"And you as well, Hades." As she approached him, she bowed her head, and he did the same. It had been millennia since the two of them had been alone—since before his marriage to Persephone, and the reminder stabbed at him. "I didn't interrupt anything, did I?"

He shook his head and took her hands, squeezing them in greeting. "No, no. My day is done. I was about to retire."

"Oh." Her smile faded slightly. "I was hoping we might talk."

"Of course." He offered her his arm, and once she took it, he led her from the throne room. The hallways were lit with everlasting torches, giving the home an eerie feel, but he preferred it. He could've easily created a light that didn't make the shadows dance, but that would've only made his loneliness worse.

Once they'd stepped inside a cozy sitting room he never had the chance to use anymore, he glanced around as she did, taking in the room. Funny how a routine could make the once-familiar strange. He summoned tea and poured them both cups, and as he sat beside her on the sofa, he saw her shift closer to him. Perhaps she simply missed him. Or perhaps she sensed how badly he needed some form of comfort.

"This place hasn't changed much," she said between sips of tea. "How are you holding up?"

"It has been a long time since anyone asked me that," he said with a faint smile, though he found no joy in either her concern or his observation. "I have been better, I suppose."

Calliope's expression darkened. "Yes, you probably have." She set her hand over his. "Is there anything I can do?"

He shook his head. "Powerful and enchanting as you are, I'm afraid there isn't anything anyone can do."

She blushed and lowered her head for a moment. Bashfulness didn't look right on her. "You're too kind."

"Hardly. It is not my fault that Zeus—er, Walter does not appreciate what he has."

Her lips twitched in annoyance, and perhaps something deeper. "No, he does not. Have you not chosen a new name?"

"I'm afraid I haven't found the time. Or discovered much of a selection."

She scoffed. "You see countless people pass through here. Surely one of them has a name you like."

"Their names are their own. I could not possibly steal it, as Diana took Ella's."

Calliope grinned. "I think she did it solely to get a rise out of her, after those comments Ella made about her and Walter."

"And you do not agree with Ella?" said Hades. "I would have thought…"

"I know what Walter does," she said with a shrug. "There's little point in fighting it now."

After eons of hearing secondhand stories of Calliope's jealousy—and occasionally witnessing it himself—that was certainly an unexpected surprise, and Hades was quiet as he absorbed her change of heart. "Have you found someone, then?"

A strange look passed over her face, and she held her chin a fraction of an inch higher than usual. "And if I said I had?"

"I would be pleased," he said, despite the bitterness that sawed away inside him. Even Calliope was finding love, yet he would remain eternally encased in loneliness until the end of time. And perhaps even then he would not be granted relief. "May I ask who this lucky man is?"

A pause. It wasn't like Hera—Calliope to be anything but direct unless she wanted something. But what could she possibly want from him? Was her new lover mortal? Did she want

Hades to spare him until she was done? "You may," she said slowly, her hand shifting toward his. "If you believe you are prepared to hear the answer."

"And why would I not—"

Her fingers brushed his, and he stopped. Calliope held his stare, her blue eyes earnest and scheming all at once, and she leaned in toward him. "You know why," she said softly. "You've always known."

Hades grew completely still, not even allowing his heart to beat. Perhaps then time wouldn't pass, and he would never have to face the inevitable consequences of this moment.

Hera. Calliope. His sister loved him. Longed for him. Coveted his company. He could feel it now, those tendrils of emotions as old as the council's reign snaking toward him. How had he missed it before? Was she really so skilled as to keep even her strongest feelings so closely guarded?

It didn't matter how she had kept it a secret. What mattered was the way she watched him, waiting for his answer with hope in her eyes and a smile dancing on her lips. It'd been so long since he'd seen her like this—as though she finally saw something good in the world that she wanted.

And it terrified him.

Even if he could entertain the notion of being with her, even if he could move past his suffocating love for Persephone, his brother would never forgive him. Such a slight on Zeus— on Walter would seem like an act of war, and he would fight until the end of the world to win back his possession.

But that was all Calliope was to Walter—a possession. A trophy. A pet on a leash he'd thought he'd tamed, but here she was, out of her cage and desperate for her freedom. And Hades couldn't give it to her.

He wanted to. Not because he loved her the way she so clearly loved him, and certainly not because he wished to start a war. But because no one deserved the kind of life Calliope had lived. No one deserved to lose herself the way she had, buried underneath her husband's pride, lost in the eternity of his wrath. After having kept Persephone for so long without allowing her the freedom she had craved, the notion of giving Calliope the very thing he hadn't given her was intoxicating. Redemption, in his own small way. A chance to prove to himself—and to Persephone—that he was not a monster, even if he knew it would be a lie.

That was not enough, though. It was not enough to give Calliope false hope that someday he might love her; it was not enough to string her along the way Zeus had. It was not enough to start a war the council could never finish. It was not enough to risk humanity and break every rule he'd made for himself since Persephone's death.

It was not enough to risk his own heart, selfish as it was. And it was not enough to give himself one more chance at happiness. Calliope may have deserved it, but he did not, and he could not see past that no matter how hard he tried.

"I am flattered," he said quietly, unable to look her in the eye any longer. She would instantly know what these words meant, but he could not find it in himself to give her even the slightest amount of hope. It would only be another cruelty. "But you are my brother's wife, and there are certain boundaries I cannot cross."

Rather than stand in indignation or hurt, Calliope tightened her fingers around his. "Please," she whispered, sounding more like a young girl than she had in a long time. "I'll explain it to Walter—I'll make sure he knows it wasn't your idea. I just—I can't live there anymore. I love you. I've loved you for longer than I've ever loved anyone, and all I'm asking for is a chance."

"That is a chance I cannot give you," he said, focusing on

their intertwined hands. A world of what-ifs in a single gesture. "I am sorrier than words can describe, but you deserve better than a life in my world. With me. I could not love you, not the way you love me, and I would rather fade than see this place choke the life out of you as it did Persephone—"

"Persephone?" She choked on the name. "Is that why you're doing this? Because of her? Because she didn't love you?"

"Partially," he allowed, and she touched his chin, forcing him to look at her. He would've expected tears by now from the waves of frustration rolling off her, but her eyes were dry.

"What if—what if she was never meant to love you?" Her tone took on a strange quality, as if she were pushing him toward something he couldn't see. "What if it wasn't your fault or hers?"

A grave suspicion filled him. "What are you saying?" he said, trying to see past her determination to whatever lay beneath. "Are you implying someone manipulated Persephone—"

"What? No, no, of course not," she said quickly. "I only mean—what if you were incompatible? What if you fell in love with someone who simply wasn't right for you? That's all I mean."

He watched her for a long moment, searching for a lie he knew was there. But because he loved her, because he wanted to see the best in her when no one else would, because the thought of her betrayal was too much to bear, he believed her. His shoulders sagged, and he slipped his hand from hers. "Regardless of the reasons, the past is the past, and there is nothing I can do to change it. I am sorry for your lot in life, Calliope. I hope someday you discover a way to leave it behind and find the life you deserve, but I cannot love you the way you want me to, and I cannot hurt you more than I already have. You will always have an ally and a friend in me. But that is all we will ever be."

There it was—the pain he knew he would eventually cause her no matter his answer. It burned like fire in her eyes, and she stood with the pride and grace of a queen. She was remarkable, worthy of so much more than either him or his brother, and perhaps one day she would find it. But today would not be that day.

"Are you certain?" she said, her hands clasped in front of her. "I will not offer myself to you again, Hades, no matter how true my feelings will remain."

He stood, inclining his head in a show of respect for who and what she was, even if the rest of the council no longer deigned to recognize it. "I will always be here for you as I was all those years ago. But as much as I treasure your company, I am afraid we can never be more than what we are now. I have hurt our family enough as it is, and I cannot allow myself to cause anyone any more strife. Especially someone I care about as deeply as you."

"And what about my feelings?" she whispered. "Don't they matter?"

He took her hand gently and brushed his lips against her knuckles. "They matter far more than my own, and that is why I must decline. I am a shell. I am a shadow. I am nothing, and you are everything."

"You aren't nothing, and you deserve love as much as I do. Don't you want it?" She was pleading now, though she did an admirable job of masking it in the commanding tone of a queen. But she was not his queen, and he would not obey her, not when it would destroy them all.

A bitter, empty smile ghosted over his features, and he bowed his head once more. "Love is all I have ever wanted in this immortal life. I have used up my chances though, and I am at peace with that. I beg you to allow me to remain so."

A moment passed, and at last she stepped back from him,

her expression unreadable. Those tendrils of emotions were gone now, securely hidden behind the barriers she had so expertly built. How long had it taken her to retreat so completely into herself? How long had she remained so, until this moment, when she had finally trusted him enough to let him in?

No matter. It was done, and he would not change his mind. The sting of rejection now was nothing compared to the agony of loss she would have felt centuries or eons down the road if he had accepted her proposal, and he had to content himself with that. She would not be grateful now, or perhaps anytime in the near future; but someday, when she had found her happiness, he hoped she would remember this moment and see the future he had allowed her to have. The future he had wanted her to have.

"I hope you visit, though I understand if you do not," he said quietly. She swallowed.

"I will do my best," she allowed. "But now I must go."

He nodded once. "I will escort you out."

"I know the way." She curtsied once, and he responded with a deep bow. "Take care of yourself, Hades. And find a name before Walter grows more upset than he already is."

"I will do my best," he murmured. "Do you have any suggestions?"

Calliope eyed him, and there was something calculating about her gaze. But when was there not? At least her heartbreak had vanished to a place where Hades could not see it. "I have had the privilege of spending time in England, where I have watched many kings rise and fall. Some are silly, pompous and far too enamored with their titles and the art of war, but some truly love their people and care for the well-being of their country. A particular favorite of mine reminded me a bit of you. He was called Henry."

"Henry." He mouthed the name to himself a few times, allowing himself to adjust to the sound of it. He'd met many Henrys, of course, though perhaps not the one she spoke of. But the name was common enough that he felt certain it would not stand out. He could be himself without the myths tainting every step he took, and no one would hear his name and fear death. It would be a relief to rid himself of such a burden. "Very well. Henry it is."

Calliope smiled, and this time it was genuine. But before long, her expression faded into one of sadness once more, and she sighed. "Take care of yourself, Henry."

"And you," he said, moving to kiss her on the cheek as he had countless times before, but she stepped away. Her barriers slipped for a moment, and the pain he had feared spilled through. It did not match the agony that had flooded him since Persephone's death, but pain was not a contest, and hers was as real as his own.

He watched her go, slipping out of the room before he could bring himself to say goodbye. Even if she returned someday, it would never be the same, and already he mourned their friendship. But it was for the best. For both of them. She deserved a life he could never give her, one filled with sunshine and love, and he would never forgive himself for hurting her as he'd hurt Persephone.

Closing his eyes, he slipped through space and returned to his bedroom to dream of the life he'd lost. Perhaps one day he would be more than a shadow; perhaps one day he would find his own happiness in whatever new form it might take. Until then, however, he would be content with his dreams.

His mind whirled with the possibilities of what small memory he would find comfort in tonight. But though time flowed around him, forcing him to go with it, his heart remained still. And it would now for always.

DEFEAT

Henry could not pinpoint the exact moment he gave up. It crept upon him like a thief in the night, stealing away his future piece by piece until he had nothing left. Maybe it was not one small thing—maybe it was an eternity of small things combining to form the perfect storm. Or maybe it was nothing at all.

Whatever it was, after that moment had come and gone, it took him another hundred years to gather the courage to approach the council with his decision. He knew in his heart of hearts that no matter how much they claimed to care for him, they would not take this well. Even though he wanted it, even though he was ready, they would see it as another burden on them—one none of them was ready for. And though he felt guilty for what he was about to do, he stood in front of the gathered council in Olympus, casting around to look each of them in the eye.

"I wish to fade."

The words he'd practiced for so long in his head slipped out as if they were nothing. And given the council's silence, for a long moment he wondered if perhaps he really hadn't said anything at all.

"Fade?" said Walter, as if he were speaking in tongues.

"Yes, fade," said Henry with utmost patience. He'd expected this. "I understand my role in this world is great, but I cannot bear to face eternity any longer. We have all lived countless lifetimes, and I wish to end mine now."

"But—why?" said a small voice beside him, and Henry looked down at Demeter—Diana. They hadn't spoken much since Persephone's death, but their bond was still there, having grown even stronger in the everlasting fires of grief. If she did not understand, he had no hope of convincing the others, either.

He looked her straight in the eye. "I am alone. Up here, you all have each other, but I have no one. And despite my best efforts to be the king my subjects need me to be, I can no longer endure it on my own."

"You can no longer endure what?" Calliope's voice rang out, much steadier than his own. "You can no longer endure your rule without a queen? Or you can no longer endure your existence without a companion?"

There was a sly tone to her question, but Henry ignored it. If she was implying she could stay with him, either as his queen or his companion, he would not have it. Nothing had changed in the past four hundred years.

"Both," he said simply. "As a king, the influx of new subjects is far too much for me to handle on my own. And as a man, I can no longer endure being alone."

"But surely there must be another way," said Diana, reaching for him. He allowed her to take his hand. "James knows the inner workings of the Underworld. Perhaps he could—"

"No." Henry spoke as gently as he could, but he would not work side by side with James no matter what the stakes.

"I have made my decision, and if you wish for James to take over my position after I am gone, then so be it. But I wish to step down from my throne now."

"And we will not let you," said Calliope.

"With all due respect, sister, you are not the head of this council," said Henry, and despite the look of utter shock on her face at his dismissal, he looked to Walter for the final word. His brother may have been the epitome of pride, but if he loved Henry at all, he could not deny him this. It was his life; his eternity to spend as he wished. And he wished to step down and fade.

Walter said nothing for a long moment, his eyes locked on Henry's. "Is this what you truly want? To abandon us? To succumb to cowardice over a few lonely centuries?"

"Over an eternity alone," corrected Henry.

"Because you are not willing to go out and find a new queen."

"Because I cannot."

"Your unwillingness to move on does not mean the rest of us should be punished."

"And your unwillingness to move on does not mean I should be punished, either," said Henry. "Allow me to be clear—this is a courtesy. For now, I am willing to wait a century before I fade, in order to give the council time to train my replacement. If you will not give me your blessing, then I will step down immediately."

Silence. Walter's lips formed a thin line, and in the throne next to his, Calliope looked as if she were near tears. But what did they expect? He was not one of them. He never had been. He had already lived the happiest years of his existence, and his duties were simply no longer enough to keep him here.

Beside him, Diana rose, sandwiching his hand in hers. "Brother," she said in a voice meant only for him. "I understand your pain. I carry it, too, and I wish for nothing more than to move beyond it. But fading is not the answer."

"It is for me," he said quietly.

"But there must be some solution. Something you would stay for."

He closed his eyes, and an all-too-familiar face appeared in his mind. The same one that had haunted him for nearly a millennia. "You know the answer to that," he whispered.

Her throat constricted. She did. Of course she did. "And what if I were to find you a new queen?"

A new queen. The idea was so preposterous that he nearly smiled. "I have no desire for a new queen, or a new companion. That part of my life is over."

"Is it?" Something flashed across her face, a determination he knew all too well. "What if we agreed with you, brother? What if we allowed you to transition your realm to another for the next hundred years, under the assumption you will fade at the end of it—but in return, you allowed us to find you a new companion?"

His heart sank. Another game. "I would never be able to love her, not the way she would deserve."

"How can you be so sure?" Before he had the chance to protest, Diana turned to the others. "I say we accept our brother's choice and allow him one hundred years to get his affairs in order—with the condition that during this time, he also allow us to find him a new bride. Someone he can love, who loves him in return. Someone who can help him rule. Someone who will give him a reason for staying."

A murmur rippled through the council, and Aphrodite— Ava was the first to nod her agreement. "I think it's brilliant," she said. "I bet between us, we could find someone who'd be perfect for you."

Her enthusiasm was contagious, and soon enough the others

had joined in, planning in low, excited voices. Their words were nothing but buzz to Henry as he watched his plans slowly slip away. They could say they would uphold his choices as much as they wanted, but eventually, as the decades passed, they would find a way to trap him here.

But the hope splashed across Diana's face gave him pause, and at last he exhaled, his shoulders sagging. He would give his sister this, and if they did break their pact, then he would do as he'd promised and step away regardless. This was his choice, and he would not allow them to take it from him.

"Very well," he said. "One hundred years. That is all the time I will allow. At the end of that hundred years, if we do not agree upon a suitable queen to rule at my side—" he could not bring himself to say *wife* or *companion* or *lover* "—then I will step down from my role as King of the Underworld, and I will fade."

"So be it," said Walter. "Sister, I entrust in you the task of finding our brother a suitable wife. Ava will help you."

Diana nodded, more radiant than Henry had seen her in an eon. "I will find someone," she murmured, once again for his ears only. She brushed her lips to his cheek, and he ducked his head, focusing on the sunset floor. "I've made many mistakes in my existence, but this will not be one of them, I promise you that. I *will* find you someone. Not just someone—but the person you have deserved all this time."

He managed the faintest of smiles. It was no secret she blamed herself for what had happened with Persephone, and if it allowed her to cast aside her own guilt, then Henry could not deny her the chance to do this. But the ache inside him, an eternal fire that turned every last piece of his happiness to ash, would not be extinguished by a stranger. Even if Diana was right, even if there was someone out there who was his match in every way, who was somehow more a soul mate to him than Persephone, she would not be able to heal him. No one could.

He would give Diana this chance though, because he loved her, and because she had been through enough already. She deserved this as much as he deserved his own choice, and it was the least he could offer her before he succumbed to oblivion.

INGRID

For three years, Henry waited.

He knew a girl was coming; Diana was relentless in scouring the world, and it would only be a matter of time before she found someone for him. And while he waited, he dreamed of who she might be. Young, old, funny, stoic, happy or as miserable as he was—anything was a possibility, but whenever he tried to picture her face, he only saw Persephone's.

Was it even ethical to ask a mortal to be his queen? To put her through the test and demand she give up half of eternity if she passed? And what would happen if she failed? Diana had sworn he didn't need to worry about any of it, but of course he did. If he was going to be the reason this girl, this woman, left everything she knew behind, then he had no choice but to give her a happy ending one way or the other.

At last Diana came to him early one evening, while a few souls still lingered from the latest batch James had led in. It'd taken him three days to get through them—two days longer than it had only a millennium ago, and he couldn't bear to think of how many souls were out there waiting for him to get to them. There was no hurry, of course, but he was miserably behind. And they deserved their eternities.

"Brother," she murmured, giving him a kiss on the cheek. "You look well."

That was a lie and they both knew it, but he allowed her that much as he kissed her in return. "As do you. I assume you bring news?"

"I do." She stepped back enough to look him straight in the eye, a mischievous smile dancing on her lips. "I found her."

For a long moment, Henry was quiet. He'd known this was coming, of course, but to hear her say it—to acknowledge the fact that there was a girl out there who Diana thought would be a match for him...

"Who is she?" said Henry at last, and Diana squeezed his hand.

"Her name is Ingrid, and she's beautiful. She has an easygoing temperament, she's loving, cheerful, and Theo is certain she's the one."

Theo, Apollo, who had access to the oracles of the world. If Theo thought she was the one, then not even the Fates could argue. "Very well," said Henry. "Will you be bringing her down here?"

"You will be meeting her up on the surface," said Diana. "At an orphanage in New York City."

His eyebrows shot up. "An orphanage? Is she a patron?"

"No, she's a resident," said Diana with the patience of a mother explaining something quite simple to her son. "And she has no idea you're coming."

A resident, which meant she was an orphan—a child. His sister was setting him up with a child. "How old is she, exactly?"

"She turned seven last week."

"*Seven?*"

"Naturally I am not suggesting you begin courtship immediately," she said. "Until she's of age, at the very least. But I thought perhaps if she grew up knowing you, if somehow you were able to work your way into her life—"

"As what, an uncle? A father figure? Perhaps that sort of relationship is acceptable within our family, but for a mortal child—"

"Would you allow me to finish before you interrupt?" said Diana with a huff, and Henry scowled, falling silent. "Thank you. Now, James will cover you down here. And don't give me that look—he's the only one who knows the Underworld well enough to do so. Besides, he needs the practice, in case we fail." But from her tone, it was obvious she didn't think they would. "In the meantime, I thought perhaps it would benefit you best to integrate yourself into the orphanage, as well. As a child."

He narrowed his eyes. She wanted him to start a relationship with a lie. He should've expected nothing less, but the thought of manipulating a child into loving him, only to snatch her away from the surface when she was old enough to marry…perhaps that was something Walter would have done, but Henry liked to think he was better than that. "And what is the harm in waiting until she is older?"

"By then, she may have found a reason to turn you down," said Diana. "And rather than take that chance, it wouldn't be such a terrible thing to befriend her, would it?"

"I would rather not," he said flatly.

"You promised you would try, and that's all I'm asking of you. I'm not suggesting anything salacious or immoral. I'm merely suggesting you give her a chance as a friend," said Diana. "I'm a mother myself, if you care to recall, and I would never condone you taking an interest in a child. But I also know you would never do such a thing, and I realize there is a distinct possibility that even if I do find you a queen, she may be nothing more than a friend to you. I am willing to take that chance. A queen and a simple confidante is better than no one at all."

He sighed. "And you swear that if she and I do not get on as friends, you will not pressure either of us any further?"

"I swear." She squeezed his hand. "Now come. Let's go meet her."

The trip up to the surface was nothing special, but as they appeared in the streets of New York City, panic began to spread through Henry, numbing his entire body. The streets were crowded with the bustle of men and women going about their day, avoiding the horse-drawn carriages passing them by at alarming speeds. And—Henry blinked—horseless carriages that seemed to move of their own accord. Despite his wonder, he couldn't stop and enjoy it, not today. Swallowing his nerves, he took the form of a boy not much older than Ingrid, and Diana held his hand as a mother would.

The orphanage wasn't far, and soon enough they entered the narrow building. Squished between two other dwellings, the only natural light came from small windows in the back and front. The rest was lit with a type of lamp Henry had never seen before.

"Ah, Diana," said a woman's voice from the floor above them. Henry craned his neck as a matronly woman who reminded him of his sister Sofia descended the stairs. "Is this the boy?"

His sister nodded. "His name's Henry. He won't tell me anything more than that."

"Oh, my dear." The woman knelt in front of him, and Henry eyed her, shuffling his feet in an attempt to adjust to his new body. He'd changed forms before, of course, but never with this level of deception in mind. "You look half-starved, you poor thing. I'm Matilda. Why don't we get some warm bread in you before you join the other children?"

As she touched his shoulder to guide him up the stairs, Diana let go of his hand, and Henry scowled. *Is this your plan? Leave me here as one of them?*

I don't see you suggesting anything better. He could hear the smugness in her tone, and he sighed.

How will I know which one she is?

Oh, you'll know. If you have any questions, dear brother, you know where to find me. And before you immediately reject her, do yourself a favor and give her a chance. You never know what might happen.

Henry may not have had access to an oracle as Theo did, but he was relatively sure this was little more than a stab in the dark. To say a little girl would be compatible with him was madness, and though he understood his sister's desperation, this was taking it too far.

He would leave—he'd be doing her a favor, really, allowing her the chance to live her life as she should have, without the heartache an eternity with him would bring. He had promised Diana he would try, but to what end? To trap this girl in the Underworld? To force her to be his friend when all she wanted was her freedom? It helped that she had no family to miss, certainly, but he could not be their replacement. He'd already made that mistake once.

Matilda led him into a room with two neat rows of a dozen beds pushed close together. "Here are the others your age," she said. "Why don't you join in while I find you something hot to eat?"

Henry didn't reply. Instead he scanned the other children, searching for a girl who might be called Ingrid. A few of them stopped playing to stare at him, both boys and girls, but there didn't seem to be anything extraordinary about them.

And Diana would choose someone special, of that Henry was certain.

But they all looked ordinary. Clean, well cared for, certainly, but no one stood out. They played in three groups, each having claimed a third of the room, and none of them asked him to join them. Not that he needed their permission, of course. It was ludicrous to think that he, Lord of the Underworld, could be bested by a roomful of seven- to ten-year-olds, but here he was.

"You're Henry, aren't you?" A high, almost musical voice sounded from the doorway, and he turned. A girl with two blond braids stood behind him, holding a bowl of something that smelled like broth. And though he'd been looking for her, the shock of seeing her for the first time made the blood drain from his face.

This was Ingrid. He knew it as well as he knew himself, and though she didn't appear to be anything but ordinary, everything about her called to him. The kindness in her blue eyes, the bashfulness in her cheeks, the way her small size made him want to protect her against every bad thing that had led her to this place. In her he saw something—something wiser and deeper than the others, something he couldn't explain. But it was there. That much he was sure of.

"Y-yes, I'm Henry," he said, surprised by how high his own voice sounded. Had he ever been this young before? He was certain he hadn't. "Is that for me?"

The little girl nodded, and he took the bowl, careful not to spill. It wasn't the sort of rich fare he was used to, but there was something distinctly homey about the scent that wafted from his meal. A soaked biscuit floated in the center, and the little girl turned red upon noticing it.

"Oh! I'm sorry. I can get you a new one." Her hands were halfway to the bowl before Henry pulled it back.

"No, it's fine," he said. "It smells good." Sinking down onto the wooden floorboards, he gestured for her to join him. "What's your name?"

"Ingrid," she said with a slight accent he couldn't place, and she sat down beside him. She eyed his bowl hungrily, and without a word, he offered it to her.

"I'm not really that hungry," he said, and despite her hesitancy, she allowed herself a spoonful, along with a bit of the soaked biscuit. "Didn't you eat?"

She shrugged. "Wasn't hungry before," she whispered. "Had a funny feeling, and my stomach was all twisty."

He didn't know how to interpret that. Had Ingrid known he was coming? Could she sense it somehow? Did she know, even now, that there was something about him, as he knew there was something about her?

"You can have all you want," he promised, and after she sneaked a look at the others, she dug in with fervor, stopping only to take a deep breath. He watched her with a small smile, reminded vaguely of Cerberus at mealtime. But despite being so young, she managed not to spill a drop.

"We should be friends," she said between mouthfuls, with the shy boldness only a child could get away with. "I don't really have many."

"I'd like that," said Henry. "I don't have many, either."

"You're my friend now." After sipping up the last few spoonfuls, she finally set the bowl aside. She hadn't left so much as a soggy bite. "And we'll be good friends, won't we?"

"The best," promised Henry. A moment passed, and she watched him with those ancient eyes of hers, as if she could see right through him. As if she knew exactly who and what he was.

"Why are you here?" she said without preamble, and Henry

hesitated. Did she know after all? Or was she simply asking about his supposed parents?

"Why are *you* here?" he said

"Because," she whispered, "I want a family."

Henry smiled. "That's why I'm here, too."

"Good. Everyone needs a family." She hugged his arm and all but dragged him to his feet, surprisingly strong for such a small girl. "Come on, I'll show you my doll."

With the same patience Diana had shown him only minutes before, Henry let her pull him away. It was strange, and no matter her age, he could never see himself loving anyone else the way he'd loved Persephone. But perhaps being friends wouldn't be such a bad thing, after all.

On Ingrid's eighteenth birthday, he finally told her who he was.

After eleven years by her side, he knew her better than he knew himself; he knew she would cry. He knew she would be confused and ask more questions than he could possibly answer.

What he hadn't expected was her acceptance.

Despite his deception, somehow she'd taken his hand, kissed his cheek, and asked to see the Underworld. For him to show her his world and everything he'd ever known before he'd met her. At first he'd been tempted to comply, but he'd never brought a living mortal down there before, and some fundamental part of himself refused.

Instead, as the tests began and the members of his family began to watch her, he reopened one of the long-dormant manors he'd built for Persephone. It was the least he could do, giving her a place on the surface where she could stay when the Underworld became too much. He wouldn't make the same mistakes with Ingrid. She would not be Persephone, and no matter what it cost him, she would be happy.

And so, he thought, would he. Their friendship was just that—perhaps to Ingrid it was more, but he still didn't have it in him to take her as a true wife. He loved her dearly, more than he'd loved anyone since Persephone, but it was a platonic love. And whether or not she accepted it, he could never quite be sure.

"So," said Ingrid one day as they walked through the gardens of Eden Manor. "If you're really Hades, and I'm supposed to be the new Persephone, then where are the pomegranate seeds?"

"The...what?" said Henry.

"The pomegranate seeds. You know, how in the myth, Persephone eats a bunch of seeds while she's in the Underworld, and that's why she has to stay down there with you."

Henry stared at Ingrid blankly. "Persephone liked pomegranates, certainly, but I'm afraid the story you've heard isn't what really happened."

"Well, of course it isn't," she said, rolling her eyes. "You didn't kidnap me, after all."

He nearly choked. *"Kidnap?"*

"You really don't know, do you?" Ingrid took his hands and sat him down on the nearest bench, and in the warm breeze, she told him everything she knew about the Persephone myth. And the more she spoke, the more Henry realized it really was nothing more than a myth that held next to no truth. Was that really what the world thought of him? What Ingrid thought of him?

Once she'd finished, he told her the real story, every last painful moment of it. From agreeing to the arranged marriage to their disastrous wedding night to Persephone's affairs. Especially with James.

And rather than ask question after question as she usually did, Ingrid remained quiet. He'd never told anyone before, not like this, not as if it was ancient history. A small piece of his burden lifted away with each word he spoke, and once he was finished, he felt strangely empty. Not healed, but as if there was room for more now.

"I'm sorry," she said quietly. "It's terrible, what you had to go through."

"I'm afraid I brought it on myself," he said with a small, sad smile, and Ingrid furiously shook her head.

"You're crazy. Of course that isn't your fault. You were as much a victim as she was, and you didn't—you didn't do anything *wrong*. She's the one who broke your heart."

"I am the one who forced her into marriage to begin with."

"No, her mother forced her into marriage. You did everything you could to make an awful situation livable for both of you." She shifted closer to him on the bench, her hand sliding up his arm to settle on his shoulder. "I get why you don't love me the way I want you to, and I won't ever pressure you, I promise. But do yourself a favor and at least try to move on, would you? Even if we're only ever friends, we could be happy. Really, really happy."

"I would like nothing more," he murmured, pressing a kiss to her cheek. "Persephone is my past, one I cannot ever forget. But you, Ingrid, are my future. And for the first time in an eon, I do not dread it."

Ingrid leaned toward him, brushing her lips against the corner of his mouth. It was such an intimate gesture that Henry nearly moved back, but he couldn't. Not when it could mean losing Ingrid. "You better not," she murmured with a playful smile. "We're going to be happy together—you know that, right?"

"I do." Or at least he hoped so.

"Good." Another grin, and her blue eyes sparkled. "Now, I'm serious about those seeds. There has to be a ceremony to make this all official. That's the only way you can do it, you know."

"Is that so?" he said, amused, and he clasped her hand in his. "Very well. For you, I will do it."

She squealed and threw her arms around his neck. "Can I wear a dress? A really pretty one?"

"The most beautiful dress you can think of," he promised, kissing her knuckles. "You can have whatever you want."

Her grin relaxed into a warm smile, and she cupped his cheek. "Hasn't anyone told you? I already do."

Her words were a greater salve than any medication in the world, and he gathered her up, holding her in the sunshine. They would be happy together. Perhaps not as happy as he'd once wanted to be with Persephone, but Ingrid was all the things Persephone never was. And Henry knew exactly how lucky he was to have found her.

The weeks passed until finally it was the night of the ceremony. Ingrid had planned every detail, from her dress to the food to where the council would sit. They had obliged her at Henry's request, though he suspected they would have anyway, considering how pleased they seemed to be at the prospect that he wouldn't fade. Regardless, everything was falling into place. Only three more tests, and she would finally be one of them.

As the council arrived and settled in the throne room, Henry headed toward Ingrid's suite. He was on edge, his nerves frayed and his stomach doing flip-flops, but he did his best to appear as calm and composed as he normally did. Even if Ingrid did not make the best of impressions on the council, it didn't matter what they thought of her. What mattered was that she pass the tests, and so far she was doing marvelously. Everything would be all right.

Knocking on her door, he waited, expecting she was putting the finishing touches on her hair. She wouldn't be late, after all, not to her own party. But as the seconds ticked by with no answer, he knocked again.

Silence.

"Ingrid?" he called. Had he perhaps missed her on the way to the throne room? No, there was only one direct path, and she had no reason to take another. "Ingrid, I am coming in."

Opening the door, he didn't know what he expected. Ingrid curled up in bed, perhaps, struck down by anxiety. Or her with pins in her mouth, putting the finishing touches on her hair.

What he did not expect was to see her crumpled on the floor, lost in the layers of her yellow dress. And bleeding from the head.

He was by her side in an instant, his body numb as he searched her for signs of life. But as soon as he'd spotted her, he'd known: she was gone. His best friend was dead.

A scream unlike any other ripped through the halls of Eden Manor, and it took Henry several moments before he realized it was him. He cradled her body, trying to will life back into it, but the bubbly girl he'd loved was lost.

"Brother?" Diana's voice whispered toward him, and the air beside him shifted as she appeared. "Oh. *Oh*. Is she…?"

He nodded, his eyes filled with tears and his throat closed. He clutched her fragile body to his chest, his fingers tangling in her blood-soaked hair. This wasn't an accident. She was in the middle of the suite, far from anything that could've caused so much as a knock on the head, let alone a fatal injury. And her skull was all but crushed.

"Who did this?" Walter's voice rumbled behind Henry, but he didn't turn toward him. He couldn't move.

"I don't know. Perhaps she fell," said Diana tightly, but even as she said it, Henry heard the doubt in her voice. Not even she believed it.

As she set her hand on his shoulder, he shrugged it off. This was his fault—if he hadn't let Diana convince him to do this, if he had just stepped down and faded as he'd wanted, Ingrid would still be alive. She would grow old, she would have children and she would have a full and satisfying life. But because she'd had the misfortune of knowing him, she was nothing more than a lifeless body now.

Calliope knelt beside him, her eyes huge as she clasped her hands between her knees. "Henry?" she whispered, but he couldn't bear the pity in her voice. They were all there now, the entire council watching him, some horrified and others grimly neutral.

"Leave," he said thickly. "I will have no more of this."

He expected a fight, but miraculously they all backed away, disappearing one by one. And once only he and Diana remained, he looked at her, her face swimming through his tears.

"Please go," he whispered, rocking Ingrid's body back and forth. Diana touched his cheek, her own eyes red.

"I'm so sorry, Henry. I'll find another girl—"

"I don't want another girl." His voice cracked, and he turned from her, burying his face in Ingrid's hair. She grew colder by the second.

"Henry, you must—"

"I will not risk another life," he said, and she took a deep breath, releasing it slowly.

"Very well. Then I will have another daughter."

"No."

"I've been thinking about it anyway, and if you don't want to risk another girl's life—"

"I said no."

She sniffed. "Those are your choices, Henry. You may either allow me to select another girl, and we will do our utmost to protect her now that we know there is a threat, or I will have another child. It is up to you."

He shook his head as tears streamed down his cheeks. She didn't understand. How could she, when her goal was to keep him in this hell of an existence? "I wish to fade."

"I'm sorry, brother, but you gave us a hundred years," she said in a gentler voice, placing her hand over his. "We all love you too much to give up."

He closed his eyes, struggling against the flood of anger and guilt and sadness inside him. "You will not have a child because of me. Any daughter you bring into this world will live the life she wants, and you will not force her to be with me. You owe Persephone that much."

Diana swallowed, growing still for a fraction of a second. "And you will allow me to choose another girl not only so we can find you a companion, but so we can flush out the killer and bring them to justice. You owe Ingrid that much."

The knife her words formed burrowed deep within him, becoming as much a part of him as his very essence. And as she stood and walked away, her bare feet silent against the thick carpet, he knew she was right. He owed Ingrid everything— even if it meant losing himself in the process.

Eleven girls.

That was how many he lost. After Ingrid, it was Charlotte; after her, Maria. And so on and so forth, as each name and face scarred another part of him until there was nothing left inside him but guilt and misery.

Some girls made it only a few days. Others, weeks—and the worst deaths were the ones who made it months, who came so close to the halfway point that he nearly let himself hope. But no matter how well protected they were, no matter what security measures he implemented, they always turned up dead. Some were clearly murder; others were questionable, with no visible signs of struggle or attack. Diana, Walter and other members of his family were certain they'd cracked under the pressure of the tests, which had never been meant for mortals. Henry wasn't so sure.

After each girl, he tried to fade. And after each girl, another member of the council convinced him to keep going. Murder after murder, body after body, he selfishly allowed another girl to risk her life for him in hope that perhaps this time, they would discover the killer. Perhaps this time, they would win.

They never did.

"How did it happen this time?"

Henry tensed at the sound of her voice, and he tore his eyes away from the lifeless body on the bed long enough to look at her. Diana stood in the doorway, a beacon of calm in the middle of the storm that was his existence, but even her presence didn't help rein in his temper.

"Drowned," said Henry thickly, turning back to the body on the bed. "I found her floating in the river early this morning."

He didn't hear her move toward him, but he felt her hand on his shoulder. "And we still don't know…?"

"No." His voice was sharper than he'd intended, and he forced himself to soften it. "No witnesses, no footprints, no traces of anything to indicate she didn't jump in the river because she wanted to."

"Maybe she did," said Diana. "Maybe she panicked. Or maybe it was an accident."

"Or maybe somebody did this to her." He broke away from her, pacing the length of the room in an attempt to get as far away from the body as possible. He hadn't known Bethany nearly as long as he'd known Ingrid, but the pain still slithered through his body, choking the life out of him. "Eleven girls in eighty years. Don't tell me this was an accident."

She sighed and brushed her fingertips across the girl's white cheek. "We were so close with this one, weren't we?"

"Bethany," snapped Henry. "Her name was Bethany, and she was twenty-three years old. Now because of me, she'll never see twenty-four."

"She never would have seen it anyway if she'd been the one."

Fury rose up inside of him and threatened to bubble over, but when he looked at her and saw compassion in her eyes, his anger drained away.

"She should have passed," he said tightly. "She should have *lived*. I thought—"

"We all did."

Henry sank into a chair, and she was by his side in an instant, rubbing his back in a motherly gesture. He tangled his fingers in his hair, his shoulders hunched with the familiar weight of grief. How much more of this was he supposed to endure before they finally let him go?

"There's still time." The hope in her voice stabbed at him, more painful than anything else that had happened that morning. "We still have decades—"

"I'm done."

His words rang through the room as she stood still next to him, her breathing suddenly ragged and uneven. In the several seconds it took for her to respond, he considered taking it back, promising he would try again as he'd done so many times before, but he couldn't find it in himself to do so. Too many had already died, and she knew it. He'd stopped fighting after each death, his thirst for justice growing stronger with each soul he had to usher through the Underworld, but this time was different. This time he meant it.

"Henry, please," she whispered. "There's twenty years left. You can't be done."

"It won't make a difference."

She knelt in front of him and pulled his hands from his face, forcing him to look at her and see her fear. "You promised me a century, and you will *give* me a century, do you understand?"

"I won't let another one die because of me."

"And I won't let you fade, not like this. Not if I have anything to say about it."

He scowled. "And what will you do? Find another girl who's willing? Bring another candidate to the manor every year until one passes? Until one makes it past *Christmas?*"

"If I have to." She narrowed her eyes, determination radiating from her. "There is another option."

He looked away. "I've already said no. We aren't talking about it again."

"And I'm not letting you go without a fight," she said. "No one else could ever replace you no matter what the council says, and I love you too much to let you give up. You're not leaving me any other choice."

"You wouldn't."

She was silent.

Pushing the chair aside, Henry stood, wrenching his hand away from her. "You would do that to a child? Bring her into this world just to force her into *this?*" He pointed at the body on the bed. "You would do that?"

"If it means saving you, then yes."

"She could *die*. Do you understand that?"

Her eyes flashed, and she stood to face him. "I understand that if she doesn't do this, you *will* die."

Henry turned away from her, struggling to hold himself together. "No great loss there."

Diana spun him around to face her. "Don't," she hissed. "Don't you dare give up."

He blinked, startled by the intensity in her voice. When he opened his mouth to counter, she stopped him before he could speak.

"She will have a choice, you know that as well as I do, but no matter what happens, she will not become *that,* I promise you." Diana gestured toward the body. "She will be young, but she will not be foolish."

It took Henry a moment to think of something to counter her, and when he did, he knew he clung to false hope. "The council would never allow it."

"I've already asked. As it falls within the time limit, they have given me permission."

He clenched his jaw. "You asked without consulting me first?"

"Because I knew what you would say," she said. "I can't lose you. *We* can't lose you. We're all we have, and without you—please, Henry. Let me try."

Henry closed his eyes, knowing that he couldn't fight this now, not if the council agreed. He tried to picture what the girl might look like, but each time he tried to form an image, the memory of another face got in the way.

"I couldn't love her."

"You wouldn't have to." Diana pressed a kiss to his cheek. "But I think you will."

"And why is that?"

"Because I know you," she said, "and I know the mistakes I made before. I won't repeat them again."

He sighed, his resolve crumbling as she stared at him, silently pleading. It was only twenty years; he could make it until then if it meant not hurting her more than he already had. And this time, he thought, glancing at the body on the bed once more, he wouldn't repeat the same mistakes, either.

"I'll miss you while you're gone," he said, and her shoulders slumped with relief. "But this is the last one. If she fails, I'm done."

"Okay," she said, squeezing his hand. "Thank you, Henry."

He nodded, and she let go. As she walked to the door, she too looked at the bed, and he swore to himself that this would never happen again. No matter what it took, pass or fail, this one would live.

"This isn't your fault," he said, the words tumbling out before he could stop himself. "What happened—I allowed it. You aren't to blame."

She paused, framed in the doorway, and gave him a sad smile.

"Yes, I am."

Before he could say another word, she was gone.

KATE

Katherine Winters was born on a sunny September morning mere weeks before the autumnal equinox. And as soon as he received news of her birth, Henry retreated to the Underworld for the next several years, hiding himself away from the knowledge that her death would inevitably be on his hands, as well.

While Diana had taken on a mortal life to raise her daughter, the council was never far, watching over Kate as if she were their salvation. Though they never spoke about her directly to Henry at his request, he caught snippets of conversation about her progress. About how her birth had gone; her first day of school; about how Diana was living amongst the mortals, blending in as if she'd always been one of them. And despite his distance, even he could tell how happy they were together. Diana finally had the life she deserved, and he could not have been more thrilled for her.

But as pleased as he was that she had finally moved on from her anguish over Persephone, he could not ignore the fact that one day soon, he would take that happiness from her, as well. And the closer they drew, the more he thought about it, and the more he thought about it, the harder he begged Diana to let him go. To give her daughter a life she deserved, one where she could choose her fate. But no matter how he protested, Diana insisted again and again that Kate would have a choice; that she would be the one to choose to be with him, and if she did not want to try, then she would be free to live her own life.

Henry knew better, though. Even if Kate said no when she came of age, the council would find a way to manipulate her into it, and the very thought of her following in her sister's footsteps made him sick. But the die had been cast, and her fate was sealed. She would be number twelve.

"You should go see her," said James one evening, as Henry sat in his office with Cerberus slumbering at his feet.

Henry raised an eyebrow and peered at him. "And you should not be here."

James shrugged. "Gonna be my realm soon anyway, so I don't see why it matters."

"Is that so?" said Henry.

"Well, yeah. Unless you think this will work."

Henry was quiet. He hoped it would work, but deep within his mind, in a place he rarely allowed himself to visit, he knew it wouldn't. They had done everything they could do to protect Bethany; he couldn't possibly see what would be different about Kate. "Why are you here, James?"

"To make sure you have the chance I didn't," he said, shoving his hands in his pockets. "Even if something does happen to Kate, she's a great kid. And you're an idiot if you waste any more time avoiding her."

He narrowed his eyes. "How dare you speak to me that way—"

"How dare *you* give up on Kate before she even has the chance to try." James drew himself up to his full height. "She's stronger than you know, and if she beats this, how do you think she's going to feel, knowing you spent the first part of her life so sure she'd die that you couldn't even bother to meet her?"

"I doubt she will care," said Henry icily. "Considering Diana is raising her as a mortal."

"She'll find out who she is one day. We're all busting our asses to protect her, making sure she's never without one of us—even Ares is stepping up. But you can't bother because you're too much of a coward."

"I am not a coward." Henry stood, digging his fingertips into the hard wood of his desk. "I have watched eleven other girls perish because of me, and each one of them hurt as much as the one before. I do not enjoy the thought of Diana's daughter falling victim to the same fate because of me."

"Then do something about it. Guide her. Protect her. *Help* her. Don't hide down here acting like she doesn't exist," said James, and for a moment, his voice hitched. They weren't only talking about Kate anymore, but any remorse Henry felt for keeping him from his friend all those years ago had long since evaporated. "Even if something does happen to her, appreciate the time you have with her. Don't ignore her in hopes that'll make it hurt less. We both know it won't."

Henry clenched his jaw. "You have no right to tell me what to do."

"And you have no right to act like she's dead already."

They glared at each other for the better part of a minute, neither willing to budge. A knot of frustration formed in Henry's throat, rendering him silent regardless, and at last James sighed.

"It's her seventh birthday today," he said. "I'm not saying you should stay with her like you stayed with Ingrid, but I am saying it wouldn't hurt if you went to see her. Diana would appreciate it. After all she's doing for you—"

"Don't," said Henry, forcing the word out through his tight throat. "She is doing this for Kate, not for me. Kate will have a choice."

"Then go give her that choice," said James, and he inclined his head. "Central Park. Sheep Meadow. They'll be there until sunset. Cerberus might appreciate running around and stretching his legs. Can't imagine he gets much of a chance down here."

With that, he turned on his heel and marched out of Henry's office, leaving him in a cloud of self-hatred and uncertainty. What would it hurt, really, to see her? She was a child, yes, but he had no feelings for her other than the unyielding desire to protect her from harm. How could he do that when he didn't even know what she looked like? And if James was right, if she did question his belief in her when she was old enough to know who she really was...

But what if she too died? The odds were against her. Any connection they formed would put her in certain mortal peril. How could he do that to her, knowing her chances of survival were so slim?

Then again, what better way to protect her than to be with her always?

He was halfway to the surface before he'd made a conscious decision. The warm sunshine hit his face as he appeared in Sheep Meadow, and at his feet, Cerberus shook off the Underworld gloom.

"What do you think?" said Henry, reaching down and giving his dog a pat. "Up for finding Diana and—"

Cerberus let out a loud woof, and before Henry could create a leash, he took off. Swearing, Henry followed, darting between small clusters of people enjoying the late-summer sunshine. No one seemed too bothered by the sight of a huge dog dashing through the crowd, followed by a man dressed in all black. Then again, it was New York.

Another bark, and Cerberus skidded onto a blanket, diving headfirst into a carefully laid-out picnic. Henry swore and hurried over, careful to appear as if he were breathing heavily.

"I'm sorry," he said. "My dog, he slipped his leash and—"

He stopped cold. Sitting on the blanket among the ruins of what had once been a small feast was Diana. And beside her, giggling as Cerberus snuffled into her hair, was a little girl.

Kate.

Her brown hair hung in a loose braid down her back, and her blue eyes and the smattering of freckles across her nose reminded him so much of Persephone that for a moment, he really was breathless. Whether Diana had done it on purpose or not, she had all but re-created the daughter she'd lost. But there was something about her, something he couldn't describe—something so fundamentally different from her sister that in the space of a single heartbeat, Persephone faded from his mind completely.

Kate didn't seem to be at all bothered by the fact that her birthday picnic had been destroyed by a dog three times her size. She gave Cerberus a kiss on the nose and turned to look at Henry, her eyes meeting his. He froze.

She may have been seven, but there was something eternal about her gaze. As if she could see all his thoughts, his hopes, his fears, his pain in one look. As if she understood every moment he'd existed. She may have been mortal, but she was without a doubt the daughter of gods.

"It's all right," said Diana, her voice warmer and fuller than he'd heard it in eons. "It looks like he managed to miss the cupcakes."

"Cerberus, come," said Henry, and he trotted obediently to his side. Henry ducked his head as he hooked a leash up to his dog's collar, trying to hide his shock. "Again, my apologies. If there's anything I could do to make it up to you…"

"Really, it's no trouble," said Diana, and she wrapped her arm around her daughter's shoulders. "Just an excuse to gorge ourselves on cupcakes, really. We'll get hot dogs on our way out of the park."

"At least let me pay for those," he said, because any mortal would insist on the same, but Diana shook her head.

"If you want to help, you could take a few pictures for us," she said, offering him a camera. "They never turn out quite right when I take them."

Henry took the camera, a modern kind that felt lighter in his hands than he expected. "Of course," he said, and he peered through the lens. Even now, Kate stood out like a beacon to him, as if she were the only flame in a world of dark.

He would protect her. He would kill for her. He would fade for her, if that's what it took to make sure she had the life she deserved. And even if he never loved her the way Diana wanted him to, he would still show her the affection and respect she deserved.

"There," he said roughly once he'd taken an entire roll of film. "You both look stunning."

Kate grinned and tried to lick off the purple frosting that had somehow wound up on her nose. "You're funny," she said, fixing that infinite stare on him. "Mommy, can he get hot dogs with us?"

Diana looked at him, and he hesitated. He wanted nothing more than to spend more time with them, but to what end? She was a little girl. It wouldn't do either of them any good for him to befriend her now, as an adult. And he would serve her better by protecting her from afar.

"Thank you," he said, and he handed the camera back to Diana. "But I'm afraid I have to be somewhere. It was a pleasure meeting you. And happy birthday, Kate. I wish you an infinite number more."

Kate giggled again and blew him a kiss. As Diana laughed and gathered her up in another embrace, Henry walked away. He hadn't expected that. He hadn't expected leaving her to be one of the hardest things he'd ever done. But if he had his way, he would make absolutely certain that he would never have to do so again.

When he returned to the Underworld, a parcel awaited him on his desk. Curious, he unwrapped the shimmering purple paper, wrinkling his nose with distaste. Who would possibly send something like this to him?

The moment he set eyes on what lay beneath, however, all question of the sender flew out of his head. Nestled in lavender tissue paper was a black-and-white picture of Diana and Kate, both holding cupcakes as they laughed together in Central Park. Diana must have been the one to frame the image, and it shimmered in the candlelight, a reflection in the making. All it needed was him.

It'd been a long time since he'd made a reflection—an image that was more a wish than reality. But to him, this was both. In it, he saw his future; a life he might one day have, if he fought hard enough for it. If he protected Kate. If, when the time came, he gave her a reason to choose him.

He tucked the reflection into his pocket and took a breath. Until then, there was something he had to do.

"Where are we going?" said James warily as Henry led him down the aisle of the throne room. They entered the antechamber together, and though Henry had spent much of the past thousand years avoiding him at all costs, he offered James his hand.

"Trust me."

James eyed him, and while Henry couldn't blame him for his uncertainty, he was rapidly growing impatient.

"If I was going to do something terrible to you, I would have done it centuries ago," said Henry. "Now come on. We don't have all day."

At last James took his hand, and the moment he did so, Henry pushed them both through the quicksand space between the antechamber and where he wanted to be. It was never a pleasant journey when he was dragging someone with him across such a large distance, but at least James knew better than to fight it.

When Henry opened his eyes, they stood in the middle of an eleventh-century castle. Henry wouldn't have known it from any other, but the moment they landed, James's mouth dropped open.

"Is this…?" he said, and Henry hesitated.

"I realize we have not been as close as we once were, and I fear there is simply far too much history between us to ever allow things to be easy once more. But we are still family, and…" He paused. "It was cruel of me to keep this from you, no matter the past. Everyone deserves happiness, even if it can only be found among the dead. While I cannot promise you I will always be on stable ground, I will take steps to ensure you can visit whenever you wish."

James gaped at him, speechless, and Henry grimaced. He hated that look. As if it were so shocking that he would ever do something kind.

"Go," he said. "I will be here when you are finished."

"I can't—" James hesitated, and without warning, he lunged forward to capture Henry in a hug. "Thank you."

It had been a very long time since any member of his family had dared touch him in such a way, and Henry awkwardly gave him a pat on the back. "You are welcome. Now go, before I change my mind."

Releasing him, James gave him a boyish grin and took off down the corridor, guided by whatever power he had to know exactly where his destination happened to be. Out of curiosity—or perhaps the desire to prove to himself that happiness in the Underworld was possible after all—Henry trailed after him.

James turned into a room filled with sunshine, and though it couldn't have been natural, a tree grew in the middle of the stone floor. Henry stood in the doorway as James approached a dark-haired girl who sat underneath the low-hanging branches. She munched on an apple and spoke in low tones with a woman who resembled her far too closely to be anyone but her mother, though the instant she noticed James, she lit up.

"James?" said the girl, her bright eyes widening. She flung her arms around him and kissed him soundly on the mouth, not the least bit bashful. "It's about damn time. Do you have any idea how long I've been waiting for you to come get us?"

"Tuck," he breathed, staring at her as if she was the most beautiful thing he'd ever seen. There was something sad about the way he murmured her name, something that reminded Henry far too much of himself. Sometimes it was hard to remember he wasn't the only one in pain.

James gathered her up, wrapping his arms so completely around her that she couldn't have escaped, if she tried. They remained intertwined for a long moment, murmuring things Henry couldn't hear, and he averted his gaze. He would have given anything to have that. Anything.

At last they broke apart, and Tuck looked at him with shining eyes. She clearly adored him. "This is my mother," she said. "Mother, this is James, the boy I was telling you about."

James greeted the woman as if they were old friends, pulling her into a hug, as well. "You have a brilliant daughter. Tuck's the most amazing girl I've ever met."

"Of course she is," said the woman, laughing. "And from what she's told me, you're not too bad yourself."

The three of them talked for a few moments longer, and at last James pulled something out of his pocket. "I've been holding on to this for you," he said, and he offered a small pendant to Tuck. "Thought you might like to have it."

She took the necklace with shaking hands. "You held on to it all this time?"

"Of course," he said, the tips of his ears turning pink. "Anything for you. I'm yours and you know it."

As she kissed him again, Henry took his leave, stepping back out into the dim corridor. As much as he despised James, to see him find happiness despite his tragedy gave Henry something he hadn't had since Ingrid. It gave him hope.

Pulling the reflection out of his pocket, he gazed down at Kate's face, memorizing every feature. He would be hers as well, and despite whatever trickery the council had planned, he'd be there to watch over her. No matter her fate, she would have a fair shot at the life she wanted, even if that life didn't include him. He would make sure of it.

He'd lost everything that had ever mattered to him, but as he listened to the sounds of James and Tuck's laughter, an odd certainty settled over him. If Kate somehow succeeded where the others had failed—if she chose to give him a second chance—then this was only the beginning. His existence felt like an eternity, and in many ways it had been. But perhaps she would finally allow him to close the book on the worst chapter of his life. And perhaps she would be the start of the best.

Tracing her features, at once so like Persephone's and yet

so very different, he allowed himself a smile. In her, he saw possibility. In her, he saw his future.

And when she was ready for it, he would be, too.

★ ★ ★ ★ ★

The Spellbound Novels

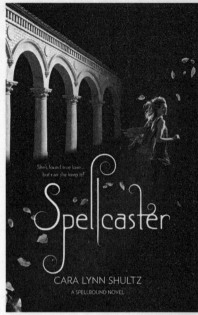

In this contemporary series of spells and magic, curses and love, new-girl Emma Connor faces snobs and bullies at her elite Manhattan prep school. When the hottest boy in school inexplicably becomes her protector, Emma finds her ordinary world changing and a new life opening to her, filled with surprising friendships, deadly enemies and a witchy heritage she never suspected.

AVAILABLE WHEREVER BOOKS ARE SOLD!